Secrets

of a

Spinster

Secrets

of a

Spinster

Rebecca Connolly

Phase Publishing, LLC
Seattle

Text copyright © 2016 by Rebecca Connolly
Cover art copyright © 2016 by Rebecca Connolly

Cover art by Tugboat Design
http://www.tugboatdesign.net

Phase Publishing, LLC first paperback edition
June 2016

ISBN 978-1-943048-08-3
Library of Congress Control Number: 2016940389
Cataloging-in-Publication Data on file.

Acknowledgements

To my beautiful, talented, and incredibly brave Aunt Laurie, who has always supported and loved me, understood me on a very special level, and inspires me on a daily basis. For your courage and your faith, for your ability to find joy even in the darkest times, and for the light and laughter you bring to the family. I am honored and beyond blessed to know you, and to have you in my life forever.

And to Cadbury's Royal Dark Mini Eggs, as a massive apology for my ignorance to the existence of such a radiant gift. You are addictive, guilt-inducing, and divine. And I adore you without shame.

Thanks and cheers to Christopher Bailey and Phase Publishing for all of the craziness they patiently endure in working with me and keeping things running smoothly. Deborah Bradseth with Tugboat Design for an exquisite cover that makes everything perfect.

Whitney Hinckley for enduring the stress that is editing of my stuff and still liking me in spite of it. The A-Team for indulging in my whimsy and obsessive behaviors and plying me with Snickers when I get hangry.

Thanks to the family for all your support and excitement. You're my favorite.

And finally, thanks and chocolate kisses to my Musketeers. You know I'd be lost without you, and all of the cheesecake in the world couldn't make up for it. Well, maybe some cheesecake. Let's be real.

Chapter One
London, 1819

There was something to be said for being a spinster.

It allowed one to escape from tiresome wretches and fawning fools, as nobody universally declared a spinster was of the smallest bit of interest to anybody. One could listen to all manner of conversations without anyone thinking anything of it at all, which made for delightful gossip, should anyone have cared to ask.

Party invitations were few and far between, which was usually quite a relief as very few parties were actually worth attending. Balls were opportunities to secretly snicker at those who couldn't dance, and to observe the attempts of nearly every person from sixteen to forty-five to gain the affections of a member of the opposite sex. Nobody called, nobody wrote, and one could move about quite freely without the merest sniff of a scandal. It was quite liberating.

Unless, of course, one had the desire for attention or parties or dancing or visitors.

Then it could be quite lonely.

But those moments were exceptionally rare for Mary Hamilton. She rather enjoyed the quiet and being left to her own devices. And really, she was so well thought of that she received a good many more invitations than your average spinster, though not enough for her to consider herself popular.

Take this evening for example. Here she stood, aimlessly lingering along the western wall of the very fine ballroom in the home of Lord and Lady Carteret, whom she had only met possibly once in her entire life. She had very nearly declined their invitation, but her sister had been driving her so completely mad the whole of the winter that an early spring soiree was a welcome distraction, and she accepted, against her better judgment.

The melee of the dance was a welcome reprieve from the plaintive whining of home.

Mary sighed a little to herself as she took her thoughts away from her sister and attempted to appear interested in what was going on around her. She would have to give a full report when she returned, and experience had taught her that the particulars were important. She began cataloguing various details; Lord Frampton's ill-fitting waistcoat, Miss Dawes' shocking neckline, Mr. Peter Tolley's inebriation, Lord Devereaux's evading of debutantes, Lady Greversham's unnecessary walking stick intentionally interfering with the servants' duties… All in all, it seemed a very typical London party.

And yet, for the strangest reason, Mary found herself wishing she might dance this time. It was completely inexplicable, as she was really not very good at it, but it had been a very long time.

Alas, she was a spinster, she reminded herself, and quite profoundly so. Dancing could not be anticipated.

"No one to dance with you, Miss Hamilton?" came a low voice near her.

She turned with a quick smile to the cheerful and dreadfully handsome Earl of Beverton. "Not today, my lord," she replied with a curtsey. "But I have learned not to expect it."

His smile turned a trifle sad. "Well, the day is not over yet, and my wife is not dancing in her condition, so perhaps you would favor me with this one?"

She quirked a brow up at him. "Do you pity me, my lord?"

He immediately shook his head, dark eyes twinkling. "Never, my dear Miss Hamilton. I simply cannot tolerate fools and simpletons. As you are neither, a dance with you would be rather enjoyable, I think. So will you?"

"Only if you don't mind trodden toes," she said with a hint of apology.

"I don't."

She smiled and placed her hand in his open one. "Then I shall, with pleasure."

He nodded and led her out to the floor, where other couples were beginning to take their place. The music struck up and as Mary began the movements, she could not resist the urge to smile. She had not expected the earl to ask her to dance, but she was not surprised. The earl and his wife had somehow become friends of hers after they'd met last summer, and now she was always being looked after.

"I am surprised to see you here tonight, my lord," Mary commented when she was near him again. "Weren't you in the country this winter?"

"For most of it, yes. But when the weather cleared, Moira desired a bit more, shall we say, entertainment. She is anxious to do as much as she can before her time comes." He looked rather exasperated about it, even if he was smiling still.

Mary laughed and spun with the other ladies. "Is that why you've come tonight? To entertain your wife?"

"Partly. But I also had no idea who Lord and Lady Carteret were, and I couldn't exactly refuse an invitation if I didn't know whether or not I should."

Mary nodded. "Very wise, my lord." They shared a brief grin.

"I thought Geoff would be here this evening," the earl remarked as the dance took him around her.

She shrugged as she placed her hands in his for the next movement. "I assume he's not in London yet. He often gets distracted on his way in."

The earl laughed once. "That does tend to happen when Duncan is around. But then, we all know how Geoff hates London. I really have no idea why he still comes."

"Nor do I, but if he didn't, I would have no visitors at all, so it suits me just as well."

He gave her a teasing look. "Now, Miss Hamilton, are you fishing for company?"

"Not at all, my lord," she replied with a smile. "My sister and I are quite cozy in our house. It's a pleasure to be able to hear oneself think."

That seemed to surprise him. "I think the silence would be a bit deafening."

"I don't mind." And she didn't. Not really.

Well, not all the time.

The earl hummed a little. "Well, perhaps I will let Moira come around, just to entertain you."

Mary looked up at him with concern. "Should she do that? Isn't she very near her time?"

He snorted softly. "Yes, but she won't rest any more than she thinks she needs. It's driving me mad. At least if she is with you, I'll know she's not doing anything reckless."

She smiled in response. "Not very reckless, at any rate," she teased.

He inclined his head, returning her smile. "If she feels like seeing you, I will allow her."

"It's not necessary, really." If Moira injured herself or her child on a visit to her, Mary would never forgive herself.

He raised a brow. "She will do it regardless. You know her nature. And if I know my wife, and I do, she will bring Kate with her."

That was undoubtedly true.

Mary bit her lip in thought, fighting a smile. "I think I'll need more pastries, then."

The earl barked out a loud laugh that turned many heads in the ballroom. "I hope you've stockpiled enough, Miss Hamilton. They will eat you out of house and home. Now, let us see if we can find you some more dance partners for this evening."

"Oh, good! You're back!"

Mary barely suppressed a heavy sigh as she handed her cloak off to Winston, who wisely had no expression, but shuffled away quickly.

"Yes, Cassie, I'm back."

"How was it? Who was there? Tell me everything!" Her sister

literally jumped the final two stairs as she raced towards Mary, then seized her arm and pulled her into the sitting room, where a rather large fire was crackling. Mary gratefully approached and held her hands out to warm them.

"Calm yourself, Cassie, for heaven's sake. It was a ball, not a festival."

Cassandra snorted and tossed her curly blonde hair over a shoulder as she sank onto a well-worn settee. "You have absolutely no taste in social occasion."

"I have taste enough," Mary retorted. "I merely do not appreciate the spectacle people make of themselves."

"Who made a spectacle?" Cassie inquired with rampant excitement, leaning over the arm of the settee.

Mary laughed and gave the report she had prepared in the carriage on the ride home, being sure to elaborate on the bits she knew her sister would find most interesting. It was much to her credit that she knew exactly what to say and how to say it so that it would satisfy Cassandra's enthusiasm. Or perhaps it was just from practice.

When she was finished, she took a seat across from her sister and put a hand to her brow, a new headache beginning to form.

"I can't believe Lady Raeburn is back from Paris this early," Cassandra commented in an awed voice. "She never stays anywhere less than four months, and she only went just before Christmas. What do you think she means by it?"

"Perhaps she was dissatisfied with the selection of hats."

"Mary," Cassie moaned in exasperation. "Don't be a toad. I thought you liked Lady Raeburn."

"I do, very much so. But I see no reason to speculate as to her reasons for coming back to England where she lives." Mary gave her a hard look, which she tempered with a weak smile.

"Well, Mr. Gerrard lives in England, too, but he hasn't been seen in Society for two years!"

"He was there tonight as well."

"He was what?" Cassie shrieked, her hands flying up to her hair. "You mean to tell me that Mr. Gerrard... Christopher, mind you, not Colin..."

"As he is the elder of the Gerrard twins, I do believe I know who you mean when you merely say Mr. Gerrard," Mary remarked dryly.

Cassie waved her comment off impatiently. "Mr. Christopher Gerrard back in England. What did he do? Who did he dance with?"

"I have no idea. I saw him come in, I saw him exit. I didn't watch him the whole evening."

"You are positively hopeless, Mary!" her sister moaned as she dramatically flung herself out on the settee.

"Yes, so I have been told."

Cassie rolled her eyes and sniffed dismissively. "Well, what did you do the entire night? Sample the punch? You ought to be an expert on the subject by now."

Mary sneered playfully. "I was preparing reports for you. I could not possibly have time for anything else."

"Come on, Mary," Cassie groaned, "be serious. Did you dance at all tonight?"

"Yes, as a matter of fact, I did."

"Oh?" Cassie sat up and eagerly folded her hands in her lap. "With whom, pray tell?"

Mary smiled secretively. "The Earl of Beverton. The Marquess of Whitlock. Lord Beckham. Lord Cartwright."

"Mary!" Cassie said, groaning yet again. Really, she was getting quite good at it. "You cannot always dance with married men."

"I can if they are the only ones who ask me," she quipped, grinning.

"Perhaps if you did not match the draperies in dress and manner, someone else would."

"Perhaps if I cared, I would do so."

"You will never get married."

"I'll survive."

Cassandra made a noise of disgust and rose. "You know, you are far less agreeable when Geoffrey is not around. I quite tire of the sight of you."

"I'll survive," Mary said again as her sister left the room. When she could no longer hear the petulant footsteps on the stairs or above her, she allowed herself to sink down into her chair and removed her slippers from her feet. Being neither old nor delicate, she rarely was able to sit during a party where there was dancing. It was rather tiresome for her poor feet, particularly when they were so out of practice.

She sighed to herself and closed her eyes. That made two individuals tonight who seemed to associate her presence with Geoff's. Not that she ought to be surprised, as they did tend to be at the same events and with each other. She received far more attention when he was about. It seemed she was only noticed if he was there.

She could hardly blame them for that.

Geoffrey Harris was the darling of Society, the crème de la crème of all bachelors. He was also the one bachelor who seemed entirely uninterested in marriage. This, of course, made him all the more tempting for the eager and determined mothers of Society, as Mary was constantly reminding him as he continued to evade each and every one.

They were the best of friends and had been since they were very young. They laughed, they bantered, and there were no secrets between them.

Well... almost no secrets.

Mary had the greatest secret of all; she was once in love with Geoffrey Harris.

It was really quite sad. She had spent most of her life alternating between feelings of helpless infatuation and complete adoration, with the slight venture into hopeless longing on occasion, topped off with a spattering of simple platonic affection. She always thought extremely well of him, and from time to time thought herself very much in love with him. At ten, it was love. At twelve, it was not. At eighteen, it was very much love again. And now, at twenty-seven, she could safely say she was most definitely not in love with him any longer.

She wasn't.

Why, she was even comfortable enough to tell Geoff when he looked especially attractive without the slightest hint of heart fluttering or cheek flushing. If those weren't signs of romantic indifference, she didn't know what was.

But she had never told him that she had been occasionally in love with him. Why, she could not have said. It could have been because admitting that she'd ever had those feelings for him would make her no better than the rest of the idiotic females who fawned over him. It could have been because she was embarrassed by the sheer volume of paper she had wasted in her journals, pining for a young man who would never see her beyond their friendship. It could have been that she was afraid of anything changing in their relationship.

Whatever the reason, she hadn't told him, and had no plans to ever do so.

She couldn't risk it, not when he was the best person in her life.

Oh, she had her family, but they were not particularly close. Her parents had removed themselves to Italy indefinitely and wrote faithfully once a month; her other siblings came to London only when they had to, and wrote only when they had things to say. It was just her and Cassandra in the London house now, shockingly without any elderly relative or companion. But nobody paid attention to the Hamiltons enough to care. London was full of other excitement, and to be perfectly honest, Mary was bored with it. The only thing that ever amused her here was Geoff.

"Miss Hamilton?"

She turned her head towards the sound of Winston's gravelly voice. "Winston, have you not gone to bed yet?"

He smiled kindly. "No, Miss. Should I have?"

"Yes, you should! It is late and I'm not in need of anything."

"Are you quite sure?"

"Yes, yes, to bed," she said with a wave of her hand.

He bowed. "Very good, Miss. Oh, and Miss? There is a note for you in the study."

"Thank you, Winston. I will take care of it."

The butler bowed once more, and then left, and Mary released a tired sigh and forced herself up out of her chair, which creaked loudly. She frowned at the threadbare piece of furniture, and wondered why she had not replaced it yet.

She walked into the rarely-used study where the note sat unopened on a tray. A small smirk flashed across her face. Cassandra either had no knowledge of its existence or had recently developed a heretofore unheard of sense of privacy.

She suspected the former.

She recognized the handwriting immediately and could not help but to grin as she broke the seal and began to read.

My dearest Goose,

I can only imagine how long the winter has been for you without me. Has Cassie driven you mad yet? I don't envy you being locked away in a house with only her for company. I hope someone has visited you, or else I shall have some serious reservations about the intelligence of London society. I apologize for my very long absence, I truly had thought to only be away one month, and here it is four. You may blame Mr. Bray, if you would be so kind. But never fear, Goose, I am returning to London to entertain and delight you as we speak. I imagine we shall arrive Tuesday, assuming my companion is not further distracted by his own shadow.

Yours ever faithful,
Geoff

P.S. Prepare Cassie for news of Wyndham. He's become a rising star in the Navy, and his name is bound to be bandied about London again very soon.

Mary sighed heavily, her smile now gone. The girl already cried enough about her "poor Simon", and heaven knew she had endured quite enough on the subject from the whole of London and Lieutenant Wyndham's family as well.

Cassandra had broken the heart of one of the most eligible bachelors London had ever known a year and a half ago and caused his escape to the sea and His Majesty's Navy, and Society had not been kind to her for it. Nearly all of her friends and associates had abandoned her, which left the energetic girl a virtual pariah whenever she managed to leave the house.

What surprised Mary was just how vicious the general populace could be to a girl who was not actually ruined. Cassie was never invited anywhere, unless by the very few who were still her friends. If she did go out, there were comments and whispers and insults so thinly veiled they were nearly blatant. So she usually stayed at home, shut away from everyone, and continuously, and very vocally, mourned her state.

As far as Mary understood from Cassandra's many emotional outbursts during that time, the man had poured his heart out to her and instead of accepting him as everybody had expected her to, she had claimed she was too young and had no desire to be a Navy wife, but she would be glad to have him if he gave that up and waited a year besides. Simon Wyndham, though generally a very patient and understanding man, had refused to do so and stormed out of the house.

Three hours later, Cassandra had changed her mind and begged Mary and Geoff to find him. But all their efforts had been in vain. Wyndham was gone back into danger and the sea, and his family blamed Cassie entirely. And thus began her societal downfall, which she had yet to recover from.

Raising all of that up again would make things exceptionally worse. Again.

She placed the note in a drawer of the desk with a sigh, then put out the candles and made her way up the stairs to her bedchamber, smiling at the thought of Geoffrey coming back.

Life was always more entertaining when he was around, and she was determined that this season would be the most entertaining of all.

For she would be leaving London after it ended, and she had no idea of ever returning.

Chapter Two

"Remind me why we've come back to London again?"

Geoffrey Harris glanced over at his travelling companion and good friend, Duncan Bray, whose grumbling had been the only thing Geoff had heard all morning. Duncan was not naturally an unpleasant man, but London and its prospects had that effect on them both.

"Because the season will begin soon?"

His friend threw back his head and laughed. "Wrong. Neither of us is nearer to marrying than Colin is. This annual march of the debutantes is as entertaining as your left boot."

Geoffrey sighed with infinite patience, though he knew his friend was right. "Because your sister is there, already breaking the heart of every man in London?"

The frown that Duncan tossed at him then was truly remarkable, and very fierce. "We are not talking about Marianne. She is far too flirtatious for her own good, and she will be dealt with."

Geoff held up his hands in surrender. "All right, all right, we won't speak of it. Well, how about the fact that your aunt has returned to London almost two months earlier than expected? That's very nearly a summons for you, isn't it?"

"What Tibby decides to do with her time is her own business," Duncan muttered awkwardly. "I would never come racing to her side simply because she is there."

Geoffrey laughed at his friend's discomfort, knowing that Duncan's denial was just for show. He really was devoted to Lady

Raeburn, one of the most unique women that Geoffrey had ever met. She was also unfailingly generous and good-hearted, doted on Duncan and his sister like they were her own, and had even arranged her inheritance between the two of them.

"Don't we have any other reason to be coming?" Duncan asked as their horses trotted along anxiously as they neared the city.

"Of course, we have," Geoff retorted. "Nathan and Derek are already here, Colin ought to be soon, if he isn't already, and this is what England's gentlemen do at this time of year."

"Being a gentlemen is sounding less and less like something I'd like," Duncan muttered, "but I suppose you're correct. When are we all meeting up?"

"Day after tomorrow, I think. Nathan has volunteered their house for us. Unless Moira delivers, and then I wouldn't be so sure."

Duncan snorted. "I think we would still go. I cannot imagine Nathan would be calm enough to endure that alone."

"Probably not," Geoffrey agreed. "Do you know if Derek and Kate are renting or are they staying with someone?"

"Renting, I believe. They have razed the remnants entirely, you know. Not that I blame them, there wasn't much left worth saving."

They both fell silent. Late in the summer, the home of the Marquess and Marchioness of Whitlock had been destroyed by fire, and they had been there to witness most of it. Thankfully no one had even been injured in the blaze, due to Kate's quick thinking and authoritative personality, but the memory of it had affected all of them. It could have been so much worse.

"I wonder if Colin is here yet," Duncan mused as they neared their friend's house, which was lit as if he were.

Geoff shrugged off his negative thoughts from before and smiled. "Well, it won't hurt to check, will it?"

"With Colin, you never know," Duncan returned darkly as they reigned in and dismounted.

Duncan knocked rather soundly, and they were let in almost without a word, which surprised both of them. Surely the servants would not let them in of their own volition if their master was not in residence purely because they recognized them…

"Well, the two of you are a sight for sore eyes!"

Duncan and Geoff grinned at each other as the unmistakably exuberant voice of Colin Gerrard met their ears. It was not two seconds before his person was before them, smile at the ready, dark hair slightly disarrayed, as if he had run from his room to greet them. Which he very well may have done.

They shook hands, then entered a near room and were seated barely thirty seconds when a maid entered with some food.

"What in the world is this?" Duncan asked with a laugh as he helped himself to a bit of the light repast. "You couldn't possibly have known we were going to descend upon you today. We hardly knew we were until about five minutes ago."

"I keep my house in readiness at all times," Colin replied smartly, his smile still fixed in place.

"Surely not," Geoff protested. "You never said a word to the servants while we stood there, we would have heard you."

Colin sighed in disappointment. "Must you always take the fun out of everything, Geoff? Very well, I saw you coming. I told the servants to let you in and bring some food. There, are you satisfied?"

"Not nearly," Duncan grunted as he reached for more food. "Geoff hardly let us stop at all, so keen was he to be in town. I'm famished."

"For heaven's sake, man, if you are so starved, go down to the kitchens!" Colin cried with a laugh. "Perry is down there and he will get you something proper, not this light dribble. Had I known you would be in such a state, I would have taken us all down there instead!"

Duncan stood and bowed very deeply in gratitude. "I shall take myself down to plunder your pantries, then."

"Eat up, my friend," Colin said with a wave. "You are going to need it," he added in a softer voice, smiling a little.

Duncan froze, and turned back. "Why?"

Colin's mischievous smile deepened. "Marianne is on quite a rampage. I think she had ten callers last Tuesday alone."

"It's not even the start of the season yet!" Duncan cried, leaning on the doorframe. "How can she possibly...?"

"Because she encourages everybody, you know that," Colin interrupted, his humor diminished. "She loves to flirt and receive attentions, everybody knows, and there are more than enough men in London willing to follow her to Africa, should she have any ideas to do so."

"Is she that obvious?" Geoff asked, wincing.

"Very," Colin admitted. "It's borderline outrageous. There have been comments. Not harsh ones," he hastily added as Duncan began to look murderous. "Just comments in general."

"Have you spoken with her?" Duncan asked as he rubbed his brow.

"Not directly, no. I have spoken with Mrs. Lansfield, but she is only a chaperone, and I think she likes Marianne's behavior."

"You could have spoken with Marianne directly," Duncan told him with a look. "Any of you chaps could, she respects the lot of you."

Colin snorted. "Not me. Not that I blame her. Besides, I'm not a big and imposing and terrifying brother who can put the fear of God into her. I am merely a lookout."

Again, Duncan sighed. "Very well, I'll address it. But I'm eating here first. Lord knows what she will have going on in my own kitchens." He pushed off of the wall and headed on down the hall, leaving Colin and Geoff alone.

"I don't envy him a younger sister," Geoff remarked with a shake of his head. "Especially not one with Marianne's temperament."

"Nor I," Colin agreed with a chuckle. "Speaking of sisters..." he said suddenly, giving Geoff a look.

Geoff raised his brows and returned the look. "Since when do you care what Franny is doing, Colin? She's married with six children and far too old for you anyway."

"I wasn't talking about Franny," Colin said very seriously, which was always a hint that what was about to be said was either unpleasant or downright horrifying. "I was talking about Cassandra Hamilton."

"Cassie?" Geoff asked in confusion. "She's not my sister."

Colin snorted. "Not all family is blood relation. You watch over those Hamilton girls as if you were their guardian, if not one of their brothers."

Geoff sighed and sat back. "This is true. Very well, what about Cassandra?"

"She hasn't been seen all winter. Not that people care beyond the fact that they need to talk about something, but she's not gone out at all."

"How do you know this?" Geoff asked him, worry knitting his brows.

Colin smiled faintly, though his blue eyes showed understanding at Geoff's distress. "I keep my ears open for everything, and I have my sources. Besides, Kit came back to town this winter and he mentioned seeing Mary at a party the other night, but not Cassandra. He found that odd, as Mary is not nearly so keen about social activities as her sister."

"No, not by half," Geoff murmured, pinching the bridge of his nose between his fingers. "What do your gossips say about Cassie these days?"

"Same as they always have done," Colin said with a shrug. "I keep thinking it will die down, but Wyndham's sister Felicity came out last season, you remember, and she is everywhere these days, and whenever she is…"

"…the comments continue," Geoff finished with another sigh. "I hate London."

Colin smiled thinly. "Yes, I know." He leaned forward and rested his elbows on his knees. "What are you going to do?"

"Well, since I cannot force them to stop talking about her…"

"Not likely, no. Everybody likes you too much to take you seriously," Colin commented with a snort.

Geoff rolled his eyes. "At least my reputation is a good one."

That brought a grin to Colin's face. "Touché."

He sat forward and rubbed his hands over his face. "What if I just throw caution to the wind and take her somewhere myself?"

"Alone?" Colin winced. "I don't think so. What about Christian?"

"My brother?"

Colin nodded immediately, looking thoughtful. "What if you and

Christian take both girls to the theater tomorrow? Nobody would think very much of the Harris brothers escorting the Hamilton sisters, everybody knows how close your families are. And Christian is so fresh to Society that nobody's had time to think anything of him at all but his family's reputation, which, thanks to his wonderful, kind, good-hearted, gentleman-like brother," he paused to indicate Geoff a touch dramatically, to which Geoff merely smirked, "is nothing less than immaculate."

"He does have other brothers, you know," Geoff muttered, feeling more than a little embarrassed by the exuberant, if mocking, praise from his friend.

Colin shook his head, still grinning. "The other three have nothing on your reputation, Geoff, and you know it." He sat back with a satisfied sigh. "I knew it was a brilliant idea, I ought to trust myself more often."

That would not have been entirely wise, but Geoff thought it best to say nothing. After all, this was Colin's home, and if he thought himself so very clever within its walls, then who was Geoff to tell him otherwise? And it really was a good idea. Colin was a good deal cleverer than people gave him credit for. But that, too, was not to be spoken of.

"So your brother is back in London, is he?" Geoff asked as he relaxed further into his chair. "I thought Kit was determined to avoid town forever."

Colin shrugged and helped himself to some more food. "So did I, but suddenly last week, there he was. You know, you would never think it, but he is actually one of my chief sources of gossip."

He was right, Geoff didn't think it. "How is that, exactly?" he asked with a laugh. "Your brother never speaks badly of anybody. He barely speaks at all."

"I didn't say he joined in the gossip," Colin said with a wag of a finger. "He just hears everything and tells me about it. He can be quite elaborate when he chooses to be."

Geoff gave him a disbelieving look. "I find that very hard to believe."

"Would you like a demonstration?" Colin asked politely, his eyes sparkling mischievously.

"I think that would be called for under such circumstances."

"Well, then," Colin began smugly, rubbing his hands together, "here you are: Mary Hamilton was at the party at Lord and Lady Carteret's Thursday evening. She spent most of the night near the west wall, near a window with dark green draperies. She wore a grey dress and a gold chain. She danced exactly four times."

"Did she, indeed?" Geoff interrupted, feeling a small burst of pleasure. "With whom?"

"Nate, Derek, Beckham, and Cartwright." Colin recited, his smile becoming just a touch pitying.

For a moment, Geoff said nothing. "That's it?" he asked finally.

"That is it, I'm afraid. Four dances, all with our married friends and her godfather."

"Blast," Geoff cursed with a wince. "Not that I am ungrateful, but why doesn't anyone see her like I do?"

Colin did not answer immediately, but at Geoff's attempt at a murderous expression, he fumbled. "I haven't the foggiest, Geoff. I don't know her very well at all, but I know you think very highly of her, so that's enough for me. I think very highly of her. Very highly, indeed."

"You'd better think highly of her," he growled as he looked down at his fingers.

"D'you know, Geoff, I think that's the first time I have seen you so defensive."

Geoff looked up at him, ready to lash out, but he saw genuine curiosity in Colin's expression and exhaled softly instead. "If you had a very good friend who was someone well thought of, but generally ignored…"

"Funny, I have a twin like that…"

Geoff acknowledged this with a nod. "If this friend were to suffer through pitying and comment and the embarrassment of being passed over and dismissed, would that bother you?"

Colin opened his mouth, but Geoff continued.

"And if this very good friend had a sister who, through her own childish fit of flightiness and rash thinking, made a decision that the whole of Society chose to constantly remind her of and cut her for, wouldn't you do what you could for her?"

Colin's mouth, which had never closed, hung gaping.

"You're right, Colin, in saying they were my sisters. I know them better than my own sister, as strange and probably disgraceful as that sounds. I seem to be one of very few people who can see beyond what Society does and value what is there."

Silence met his ears and, more than a little worried, he glanced up to find Colin still gaping. "What?" he asked roughly.

Colin finally closed his mouth, then thought for a moment. "I have two things to say. One, that was the most impassioned speech I have ever heard you give in the whole course of my life, and I have known you for a decent portion of the course of my life."

"Colin..."

"Two... you are right."

Geoff was surprised, to say the least. "I am?" he asked.

Colin nodded. "Perfectly. I may not show it much, but I don't appreciate the way some speak of my brother. Many think him very respectable, some think him very mysterious, but there are some who feel the need to spread rumors and make mischief, and bandy about my twin's name. It drives me to distraction. I understand, Geoff."

"Yes," Geoff said slowly, watching his jovial friend's sudden somberness with interest. "Yes, I see that you do."

They sat in silence for a long moment, each of them lost in their deep and rather unpleasant thoughts.

"I'm terribly sorry, I thought Geoff and Colin were in here, not two gravediggers," Duncan joked from the doorway, looking at the two of them with amusement and a little worry.

Both shook themselves and looked over at him. "Have you eaten your fill?" Colin asked with a wild grin that hid any hint of his former dark thoughts.

"You know better than that," Duncan scolded, smiling a touch. "It would take more food than you have to fill me."

"Of course, of course, all the food in London would hardly suffice for you," Colin replied with a nod.

"Everything all right in here?" Duncan asked, looking between

24

the two once more. "You looked as if somebody might have died."

Geoff smiled. "Nobody died that we know of. Colin and I were merely talking about the idiocy of Londoners."

"And you couldn't wait for me? I thrive upon berating Society as a whole!"

That broke any of the remaining tension and the three of them laughed for a long while, then began discussing more pleasant, light subjects.

Duncan and Geoff parted ways as they left Colin's home, each having his own tasks to complete and people to see. Geoff, for one, was anxious to be safely ensconced in his home rather than relying on inns and the hospitality of others as he had been doing of late.

He had spent the last few months with Duncan, who was fond of travel and didn't care when he did so or if the location were remotely interesting. Why Geoff had accepted, he still didn't know. He was much more prone to staying at home, enjoying comfortable evenings with friends, and leaving the adventures of life to those more energetic than he.

But when his friend had come to him and invited him along, he agreed to go. After all, Nathan and Derek had married, or rather, in Derek's case, had decided to actually enjoy his marriage, and Colin… Well, they had long since learned that travelling with Colin was not exactly a wise idea. He was not as hardy as he supposed himself to be.

What had initially been thought to be a month long excursion had now been four, thanks to Duncan's eagerness and Geoff's disinterest in complaining. He was impossibly tired and really had no desire to be in a saddle again for a very long time.

The season would start in a matter of weeks, and then he would have to have his guard up again. Every year some desperate girl, or her even more desperate mother, would try to get him to court and marry her. Those who had been around for a while or had daughters who had left the Marriage Mart with success knew his inclination and so they had ceased attempting to gain his attention. He very much appreciated those people.

He sighed as he neared his home and tried to think of something to look forward to. At least Mary would be around. She was the one bright part of those blasted things. She would voice the things he would only think, and the two of them would laugh as quietly and delicately as possible, which was proving to be harder as the years went on. She was quite an unusual woman. She never complained that she rarely danced, though he danced with her every chance he could. She cared little for fashion, which was a little refreshing, if not outright astounding. She was a rare one, his Goose. One of these days, though, one of them would marry, and that would be it.

But neither of them were so now, and that was good enough for him.

As long as Mary was around, London would always be worth visiting.

He smiled to himself and pushed his horse on a little faster, remembering his plans for taking the girls to the theater tomorrow evening. He loved taking Mary to the theater.

It was one of the few things in life she actually, and very vocally, detested.

London was looking brighter already.

Chapter Three

"*I* am so bored," Cassandra moaned morosely from a sofa in the corner, setting aside the needlepoint she had been attempting to complete for nearly three years now. Cassandra was always bored and had no patience for needlework.

Mary barely refrained from rolling her eyes and brought her eyes back down to the book she had been reading. There always seemed to be some sort of interruption whenever she got anywhere good in something as delightful as *Pride and Prejudice*. It was really quite annoying.

A mournful, desperate sigh was heard a few moments later and Mary closed her eyes and gathered all of her patience, then set her book down and looked over at her sister. "What is it, Cassie?"

Her sister adopted a look of feigned surprise and her pale blue eyes went wide. "Oh, I'm sorry, could you hear that?"

Mary smiled tightly. "Yes, Cassie. I would much rather ignore you and continue reading, but as your sighs are very distracting, I cannot. What is it?"

She looked as though she would argue the point, then decided against it. "I only wish there was something to do! I can't just sit here and pretend to work on this wretched thing anymore."

"Try reading," Mary suggested dryly.

Cassandra shook her head. "It gives me a headache."

"Play the pianoforte."

"I don't feel like it."

"Go for a walk."

"It looks like rain."

"Sketch something."

"No."

Mary sighed and closed her book. "Cassie, you are being more surly than normal. You are being difficult and juvenile, which is not like you. You hardly ate anything at breakfast, you have not sat still all morning, and you are quite frankly putting me at my wit's end. What in the world is the matter with you? Are you determined to be miserable?"

Instantly, her sister clamped her lips together in a thin line and looked away. Mary frowned at that. While Cassandra was a little dramatic and sometimes rather childish, she never hesitated to speak.

"Cassie?"

Her sister wiped at her eyes and shook her head.

Mary rose from her chair and sat next to her sister, forcing her to meet her gaze. "Cassie."

Cassandra said nothing for a long moment, then said, in a very low voice, "I received a letter this morning. From Felicity Wyndham."

Mary slowly let out a breath. "What did she say?"

Cassie swallowed. "That she expects to be married by the end of the season to Mr. Patrick Gray. He is the gentleman from Shropshire who has…"

"Twenty thousand pounds, yes I know," Mary interrupted. "So what is the problem? Shouldn't you be happy for your friend?"

"I am," Cassandra said slowly.

"What is it, then?"

"She… she wants me to be there, but doesn't know how her mother would feel. Or Society."

In Mary's very humble opinion, Mrs. Wyndham and the rest of Society could take their feelings and toss them in the stables with the horse droppings. But this was probably why Mary would never get married. These wild opinions, however humble or true, were far from proper.

"I should never have refused him, Mary," Cassie whispered, fresh tears forming. "I loved him so much and he loved me, and he wanted to spend the rest of our lives together. And I said no!" She dissolved into sobs, and Mary gathered her up as best as she could, wondering how long this would go on.

"Cassie," she tried to soothe, running her hand gently over her sister's hair, "you know why you refused him. You hated the idea of being a Navy bride. And you were eighteen, hardly old enough to make such an important decision."

"He said we could wait! He asked if I would wait for him! I could have waited, Mary, I could have!"

"But you hate the sea."

"But I love him!"

Mary tried not to sigh again, but she was quite at a loss as to what to do. Every now and again since that fateful day when Cassandra Hamilton refused Simon Wyndham, there were moments of complete abandonment of emotional self-control, and Mary had tried everything from suggesting she run after Lieutenant Wyndham to volunteering information about a lovely convent in Yorkshire. No suggestions had ever been taken well. So she was left to just repeating the same inane arguments that Cassie herself had made before, which had sounded ridiculous to Mary the first time she had heard them.

And it always ended just like this, with Mary holding her brokenhearted sister, who was destined to be as dramatic about this in ten years as she was now. And every time, Mary ended up wishing she knew what she could do to make it all go away.

"Cassie, we really need to find a way to stop all of this," Mary said as she rubbed her sister's back gently.

"Stop all of what?" she sniffled, pulling back.

Mary gave her a look that should have told her, quite plainly, that she did not believe her ignorance at all. "I know you are hurt, but there is no reason to give up your future."

"Simon was my future!" Cassandra wailed, flinging herself back onto her rather forcefully. "I am nothing without him. I cannot go anywhere, I cannot see anyone, and no one will ever love me again!"

Mary groaned inwardly and, this time, did not refrain from rolling her eyes. At first, this behavior had worried her, as had the moments of listlessness and desperation to never be alone. Now it merely drove her mad.

But she could not very well let it alone. Whether she liked it or not, Cassie depended on her. The rest of the family had given up on the both of them, and so she had to do something.

"Here's a thought," Mary said after a moment, knowing she would regret her words later. "I have had enough with London and all its frivolity and bustling idiocy. I've already been thinking that this is going to be my final season before I hang up my dance card for good. What if I make a lark of it all, and I prance around like a debutante for the whole of it?"

The wailing ceased and her sister stilled. "A debutante? How do you mean?"

"Exactly the way it sounds. I will mold myself into the same sort of girl that fills every dance hall during the season."

"Do you mean... you will flirt and look ridiculous and simper?"

Already the regret started in. "Yes," Mary agreed with a wince.

"And you will get all new gowns and change your hair?"

Mary closed her eyes on a reluctant sigh. "Yes, and I will bite my tongue."

"You don't speak at all in public."

"I mutter," Mary admitted grudgingly. "Anybody in the vicinity would hear." And have heard, she thought to herself. More than one unsuspecting patron of society had choked on a beverage when in her presence and had been privy to her snide remarks.

"Will you go to more events? Balls and parties and the theater?"

"Yes." She bit the inside of her cheek at that concession, but if it really were her last season, why not? "But you must come with me and get out yourself. You must agree to that or I will not do it. That is my one condition."

Cassandra looked unconvinced, trying to find the trick in this plot.

But Mary was quick. "Somebody has to laugh at me and remind me who I really am. Think of how ridiculous I will be."

Her expression cleared and she giggled. "Oh, heavens, that will be a sight." She sniffled once and smiled just a bit. "That would cheer me up a great deal, Mary."

"Well, I do live my life to please you."

Cassie flashed a brief grin. "Very well, I agree." Then she sobered. "What if we both end up lonely, alone, and old, Mary?" she asked quietly and very seriously.

"I probably will," Mary said without concern.

That somehow coaxed a hint of a laugh from her. "Oh, Mary, how can you be so droll?"

"I have worked very hard at it," Mary assured her. She took her sister's hand in her own. "I may end up alone and old, Cassie. I know very well that being twenty-seven and remarkably plain limits my options. But you don't have to. You are young and beautiful and bright. You can have everything."

"I don't think there is anything left for me," Cassie replied, sounding the most serious Mary had ever heard her. She sat back and sniffled, wiping at her nose with the back of her hand. "We are quite the pair of miserable spinsters, are we not?"

"It would appear so," Mary admitted. "But I refuse to call you a spinster until you are at least twenty-five. No woman was ever a spinster at one and twenty."

"One who shall never be happy again is," Cassie muttered with finality.

Mary tried not to stiffen at her sister's continued despondency, but she couldn't help it. "The difference between your situation and mine, Cassandra, is that you had a man confess his love for you. I never had any man try." She rose quickly and removed herself back to the chair she had vacated and picked up her book again, beginning where she had left off, her sister remarkably silent.

It was not until Miss Elizabeth Bennet had reached the grounds of Pemberley that Cassie spoke again. "I am so bored. Where is Geoffrey? He always cheers me up."

This time Mary did sigh aloud and rolled her head back to look at her sister. "He is off with Mr. Bray, Cassie, as I have told you. And I think that Geoff has quite a good deal more pleasant things to do than being forced to entertain the spinsterly Hamilton sisters like a strange performing monkey."

"Not really," came a low, rather well-known voice that sent a smile careening off of her cheekbones.

"Geoffrey!" Cassie cried in delight, leaping from her seat and racing to the doorway in which the owner of the voice currently stood.

"Your own personal performing monkey, at your service," replied Geoff, a smile evident in his tone.

Mary rose from her chair, tossing her book down onto it, and allowed herself an overt examination of her best friend, who was now being joyously mauled by her sister.

He looked well, which was not surprising, as he always looked far too well for her taste. But today the color of his waistcoat magnified the blue of his eyes, and his blonde hair looked ever-so-slightly ruffled, which was not usual, but suited him well. The challenges of having an attractive best friend were many, chief of which was that one always wanted to look at him. And often did so.

There was no shame in that, surely.

"Well, I do love being warmly greeted, but this is certainly a change," Geoffrey chuckled as he extricated himself from Cassandra's hold. "What was that for?"

"I am hardly sufficient entertainment for my sister today," Mary said with a melodramatic sigh. "She is bored beyond reason and since I am the least exciting person we all know, any change in the situation is a relief."

"Oh, come now, Mary, I hardly think you are the *least* exciting person we all know," he scolded with a smile as he came over and took her hand. "As it happens, I know for a fact that there are quite a number of people who are less exciting than you." He quirked a brow and gave her a teasing bow of greeting.

"That is because you are deluded into thinking that the random mutterings of a runaway mouth are amusing," Mary replied as she curtseyed, priding herself on her wit.

He snickered and dropped himself into the chair nearest her. "That's not why, you goose. I just know all of the stories about sweet Mary Hamilton that might not live up to her reputation." He smiled up at her proudly, and she rolled her eyes and sat back into her chair.

"You know that every single one of those stories happened

because you spurred me on," Mary argued, unable to help smiling herself.

He shrugged. "That's probably true. And speaking of stories…" He leaned forward and gave her a look. "When were you going to tell me that you spilled the true details, to which you were sworn to secrecy, of my little fountain prank to Diana Beckham?"

Mary's brain froze and her lips parted in shock. That had been years ago. He was never supposed to know that she had let the secret slip. "She was not Diana Beckham then," she said in a small voice.

"Mary."

She sighed and sat back in her chair. "We were sixteen, Geoff. Diana had come over and we were just…" She paused and threw him a severe look. "Have you ever tried keeping a secret from Diana?"

"I have never had to," he offered with another shrug.

"It's not possible. But I swore her to secrecy as well, Geoff, I swear."

"Mary!" Geoffrey cried in dismay. "You know Diana cannot keep secrets from Derek! The rest of the world, maybe, but not Derek!"

"So she told her brother," Mary said without concern, trying not to smile. "Why is that so monumental?"

"Because Derek Chambers cannot keep a secret from anybody." Geoff sighed and frowned over at her again. "What, was twenty pounds not good enough for you?" His tone was severe, but there was a twinkle of mischief in his eyes.

She smirked at him. "In case you have forgotten, there are many secrets that you have paid me to keep silent about over the years, the rest of which have been kept so. Now, if you wish me to reveal those secrets to, oh, say, Colin Gerrard, then…"

"You wouldn't," Geoff stated in a would-be calm voice, though there was real panic in his eyes.

She quirked a brow. "I might."

He swallowed hastily.

"As amusing as watching the two of you bicker like cats is," Cassandra announced from her side of the room, "I am still bored."

Geoff met Mary's eyes and the two of them shared a secret smile.

He looked back to Cassandra and smiled more broadly. "What if I were to escort the two of you to tonight's performance of *The Marriage of Figaro* at Covent Garden?"

"Really?" Cassandra cried happily.

"Really?" Mary asked with no small amount of reluctance.

"Be nice," he hissed out of the corner of his mouth. "Really," he said louder, grinning for Cassandra's benefit.

Cassie happily danced around the room for a moment, then stopped. "But who will be my escort?" she asked with concern. "You cannot bring two women with you to the opera, Geoff."

"I would never do anything so shocking," he replied drolly. "Christian will accompany you, if you don't mind."

"Oh, good!" she cried, clapping her hands. "I love your brother. Does he care for opera? I can never remember."

"He does," Geoff said with a nod. "And he speaks German very well."

"Geoffrey," Cassandra scolded impatiently, hands on her hips. "*The Marriage of Figaro* is an Italian opera."

"Oh dear," he replied in apparent confusion. "Then Christian will not be very helpful at all."

Cassandra sighed even as Mary snickered behind her hand. "Geoffrey, it's a good thing you are practically family, or I would probably not even be friends with you."

"Then I am excessively grateful for our closeness. At any rate, Christian is looking forward to seeing the two of you again." Geoffrey smiled fondly between them. "He doesn't go out much in Society yet, so make him behave, won't you?"

Cassandra grinned. "I shall do my best. But if he is anything like his older brothers, he will be rather difficult to manage."

Geoffrey looked outraged. "Difficult? I hope you are not including me in that broad assessment! John and Charles and Phillip, maybe, but certainly not me!"

Cassandra rolled her eyes and left the room with an airy, "No, never. Of course not."

"Does Christian know that he has been spoken for this evening?" Mary asked Geoffrey when they were alone.

"Of course not," Geoffrey told her with a snort. "The poor boy thinks that being freshly nineteen years old makes him a man, and so he was off very early with Derek and Nathan to discuss purchasing a horse from Dennison's. I haven't seen him since last night."

Mary shook her head in amusement. "I can't believe he is so old already! It seems like yesterday he was following you around like a little puppy."

"That was yesterday."

Now she couldn't help laughing out loud. "Cassie is right, you are difficult."

Geoff looked appropriately wounded. "I am hurt. From my best friend, even? This is too cruel."

"Oh, come now, Geoff," she laughed, pushing at his shoulder. "You know I love you like a brother."

Now it was he who laughed. "Please, Mary, I know for a fact that you love me much more than you ever loved your brothers."

She grinned. "This is true. You are the brother I would have liked to have, had I any say in the matter."

"Yes, well, I'm rather glad I'm not your brother," he said with a shudder. "I might have inherited that nose of your mother's."

Mary laughed loudly and clamped a hand over her mouth. Then, adopting a serious and would-be offended expression, asked, "What are you trying to say about my nose?"

"Nothing at all. You were blessed with a perfect nose."

"Well, that's that, then," she sighed, throwing her hands up. "My one perfection is the nose that is not my mother's."

"That's not all," he said softly, with a gentle, reproachful smile.

She felt a jolt of surprise and looked at him. "Really? What else, then?"

He looked her over thoughtfully. Too thoughtfully.

"Be careful," she warned. "Take too long and I'll doubt you."

He opened his mouth instantly.

"Answer too soon and I will know you're lying," she said quickly.

He frowned up at her, and she only lifted a brow imperiously.

"Your brows," he said finally, with perfect timing.

She jerked in surprise. "I beg your pardon?"

"You have the most perfect, expressive brows I have ever seen." She started to smile, just a little. "You're joking."

"Never," he promised somberly. "I swear, they really are magnificent."

Now she grinned. "Is that your favorite part of me, Geoffrey?"

He shrugged lightly and stood, seeing himself to the door without answering her. "You had better get some rest, Mary. We're off to the opera tonight."

She groaned and rose to glare at him. "Did you have to pick the opera, Geoff? You know I hate it."

He grinned the same mischievous grin he'd worn since he was seven. "I do know. That is why I am escorting you. I love how you hate it."

"You are evil."

"But you love me, Goose, and you know it." He winked and left, laughing merrily to himself.

She shook her head and laughed as she returned to her book, hoping it would distract her until tonight. She would have to tell him of her season plans eventually, and she was not looking forward to that at all.

Perhaps he would not think it a so very dreadful idea. Perhaps he would even help her. Lord knew she would need it.

There were those people who would think she would be doing all of this for attention, for one last chance to get a husband for herself.

Those people were silly, nonsensical fools. She had stopped wanting attention, and a husband, long ago. She was far more sensible and realistic now than she had been then, and it was nobody's business but her own if she wanted to have a bit of harmless fun now that she had come to the end of her time as a marriage prospect.

After all, a very plain woman of twenty-seven had very little reason to hope for more.

Chapter Four

$\mathcal{G}$eoffrey Harris did not enjoy opera.

In fact, there were few things he hated more than opera.

And yet, here he was, dressed in his finery, in a carriage with his brother to get Mary and Cassandra expressly for the purpose of going to the opera.

Even now, it seemed ridiculous to him, but people went to the opera, despite his personal aversion to it. It was a customary thing to do as the season started, and he did so love taking Mary anywhere she did not enjoy being.

If there was one thing he had learned about her from a very early age, it was that she was not nearly as sweet and docile as people took her for. She just had an uncanny ability to bite her tongue, which she thankfully refrained from doing when he was around. It made everything so much more enjoyable.

It might have seemed odd to some that the fourth son of a wealthy and well-respected family should spend so much time with the oldest daughter of an equally wealthy and respected family and not have married her, but it had never crossed his mind.

Not really, anyway.

Once or twice it had entered his mind that perhaps they should marry each other simply because it would be easy and they would probably never like anyone better. But such was hardly a suitable reason for marriage, though he knew many married for and with far less. He could not, and he knew Mary would not.

It didn't take long for them to arrive at the Hamilton townhouse, and even less time for them to collect the girls, who had been impatiently waiting for them just inside the door. Well, Cassandra had been impatient. One look from Mary told Geoff that she was still angry with him. He bit back a grin at that.

Christian and Cassandra immediately began chatting excitedly on one side of the carriage, while Mary maintained a stony silence and spent most of the trip to the theater looking out of the window.

"You're not going to be silent the entire night, are you?" Geoff muttered out of the corner of his mouth.

Mary only shifted further away and tightened her jaw.

He sighed heavily and leaned back. "You'll never make it, you know. You won't be able to bite your tongue that long. Eventually, you will have to speak to me."

Her silence only made him smile more.

"I fail to see why you're angry with me at all," he grumbled. "Especially when you know I hate these blasted things every bit as much as you do."

Mary twitched as though she would speak, but settled for just giving him one very pointed look.

"Why did I do it, then?" he asked, reading her expression perfectly. "Because your sister loves it, and she needed to get out."

Mary sighed and dropped her shoulders, glancing over at her sister, who was still brightly conversing with Christian, looking happier than she had in weeks.

Unable to give up his mischief, Geoff went on. "And you know that I cannot resist taking you to things we hate purely for the sake of your delightful commentary."

As he suspected, the glare snapped right back into place and despite his teasing, he was slightly afraid of it. Did she have any idea how potent that glare was? Had any other person in the world ever received that glare? If they had, Mary's reputation wouldn't be nearly as sweet as it was.

They arrived at the theater with a line of other carriages, but Cassandra was so eager she reached for the handle of the carriage door at once.

"Cassie," Mary warned softly.

Her sister gave her a withering look. "Yes?"

Mary gave a tight smile. "Patience."

She rolled her eyes at Christian, which made him chuckle.

Geoff almost said something glib about it to Mary, but saw how suddenly tense she was. "Mary," he murmured so softly that the others hadn't a hope of hearing him, "what is it? Surely you don't hate the opera that much…"

"No, it's not that," she hissed, leaning a bit closer and matching his tone.

"Then what?"

The carriage stopped and a footman opened the door with a bit of flourish that the older, more sensible pair could have done without. Cassandra and Christian disembarked and moved on without them.

"I hate this," Mary told him softly as he exited and blocked her view.

He took her hand and helped her down, but glanced about and could already see the patrons that had yet to enter begin to whisper to each other, some behind fans, some without such discretion.

At once, Geoff understood. While Cassandra was the target of the whispers, Mary felt the impact.

"It will be all right," he whispered as he looped her hand through his arm, pulling her closer. "I promise."

Her only response was a tight nod, and a brush of her fingers against his arm.

Mary felt beads of sweat begin to form behind her ears as she and Geoff followed Cassandra and Christian to their box for the evening. The gossips were in fine form tonight, though it was nothing she hadn't already heard before. But her fingers itched uncomfortably against the fabric of her gloves, and she forced herself to breathe calmly through her nose. It wouldn't do to lash out at Society's finest like a wild beast.

"How dare she show her face in public! What is she thinking?"

"And do you see her now with the younger Harris boy? So appalling. I hope he has the sense of his brother."

"Oh, he does," spoke up a deep voice that nobody expected to hear, causing several patrons to jump. "That's why he is with Miss Cassandra Hamilton tonight. Only the finest quality can be seen with the Harrises, I can promise you that."

Mary breathed a small sigh of relieve at the sight of Duncan Bray coming towards them as he pushed through some of the crowd, a beautiful brunette on his arm. She very nearly slumped against Geoff as the gossips went back to whispering, but this time their focus on Duncan.

"Good evening, Harris," Duncan greeted as he approached. "Christian. Miss Hamilton, Miss Cassandra."

"Good evening, Mr. Bray," Mary replied with a grateful smile.

"Fine sense of timing you have there, Duncan," Geoff said, grinning himself.

"Funny how that works, isn't it?" Duncan returned with a brief quirk of his brows. He turned to the young woman at his side. "I don't believe, Miss Hamilton, Miss Cassandra, that you are acquainted with my sister, Marianne."

"No, we are not," Cassandra said with a kind smile. "But I think we've seen each other on several occasions."

Marianne smiled back, displaying what were quite possibly the most perfect teeth Mary had ever seen. "Yes, I believe so. It's a pleasure to meet you both. And I will have you know that I purposefully have trodden upon Mrs. Smythe's skirt tonight, horrible, gossiping old wretch, but it is unlikely that she is aware of it, given the sheer yardage of material required to make a full skirt for her."

Mary jerked her hand to her mouth to cover the snort that nearly escaped. Cassandra merely clamped her lips together and bit down hard.

Marianne continued as if nothing was amiss. "I think that she will find her skirt hanging just a little off center for a while."

"How hard did you trample it?" Mary asked through her restrained laughter.

"I don't know how hard," she said with a mischievous smile.

"But it was repeatedly done. I hope she will learn to keep her gaping mouth shut one of these days, but she seems to enjoy catching flies with it, so I must do what I can to aid the world in retiring her shortly."

Laughter rang out from the group, and then they heard the tuning of instruments and made their way to their seats, amidst further whispers that no one was heeding any longer. Duncan and Marianne were in the box next to them with their aunt, Lady Raeburn, who was really quite terrifying, even if she was delightful in every way. But Marianne was immediately transfixed by the musicians, and so only Duncan had to suffer conversing with her. He was generally a stoic man, but his longsuffering glances toward their box did not go unnoticed.

"I pity him," Geoff said with a sigh.

"Why?" Mary laughed. "I adore Lady Raeburn! She is the most unique woman I have ever known." She smiled and inclined her head as the lady in question looked her way.

"You've never had to sit with her in a restrictive area," he muttered darkly, though with a smile. "Rather like being a prisoner of war, I expect."

"Oh, Geoff, did Mary tell you?" Cassandra whispered across Christian as the overture began. "This is her last season and she is going to transform herself into a debutante for it! Can you imagine?"

Mary closed her eyes and groaned softly. She had hoped that her sister would either forget all about her rash promise to embark on such insanity, or that she would be able to confide in Geoffrey about it at time when she actually felt brave enough to do so. Now was hardly the time or place she had envisioned sharing her plans with him.

"Oh, is she?" he asked softly, giving Mary a curious, questioning look.

"I hardly think we need to discuss this now," she hissed through her teeth as the music grew louder.

"Oh, really, as if you are actually listening," he scoffed as he leaned closer. "Come on, Mary. Your last season? Really?"

She sighed and nodded.

He gave her a serious look. "You aren't saying this to indulge Cassie, are you? I know she's been shut away all winter of her own accord, and I know your inclination to protect her."

She nearly laughed at how well he knew her. She gave a slight shrug of one shoulder. "No. Well, not entirely. I've been thinking about it for some time. I've... I have never enjoyed London all that much, and it's hardly been worth the effort I've put in to be a part of the hustle and bustle of the season." She looked over at him and allowed the weariness she had been feeling for so long to show. "I'm tired, Geoff. I want to retire somewhere in the country and live quietly for a while. Perhaps not forever, but for a time, at least."

"So you are giving up on the Marriage Mart, then."

She met his eyes. "I'm twenty-seven, Geoff, and long past having hope in it."

That seemed to sadden him and he took her hand in his and squeezed it softly. "Then your final season it shall be. Will you close up the house?"

She sat back just a little, allowing him to retain a hold on her hand. "I don't know yet. I think so. Cassie will need to come and visit every now and then, as she is so fond of city life, but she never goes anywhere without me anymore, so I'll have to return as well. I worry about her, Geoff. If she's not going to partake in Society, she will end up miserable, bitter, and alone."

"You know she'll be happy again eventually," he murmured encouragingly, his eyes drifting past her to glance at their younger siblings, already entranced with the show. "Look at her tonight. She is fairly glowing."

"You don't see her when all the frivolity has past," Mary returned with a hint of bitterness. "You've never sat up with her until she has cried herself to sleep. She has moments of pleasure, but then they are gone, and she remembers to mourn all over again." She glanced over at her sister and frowned. "And it doesn't stop," she whispered.

"Hence your willingness to parade around as a debutante just to entertain her. To get her back out in Society."

She winced and looked over at him. "I know, I should never have said something so ridiculous..."

"I think it's a marvelous idea," he interrupted with a grin.

"You do?"

He nodded, now turning to face her. "Why not make this a grand season? One last hurrah, if you will. We could make a fine joke out of it all."

"We?" she asked with a quirked brow.

"Mm-hmm," he nodded again. "I am assigning myself as your permanent escort for the season."

She laughed out loud, received murderous glares from numerous people, and clamped her hand over her mouth. When she had quieted herself, she turned to the still snickering Geoff and removed her hand. "You cannot be serious. You won't catch a wife if you are always with me."

He scoffed. "Please. As if I have been hunting of late. One season of larking about with you is not going to doom me to a life of bachelordom. And you cannot go gallivanting all around London without a proper escort. Where you will go, I will go, and it will undoubtedly be the best time either of us has had in a long time."

The opera began in earnest then, and they were forced to be silent, but Mary found herself almost buzzing with a newfound excitement. She leaned closer to Geoff and whispered, "You'd better prepare yourself. Cassandra is forcing me to get new gowns and change my hair and fit myself with all sorts of fine frippery. What do you think of that?"

He leaned away and shook his head. "I'm not going to comment on that. I have nothing to say on the subject of your fashion."

"No comment from you? Really?" she asked, a bit surprised.

"No comment. Really," he repeated, still focused on the stage.

"Mary, please!" Cassandra hissed from her other side.

Mary resisted glaring at her, and leaned closer still to Geoff. "Why?" she whispered.

"Because I like you just as you are, you goose," he replied in a low voice, smiling as he squeezed her hand. He slid a sideways glance at her. "And despite what you might think, I am not a woman, so fashion is not my forte nor my interest."

She sat back against her chair with a slight huff. "Well, you are no help at all," she muttered.

He grinned and released her hand. "Never said I was going to be, did I?"

Mary rolled her eyes and pretended to be upset, but that only lasted for so long, and she found herself smiling. Perhaps this would not be so bad after all. Geoff and Cassandra would be with her all the time, so they could keep her sensible when she would be driven mad with the whole project.

She had no doubts at all that she would be completely insane within a week.

She allowed herself to relax and focus on the performance, making sure to whisper comments to Geoff as the situation called for, and grinning to herself with each of his snickers. But really, she had one other secret she had never told him that made this whole evening that much more agreeable.

She actually truly enjoyed opera.

Chapter Five

"*I* cannot believe I let you talk me into this. What in the world was I thinking?"

"That you were through imitating wallpaper in both behavior and dress and wanted to be a viable member of Society?"

Mary glared at her sister as the two of them walked briskly towards Cassandra's favorite dress shop, which was not Mary's favorite, but according to Cassandra, that was precisely why they were going there.

Some girls no doubt enjoyed being poked and pricked and measured in the most embarrassing ways all for the sake of their own fashion, but Mary was not one of them.

"Why can't I just pick some ready-made gowns and wear those?" Mary complained as her sister very nearly dragged her along the bustle of Bond Street as they approached.

"Because any woman with any desire to catch any man will dress herself in the most flattering and well-fitted gowns she can so as to bring as much attention to her form and figure that she can."

"Ah, but I don't…"

"If you are going to be a debutante, you must at least pretend that you care about what you put on yourself," Cassandra overrode impatiently. "I know you aren't trying to catch a man or attract attention, but you must have properly fitted gowns, Mary. No one in this world but me has any idea how tiny that waist of yours is!"

"Cassie, hush!" Mary hissed as they passed some ladies who

studiously avoided their gaze.

Cassandra snorted. "Oh, please, they weren't listening. I am a pox upon the city and you are universally ignored. Why would anybody possibly listen to us?" She quirked a brow and entered the store.

"I haven't a clue," Mary muttered as she followed.

"Miss Cassandra!" squealed a buxom, graying-haired woman from the back of the shop before her young assistant could do more than open her mouth in greeting.

Cassandra smiled broadly. "Good morning, Mrs. Farrow."

Mrs. Farrow trotted over with a beaming grin that rumpled her plump face. "I will take care of this one, Anna. You can finish Mrs. Smythe's order. Extra yardage on the skirt, remember."

The girl bobbed a curtsey and slipped into the back of the shop.

"My darling dearest girl," Mrs. Farrow gushed, taking Cassandra's hands and kissing her cheeks. "I have missed you ever so much. Tell me you have come back to me for a new gown, I simply love dressing you, child. Nobody wears my gowns as you do! And by the by, I never pay any attention to those horrid people who say such awful things about you. A woman has a right to her own mind, and does not have to accept a man just because he offered, although you and that Lieutenant Wyndham would have made the most exquisitely glorious babies. But pah! No more. Darling girl, what can I do for you?"

Mary stood stock-still and agape as she stared at the woman who had just managed to say a multitude of sentences without taking a single breath. And beyond that, Mary had no idea what she had just said except that this woman was truly glad to see Cassandra, which was such a rarity these days that she could not actually believe she was sincere.

And yet she was.

"Sadly, my dear Mrs. Farrow, I am not here for myself today," Cassandra said, still smiling. Then she turned and indicated Mary. "I am here for my sister, who wishes to make quite a splash this season."

Mrs. Farrow's eyebrows shot up and her lips pursed. "Oh," she said after a long pause, which was not exactly the sort of encouragement that Mary would have liked at this moment.

She looked over to Cassandra with a pleading expression, and not a touch of "I told you so" in her eyes, but Cassandra merely smiled and put her arm through Mrs. Farrow's and said, "I think she has great potential, don't you, Mrs. Farrow? She is like a blank canvas, awaiting your artistic touch."

At those words, Mrs. Farrow's brows snapped back down, her lips formed a smile Mary had seen on many cats, and her free hand tapped her chin thoughtfully. "Why, yes, I think she has potential indeed." She nodded as if just coming to this decision herself, then whirled around. "Anna! I need you after all!"

Cassandra took Mary's hand, grinning, and pulled her along to follow Mrs. Farrow as she waved them towards the back.

"This is a very bad idea," Mary whispered, wiping her now clammy palms on her dress. "She is going to put me in some awful feathery hat and a dress I cannot breathe in. This is a very, very bad idea."

"No, this is a very good idea," Cassandra corrected, squeezing her arm. "Mrs. Farrow will not put you in feathers, she has more taste than that. And breathing will not be restricted at all, I promise. You can have your own input, you know."

"Why bother? You will override my protests anyway."

Her sister smiled wickedly. "This is true. But I won't be completely tyrannical. It could be fun, Mary."

"Not likely."

Cassandra sighed and rolled her eyes. "Well, cheer up anyway. I have a surprise or two for you, and you had better enjoy them."

"Again, not likely," Mary replied. Really, she was beginning to feel slightly nauseated and overheated. Surely that was not normal.

For the next several minutes, which felt like hours, Mary endured the sheer embarrassment of being forced to strip to her undergarments before this woman and measured where she knew she had never been measured before. She could feel her cheeks flaming, but opted to keep her mouth shut. As Mrs. Farrow was such an admirer of her sister's, perhaps the price of these gowns would be less than previously anticipated.

Provided Mary managed to not insult the woman before the appointment was over.

"Now, this dress over here is already made up, but I think it will suit you very well," Mrs. Farrow was saying as she helped Mary step into it.

"Oh, Mary would love to try any ready-made dresses you have, Mrs. Farrow," Cassandra broke in kindly. "She is so thoughtful, she would hate to make you fuss so much just over her specialty gowns. And all your gowns are so exquisite, I know any of them will be perfect."

Cassandra had a gift, Mary decided, and she shot her sister a grateful smile, to which she replied with a wink.

Mrs. Farrow's cheeks colored, and her smile grew more satisfied. "What a kind thing to say, Miss Cassandra! You are always so kind. And Miss Hamilton is too gracious, but it is no trouble at all to make her full new gowns. Let us try this one, and then I will show you some of the others that are ready, and we can alter them for you right here and now, so you may take some home with you. Oh, you sweet girls, I adore you both!"

Mary managed to smile, but her tongue was aching from biting it so hard. At least she would be getting some dresses already made. That should cut down on the number of fittings she would have to come in for.

She glanced down at the dress she was currently wearing, a very pretty pale green muslin, and she found herself smiling just a little. It was neither audacious nor ridiculous. In fact, it was quite simple in cut and color, and she would be comfortable wearing this on a regular basis.

Unfortunately, her smile was caught.

"Ah! She adores it!" Mrs. Farrow cried jubilantly, clapping her hands. "Come, let us take you out to the mirrors." She seized Mary's hand and pulled, and Mary, try as she might, lacked the strength to resist.

"But, Mrs. Farrow," she panted, "I don't wish to be seen."

"Oh, you sweet girl, don't worry! It is all arranged, there are better mirrors in the back, away from the windows. No one will see you but us," Mrs. Farrow soothed, patting her hand.

Well, there was that, at least. She breathed a little easier and stopped resisting so much. She was already dreading her first appearance as this new version of herself. What in the world would people think?

"There now, Miss Hamilton, just step on up there and take a good look at yourself," Mrs. Farrow ordered as they reached the mirrors.

With an inaudible sigh, Mary did so, and felt her breath catch ever so slightly. Not that she looked especially stunning or that she had been magically transformed, for she was still herself, which was neither stunning nor magical. But she looked...

"That suits you very well, Mary."

Her cheeks paled and she turned towards that voice she knew so well. Taking a seat with a perfect view of her was Geoff, and he was smiling broadly.

"What in the world are you doing here?" Mary barked, placing her hands on her hips.

"Erm, surprise?" Cassandra said with a giggle as she came into view.

Mary whirled to face her. "This is your surprise?"

"A rather grand one, I should think," Geoff mused as he set his hat down on the floor and removed his gloves.

"Hardly," Mary snorted, not turning towards him. "Cassie, I don't want to be seen by anyone!" Least of all by him, she thought.

"Geoff is hardly anyone!" Cassandra protested, mirroring Mary's pose. "He is your best friend and an objective set of eyes and he will tell you exactly what he thinks."

"I will indeed," Geoffrey broke in, still smiling, "but only insofar as it matters. I won't tell you what you should or should not do."

"Then what good are you, Geoffrey?" Cassandra asked in exasperation, flinging her hands in the air. "She won't do anything of her own volition."

Geoffrey shrugged. "That's what you are here for, Cassie. I'm here for support and approval, you to decide and dictate. I don't care about gowns and finery. I only wear what my valet tells me to."

"Ugh, men," Cassie groaned and turned to Mrs. Farrow, who gave her a sympathetic look.

"I don't know about this," Mary said as she bit her lip. "What will people say?"

"Why should they say anything?" Geoff asked with a shrug of one shoulder. "It's not as though you're indecent. Or will you be later?" He looked between the ladies, his face a mixture of teasing and curiosity.

"No!" Mary immediately said.

"Yes!" Cassandra and Mrs. Farrow chimed in at the same time.

"No!" Mary said again, glaring at the other two women.

Geoff chuckled and sat back. "This is going to be entertaining. Get on with it, Mary."

She huffed and turned back to the mirror. "Very well. But you make any snide comments, Geoffrey Harris, and I swear I will…"

"Yes, yes, you will plague my heart out and stuff my entrails with cabbage, I know," he said with a dismissive wave. "I accept your terms. Now get on with it, Goose!"

A small smile ticked at Mary's cheek, which was quickly snuffed out when Mrs. Farrow came up behind her and patted her sides. "Now, my dear, let me show you how it would look with alterations."

"Oh, no, Mrs. Farrow, it's just…" Mary tried, but there was no stopping the woman.

She took at the sides of the dress and pulled tight, revealing the slim waist Mary had never thought much of. "If we do this, can you see what it does for that marvelous figure you are hiding?"

Mary couldn't say anything. She did see. She could not *not* see.

"Good heavens, Mary. I had no idea you had that figure," Geoff commented.

She glanced at him in the mirror and saw the arrested look on his face. "It appears that I do," she said slowly, uncertain as to what he meant.

His eyes flicked to hers and he nodded slowly, smiling a little. "So it does. It suits you well."

She returned his smile, relieved. "So you think I should cut the gowns like this, then?"

He immediately sat back again and shrugged. "If you like it, then yes. I told you before, Mary, I'm not going to tell you what to do. I like you just as you are."

She was torn between screeching in aggravation at his lack of help, and giving him a hug for being her loyal friend. Then she heard Mrs. Farrow and Anna give matching fluttery sighs and she frowned. Aggravation it would be.

"Fine, you unhelpful louse," she growled, which made him grin. "Cassie. You tell me."

Now it was Cassandra who looked surprised. "Really, Mary? There is no question. Absolutely yes."

"Then I suppose I will," Mary sighed. What was the point?

Anna and Mrs. Farrow clapped their hands and Cassie grinned.

"Excellent," Mrs. Farrow squealed. "Let us pull some more, shall we?"

With that, Mary was yanked from her pedestal and thrust out of sight as they went to work. Geoff waved to her as she left and she made sure to stick her tongue out at him. He should not be enjoying himself as much as he was.

Four more dresses were forced on her, and each time she would be paraded back out to look at herself in the mirrors, and for Geoffrey to see. Time after time he either nodded or shrugged, neither of which told anybody anything. But he continued to smile, no doubt thinking this all a very fun game. As for Mary herself, she was moderately pleased. Some of the dresses were quite simple and elegant, and she thought she could bear being seen in them.

But the day was still young. Who knew what else she would endure?

As she stepped out in her fifth dress, there was a commotion from the front of the store. Mrs. Farrow sent Anna off to investigate, and she returned with three women, one of which was so large with child, it was amazing she was still with child at all.

"Mary!" Moira, countess of Beverton, called out with a wave, her other hand protectively shielding her incredibly swollen abdomen as she made her way towards them. "So sorry we're late, we meant to be here sooner, but here we are at last!" She nearly knocked over a mannequin, but thankfully, Kate, the marchioness of Whitlock, was right behind her and caught it.

"Steady on, Moira," the dark haired beauty teased. "You'll leave nothing standing if you don't sit down."

Moira scoffed and shook her fiery hair even as she nodded to Geoff. "It's not my fault I'm this large. Blame that husband of mine, you've seen what a massive beast he is. Good morning, Geoffrey."

"Moira. Kate. Lady Beckham," he said, nodding to each in turn.

The third woman laughed and helped Moira sit, and then did so with Kate, who also had a suspiciously swollen abdomen, but hid it well. "Really, Geoffrey, after all these years you still won't call me Diana?"

He smiled and bowed. "My apologies. Good morning, Diana."

She nodded and took her own seat, then glanced up at Mary. "Hello, dear. That is a very pretty color on you. I love what it does for your eyes."

"Oh, Mary, you must get that one," Kate agreed with a nod. "Truly, you look splendid."

Mary was still staring at the three of them in shock. "What are you three doing here?" she finally managed, knowing she sounded rude.

"Helping you find your new dresses for the season, of course," Moira told her with a laugh. "Really, Mary, I think this is the best idea in the world. I hope to be able to see you as a debutante, but if not, I know the girls will tell me everything."

Mary looked over at her sister, who was grinning. "Cassie…"

"Surprise," she said again, in a small voice.

Mary closed her eyes and breathed through her nose very slowly.

"She doesn't want us here," Moira whispered loudly to the others.

"We knew she wouldn't," Diana whispered back, "but we're staying anyway."

"It's not that," Mary said, opening her eyes. "I just… I already feel ridiculous, and to have people see me…"

"Mary," Kate said kindly, "we are not people. We are your friends. And Moira was driving Nathan mad, so she needed to do something, and sitting here with you is much better than sitting at home with a worrying Nathan."

Mary smiled and quirked a brow. "Moira, surely you ought to be resting…"

Moira took a sip of the tea that Anna had brought to them. "Nonsense. A bit of walking is good for me and for the child. Now, step on up there and take a look at yourself. The girls are right, that blue simply makes your eyes shimmer."

Knowing it was pointless to resist all of the women in the room, Mary stepped on the pedestal and took a deep breath of resignation.

"I think that now would be a fine time for the man in the room to quit this soiree," Geoff said as he rose from his seat. "I think you have all the help that you need here."

Mary turned to face him quickly. "No, don't go. Really, it won't be that bad."

He chuckled. "This coming from you? You are barely making it through, so great is your suffering."

She bit her lip and waved him over to her.

He obediently came and tilted his head up at her. "What is it, Goose?"

"I need you to stay," she whispered, feeling her heart race with a bit of panic.

His brow furrowed and he took her hand. "Are you all right?"

She nodded, but gripped his hand tightly. "I need you to stay, Geoff. I am very out of my comfort here. Everybody is telling me what to do and I just can't…" She struggled for words and swallowed.

"You don't have to go through with this, you know," he murmured, knowing the others couldn't see his face. "The whole season of this game, it isn't necessary."

"I know. But look at Cassie, Geoff. She is out in public, and she is glowing. She is holding up her end of the bargain we struck. I cannot back out. I won't. I'll do it, and will attempt to smile through the whole of it." She took a steadying breath. "Just… just don't go. Please."

He looked at her for a moment, then smiled. "Very well, I'll stay. But you will owe me."

She smiled back at him, relief washing over her. "I will and I do, and I will gladly pay it."

He lifted one brow, and his blue eyes twinkled a touch dangerously. "Oh, you shouldn't say that before you know what I will require."

She rolled her eyes and pushed at his chest with a laugh. "I am not afraid of you."

"I think you should be, Goose," he said, winking as he stepped back. "I think you should be." He sat back in his chair and indicated that she continue her modeling.

Mary nodded regally and turned, then saw in the mirror the expressions on all three ladies' faces. Suspicious, curious, and intrigued. Oh dear.

The rest of the morning passed rather the same for Mary, though each dress she tried or was fitted for was different and unique and certainly elegant, and not so very far out of her own tastes. At least, compared to what it could have been. Her friends had very distinct opinions about her gowns and even, saving Moira, rose on occasion to suggest various alterations to Mrs. Farrow, who simply delighted at having three such wealthy and respected ladies in her shop at the same time. Moira merely voiced her opinion from her seat, which was quite enough.

But even Mary, reluctant though she was, had to admit that Mrs. Farrow knew what she was doing. Never had Mary felt so... pretty. There was no other word for it. Being fussed over and complimented was something she thought she could get used to, and when she saw what it brought her, she almost felt that she was worth being fussed over. She had never thought that something as simple as a dress could have that effect.

Geoffrey had been nearly silent the entire time, which suited Mary. She could see in his face if he especially liked something or not, but unless he was asked a direct question, he said nothing. It didn't matter to Mary if he said anything at all. He was here, keeping her steady, and that was all that mattered to her.

"Oh, Miss Hamilton," Mrs. Farrow gushed as she raced back into the dressing area and interrupted her thoughts. "I have found one more gown that is not entirely done, but the girl who had ordered it changed her mind or eloped with a stable hand or something. I think will fit you perfectly. Will you try it?"

Mary looked at the dress, a deep blue ball gown that was almost purple in its richness. It was a little more elaborate than the others, but tastefully so. She fingered the material, and found herself nodding. There was something about this dress that she loved, which was an entirely new emotion for her.

Mrs. Farrow and Anna helped her get it on, and Mary held her breath for their reactions. After all, they were the experts and she the novice. Her own thoughts counted for very little.

"It fits perfectly," Anna breathed, her eyes wide.

"I knew it would!" Mrs. Farrow sighed. "As I said, it is not entirely finished, but it is quite good enough to show your sister and your friends."

Mary let out a breath, then nodded. She closed her eyes, then stepped out into the room and heard a collective intake of breath from the girls, but no other sound. She looked at them all and found them all staring with open mouths.

"Well?" she asked a touch nervously.

"Oh, Mary," Diana breathed, starting to smile. "You look incredible."

Mary was stunned. Diana was never one for flattery. "I do?"

"You do!" Cassandra squealed, her hands covering her mouth as she very nearly danced where she stood.

"You have to take this one," Moira said, dabbing at her moist eyes. "If it can make the emotionally unbalanced and very large woman cry, then it's a sign."

"You're not the only one," Kate laughed, pulling out her handkerchief. "It's beautiful, Mary. Exquisite. I want one."

Everyone in the room laughed, except one. Mary looked past the women to Geoff, who looked rather thunderstruck.

"Geoff?" Mary asked uncertainly, for once wanting him to say something besides his customary "if you like".

He looked her up, and then down, his expression never changing. It seemed as if the entire room held its breath as he examined her. Mary felt her heart pounding furiously in her chest, and thought it very likely she would die before he said anything.

Finally, he met her eyes, his customary smile spread, and he said, "Mary, you have to get this one. Honestly and truly, you do."

The room nearly exploded with cheers and Mary released the breath she had been holding, and allowed herself to grin. If all else failed her, if the season turned out to be a grand disaster for her, at least she had this one gown that made her feel the slightest bit magical.

Perhaps fashion was not so bad after all.

"Wonderful!" Mrs. Farrow cried again, coming over. "Now let us see what we can create for ourselves, hmm? And then we must find bonnets and gloves and coats and stockings and slippers and, of course, undergarments..."

Mary restrained a groan.

Never mind.

Chapter Six

"*S*omebody say something to distract him."

"Distract him? How are we going to do that? It's not even mine, and I can't be distracted."

"Yes, but you will soon have one of your own, so it affects you differently."

"What's all the whispering?" Geoffrey asked his friends as he approached, handing his gloves and hat off to a servant standing nearby.

Derek turned with an oddly strained expression. "Moira is... ah... she is..." He looked to the others for help.

Colin rolled his eyes and said, "The baby is coming."

Geoff turned on his heel, but was stopped by a pair of hands clamping onto his shoulders. "I really don't think I need to be here for this," he protested as Duncan turned him around again.

"None of us do," Colin sighed as he flung himself into a chair and rubbed his brow. "But Nate asked us to come, so here we are. I think this qualifies us for the best friends ever."

A cry that was somehow both hoarse and shrill echoed down to them, and everyone flinched, but Nathan, whom Geoffrey had somehow missed before, groaned and clutched the doorframe harder, his knuckles so white it was unnatural.

"How long has he been like this?" Geoff murmured to Duncan.

"I don't know," he replied. "I've only been here ten minutes myself."

None of the others had any answers either. They all looked at Nathan, but he was so fixed on that room upstairs that an army of giants could have marched into his home and he wouldn't have noticed. He barely even blinked, and gave no hint he heard a single word of their conversation.

"We probably should distract him," Duncan said softly, his brow furrowed in concern.

"And how would you suggest we do that?" Geoff asked in a whisper, doubtful that Nathan would listen to any of them.

"I fail to see why any of us are bothering to keep our voices down," Colin said in his normal voice. "He's not paying attention to anything we say, so there is really no need."

"Just because I'm not responding, Colin, doesn't mean I cannot hear," Nathan replied in a tense voice, though he smiled just a bit.

"He lives!" Colin cried and jumped from his seat. "I feared you were lost to us. What shall we do, Nate, hmm? Go for a ride? Have a few drinks? Fence in the foyer?"

"No."

"Come on, what if we go four against one? Duncan doesn't mind."

"Duncan surely does!" the man in question broke in.

"Come on, Duncan, it's for Nathan," Colin pleaded. "Do your friend a kindness, won't you?"

"I don't need distraction, nor do I need Duncan to play pincushion," Nathan said, not looking at them. He let go of the doorframe and started pacing. "Why haven't I heard anything? I should have heard something. What if it's all going wrong? What if she needs me and I'm down here with you lot?"

"It's Moira, Nate. She would let the world know if she needed you," Geoff assured him.

Nathan apparently did not hear him.

"I should be up there," he muttered, still pacing. "I should be with her."

"So why aren't you?" Colin asked, having lost his juvenile air. "If you're mad enough to actually want to be up there," he paused to shudder for effect, "which I do not understand, why are you down

58

here with the rest of us sensible creatures?"

Nathan looked pained and finally met their eyes. "She kicked me out."

Geoffrey bit his lip to keep from laughing and saw the others doing the same. Colin was struggling the most.

"Oh, fine, laugh if you will," Nathan growled irritably. "You all will feel very different when it's your wife."

Derek sobered up immediately. "That's not far off for me," he murmured, glancing apprehensively up towards the bedchambers.

Colin caught the look and laughed. "Oh, please, Derek, you have nothing to worry about. It's Kate. She will issue a command and your child will come walking out."

That seemed to break the tension, and all laughed.

"Come on, Nathan," Duncan said, putting his arm around his friend's shoulder. "Let's get some food. Worrying here won't do any bit of good."

Nathan sighed and nodded. "That's what Moira said upstairs, and why I'm now down here, but I couldn't help myself. How that woman can be so calm about this whole thing is beyond me."

"One of the great mysteries in life, I expect," Colin added with a nod, sending a servant to bring some food up from the kitchens.

"What, birth?" Derek asked as he took a seat.

"No, women."

Geoffrey rolled his eyes and sat down himself. "You will never marry, Colin."

Colin grinned, his blue eyes glinting. "Oh, and you are one to talk? When was the last time you courted anybody?"

"Lydia Fawcett, and it was 1813, I think," Derek recited, leaning back and smiling.

"How could you possibly remember that?" Geoff asked with a laugh.

"Because you were so entertaining to watch," he replied, indicating the nods from the others. "You were a sight to behold."

"And nobody has seen that side of you since," Duncan sighed mournfully.

"And how is the lovely Mrs. Arnett these days?" Colin folded his arms, looking mischievous. "What does she have, four children now?"

"So, Nathan, how was your winter?" Geoffrey asked in a loud voice, to general laughter.

"Very enjoyable, thank you, aside from a pregnant wife who will not listen to reason." Nathan groaned again as another cry could be heard from upstairs.

"Kate is going to kill me," Derek hissed, his eyes screwing up against the sound.

"Ah, the food is here!" Colin nearly yelled as a servant entered, looking wildly confused at the state of the men. "You are an angel, my dear," he told the girl, who blushed and bobbed a curtsey, then exited.

Duncan and Colin busied themselves with the food, while the other three didn't touch it.

"How long have you been in town, Nathan?" Duncan asked around a mouthful of food.

"Three weeks," he replied, looking gratefully at Duncan. "Moira was bored with Beverton House, so we came here. Went to a party at Lord and Lady Carteret's the other night. Which reminds me," he said, turning to face Geoff. "I like that Mary Hamilton of yours."

"Oh, really?" Geoff replied sarcastically.

Nathan gave him a hard look. "I know you've thought highly of her all your life, but I didn't know her. She's sensible, witty, and good tempered. I used to think her totally reserved, but she merely chooses when and where to open up, and to whom, which makes her a good deal wiser than other members of society, male or female."

Geoff sat back with a satisfied smile, pleased with the assessment. "She's going to play the debutante this season. Balls and the theater and flirtation and the whole bit."

Across the room, eyes widened and brows rose, but only Nathan spoke. "Is she now? That will be an interesting change."

Geoffrey frowned. "Interesting?"

Nathan seemed to choose his next words with a great deal of care. "The thing about Mary is that no one really knows her until they get to know her. She's a mystery wrapped in the assumptions of society. Changing that will change everything else."

"It will be a laugh," Geoff corrected a little strongly.

Nathan shrugged. "If you say so."

"She's one of my best friends," Geoff told them all, feeling defensive. "Don't you think I know what will be a laugh with her and what will not?"

"If you say so," Nathan said again.

Nobody looked remotely convinced of anything.

Another loud yell was heard from upstairs and again, all of them winced.

Nathan put his face into his hands. "I cannot bear this. It's no use."

"I am going to die," Derek moaned to himself with a shake of his head, apparently not hearing Nathan.

A soft clearing of the throat brought all of their heads up to the maid at the door.

"Yes?" Nathan all but barked.

"My lord, she is asking for you," the maid said, wringing her hands a little.

"She is?" he whispered, looking a little pale.

She offered an apologetic wince. "Erm... demanding would be a better word."

"But she kicked me out earlier."

"She said she's changed her mind, and that if you have half of one, you'll be up there before she has to ask again." She smiled a little, looking somewhere between wanting to laugh and wanting to run.

Now the snickers were full blown laughs, but Nathan was off like a shot, moving faster than any of them had ever seen. And Nathan could move very fast indeed.

"Well, I suppose now would be an appropriate time to take a nap," Colin sighed, sliding down in his chair and resting his head against the back of it.

"I think that sounds like a very good idea." Duncan nodded and he took up position on the sofa and closing his eyes.

"I think..." Derek began, standing shakily, "I think I need to go home and hold my wife."

"Tell her hello from me," Colin said without moving, except for the wide grin that appeared on his face. Derek paid him no mind, as usual, and left with barely a nod to the rest.

Geoff smiled to himself as he sat back in his chair. There was nothing else that needed his attention at the moment, the least he could do was get his rest in while waiting for his friend to become a father.

If Mary was going to be as involved in society this season as she seemed determined to, he was going to need all the rest he could receive now.

Nathan's words of doubt nagged at his mind repeatedly, but he brushed them aside as quickly as they came. Things would be fine, not to mention hilarious, they would see.

"Now remember, Mary, when you are at a dinner, do not slurp your soup, or wear your serviette like a cravat, or talk over someone, or eat off of your knife, it's a despicable habit."

"When have I ever done that?" Mary asked incredulously as she leaned against her bedpost, watching her sister pace her bedchamber with this instruction.

"Never, but a reminder is always useful."

Mary threw up her hands and closed her mouth. There was no use talking sense to Cassandra most days, but when she was excitable as she was now, it was impossible. And she had only just started.

Physically, and fashionably, Mary was completely prepared. The gowns and all of the additional accouterments that came with them had been finished earlier in the week, and Cassandra and Mary's new maid, Josephine, had spent the last two days perfecting Mary's hair. What exactly had been wrong with it in the first place had never been explained to her, but she bit her tongue and moved forward, as usual.

What unsettled her still was far less simple. Her entire manner of thinking would have to change. Her behavior, her reactions, her very nature would all have to change. She had to become a debutante, not only look like one. And she didn't know the first thing about that.

How would she even begin to flirt? She'd never done that, and as such, it was an area in which she was a complete novice, even at her age. She wanted to have a bit of a laugh this season, but she'd rather not be laughed at.

"When you're dancing, don't tread on the gentleman's toes, don't engage in too much conversation, as he will think you overeager, but don't be silent, or he will think you a bore, and do not forget the steps," Cassandra rambled on, lost in her own etiquette lesson, the length of her nightgown shifting audibly with her steps.

"You have always said I was a good dancer!" Mary protested with a frown.

"I was being kind," Cassandra assured her. "You are not terrible, and you are positively a better dancer than that awful Emma Hastings, but neither are you graceful."

"Hmph," Mary grumped. Dancing was the one thing she hadn't been nervous about before. After all, she danced every season. A few times. Total. She groaned to herself and shut her eyes. She should not be feeling anxiety about entering a season at twenty-seven. For heaven's sake, it would be her tenth time!

Cassandra moved to the door and turned to face Mary. "Now, when you walk into a room, do so slowly, but with confidence. Expect everyone to stop and look at you. But don't be haughty. Be delicately aware of your allure, but approachable. Don't fidget with your appearance at all. Stand tall, shoulders back, and glance around the room, as if looking for someone, but do not make eye contact with anybody. Then glide towards someone you know, preferably the marchioness or Diana, as they are so well respected. Geoffrey will be with you much of the time, but that doesn't mean he has to be your nanny. Don't hover around him, as that will keep others from approaching."

"You know, I have had a season or two before this, Cassie," Mary broke in, finally, not bothering to keep her voice calm. "I think I know how to behave in public."

Cassandra snorted and tossed her hair. "Obviously not, or you would be married by now."

Mary's mouth popped open and she stared at her sister in shock.

"I cannot believe you just said that."

Cassie shrugged. "It's the truth, and you have said no less yourself. You have absolutely no skills when it comes to social occasion."

Mary sank onto the bed with a hard thump. "Well, this is certainly enlightening."

"You've never thought yourself very good either, so don't blame me for being honest now," Cassie scolded, placing her hands on her hips.

"No, why should I? The rest of the world has been honest my whole life, I hope my family would do the same before I fell under some delusion." Mary looked away, flicking the ends of her plait irritably.

"Mary," Cassandra said slowly, coming over to sit beside her on the bed, "I thought you wanted me to be honest. I am only trying to help you, but if you have changed your mind…"

"No, no, it's not that," Mary sighed, adjusting her shawl. "I am just… I just…"

"You're nervous," Cassandra said in a soft, somewhat awed voice.

Unable, and frankly unwilling, to lie about it, Mary simply nodded.

"Oh, Mary, I'm sorry," Cassandra said, putting her arms around her and touching her head to Mary's. "And here I was rattling on about details. Why didn't you say something? I would have shut up."

"I doubt that." Mary folded her arms over her worn linen nightgown and smiled at her sister.

"Very well, probably not," Cassandra allowed, smiling back, "but I would have listened. Why are you nervous?"

Mary stiffened and shifted away. "It's nothing. It's silly, don't worry about it."

"Mary. I'm your sister. What else are we for but the silly things?"

Mary looked at her sister, for a long moment, then sighed and looked down at her hands. "I don't want to make a fool of myself."

"Why would you make a fool of yourself?" Cassie asked in surprise. "Mary, you have never been a fool."

"When I have been myself, no," she agreed. "But how can I be me and still be the debutante?"

"That is a question every debutante asks herself, I can assure you," Cassandra said with a knowing smile.

"So what is the answer?"

"I haven't the faintest idea," her sister replied with a laugh.

"Cassie!" Mary laughed and fell back onto the bed, arms around her middle.

The laughter continued for a few moments, and then Cassandra grew serious. "Mary, this is all a game as it is. If you don't want to play, no one will make you."

Mary looked at her sister, tempted to back out, despite everything. "Thank you," she replied slowly. Rationally speaking, she did not have to do this. She was content as she was.

She was satisfied.

She was lying.

"I will still do it," Mary relented.

"Oh, good," Cassie burst out, sighing heavily with relief and collapsing onto the bed beside her. "I was going to beat you over the head with your water pitcher if you backed out, especially after all the work I have put in to get you ready."

"Really, Cass?"

Her sister smiled a bit impishly. "No, not really. But I would have stolen all of your dresses."

Mary laughed and smacked her with a pillow. "Wretch. I knew it."

Cassandra giggled, then sighed. "Mary, if it will help, here is a thought for this season; pretend the whole thing is a masquerade."

That brought a bit of a frown to Mary's face. "What good will that do?"

"We are all hiding behind masks whenever we are around others. We want to be the best version of ourselves, we want to hide what we are not, we want to be liked, we want to escape." She shrugged lightly. "It is the way of things. So just change your mask. It's still you, but the mask and costume are different."

"And I have to flirt."

Cassandra grinned. "Of course, you have to flirt. That's where the fun is."

"I think you have an entirely different version of fun than I do," Mary muttered as she sat up.

"Is that what this is all about?" Cassandra asked, watching her closely. "Are you worried about flirting?"

"I have no idea how to do it," Mary admitted in a small voice.

The look on Cassandra's face was priceless and she jerked to a sitting position. "I've never heard of any such thing," she said in a shocked voice.

"Now you have."

Cassie shook herself and stood. "Well, you happen to be related to a girl who was once quite the flirt, if you recall, so I think you will find my instruction adequate for your needs."

"I think I should pass," Mary suggested.

"I think you should stand up and stop being afraid of everything that comes out of my mouth," Cassie returned, looking severe.

"Old habits."

Cassie's blue eyes rolled dramatically. "Really, Mary, you will never be able to flirt if you're going to be a troll."

"Trolls have no need of flirtation."

"Mary!"

"All right, all right, you can teach me!" she cried, standing up.

Cassie smiled mischievously. "You will not regret this, Mary."

"I doubt that," she muttered, hands anxiously gripping her nightgown.

Cassandra chose to ignore that comment. "First things first, you need to bite your tongue."

"I'm working on it."

She nodded approvingly. "Now, have you ever seen how Marianne Bray acts in public?"

"Yes…" she replied, suddenly wary. She liked Marianne, from what she knew, but she couldn't deny that she was quite a sight when on display.

"Try that."

"I do not want to be… like that!" she protested weakly, suddenly envisioning it and feeling ill.

Cassie snorted. "You would have to practice for years to be as accomplished as Marianne is. But just for fun, try it."

"I feel ridiculous," Mary muttered as she tried to adopt the mannerisms that came so naturally to Marianne Bray.

"You look it."

"Whatever happened to hold your tongue?" Mary asked with a raised brow.

"It doesn't apply to sisters."

"Where did you hear that?"

"You. Now, stand taller and glide."

Chapter Seven

It was not often that Geoffrey Harris was surprised. It simply was not in his nature. Whether it was the calmness of his character, or some deep rooted inability to be astounded, he didn't know, but surprise rarely struck him.

Until tonight.

He slowly sipped whatever it was he was drinking and stared off at nothing, albeit in the general direction of his best friend, who has already well on her way to achieving exactly what she wanted from this season.

And therein lay his surprise.

He had arrived at the Hamilton house earlier than expected, and made himself at home, as he usually did, asking Winston to inform the ladies of his arrival. Word was sent back down that they were not ready yet, but would be shortly. Three quarters of an hour later, Cassandra came down, gave him a beaming grin, and said Mary would be down momentarily.

He hoped that Cassie's meaning of the word "momentarily" was a good deal less than that of "shortly."

"How does she feel?" he had asked with concern, wondering if a rare case of nerves had afflicted her.

"You'll see," she replied with a smug smile.

"I said feel, not look," he grumped.

Cassie had only smiled again and said again, "You'll see."

Entirely unsatisfied, Geoff folded his arms and waited.

Less than five minutes later, Cassie had waved him over to the stairs excitedly. He rose from his seat and came over to the base of the stairs, and looked up.

Never before in his life could he recall surprise of such magnitude.

She was wearing the lavender gown he had seen the other day, and it had been one of his favorites. Now, however, the details were complete and it was fitted, and it was as if he had never seen it before. But it was not the dress that surprised him, beautiful as it was. It was the woman who wore it. Her tiny waist was on display for the entire world, who had never known her to have a figure at all. She was moving with a grace and elegance he had never seen in her. Her hair looked rich and thick, and it was dotted with small pearls that matched the ones now embellishing the bodice, drawing more attention there than anyone would have paid before, and the gown made it worth their while. Her complexion was rosy and healthy, and she had a glow about her that made impossible to look anywhere but at her.

For the space of an entire three heartbeats, he wasn't even sure it was Mary. Then he met her eyes and the familiar friend was there, and he could breathe a little. He took her hand, bowed very properly over it, and murmured, "Miss Hamilton."

"If she pinches my cheeks one more time, I'm going to slap her," Mary hissed through a smile.

Relief had washed over him as he glanced up at her and grinned. Things would be just fine.

Now, as he pretended not to watch her, he wasn't so sure.

It was as if she had been a natural debutante her entire life.

She flirted, she smiled, she hypnotized. There were at least seven men standing around her, all of whom had seen her before, and often, at other events and had never even looked in her direction. It made no difference to them that she had come here on his arm, in his carriage, and with his protection. They were just as keen to make a favorable impression on her as if she were the freshest female in the room. To them, he supposed she was.

"I think this is going rather well, don't you?" Cassandra asked him as she came to his side.

"Do you?" he murmured, slowly drinking again.

"Of course," she replied. "Look at how happy she is. She has never had this much attention in her entire life!"

"Mary doesn't like attention."

"Oh, please, Geoffrey," Cassie laughed, smacking his arm with her fan. "Every woman likes attention, even if she pretends she does not."

"Mary isn't every woman."

Cassandra rolled her eyes. "Honestly, Geoff, what has your breeches in a twist? I have never known you to be so grumpy. Why can't you be happy that she is happy?"

"Is she happy?" he asked in reply, tearing his eyes away from her. "Because unless she tells me so herself, I cannot believe it."

"Then go dance with her, and ask her yourself," she muttered with a snort of derision. "Don't stand in the corner like some old man, grunting about the impropriety of the younger generation."

He gave Cassandra an assessing look, then laughed. "Forgive me, Cassie. You're right. It's the change. I suppose I have to get used to it like everybody else."

"Yes, you do," she said with a nod and a smile. "Our project is working, just as we predicted. She will be right as rain, and will laugh about it with us later, you'll see."

He glanced back over and caught Mary giving him a warning look he well recognized as a rather young gentleman struggled desperately to maintain her attention. "She wants to be rescued," he said in a low voice. "Shall I save her or let her fend for herself?"

Cassie smiled rather wickedly. "Let her endure for a dance. She won't have us watching her all the time, she must learn how to escape on her own."

Geoff chuckled and held a hand out to her. "Then will you dance with me, Cassie?"

She beamed up at him, and for the present, his troublesome thoughts abated. Let Mary find her own way out of her quandary.

After all, this was what she had wanted.

Well, that was all well and good, Mary huffed to herself as she watched Geoff blatantly ignore her cry for help. She had seen the way he and her sister had debated on her fate, knowing how she was struggling, and then betray her. The two of them would have to be dealt with.

But as she watched her sister dance, to see her laugh again and smile so brightly and with so much joy, she had to admit that it might be worth it.

"Pardon me, Miss Handelin?" prodded the puppy who had been practically proposing to her for the last twelve minutes.

She put aside the cool detachment that had been plaguing her for the last hour, and gave the lad a look. "It is Miss Hamilton, Mr. Davis. If you cannot remember it, then perhaps you ought to work on that before you solicit my society. No woman will take any man, regardless of his youth, if he does not even know her name."

He went skulking off, cheeks flaming, the other gentlemen snickering in their delight.

She could have shot the lot of them.

"Well said, Miss Hamilton," an attractive man nearby said with approval. "Poor Master Davis to be so soundly set down by so fair a maiden."

Mary gave him a careful look, noting his too-extravagant ensemble, which fit perfectly, and tried to ignore the oddly vibrant blue waistcoat. "I daresay he will rally," she said carefully, reluctantly sliding her debutante mask into place. "He is too young to be serious about courting anyone, let alone someone of my years."

The man smiled in surprise, showing rather perfect teeth, which must always be admired. "I did not think that ladies referenced their age, no matter the number of years they have."

"Only those ashamed of their age for one reason or another," she told him with real honesty. Then she shrugged. "I am not."

That seemed to impress him and he inclined his head politely, then moved away.

How bizarre, she thought. He was the one man she had spoken with since arriving that she might have actually enjoyed conversing with. Everyone else was just for show. And he would just leave?

She shook her head. It was all so confusing.

"Might I have a dance, Miss Hamilton?"

She looked up into the face of the Marquess of Whitlock, and returned his smile with one of her own. "With pleasure, my lord."

He led her out into the floor and swept her into the movement with surprising grace. "How is your little project going?" he asked her, looking amused.

She rolled her eyes, which made him laugh. "If I could bear any of the conversation, I might be enjoying myself."

"Well, you seemed to be getting along with Burlington well enough."

"Who?" she asked in confusion.

"Henry Burlington," Derek said, tilting his head in the direction of the attractive, over-dressed man she had just spoken with.

"Oh," she replied absently. "Yes, I suppose I did. He doesn't seem to be interested in me at all, which makes me inclined to think well of him."

Derek laughed, then gave her a scolding look. "You will never get anywhere setting yourself down in such a way, Mary, and I won't allow it." He glanced up, one corner of his mouth curving up. "And if you will turn your head slightly to your right on the next movement, you will see where his interest lies."

Mary did so and saw Mr. Burlington watching her carefully, his expression composed, but engrossed. He looked away when their eyes met, but Mary knew instinctively that he would look back.

She quickly returned to attention to the dance, and her partner, who was smiling mischievously.

"It seems you have an admirer after all," Derek mused.

"I don't see why," Mary retorted as she made her circle around him. "I look like every other woman in the room, and the only words he said to me were a compliment on my insult and his shock on the discussion of my age."

"You will soon learn, my dear Miss Hamilton, that nothing

sparks a gentleman's interest more than a woman who takes us by surprise."

"Oh good," she muttered dryly. "Well, what is he like? Do you know? If he is a man worth entertaining, I might allow his pursuit."

Derek chortled and spun her as part of the dance. "Him? You could do better. He is the top of the fops."

That drew a surprised laugh from Mary. "Oh, I doubt that very much. He might be a bit elaborate, but…"

"He is the epitome of elaborate, my dear. Quite ridiculous."

She gave Derek a long, speculative look. "I don't believe you. I think you are toying with me for the sake of our long acquaintance, and trying to influence me for your means."

Derek grinned, looking a little surprised. "Would I do that? When it is something so important as potentially finding your future husband and securing for you the incomparable joy of matrimony?"

"God save me," she muttered in a dark tone. "This whole venture was supposed to be a laugh, and the first night I find myself more irritated than anything else. It's not encouraging. They just want me to stand there and look demure while they shower me with flattery." She closed her eyes briefly. "I'm so bored."

Derek chuckled softly. "That is because no one has danced with you yet. Present company excluded, naturally."

Mary gave him a suspicious glance as she passed around him in a movement of the dance. "Is this why you're dancing with me, Derek?"

"Precisely. Someone had to show off your talent for dancing, and what better person than myself?" He smiled broadly and Mary couldn't help laughing.

"But I have to confess," Derek said on a sigh as he turned her, "that was not my only reason for coming over to you."

Mary wrinkled her brow in confusion. "What was the other?"

Derek took her elbow as the dancing finished and pointed discreetly over at his wife, who was smiling at her. "Kate. She thought you needed a reprieve. Actually her words were, 'Go save her before she kills someone.'"

"Your wife has remarkable perception."

73

"I am well aware of it, I can assure you."

He led her over to his wife, who smiled up at him proudly. "Thank you, darling."

"Of course, my love," he murmured, pressing a gentle kiss to her cheek, then striding away towards the card room.

"What in heaven's name was that all about?" Mary murmured as Kate linked their arms.

Kate laughed and glanced in the direction where her husband had just disappeared. "I'm not entirely certain. He's been attentive and sweet and adoring for the last several days. I think it might have something to do with Nathan and Moira having little Robert last week, but he won't tell me anything. Not that I am complaining, mind you, but it's very odd."

She shrugged a little and began to walk with Mary around the ballroom slowly, nodding at various people, who whispered excitedly.

"How are you enjoying yourself, Mary?" Kate asked, as she smiled at Lady Greversham tightly. "Or are you enjoying yourself?"

"It's difficult to say," Mary replied, choosing her words carefully. "I think the shock of so much attention is preventing me from feeling anything but anxiety at the moment."

Kate patted her hand and sighed. "I think you'll have to get used to attention if you're going to pull this off. Use it to your advantage. I don't know your sister well, but I hope she hasn't been attempting to mold you into someone else."

"No, Cassie seems to want me to remain myself under this costume, but it still feels strange and unnatural to act like this."

"I know," Kate murmured, looking over at her. "Change is a painful process. Balancing who you are with who you wish to be is a never-ending struggle. But you can do it, Mary, and I trust you can do so with more poise than I had."

Mary smiled softly in response, remembering when she had met Kate during her own transformation, though she had been a witness to the old Kate, or Katherine as she always was, and the difference was truly profound.

"I think you had grace and poise enough for royalty, Kate."

That seemed to take Kate by surprise, and she smiled in return, though her eyes grew a little misty. "Thank you, Mary. That means a great deal." She blinked rapidly and laughed. "Well, do you think we have done enough parading for one evening?"

"Is that what this was?" Mary asked as she carefully looked around. Dozens, if not hundreds, of eyes were on the two of them, and she found herself wondering just how many had been watching them the whole time.

"A bit, but I really did want to talk with you alone. And if I could do that while showing you off, all the better!" She grinned rather grandly, which made Mary chuckle.

"You are conniving, Lady Whitlock."

"A marchioness with an attractive friend in need of suitors must be, my dear Miss Hamilton." Kate softened her smile and looked beyond Mary for a moment. "Now, Geoffrey is coming to save you, so I will just kiss your cheek and be on my way."

"So many saviors, so little time," Mary sighed as Kate kissed her cheek and winked.

Kate squeezed her hands. "Don't blame us for liking you," she whispered. "We can't help it."

Mary shook her head in amusement as Kate walked away, no doubt to speak with people of great importance and spreading her influence far and wide.

Derek was lucky to have such a wife.

"Well, I certainly am a fortunate man to finally catch you alone, Miss Hamilton."

Mary rolled her eyes and turned to face Geoff with a severe look. "It wouldn't have been so difficult if you had simply come over, Mr. Harris. I was not so surrounded that there was not room for you."

Geoff grinned and inclined his head towards her. "Are we pretending again or are you being serious?"

"A debutante never reveals her true intentions, Mr. Harris," Mary told him, quoting her sister to a tee, and fluttering her eyes a little. "She leaves a man guessing right until the very end."

"Ah, so she does," he replied, bowing smartly. "Will you consent to a dance, then, Miss Hamilton? I so desire to have further opportunity to guess at those intentions of yours."

Mary had to refrain from giggling, and very calmly placed her hand in his. "It would be a pleasure, Mr. Harris."

He led her out to the dance floor proudly, the pair of them remarkably composed for the laughter threatening to explode at the whispers behind them.

"Bravo, Goose," Geoff whispered. "You are better than I thought."

"It is Cassie's lessons," she murmured back as they moved into position.

"Lessons? Really?"

"Yes, really," she told him with a smile. "One cannot become a debutante overnight. It takes lessons and practice and learning to be long-suffering to perfect one's self."

"Well, you are in fine form tonight, Miss Hamilton," he said a bit louder as the dance started.

"I hardly think it appropriate for you to comment on my form, Mr. Harris," she scolded.

He shrugged. "I'm not nearly as appropriate as people think me, Miss Hamilton, and I frequently comment on things I shouldn't."

"How very shocking you must be, then! How should I reply?"

"You might say something shocking in return."

She lifted a brow rather imperiously at him as he crossed in front of her in the dance. "I have nothing shocking to say."

"Oh, I doubt that very much, Miss Hamilton," he said with a bit of a wicked grin. "I know you. You always have something shocking to say."

"Perhaps you don't know me as well as you might think."

It was now his turn to offer a lifted brow, daring her to continue.

"A lady never says shocking things, Mr. Harris," she informed him as she crossed. "She merely thinks them very loudly."

He closed his eyes, struggling not to laugh. Mary was having no less trouble, but she forced herself to not bite down on her lip.

The dance continued without much opportunity to converse further, but they said a great deal with their eyes, and it made the act of not laughing that much more difficult. When it was done, Geoffrey led her to a different side of the room than she had been previously.

"Let's see if we can't get you some more appropriate fops on this side, shall we?" he murmured as he escorted her.

"I doubt it, but why not?" she laughed, feeling a bit breathless from the dance. "That was the most fun I have had in a while, Geoff. Thank you."

"I would dance with you more, but I think a line will be forming in about forty-two seconds." He laughed to himself as he looked around.

"Oh, my poor feet," she moaned.

"I wouldn't worry for them. They are quite perfect, you know."

"My feet?" she asked with a laugh. "Don't be ridiculous. Nobody has seen my feet."

He smiled rather devilishly. "I have. Therefore, I feel expressly qualified to comment on their perfection. Each and every toe."

She blushed a bit, which made him chuckle. "Is that your favorite part of me, then?"

He shrugged and bowed low. She returned it with a deep curtsey.

"Don't cause a scandal now, Goose," he whispered, still smiling.

"You first," she replied.

He acknowledged her comment with a slight tilt of his head, then walked away, still smiling.

Insufferable man, she thought viciously as she watched his retreating back.

"Miss Hamilton," no less than three male voices said at the same time.

Mary sighed inwardly, cast one more very brief, slightly longing glance in Geoff's direction, then slipped into her debutante form again with a polite smile and turned once more to her newfound admirers.

Chapter Eight

 $\mathcal{M}$ ary sat at the edge of her bed, still in her nightgown and wrap, hair blissfully ignorant of its current woebegone state, and rubbed her tender feet with a wince. She had arrived home very late last night, or this morning, rather, and until she had removed her shoes, she'd had no idea how sore they were. A restless night's sleep was not helping matters.

This was what she should get used to? She would never survive.

She groaned and closed her eyes as she gripped a particularly tender part of her foot. She danced nearly every dance last night, which she'd never done. It had never happened in her entire life, and she couldn't honestly say that she was sorry for it. But she also couldn't deny that the change was… rather nice.

Cassandra had crowed the entire carriage ride home about Mary's victorious entrance and how lovely she looked and who stared the most, who said the vilest things, and who was most likely to begin to court her first. Mary had ignored her as her head throbbed and her toes begged for a reprieve. Geoffrey had said nothing either, but he did watch her. Not in the way that the other men at the ball had, but with a sort of concerned amusement.

"Geoffrey," she'd said sternly as she closed her eyes, "staring is rude."

"You had fun."

One eye pried itself open and glared. "Is that so shocking?"

He smiled his favorite, most mischievous smile. "No denial? You must have had a grand time indeed."

Cassandra clapped her hands and squealed. "I knew you would! I simply knew it."

"Cassie, do shut up."

Her sister smirked and sat back, looking rather satisfied.

"You did have a good time, didn't you?" Geoff asked, leaning closer.

Mary gave him a bit of a smile. "If you promise not to say anything…"

"On my life and that of my greyhound."

"…I had a good time," she admitted with a small smile. She yawned and covered her mouth with the back of her glove. "But must it go on so long? I could have been in bed hours ago."

Mary shook her head with a smile now as she remembered. Geoffrey had been a rather good escort the night before, excluding his ignoring her plea for help. He had danced with her twice, the second being a true rescue as she was nearly forced to dance a third time with Mr. Newton, who, while semi-attractive, was also notorious for his ability to bore cattle.

She regretted not being able to converse with Mr. Burlington any further. Despite Derek's rather weak warning, she was curious. He had been rather polite with her, hardly superfluous, and someone she'd expect Derek and Geoff to approve of, elaborate waistcoat notwithstanding. Burlington had maintained a safe distance from her most of the night, despite always watching, and had done nothing to make his intentions known. Provided he had any intentions at all. She could hardly imagine he had when she had no proof.

One night in and already she was having grand assumptions.

"Keep your head, Mary," she scolded herself. "Pretend the debutante, don't become one."

A soft knock came at the door, and Mary jerked. "Come in."

Mrs. Evansdale, their sweet and overprotective housekeeper, entered her room with a confused look on her face. "Miss Hamilton, I believe you have company."

Mary felt her brows shoot up to her hairline. "At this hour? I haven't even had breakfast."

"I know, Miss. I've told them such, but they are insistent." Mrs. Evansdale shrugged, then started wringing her hands together.

"If Diana and Kate expect me to behave this season," Mary huffed as she quickly pulled out her plait and got to her feet, "then they ought to wait until after I am fed before starting an inquisition."

"Erm…" Mrs. Evansdale hummed anxiously, her fingers nearly clawing at each other.

Mary looked over with concern. "Are you all right, Mrs. Evansdale?"

The plump woman bit her lip, cheeks as red as her hair. "It is not Lady Beckham or Lady Whitlock, Miss. "

Mary folded her arms and peered at her. "Then who is it?"

Mrs. Evansdale stepped aside and waved behind her. Josephine entered, bobbing quickly, looking far more delighted than the housekeeper. Her bright eyes sparkled with excitement.

"Winston says it is gentlemen, Miss," Josephine whispered gleefully.

Mary rolled her eyes and turned to the wardrobe. "Oh, bother, don't tell me Geoffrey is calling for a ride this early. I won't venture out of doors at all until I…"

"Pardon, Miss, but it is not Mr. Harris," Mrs. Evansdale interrupted as she pushed Josephine over in Mary's direction.

Mary froze and met her maid's eyes. "Then…"

"He only said gentlemen, Miss," she replied with a shrug.

"Wait. Men? As in… plural?" She clutched at her throat, which suddenly had constricted and become very dry.

"Indeed, Miss," Josephine said with a happy nod as she began helping Mary out of her night things.

Mary took an unsteady breath and released it slowly. This was all part of being a true debutante. Callers would come, and they ought to be informed that she wouldn't take calls before breakfast. Some things she would not bend on, and they needed to know it.

Josephine dropped a dress over her head and helped it on, and Mary looked at herself very calmly in the mirror. She caught sight of Mrs. Evansdale by the door, still looking uncomfortable.

"How many?" Mary asked slowly.

Mrs. Evansdale met her eyes in the mirror, suddenly terrified. "Wh… what, Miss?"

"How many gentlemen?"

"Oh, we can't say for certain," Josephine said absently as she did up the buttons. "How many gentlemen do you think can fit in the sitting room?"

Three minutes later, Mary slipped carefully down the stairs, keeping her back to the wall the entire time. Thankfully, the sitting room happened to be situated directly off of the staircase, so she should be able to sneak a peak in without too much of a risk of being seen. But having never attempted to sneak anywhere in her own home before, she had no idea if it was even possible. Did her stairs creak? Were her slippers soft enough to avoid making noise? Would the door to the room hide her enough to allow her more than a cursory glance?

Her buttons scraped against the wall and she froze, hoping against hope that the sound, horrendously loud in her ears, would be indistinguishable to others amid the sounds of whomever was in her sitting room.

No sounds other than the low murmur of voices were heard, and she relaxed, ever so slightly and kept moving. Total relaxation was not possible at this point, not when there was a roomful of men downstairs.

At last, she reached the bottom stair and she drew in a long, silent breath. Then she very carefully leaned forward and peered into the room as surreptitiously as she could.

Josephine had not exaggerated.

Mary could see almost a third of the room, as well as the gaudy mirror her mother had put in that room years ago. She had never been so grateful for something she hated in her entire life. In her line of sight, there were at least six men. In the mirror, at least four others were visible. They all seemed preoccupied, whether with their own attire, hair, or teeth, or with discussing important topics, horses it seemed, and so she was unnoticed in her observations.

She felt her heart pick up its pace and her breathing followed suit. She couldn't do this. She could not do this.

Forgoing her previous desire for silence, she raced up the stairs. Already panting, she turned the corner down the hallway, threw open Cassandra's bedroom door, and slammed it behind her as she entered, plastering herself against it. Cassie was still in bed, but stirred at the sound, blearily opening her eyes.

"Mary?" she mumbled sleepily. "Wha-er you doing?"

"Men," Mary gasped.

Cassandra blinked in confusion, rubbed her eyes, then pushed herself up to a sitting position. "Maybe I was too hasty to push you out into Society so early. You have clearly lost your mind."

Mary shook her head quickly, swallowing. "There are men in the sitting room."

"Really?" Cassie said slowly as a sly smile crossed her face. "How many?"

"Ten."

A deep furrowed formed between Cassie's brows. "That's all?"

Mary looked at her in disbelief. "That's all? That's ten times what I have ever had put together! There's no room for them all to sit down!"

"No, nor should there be." Cassie yawned, stretched, and got out of bed, padding barefoot over to her mirror. "Sitting down makes them more comfortable. Maybe we ought to remove one of the sofas," she mused as she sat down and began undoing her plait.

"Oh, Cassie. What am I supposed to do?" Mary moaned. "I'm not prepared for something like this. I don't... I can't... I think I may be ill."

Cassandra sighed, but showed no other sign of concern. "Not on my carpet, if you please."

"Cassie! What do I do?" Mary asked, her voice rasping in her dry throat. Now was not the time for her sister to be indifferent.

Her sister cast her a look in the mirror. "Go down and greet your callers, of course. What do you expect?"

"Not this!" Mary put a hand to her head and slouched against the door. "Definitely not this."

Setting down her brush, Cassandra turned and faced her. "Mary, you've never shied away from a challenge before. This whole scheme was your idea, remember. Yes, ten potential suitors in the sitting room before breakfast is more than you expected, but don't you see? This means you are a success and those men want to know more! Your task now is to weed out the ones not worth your time. You enjoy gardening. Go pull out the weeds."

Mary stared at her younger sister, who knew so much more about this sort of thing that she did. How, in all of Mary's twenty-seven years, had she learned so little? She swallowed hard, and stood up straighter. "Right. I can do this. I can be myself and still be a debutante on short notice."

"Yes, you can," Cassandra agreed, smiling slightly. "You look lovely, especially since it's before breakfast. Perhaps you might wish to scold them for it?"

"I plan to," Mary said darkly. "That is, if I can find a way to politely scold a roomful of men without offending any. The last thing I need is bad gossip going around and taking all the fun out of things."

Cassie adopted a would-be innocent expression. "Oh, are you having fun right now? I thought you were panicked."

Mary made a face at her. "Don't mock my pain."

"Oh, the sheer agony of success," Cassie muttered dryly as Mary exited. "Be graceful, dear!"

"Yes, Mother!"

Mary could hear her sister snicker as she closed the door behind her. She waited a long moment as she collected her thoughts, settled her breathing, and could manage to swallow easily. Finally, she took in a breath, released it slowly, and then made her way down the stairs. Gracefully, of course.

Composing her face into an expression of cool detachment, she entered the room, and was amused at the reaction of the men within. They all stood hastily and bowed, but not in unison. Those elaborately dressed bowed deeply, and those with more sensible clothing bowed only half as much. She noticed, with a twinge of disappointment, that Mr. Burlington was not among the gathered. It appeared that both she and Derek were mistaken in his regard for her.

No matter. She had other weeds to pluck.

"Good morning, gentlemen," she told the gathering, a polite smile on her face. "My, what early risers you all must be!"

The entire room laughed, some more loudly than others, and some rather high-pitched indeed.

She must remember to find a man whom she could stand to hear laugh. Assuming she ended up finding one at all.

She calmly folded her hands in front of her and looked around at them all. "Any of you that have come here due to your mother's insistence because she thinks I am desperate may leave now. Winston will show you out."

The butler appeared at her side in an instant, which was lovely, as the man could be a bulldog, if needed. Between her words and his expression, no one would dare lie about their intentions.

And none did. For a moment, the room was entirely still. Then a few of the men ducked their heads and exited without a word.

Mary waited until the door was closed before looking at the remaining men. They were all very different in age, in dress, and in wealth. She doubted if this particular group of men had ever been in the same place at the same time outside of a ballroom or theater. And yet all were here, in her sitting room, eagerly awaiting a word or a look from her.

What a laugh.

She fought back a sigh, and smiled instead. "Would anyone care for some tea?"

Chapter Nine

"Let me get this straight. She had Viskin, Godfrey, Oliver, and Wofford in her sitting room all at the same time?" Colin laughed and put his hand over his eyes.

"I'm surprised they did not get into a slapping match," Duncan mused wryly, shaking his head. "And that Burlington wasn't there with them."

"Burlington is interested," Derek assured them. "They were officially introduced the other night. But he has not called yet, as far as I know. He prefers a delayed approach. Part of his charm." He snorted and propped his feet up on his table, folding his arms over his chest. "I heard she also has had Timmons, Harper, Beech, and St. Martin in there."

That sobered Colin's laughter as he leaned forward incredulously. "St. Martin? Not…"

"Yes, the duke," Derek affirmed with a serious nod. "She has drawn him out of eternal bachelorhood."

"This is remarkable," Nathan said as the others tried to digest what this meant. "She really is making quite the splash, isn't she? And after that card party last night, it will get even worse."

"Wait, what happened last night?" Colin asked eagerly, looking between his friends.

"Lady Warden's card party," Geoff told him simply.

Colin winced. "Oh, no, did she try to convince you to marry Penelope again? I don't even accept her invitations anymore."

"No, she seemed more focused on Sophia this time, but as Sophia prefers men of superior intellect, we parted as quickly as her mama threw us together." Geoffrey shook his head with a laugh.

"So what happened at the party to make things get worse?" Colin asked again.

Duncan looked at him in surprise. "Haven't you heard? It's all over town."

Colin looked a bit sheepish. "I may have slept past my normal time this morning, a bit too much fun last night. I haven't seen anyone but you lot, so you must fill me in. What did Mary do?"

Geoffrey sighed and rubbed his face with his hands. "The woman is a card sharp. She won every hand of whist, loo, and cribbage, even with multiple partners and sets. She won ten pounds off of Jack Kent, and then doubled it against Thomas Granger."

"And consequently added them to her coterie," Nathan added with an amused shake of his head.

"They're not the only ones," Duncan said slowly, his eyes flitting to Geoff with concern. "I was visiting my solicitor this morning, and I overheard some things…"

"Like what?" Geoff laughed. "Is the Prince of Wales interested in her now?"

Duncan didn't laugh. "George Branson may call upon her today. As might Daniel Tremont, Charles Elliot, and Robert Henley."

That sobered the entire group. A more troublesome group of rogues couldn't to be found in the entire city, if not the country. Branson was rumored to regularly seduce maids, not to mention young innocents. Tremont had run through his fortune at least once already and about whom Geoff knew far too much, and Elliot was a dangerous man whose wife had died under some very suspicious circumstances.

And Henley… Henley might have been the tamest of the lot, but he was also the one about whom not much was known. He had only recently returned the country, following the death of his father. He had been on the continent for years, and no one knew why or what he did.

All of the men were very handsome, and all of them were equally charming.

"Elliot will not actually call," Derek corrected firmly, breaking the silence. "He will send flowers with his compliments or something first, to lure her in. He is a cunning fox."

"So she is attracting fops, card players, and rogues?" Colin furrowed his brow in confusion. "That doesn't make any sense."

"She's also got some scholars, from what I hear," Nathan said brightly, trying to lighten the mood. "Probably impressed with her strategic mind. But Mary is a wise girl, Geoff. She won't tolerate fools."

"Oh, I know that," Geoff replied with a wave of his hand, smiling. "I'm not worried. Mary can handle herself. Who would have thought she would attract so much attention just by changing her hair?"

Colin snorted. "If only it were that simple."

Everyone looked at him in surprise.

He caught their glances, and shrugged. "I don't know Mary as well as you, Geoff, or Nathan or Derek, or even Duncan. We ran in completely different circles. I'm a gossipmonger wherever I go, and she a wallflower. Yes," he overrode as his friends rose to her defense, "yes, she is, and don't bother to deny it."

No one did, so he continued.

"People never got to know Mary because she never let them. She is reserved by nature, and in public, a reserved nature is magnified. No one wants to talk with someone who is not talking to anyone, unless she is remarkably pretty or has a massive fortune. Mary is a plain girl with a decent fortune, but hardly one to brag about." He waited for more denials, but none came. "Now all that is changed."

"As I said," Geoff interrupted with a hint of frustration. "All from changing her appearance."

Colin held up a finger. "Yes and no. She found a way out of being plain, which attracted attention. But she is also talking. She is opening up. She is putting aside her formerly reserved temperament, and showing that she really would be worth the trouble. And that is what catches suitors. They are paying attention now."

Geoff shifted uncomfortably, feeling defensive. "Well, I've been paying attention to her for years."

Colin laughed. "Not like this, you haven't. Go on over to Mary's house and see what sort of attention she is receiving. You may find your eyes opened."

Geoffrey looked around at them all, and then stood. "All right, I will. And when I prove you all wrong, I'm going to crow about it for a very long time." He nodded and walked out of Derek's library with his head held high.

"He has no idea," Nathan sighed.

"None at all," Duncan agreed.

Geoffrey grumbled about his friends the whole walk to Mary's. He ought to have taken a hack, as it would have reduced the travelling time significantly, but he needed the exercise.

As if they would know Mary better than he did!

How many men truly could be so fascinated with a woman they had seen for years and had never really noticed? He shook his head and picked up his pace, wanting to hurry and see what all the fuss was about. Mary would have quite a laugh when he told her what his friends thought.

He shook his head as he walked, still laughing about the night before. He thought he knew Mary so well. How had he never known how skilled she was at cards? To beat Jack Kent and Thomas Granger! There were very few men in the country who could say they had done that, let alone any women.

He rang at the house, and Winston answered, not looking entirely composed.

"Mr. Harris, it is a delight to see you," the old man wheezed.

"Winston," Geoff greeted with a nod as he handed his hat to him. "How does our girl do today?"

Winston sighed heavily and shook his head. "It has been difficult to keep up, sir." He glanced back towards the room. "I don't know what to make of all this."

"None of us do, Winston," Geoff said with a pat on the butler's shoulder.

"Do what?" asked a cheery voice from the stairs.

Geoffrey grinned up at Cassandra as she came down. "Your

sister's sudden popularity. We were just agreeing how confusing things are getting."

Cassie rolled her eyes, but smiled. "Isn't it ridiculous? I've tried to tell her to be more firm, to pace herself, but every day she allows them all to come in. I wouldn't have thought it, but my sister is turning into quite the social butterfly."

"Surely not," Geoff protested with a laugh. "I have seen no such thing."

Cassandra gave him a look. "You haven't been watching, then. Go in and have a look."

Now genuinely curious, Geoffrey headed in that direction and even before he entered, he saw five gentlemen sitting around Mary as if she were a queen of old and they her adoring court. Oddly enough, none of the men he and his friends had just been discussing were present. At this particular moment, Geoffrey could only identify one of them. James Finley-Ashe, a scholar by definition, a notable bore by trade. He was sitting closest to Mary and was currently speaking animatedly on some subject Geoff's ears simply refused to hear.

Mary seemed to be listening to Mr. Finley-Ashe with polite interest and had not seen him yet, so he took up position in a chair in the corner of the room where he could survey the entire gathering with ease.

Eventually, one of the others said something, and the group laughed, even Mary. And it was not a polite laugh for the sake of the men, it was her genuine laugh. Geoffrey was one of few people who knew the difference. He frowned momentarily. Could Mary be enjoying all of this?

Well, if she were going to become the most sought after woman in London, he supposed he could make more of an effort to show that they spent time together. If he were fortunate, it might end up doing wonders for his romantic prospects in the future as well.

He smiled to himself and sat back in his chair, finally catching Mary's eye. She smiled just a touch, inclined her head slightly, then went back to the conversation at hand.

Almost an hour later, Geoffrey was quite certain that his lower half was falling asleep in the rather uncomfortable chair he had chosen to deposit himself in. He had long ceased trying to look pleasant and was quite certain his face would forever be frozen in this state of near-complete boredom. How in the world was Mary able to remain civil to these inconsiderate idiots? She still looked as calm as ever, her complexion rosy and glowing, her hair perfect and flattering, and her dress light and fresh. Geoffrey considered himself a pleasant man, but even he had limits.

Perhaps Mary had learned more in the last few days and weeks than he had realized. The old Mary would have been finished with tedium a long time ago, and without any concern for real politeness either. Yet there she sat, just as interested now as she had been before.

It was simply bewildering.

"My goodness, look at the time!" exclaimed one of the men Geoffrey really did not care to meet. "I am to meet with Lord Viskin's ward for Greek lessons in ten minutes!"

That seemed to be the cue, for all five men rose, paid their compliments and farewells to Mary, then left in an almost military fashion.

Only when the door closed did Geoff move. He stood, stretched, and groaned, "Oh, good, I thought they would never leave."

Mary looked up at him in surprise, as if she had forgotten he had been there. "Was it really so long?" She glanced over at a clock and her eyebrows shot up. "My goodness! I'm sorry, Geoff, I didn't mean to keep you waiting so long."

He smiled and waved a hand. "Don't worry about me. I enjoy sitting in uncomfortable chairs for long periods of time."

Mary snorted a laugh and rose, stretching a bit herself. Then she moved towards the door to the room.

"Besides," Geoff continued as he followed, "I enjoyed watching."

"Watching what?" she asked in confusion as she turned her head to look back at him.

"You." She looked surprised again, and he chuckled. "I never noticed how well you do this."

She stopped and put her hands on her hips. "Do what, exactly?"

"Play the debutante."

A bemused smile formed on her lips. "I wasn't playing anything just then."

Geoff stared at her in abject confusion. Of course, she had been playing then! How could she not have been? She was eager and interested and amused by them, and the Mary he knew wouldn't have... She'd never...

He really had no idea what she would or would not do anymore.

"But... you were listening so keenly to James Finley-Ashe," he said with a weak laugh.

Mary shrugged. "It was fascinating."

Now he laughed in earnest. "Fascinating? Mary, how much wine did you drink last night?"

With a bit of a huff, Mary frowned and looked at him. "I didn't have any wine at all last night. Did you?"

"No," he replied as his laughter faded. "But Mary..."

"Oh," she said softly as comprehension dawned. "Oh, you think I shouldn't have found Mr. Finley-Ashe so interesting because he is generally thought of as dull and boring and far too scholastic."

Something like that, yes.

"Well, I..." he began.

"I, on the other hand," Mary overrode, looking disapproving, "choose to find out for myself what to think of other people. Mr. Finley-Ashe, for example, is a very intelligent man and is as equal in stimulating conversation as any other man who is appreciated. I greatly enjoyed hearing his theories for improving farming techniques."

"Mary, you don't farm," Geoff pointed out matter-of-factly.

One shoulder lifted in a bit of a shrug. "I could learn," she said simply. She turned and continued down the hall, leaving him there in stunned confusion.

But only momentarily.

"Wait, Mary, wait," he called as he hurried after her. He wished the halls in this blasted house were not so cramped, for as she turned again, her eyes a bit impatient, he actually felt a little afraid. "Erm, I apologize for thinking so badly of Mr. Finley-Ashe?"

"Is that a question or an admission?" she asked, raising one eyebrow.

"You know, your ability to put a man on the spot is very disconcerting," he admitted with a half-smile.

She rolled her eyes, but smiled back. "Is that your favorite part of me?"

"Definitely not," he replied proudly.

"Good." She turned and entered the dining room, where a luncheon had been set. "You might as well help yourself, Geoffrey. Cassie rarely eats in here except for dinner, and with you here, it is impolite for me to eat alone."

"Oh, no, thank you, I have eaten already at Derek's," he told her as he sat. "How are you holding up under all of this?"

"Remarkably well, I should think," she replied lightly. "I admit, I was overwhelmed at first, but soon it all began to feel natural, and I find that I am enjoying myself quite a bit."

"Are you really?"

She nodded and started eating. "And no, I am not really considering Mr. Finley-Ashe as a suitor, but I do find him interesting, and his theories really do make one think more logically. But I have no intention of letting him court me."

"Well, I am relieved to hear it," Geoffrey sighed as he sat back. Then he realized what she had said and froze. "Court you? Mary, you are looking for courtship now?"

"Not in so many words," she replied slowly in between bites of food. "But when I was at dinner with Lord and Lady Danton a few nights ago, I thought…"

"You had dinner with the Dantons?" he interrupted, shooting forward in his chair.

She reared back a little, surprised by his reaction. "Yes, Lady Danton sent a note around asking if I would join them for a small supper party with a few other friends."

"When did you and Lady Danton become friends?" he asked, feeling oddly defensive.

"Well, I don't…"

"I mean, you would think that Lady Danton, as my cousin, would have informed me of a dinner party, particularly when she knows that we are friends," Geoffrey explained, feeling rather miffed at Lavinia for her lack of family loyalty.

"Oh, please, Geoffrey, you would have hated it," Mary scoffed, rolling her eyes. "It was blue stockings and academics, all of us enjoying intelligent conversation without the trouble of flirtation."

He looked at her carefully, then smiled a bit. "But you flirted anyway."

She returned his smile with a rather devious grin. "Well, I do have to practice."

"I think you have done quite enough practicing, if the number of admirers is any indication," he laughed, jerking his thumb towards the front door. "Still, I would have been glad to escort you to the Dantons, even if I had been bored stiff. I am your permanent escort, remember."

Mary chewed slowly, looking at him. "I've been meaning to talk to you about that. While I was at this party, it occurred to me that even though this may have started out as a game, it might be possible to have… other advantages."

Geoff stilled in his seat as he stared at her. Cautiously he wet his lips. "What other advantages?"

"Promise you won't breathe a word to my sister?"

He ought to have said something glib, something that Geoffrey Harris would say to Mary Hamilton, but he only managed a nod.

"Suppose I actually find a husband," she said in a low voice, her eyes bright. "I've never had opportunity like this, Geoff. I haven't felt like this since I was seventeen. Suppose one of these men that comes calling at my house or dances with me in a ballroom or regales me with farming techniques might actually be a man I could marry and have a family with."

Geoff opened his mouth, but no sound came out. Mary find a husband? Well, of course, he wanted Mary to find a husband, if possible. She deserved to find one. She deserved a family.

So why could he not feel his heart beating?

He swallowed and tried for a look of innocent surprise. "Well, that must have been a startling realization."

Mary grinned and buttered her roll. "It was. I almost fell out of my chair. I have been so used to the idea of being alone forever that it never occurred to me that this lark could actually work. Not that anybody has said or done anything that leads me to believe a match is on the horizon," she allowed, which made Geoff's heart resume a normal rhythm, "but I'm not going to rule it out either."

"And this affects my escorting duties how?" he asked, feeling a little better.

"I don't want you to have to be my nanny, Geoffrey," she told him with a smile. "If I'm not going to laugh at everything we used to, then it would hardly be good fun for you to come to things you hate just to be with me. And I hardly need you to keep me company once we are there. I cannot even manage to keep myself company these days. And if I am to be so busy, it would be rude to take up all of your time when it is hardly worth the effort."

"Mary…"

"And…what if someone else wants to take me to something?" she asked in a shy voice, not meeting his gaze.

"Ah," he said slowly, leaning back again. "Does someone?"

"Not yet," she admitted with a scowl.

He grinned. "Very well, if and when that day comes, you need only tell me and I'll take Cassie instead."

Mary laughed out loud and covered her mouth quickly. "That would be more than you could handle, but if you insist."

Geoffrey reached over and squeezed her hand. "I will always have time for you, Mary, whether I like the event or not."

She smiled back at him. "Thank you."

He nodded and removed his hand. "Would you like to go to the theater on Friday? There is a new comedy out, and I've reserved a box. We can show you off in grand style."

"Oh, that would…"

"Pardon me, Miss Hamilton," Winston interrupted gently from the door. "There is a gentleman here who wishes to speak with you. A Mr. Burlington."

Mary paused, her surprise evident. "He is?" she managed.

Winston nodded, smiling a little.

Mary also smiled, then swallowed and said, "Send him in here. I have finished, and it would be no inconvenience."

Winston bowed slightly, then disappeared.

"That's not bad form, is it?" she whispered as she and Geoff stood. "Having him come in the dining room."

"Not that I am aware of, no," Geoffrey assured her.

"How do I look?" she whispered again.

He smiled at her. "Lovely as ever."

"You are biased."

"Guilty."

Winston reappeared and bowed. "Mr. Burlington, Miss."

Mr. Burlington fairly swept into the room, his gold-lined great coat billowing slightly. He swept into a deep bow, then removed his feathered hat and set it beneath his arm. "Miss Hamilton, it is truly a delight to see you again."

Mary curtseyed and smiled politely. "And you as well, Mr. Burlington. You know Mr. Harris?" she asked, indicating Geoff.

"Indeed," Burlington replied jovially as they bowed to each other. "How do you do, Harris?"

"Tolerably well, thank you, sir," Geoff replied, though it was lost on the man as he had returned his attention back to Mary.

"You must forgive me for not calling sooner," Burlington was saying as he moved around the table towards Mary. "But you see, I never call immediately, as it would lump me with the rest of the masses. And I desire to stand out to you." He took Mary's hand and kissed it.

Geoffrey felt nauseated.

"Well, it is good to see you here at last," Mary managed, sounding a little confused, but not displeased.

"I had my new phaeton out today," Burlington told her, his dark eyes eager, "and I thought, 'It is such a fine day, would it not be lovely to have Miss Hamilton sitting beside me as we drive about the city', and it was such a capital idea that I drove straight here, determined to have you join me. Will you?"

Mary grinned and nodded. "I would be delighted. I shall go get a coat and bonnet."

"Excellent, I shall be eagerly anticipating the gracious blessing of your company by the phaeton out in front." Burlington bowed and turned his remarkably shiny shoes on their heels and removed himself from the room.

"Will you need a chaperone?" Geoff asked.

"Not at all," Burlington called from the hall. "My man sits in the tiger seat, all is quite proper, no need to fuss."

Geoffrey glowered after him, then turned to Mary, who was smiling brightly.

"I have not ridden in a phaeton for ages!" she fairly squealed as she dashed from the room.

"Mary! The theater! On Friday!" he shouted after her.

"Yes!" she yelled back. "I have a new dress that would be perfect for the theater!"

He heard her thundering up the stairs, and then moments later, heard her flying back down. The front door closed with a loud bang, and then it was silent.

Geoffrey sank back into his chair, feeling completely lost. What in the world was happening here? Mary had just said she had not given up on marriage after all, and such was her luck, it was actually possible now. And he had not missed her expression when Burlington was announced. Did all callers have that effect?

He frowned, unable make it all out.

"Would you like something to eat, Mr. Harris?" one of the kitchen maids asked as she began clearing the meal.

He looked over at her, then at the food, and then he sighed. "Yes, I would."

Chapter Ten

$\mathcal{M}$ary's ears were positively ringing. The tiny hairs at the back of her neck were sure to be standing on end, her skin was riddled with goose pimples, and it was all she could do to refrain from wincing. But she clapped politely with everyone else when Miss Walters finished her aria, and even managed to smile as the girl curtseyed in a sort of embarrassed delight.

The poor dear had no idea she could kill a man in a dark alley with that voice.

Still, it did take a certain amount of bravery to perform in front of so many people, particularly if one is not encouraged at home.

Lady Raeburn, arrayed in blue silk in all of her resplendent glory, stood and faced the gathering. "I think we shall break for a few moments, and then we will let the rest of the program commence. Refreshments are being brought in." She gestured grandly towards the doors of the music room, which instantly opened to multiple footmen, each bearing a tray.

This, too, was met with applause, but that tended to happen whenever Lady Raeburn was around. She positively attracted praise and admiration, and demanded attention and respect merely by being present.

Mary stood and smiled at Lady Raeburn, who was watching her with a curious intensity. If it had been anybody else, she might have been disconcerted. As it was Lady Raeburn, she was oddly flattered.

As was becoming common, a few men followed her. What she

had once feared was now becoming rather exciting. Who would they be? Would she know them already? Would she be surprised? She had no doubt she had lost a few of her followers as it became clearer that she actually had opinions and thoughts, but where one was lost, another two seemed to be found.

She moved to stand by Marianne Bray, who had more than a few admirers of her own, and smiled at the younger girl.

"Miss Bray, you look very well this evening," she commented. "That shade of blue does suit you so, I am quite envious."

Marianne blushed just a touch, which was too becoming on her. "Thank you, Miss Hamilton. It is a favorite of mine, but mostly because it is surprisingly comfortable. The fact that it flatters me is merely convenient."

Mary laughed, which made the men following her laugh, which made the men surrounding Marianne laugh. It was ridiculous. She could see Marianne felt the same, though she hid it better than Mary.

"Will you take a turn with me, Miss Hamilton?" Marianne asked with a polite smile. "I should love to discuss your gown at great length, it becomes you so marvelously well."

"I should be delighted, Miss Bray," Mary replied, taking Marianne's arm as they moved away. "Thank you," Mary whispered when they were alone. "I don't mind being admired, but they do tend to get in the way."

Marianne snorted a little. "They certainly do. One can never find a single moment to breathe, let alone think. And I am so tired of smiling," she moaned as she worked her jaw a tiny bit.

"Is it always like this?" Mary whispered as she glanced around, noticing just how many people were staring at them.

"Unfortunately," Marianne murmured, fixing her smile back in place. "But only in public."

"How can you keep them from calling?"

Marianne gave her a strange, almost amused look. "You cannot. Why would you want to?"

"It is getting rather crowded," Mary sighed with a small amount of embarrassment. "And tiresome. I want to weed it down, but I'm not entirely certain how."

"That, my dear, I can help you with," Marianne told her with a slightly evil grin. "You have a reputation of being sweet and kind. I do not. There is a reason for this."

Mary returned her smile, knowing the girl was right. "You are sweet and kind, Marianne Bray."

"Only in private, and very rarely," Marianne replied with a shrug. "It serves its purpose. I do good turns, but I cannot afford to be particularly endearing. It would make my attempts at popularity more difficult."

"I don't understand," Mary said in confusion.

Marianne smiled indulgently. "No, I suppose you wouldn't. You see," she began, lowering her voice, "if I were to be all kindness and sweetness, I wouldn't have half of the suitors I do. The thrill of the chase is what they like, and if you don't give it to them, they will look elsewhere. So shall I come round your place tomorrow to show you how it is done?"

Oh, why not? What harm could there be in allowing the crème de la crème of debutantes teach her how to be more discerning in her prospects? She smiled broadly and nodded. "Thank you, I would be delighted."

"Good. And I really do love your gown," Marianne told her, as she considered it. "That pink really brightens your countenance, and the cut is so fine! I'd like one for myself, but I won't imitate it."

"No doubt it would suit you better than me," Mary laughed.

"I don't think so," Marianne replied without laughing. "Give yourself some credit, Mary. Now, have you seen Kit?"

"Pardon?"

"Christopher Gerrard. I had heard he was back in town, but I have yet to see him."

Mary grinned and shook her head. "Another one of your conquests, Marianne?"

"Lord, no," Marianne insisted with a laugh. "He's an old friend, more like a brother. I'll go see if he is around. Excuse me."

Mary nodded as the girl left, and continued to smile after her. The smile faded ever so slightly as men started to flock to her again, but she managed to maintain the appropriate airs. She didn't know any of them very well, but that didn't mean she was unwilling to try.

After a few minutes, however, she was bored. Why could Lord Godfrey or Mr. Timmons or even the Duke of St. Martin not be present this evening? She could do with a few laughs. At least Mr. Burlington had promised to appear at some point. He was always agreeable. Just then, she caught sight of Geoffrey, standing alone next to one of the grand columns that decorated the room. She politely excused herself from the others and made her way over, smiling brightly.

He saw her coming and returned her smile. "What, you tired of your admirers so quickly?"

She snorted and took up a position next to him, taking a beverage from the tray of a passing footman. "Those are the most tiresome lot of the bunch. I have no idea why I have such trouble attracting sensible men at these things."

"I don't think there is trouble," Geoffrey admitted in a low voice. "I think it's merely crowded."

"Surely a sensible man would know when a woman likes the attention she receives or not." She looked over at him for confirmation, but received none. "No?"

"No."

"Why not?"

He managed a smile. "Because, my dear Miss Hamilton, you are so busy being polite and not offending anyone that you make it impossible for anyone to know how you are really feeling."

That took her by surprise. "Oh. But surely you know."

"Sad to say, but lately, I am having the same trouble."

That wasn't good. "Oh dear. So I need to be meaner?"

"It would certainly help," he told her with another smile. "But it would lessen your throng."

"That would not necessarily be a bad thing," she muttered as she took a drink. "I've just been speaking with Marianne Bray, and she told me almost the same thing. She even offered to help me."

"Be careful with that, Mary." Geoff suddenly looked earnest as he glanced at Marianne, then back at her. "Marianne is ruthless. She is spoiled and harsh with attentions she receives. More than one man has found himself entirely unmanned by her words and behavior. She's not exactly an example of consistency."

"No, but she is effective," Mary said with a shrewd look in her eyes. "I can certainly learn a thing or two from her."

"Ladies and gentlemen, if you will most kindly return to your seats, we shall begin again. And we have already had one request. Miss Hamilton."

Geoff jerked and saw Mary do the same beside him as she suddenly seized his arm. They'd long forgone the topic of Marianne and he was surprised she'd managed to remain near him for this long. Her throng waited nearby, but didn't approach, thankfully.

He'd forgotten all about the rest of the musical evening until now.

"Miss Hamilton? If you will be so good as to favor us." Lady Raeburn smiled encouragingly.

"I fear I play poorly, my lady," Mary managed, her grip on Geoff's arm very tight.

"No matter, no matter," the older woman waved impatiently. "Miss Arden can play for you. You do not play, she does not sing, it's perfect."

Miss Arden looked back at her now with a smile, which Mary returned hesitantly. Mary looked up at him with a bit of the same hesitation. "What do you think, Geoff? Should I?"

He smiled and patted her hand softly. "It's not up to me, Goose."

"Nor I, I suppose," she muttered. "I can hardly refuse Lady Raeburn, can I?" Then she smiled more broadly and made her way to the front of the room to applause.

Geoffrey leaned back against the pillar with a satisfied smile on his face. He had never told her, but he really loved to hear Mary sing. She didn't do it often, probably because she rarely had the opportunity, but he always felt it was his little secret about her. Her voice was a rare treasure in and of itself. In another life, in another

101

situation, she could have been a sensation.

His smile faded ever so slightly as he realized that this exhibition of her abilities would only earn her more suitors, and ones probably more suited to her taste. Ones that would compliment her on talents she possessed long before her transformation ever took place. It was as close to the real Mary as one could get under these circumstances.

He glanced around the room quickly, wondering if anybody present had any idea what they were in for.

The ladies conferred as to the selection, and then Miss Arden started in her accompaniment. A few notes later, Mary's heavenly voice joined in, and the entire room stilled almost as one. No one could even manage to whisper their shock as they were so captivated by the sound.

Sweet and alluring, in the most perfect tones, Mary's voice carried them all through the sad details of the song, stirring even the most hardened of hearts. Even Geoff, who had heard her sing on a number of occasions, felt his emotions rise and fall with the melody, and found it impossible to look anywhere but at Mary. She didn't appear at all nervous up there on display. In fact, he had never seen her more at ease in his life.

She was a natural. And now everyone else knew it.

Her voice filled the entire room, rang from the ceiling with its purity, sending an ethereal air cascading down on the gathering. No one even dared to breathe as she finished, the last note lingering in the air. Geoffrey had to fight to swallow, feeling as though his lungs were dry as a desert.

The applause that followed was bordering on the thunderous. Several gentlemen, even some of the married ones, leapt to their feet to applaud her, and some fool in the front shouting "Bravo!" at the top of his lungs as if she wouldn't hear him. Her cheeks flushed with pleasure and she smiled in her embarrassment.

Geoff clapped with the others, trying to catch Mary's eye to offer her a smile of approval. But so thick was the immediate thronging about her that he could no longer see her. He did see Miss Arden making her way out, none of the praise for her, and was about to go over to her himself when the crowd suddenly gave way and he could see Mary once more.

She smiled broadly at all who were around her, but none so fondly as she did Mr. Burlington, who was suddenly at her side, clasping her hand as if it were a lifeline. Mary looked up at the man with a laugh that brightened her whole countenance and gave her a glow that was indescribably beautiful. There was not a single man in the room, unattached or not, who couldn't see it.

She never looked his direction. Not even once.

Something dark and feral began unraveling within Geoff's chest. Something he didn't dare dwell on or attempt to identify. Something that sent him storming from the room, down the hall, and into the card room, where he spent the rest of the evening, silently losing money he no longer cared about to men he usually avoided.

It wasn't until someone told him that Mary was ready to depart that he remembered he had brought her, and that alone stopped his play. Without a word, he collected his sparse winnings and sparser wits, and made his way back to the music room. Mary was still surrounded by her admirers, looking as though she could endure their attentions for a lifetime.

He glowered for a moment, hoping she might notice him this time, as she had sent for him. When it was clear she would not, he grabbed the arm of a footman.

"Kindly inform Miss Hamilton that her carriage is ready, as she requested," he growled.

"Yes, Mr. Harris," the footman said obediently, surprised by his tone.

Geoff could not even bring himself to care.

He watched as the footman made his way through the throng and informed Mary, then saw her look around and meet his eye. Very briefly, he saw a light of relief enter her eyes, and the darkness in his chest lifted a bit.

After a few moments of bidding farewell to her followers, she finally made her way over to him. She said nothing, but the widening of her eyes in exasperation made him smile. He helped her with her cloak and into the carriage, and only when they were off did she speak.

"Oh, tell me I can stop smiling now!" she moaned, rubbing her face.

He chuckled. "You can stop smiling now."

"Thank you," she muttered with a roll of her eyes. "I didn't think that was going to end."

"We could have left sooner," he told her, shifting in his seat to face her. "All you had to do was say so."

She leaned her head back and looked at him. "Well, it was fine for a while. It was splendid, actually, for quite a long while. Everybody was so kind and complimentary after my song, and I have never had that before, not for something I can actually do and not pretend to do."

"What about when you sing for our friends?" he offered, feeling the need to remind her that not everybody in the world ignored her.

She waved it off. "That's not the same, and you know it. Our friends like me in spite of everything, and so one never really knows if they are being truthful or merely kind."

He frowned now, his irritation returning. "What about when I compliment you?"

"You I believe, of course," she said with a smile, "but only because I know you hate to compliment anybody if you can help it."

That offered him only the smallest of comforts.

He waited a long moment, letting the silence of the carriage speak for them both. "Well, you sang beautifully tonight."

"Thank you," she replied softly.

"I hope you enjoyed yourself."

"I did."

Another series of minutes passed in awkward silence.

"I didn't know Miss Arden was so gifted."

"Nor I. I hope others noticed besides us."

"I didn't see anyone approach her."

He heard Mary sigh with disappointment. "That's unfortunate. I'll call on her tomorrow, and set it right. Perhaps she would let me host a party and she would be able to have further opportunity to play without any… additional distractions."

Geoff smiled and glanced over at her. "I knew you would do

something, Goose."

Her eyes rose just enough to meet his. "And just this once, you were right." Then her brow furrowed. "Why didn't you approach Miss Arden yourself? You had ample opportunity."

He was not prepared to have the tables so aptly turned on him and found himself without a reply. "I... I meant to, but..."

She rolled her eyes and frowned at him. "Geoff. You could have done something."

He thought it best not to tell her that he'd been too upset with her ignoring him that he'd ignored Miss Arden. "Tell you what, Goose, you have that party and invite Miss Arden and I will be her chief admirer for the entire evening. I will be so full of compliments that you will think you invited one of your fops instead of me."

Mary snorted and sat back against the cushions. "I shall warn her to expect your attentions and to think nothing of them."

"Who says it will be nothing?" he demanded, raising a brow at her.

Mary gave him a doubtful look, then sighed and closed her eyes. "I wished that Mr. Burlington and Mr. Ashwood had stayed longer. And it would have been so nice to see Lord Godfrey or Mr. Timmons in attendance, I know they are fond of music. But I did meet a few other gentlemen this evening that I hope I shall get to know better in time."

Geoffrey stared at her in complete and utter confusion. "Correct me if I am wrong, Mary, but I thought only a few hours ago you expressed an interest in thinning your throng of admirers."

She didn't even bat an eyelash. "I still do."

"Then..." He hesitated, struggling to grasp any semblance of understanding. "Then why do you want to know more of these gentlemen?"

Mary opened her eyes and looked at him as if he had sprouted an additional three heads. "Because most of those gentlemen were a far cry better than the majority of the ones I have had to endure as yet. I'm not thinning the crowd purely for the number, I also want to ensure that the ones I do keep are ones worth spending any period of time with. Surely you can understand that."

He did. He wished he didn't, but he did. "So Marianne will help you there?" he asked, keeping his voice level.

"I hope so. She has more practice than I do with this sort of thing."

"Just be careful, Mary."

Mary laughed and tilted her head at him in the coy fashion he'd seen her adopt of late. "Are you getting protective of me, Geoffrey?"

He did not return her smile. "You don't enjoy injuring people, and Marianne does. I would hate to see you lose any respect by becoming more like her."

Mary's brows snapped together. "I hardly think Marianne actually enjoys injuring people."

"You don't know her like I do."

"You may not know her as well as you think you do."

He tossed his hands into the air. "For heaven's sake, Mary, I'm only trying to help."

"By telling me to be careful with your friend's sister because the poor girl might turn me wicked?"

"I never said that."

She snorted and shook her head. "Obviously, we aren't having the conversation you think we are."

"She has a reputation for breaking hearts and being cruel about it," he said, his voice louder than he liked, but he couldn't help it.

"At least she has a reputation and one that involves something other than being dull and lifeless!"

His jaw dropped and he reared back a little. "Are you jealous of her?"

One brow rose in his direction. "And if I am?"

"Mary, you have so much more to offer than she does! Would you rather be the brunt of scorn and disdain than the ideal of respect and propriety?"

"What I would like," Mary said, sounding very much as though she were gritting her teeth, "is to be allowed to make my own decisions about my own life and behavior without reference to anybody else or their idea of me. Marianne Bray will never know what it feels like to stand in the corner of a ballroom and wish, just once, that someone she doesn't know would dance with her for no other reason than because they want to. She will never know what it feels like to be passed over for someone more attractive or younger or better dressed. She will never understand what it feels like to be twenty-seven and never have a single man want to spend more than five minutes together in her company. And for that, yes, I envy her."

Geoffrey stared at her in stunned silence for a long moment. "Mary…" he finally said softly, reaching out.

She held up a hand to stop him. "Spare me the pity, Geoff. I'm in no mood for it."

The carriage chose that precise moment to arrive at Mary's home and she wasted no time extricating herself from the carriage and the situation without waiting for any aid. "Thank you for escorting me, Geoffrey. It was a most pleasant evening," she said as she hurried away. "Good night."

"Good night," he murmured, his brow furrowing as he stared after her. The evening had turned into quite a confusing one. They had never fought like that, had never even raised their voices at each other except in jest or calling over distances. And she had never accused him of pitying her, ever. Had he pitied her?

He respected her right to do as she pleased, and certainly without any consideration for him, he had no claim on her at all. But their plan, his plan, if he were to be completely honest, had been to attend events together, watch her ever-improving acting skills doled out on Society, and then laugh about it on the carriage rides home. Yet here she was, enjoying herself and sorting out suitors, real suitors it appeared, and speaking of courtship.

"Sir?" the coachman's voice cut into his reverie. "Sir? Shall we make for home?"

He looked up at him, only to realize that he was hanging halfway out of the carriage like an idiot and had been since Mary had bolted from it.

"Yes, Dawes, home," he instructed as he hastily reentered the carriage and took his seat.

He didn't like what was happening here. He did not like being pushed aside, particularly by his best friend. He did not like that he was so bothered by all of this, and he very much did not like that Mary was not.

Her words about envying Marianne replayed in his mind. She had never expressed herself in such a passionate way before, and had never told him how Society's treatment bothered her. He thought she had accepted it, had gotten over it, no longer cared. Now he could see that was far from the truth. She cared very much, as any other girl would. She just hid it within herself, kept her feelings inside, and put on a façade of indifference. And now she was through with hiding anything at all.

His dark and sinking feelings returned as he continued home. Things were changing faster than he could keep up with and far more than he liked.

Chapter Eleven

He was frantically running down a London street with only one thing on his mind; he was late. He had no idea how he had gotten to this point, he was never late. Was he suitably dressed? He glanced down at himself to find that while he was technically wearing the appropriate attire, he had never been in more disarray in his entire life.

He didn't care.

He was very late, and he was running out of time. He shoved open a heavy set of thick, wooden doors and turned the corner, his heart pounding so hard in his chest he could hardly breathe for the pain. He was running down the ancient stone corridor frantically, dodging in and out of faceless people, all dressed in their finery and talking so loudly he couldn't hear himself think. The walls kept shifting and changing, becoming longer, thicker, taller, more like a maze than any building he had ever known.

He had to get there in time. He had to.

"You're going to be late, Geoff," came a low, scolding voice. Duncan? He turned to face his friend, but he was not there.

No one was.

Geoff's eyes popped open and he found himself lying in his bed, just as he should be in the middle of the night. He sat up and wiped his brow, his arm coming away drenched in sweat. His chest ached as if he had actually been running through an endless corridor, and the panic... He had never felt emotion like that in his entire life. Which was entirely ridiculous, it had only been a dream about being late, and as much as he really did hate being late, he would never be so upset about it. Why should this dream give him such anxiety?

He didn't even know what he had been late for or what he had been doing or why it was so important. All he could remember was his sheer panic and terror at being too late.

Geoff swung his legs off of the bed and shook his head. He didn't normally dream so vividly. And he had never seen that corridor before. It had been old, almost falling apart, like some place they would have studied at school. Had he been in some ruins?

He exhaled sharply and pushed himself up off of the bed, walking over to the grand windows facing the east. The sky was beginning to change to a pinkish hue, the remaining clouds still the thick purple of the night. It was morning, then, not night. All the better.

He rubbed his hands over his face repeatedly, trying to scrub the night off of his face. He felt tense, ill at ease, anxious... It was almost as if he should find some warning in the dream he had just had.

Geoff snorted and shook his head. Trying to find answers in a dream that he had had only once? It was preposterous. He must have still been agitated from his fight with Mary, nothing more.

Mary was entertaining Marianne Bray along with her coterie of nitwitted admirers this morning. He frowned and moved to his bureau and pulled out a shirt and trousers, changing quickly in the dark. He would go for a ride, work out some of his agitation through exertion and fresh air, and then he would find something else to entertain his mind until the general populace would awaken.

Anything to avoid thinking about what could happen today.

He huffed in irritation and strode from the room, startling a few of the maids who were heading down to start the fires in the kitchen. He ignored them. There was entirely too much on his mind to concern himself with the thought processes and gossip mongering of his staff.

Mary had better behave herself today.

Or she would be answering to him.

"And so, of course, I said to Mr. Peters, 'What care I for your books? If I wanted to live in a library, I should do so... provided I saw very few books and very little of you!'"

The room erupted with laughter, and Mary attempted to join in, but really, she felt a little sick. Marianne had done nothing but tell stories about her suitors and behaviors, wherein the suitors were ridiculous and Marianne cold.

It was working, she could see, as some of Mary's own more sensitive admirers departed the room after a few stories from Marianne. It might not even take bad behavior from Mary herself to thin the throng. Being associated with Marianne on a more intimate level and not condemning her actions seemed to suffice.

It had not taken long for her to see that Marianne was a good deal like Cassie and not in an admirable way. They were both over-emotional, highly impulsive, and prone to rash action. They were too young to understand consequences of their actions on a grander scale, and had no wish to adhere to the proper confines that had long kept Society thriving.

In short, neither of them had any sense at all. But Mary couldn't say the same thing about herself. She had spent the last eleven years of her life specifically cultivating good sense, the latter half of those years against her will. It was what made her such a well-thought-of fixture in certain circles. Mary Hamilton was a name that may not have commanded respect or amorous admiration in the past, but one could always expect good sense and proper behavior, and that was something of a rarity in London these days.

She shook her head and looked over at Marianne, who was thriving in her element. What would it be like to be so confident and poised under the pressure of so much attention? Mary was still learning how to sit still in company such as this, let alone appear so collected.

Marianne turned to her with a brilliant smile. "What about you, Miss Hamilton? What are your thoughts on books and literature and scholars?"

She was slightly caught off-guard at being so suddenly addressed, but she somehow managed to stay composed. She offered a delicate smile, which she had been told was always an excellent way to stall for time. This was supposed to be her opportunity for exposing a harsher side, and she was fairly quaking beneath her carefully constructed outer shell. Mary allowed her smile to grow and she tilted her head in the manner her sister had praised as being 'positively regal'.

"I find I tend to be accepting of literature in general. I happen to be a great admirer of books and the literary arts, much to my mother's dismay. She thought I would become a blue-stocking, so often had I my nose in a book." She tucked her chin in a bit and fluttered her lashes as if in embarrassment.

The gentlemen in the room laughed in a sort of befuddled adoration, which Mary thought was positively idiotic.

"This does not mean, however, that I want to discuss any literature at great length," she said, turning her gaze slightly severe. "I could care less about the wild beasts of Africa or the growth cycle of a hibiscus in Paris or the history of Prussian rulers, and every time I have to sit and bear such tedious sermons on any other appallingly tiresome topic, I feel tempted to faint clear away so as to avoid the discussion altogether."

The room fairly erupted with laughter now, save for a few suddenly pale-faced men in the back.

"And so I am left to wonder," Mary continued, avoiding the eyes of those particular men, "if they even realize that such topics will not only bore their listener to within an inch of insanity..."

More laughter, more pale faces.

"...but will also make it so impossible that they will ever marry that the majordomo at Almack's will neglect to even announce them, not even for the fortune of the Duke of Ashcombe."

Guffaws and chortles exploded from the remaining men, some of them laughing to such excesses that they were incapable of remaining upright. Mary glanced over at Marianne, who was laughing, but also winked at her in approval. It should have made Mary feel extremely pleased, but the sight of four men slipping out of the room kept her amusement at bay.

"Oh, I quite agree," Marianne sighed when the volume had returned to a more acceptable level. "If I must endure conversation with a particularly learned man, the conversation ought to be short and never vary from topics I am well versed on; dancing, music, and beauty."

Applause rang out, and a few shouts of "Bravo!" and "Well said!" echoed in the room.

Mary barely avoided rolling her eyes, and was impressed that she didn't succumb to her impulse to give Marianne an incredulous look. Why in heaven's name would the girl want the entire world to think of her as being shallow and vain when she knew otherwise? Mary could still remember the venomous thrill that had lit the girl's eyes that night at the theater when she told them what she had done to Mrs. Smythe in their honor.

But here she was, content to be thought nothing more than a pretty face without heart or feelings.

"I heard tell, Miss Bray," one of Mary's most devoted suitors began, "that, as we are speaking of those who bore rather than court, you at one time received the attentions of Mr. Gerrard."

There was no hiding the lurch that Mary felt at those words and she only barely managed to avoid actually whipping her head around to look at Marianne.

Mr. Gerrard? As in… Christopher Gerrard? Or, as Marianne herself had called him just last night, Kit…

Marianne's face paled and her smile froze into more of a grimace. "I…"

"I further heard," the man, whose name still escaped Mary at the moment, continued, "that he was so distraught by your treatment of him that he fled London, and you remain the single reason he has for avoiding the season and London altogether."

Marianne swallowed, her throat visibly constricting. Her hands, so calm and collected before, were twitching and fidgety and wringing with each other so tightly that Mary feared she would do them harm. Her cheeks, so elegant in their prominence and location, now appeared almost gaunt with the sickly pallor they were rapidly adopting.

"Pray, tell us, Miss Bray," the man almost sneered. "Is that so?"

Mary had no idea what truth there was in the gentleman's statement, if any, and she didn't need to. If anyone had told her they could make Marianne Bray look like the small, delicate, helpless creature before her, she would have laughed in disbelief.

But there was absolutely nothing humorous about the situation at present. She needed no other excuse.

In an instant, the man's name returned to her memory.

Mary assumed the most severe expression she could and employed every ounce of her strength behind it. "Mr. Townsend," she said, her tone icy cold, "you will cease your abuse of my sweet friend and swallow any further falsehoods you may have swirling about in that miniscule brain of yours."

The previous buzz of interest in the room stuttered to absolute and stunned silence, and all eyes were upon her.

Mr. Townsend looked as though he had just been slapped in the face by his mother. His mouth gaped, his eyes were wide, and all color had drained from his skin.

"You will furthermore remove yourself from my home at this moment and permanently," she continued, fury boiling in her veins. "And the next time you will be permitted to approach Miss Bray or myself in any capacity at all, you will present Miss Bray with an apology so sincere it would make confession look like a masquerade liaison."

She could have dropped a pin on the carpet and it would have rung like a gong. Several other men in the room were swallowing with difficulty.

"And make no mistake, Mr. Townsend," Mary said, lowering her voice to a darker tone, "I will be informing Mr. Bray about your comments just now."

If possible, Mr. Townsend's face went a shade paler, and he faltered slightly. Someone in the back of the room gasped.

"And given that Mr. Bray is a very dear friend of mine," she went on, fibbing slightly, "I have no doubts he will believe every word I say. And I would expect him to pay you a visit in the very near future."

Really, the way his face could be completely devoid of color was impressive. She could sell tickets to such a spectacle.

Satisfied that he had received quite enough torment for one afternoon, she raised one brow and picked up her teacup as if she had only corrected his grammar. "You are dismissed," she said in a sweet voice as she sipped.

Townsend fled from the room without a word. Mary chanced a look at Marianne, whose expression was rapidly regaining color, but whose eyes remained downcast.

Mary set down her cup and looked at the gathering. "We quite tire of the lot of you. Leave us be, and kindly mind your tongues about what you've heard here."

There was a stampede of men for the door, all of whom vowed repeatedly that they would be silent. When the last man had vacated the premises, Mary sighed and dropped her shoulders and her act.

"Thank you," Marianne murmured softly from her side.

Mary turned to her and saw that, much to her surprise, the girl was flushed and looking very young. She reached out and gathered Marianne into her arms, holding her close.

She was stunned to find Marianne clinging to her tightly, resting her face in Mary's shoulder, and taking slow, deep breaths. There were no tears, for which she was grateful, but then, Marianne Bray was far too composed to ever let tears be shed in public.

After a few minutes, Marianne released her and sat back. "I'm sorry about all of this," she said, her voice regaining its usual, confident air.

Mary eyed her carefully. "Not at all. I think I handled it well enough."

Marianne grinned broadly, which was, again, unusual. The girl never exposed all of her teeth when she smiled, stating that it was too eager and not flattering. Mary disagreed. Her smile when it was full and unrestrained was a wonder to behold.

"I daresay you did!" Marianne exclaimed, bringing Mary out of her sudden stupor. "I've never seen men move that fast in all my years."

She thought it best to refrain from mentioning that, in this case, the phrase "all my years" really didn't add up to very much.

"What was that, Marianne?" Mary asked as gently as she could.

Briefly, Marianne's face faltered, but in an instant it was controlled again. "Oh, just some rumors. You know how Society can be."

"Marianne."

She met her eyes and sighed heavily. "Very well, I suppose I can tell you, but only if you promise not to tell Duncan."

Mary shook her head. "I will tell him what happened today, Marianne. He's your brother and your guardian and he..."

"I don't care about that," she interrupted with a wave of her hand. "Tell him what Townsend said, by all means. But don't tell him what I am about to tell you. He... he would think less of me, and I couldn't bear that."

Mary considered that for a long moment, and then nodded. "Very well, I agree."

Geoff sat at his usual table at the club, surrounded by his friends, not hearing a word they said. Ever since he had risen this morning, his head had been positively ringing. He felt as if he had imbibed too much the night before, yet he was as sober as he had ever been. He stared off at nothing, too tired to even think. The only thing he had processed was that Nathan was at home with Moira and their new son. Again.

"Hello, Geoff?"

"He is looking a bit peaky, isn't he?"

"You look peaky, Colin."

"Shut up, Derek."

"Geoff!"

"What?" he asked suddenly, shaking himself out of his stupor.

His friends all stared at him in confusion.

"What?" he asked once more.

"We have been trying to talk to you for nearly five minutes,"

Derek said with a rise in one very ducal brow.

"Thought you had off and left us for the next world," Colin offered as he sat back in his chair, sending it to the back legs.

"Aside from the fact that he is still breathing," Duncan said with a roll of his eyes. He looked back to Geoff. "Where are you at the moment, anyway?"

"Probably back in my bed," he admitted with a heavy exhale.

Colin grinned, as only Colin would.

"Mind out of the gutter," he growled to Colin, who only shrugged. Geoff turned back to Duncan and Derek. "I slept horribly. Had this dream…"

Again came Colin's grin.

Duncan cuffed Colin on the back of the head, sending his chair crashing back down on all four legs.

"Go on," Derek said as if nothing had happened.

Geoff quickly recounted everything he could about the dream, and found himself unable to infuse the story with the same depth of panic and emotion he had felt. As a result, the whole thing came out sounding wholly pathetic.

He looked up at them with a slight wince when he finished. Derek and Duncan looked confused, and Colin pretended to be asleep.

"That's it?" Derek asked finally.

"Why wasn't I there?" Duncan asked, wearing a puzzled expression.

Colin let out a particularly loud snore.

"I can't explain it," Geoff told them in frustration, rubbing a hand over his face.

"Obviously," the sleeping Colin said.

Geoff gave him a look that he would not see. "It was the most panicked I have ever felt in my entire life," he told the others. "I was just running and all I could think about was that I was going to be late… Too late…"

"Where were you?" Derek asked, the wrinkles disappearing from his brow as his concern abated.

"I don't know," Geoff admitted.

"What were you late for?" Colin asked on a would-be patient sigh.

"I don't know."

"Were you looking for someone?" Duncan asked him.

"I don't know." Geoff gave them all a weak smile.

Duncan huffed and gave him a look. "Well, what do you know?"

Geoff shrugged and sat back in his chair, suddenly just weary of the whole affair. "I was late and I was panicked... no, more than panicked, I was absolutely terrified. As if my life depended on my being on time. No idea why."

"You need to get out more," Colin announced, opening his eyes. "I thought after you started being Mary Hamilton's permanent escort for the season..."

"I don't want to talk about Mary," Geoff muttered, shaking his head. In fact, he had spent the majority of his morning avoiding the topic altogether.

Now it was Derek who grinned. "Not having fun, Geoff?"

"You know what they are saying, don't you, Geoff?" Colin jumped in, leaning forward eagerly.

He didn't want to know. He did not.

"They are saying even with your history, Mary doesn't want to spend time with you."

Geoffrey felt his jaw drop as he continued to stare at Colin in disbelief. Out of his peripheral vision he saw Derek and Duncan do the same.

Colin nodded, his smile fading slightly, because, really, this was not that humorous. "They say that you cannot keep her sufficiently entertained and that you have actually become a devoted follower that she won't give the time of day to."

Geoff closed his eyes and released a slow breath through his nose. He didn't care what Society thought... He didn't...

Who was he kidding? He did.

Over the noise of his friend's uninhibited sniggering, he cleared his throat. "Did you know that Mary is talking with Marianne this morning about how to be a better debutante?" he said suddenly, turning to Duncan.

That got the attention of the entire table. Mouths gaped.

One of Duncan's thick brows rose. "Excuse me?"

"Marianne has agreed to help Mary 'thin the crowd'," Geoff told him, his voice sounding a little petulant.

Derek and Colin looked at Duncan without saying anything.

"Has she now?" Duncan said slowly, his low voice seeming to rumble from the middle of his chest outward.

Geoff nodded with a shrug. "Mary told me herself. She was quite pleased. She wants to be able to act as Marianne does when she chooses, apparently."

Duncan winced, and he wasn't the only one. "Not sure that is such a good idea. It will work, I'm sure, but my sister has no idea what people actually say about her."

"I know," Geoff said morosely as he set his elbows on the table and put his face in his hands. "I don't want Mary becoming like her."

Silence met his ears and he moved his fingers. Duncan was frowning deeply, and grimaces graced the faces of the other two.

Geoff realized his error and looked at Duncan with a cringe of his own. "No offense?"

"Right…" Duncan said with a snort and a shake of his head, "Well, I can talk with Marianne, but it hasn't done any good yet. She doesn't listen to anybody, let alone her overprotective and overbearing big brother."

"I always thought Mary was a girl with sense and judgment," Derek said, turning serious. "It would disappoint me, and I know Kate as well, if she were to suddenly become less than what she is."

Geoffrey nodded slowly. That was his chief concern as well. This trick of Mary's, as entertaining as it had begun, was fast losing its appeal.

"She won't talk to me anymore," he confessed to them. "Not the way we used to. She's hiding things, she's changing her mind, she's…"

"Treating you like any other woman might?" Colin finished, giving him a raffish grin.

Geoff opened his mouth, then closed it again. Was that what it was? Their connection was fast becoming a thing of the past because she was losing what made her stand out to him. What exactly that was he could not put his finger on, but he found himself wishing that things would go back to the way they were, when she was largely ignored and only he knew who she really was.

He wasn't even sure he knew her anymore.

"Tell you what," Colin said, holding up a finger. "I'll go over to her house today and pretend to be a candidate. I'll keep an eye on the men that are there, see what Marianne has got up her dainty little sleeves for Mary, and report back to you all everything I find."

Geoff looked at him with skepticism. He knew Colin too well. "Will you be a suitor or a spy?" he asked slowly.

Colin shrugged. "Whichever gets me the better outcome. I can be very charming," he added with his best roguish grin.

Geoffrey Harris did not glare often; he was too polite and considerate for that. And so it didn't come as much of a surprise to him that when he cast a very unexpected, very long, very dark glare at one of his oldest friends, there was an equally unexpected reaction.

Colin's grin faded and he cleared his throat, hastily standing up. "I, uh, I have just realized that I am… late… for something…" He threw a few coins on the table and left without looking at any of them.

"Bravo, Geoff," Derek commented with a smile of his own. "He hasn't moved that fast since Clara Maxfield learned he could waltz."

Derek and Duncan chuckled, but Geoff found that his sense of humor was not in full bloom. His glower remained fixed in place.

"Stop worrying, Geoff," Duncan said with a hand on his shoulder and a rough shake. "Mary is too smart to become a complete debutante, and Marianne won't be able to change her beyond hope."

"It's true," Derek offered. "And as for what the gossips are saying, who cares? They think Colin is an angel, and we all know what a load of rubbish that is."

That, at least, managed to coax a smile from him, and he found himself starting to relax a bit. They were right; he was worrying for nothing. He would see Mary on Friday for the theater, and underneath her disguise, she would still be his same, wonderful, dependable Goose.

As she always was.

Chapter Twelve

Geoffrey paced in the foyer of Mary's home absently, hiding a yawn behind his gloved hand. He had had the exact same dream twice more and each time he got a bit further down the blasted corridor, but never saw the finish, never knew what he was running for, or why it was so important. He never felt refreshed after that dream and he couldn't sleep again after waking from it. The lack of sleep was starting to get to him, not to mention showing on his face. His brother had let him in on that point of fact none-too-gently this morning at breakfast.

He was also far touchier than his usual temperament allowed. That had been Duncan's contribution, which had not been received well. What had been said in the club, and by Mary herself the night of the musicale, had only festered with the time passed. He was half tempted to interrogate Mary in the carriage on the way to the theater.

Assuming she actually showed.

He had been waiting nearly a quarter of an hour and his patience was wearing thin. Winston had let him in, which should indicate that all was going to go according to plan, but Geoff was not entirely sure he could fully trust Winston to be loyal to him.

He exhaled sharply and looked up the stairs once more, tempted to run up and fetch Mary himself only to find that she was at last making her grand descent. As angry and irritated as he was with her, he couldn't help but be awestruck at the spectacle she presented.

Her gown was a rich midnight blue that seemed made from the

night sky itself, with the very stars in the fabric, all of which shimmered in their own time as she moved. It was a tight-fitting gown, but not boldly so. Just enough to emphasize her remarkable figure, and to hint to any admirers the quite desirable possibility she had the potential to present. She would have no shortage of attention tonight; he highly doubted the eyes of those in attendance would look anywhere else.

Faintly it occurred to him that he had seen her in this dress at the shop that day, though he could hardly believe it. Mrs. Farrow had obviously completed her work on it and tailored it to Mary's taste and style, and the end result was breathtaking. He was not one for appreciating fashion regularly, but he could see a very great reason to petition to have Mrs. Farrow named a saint.

Gradually his eyes reached Mary's face and found her complexion positively glowing. When had she become such a stirring beauty? It seemed that more of the stars had found themselves lost in her tresses, which were delicate and smooth and begging to be toyed with. And her eyes held the remaining stars in them as they danced with excitement.

"Do I pass your inspection?" she asked in musical tones, a small smile toying with the edges of her lips. "You have been at it long enough."

He shook himself out of the fog he had so suddenly found himself ensconced in, and bowed slightly. "Indeed. I am no match for my companion tonight, and no one will remember that it was I who attended her."

Mary laughed and reached for the wrap that one of the maids held out for her. "Come now, Mr. Harris, nobody remembers the men who escort any woman to these sorts of things. Has anyone ever noticed you before?"

He frowned at her back as she exited the house. Her statement was probably true, but he had not expected that from her. He had meant to pay her a teasing compliment, and perhaps receive one in return, as they had done for so many years. Yet she had doled out a veiled insult, not harshly, but coyly… Just as Marianne would have.

He followed her quickly, donning his hat and entering the

carriage, sitting opposite her once more. He rapped on the carriage, and fixed his eyes upon her with no small degree of criticism as the carriage began moving.

Mary studied and readjusted her gloves aimlessly, never once looking at him. But he never got the sense that she was ignoring him. It was more as if he was not even there.

He waited as long a time as he could bear to, and when she still took no notice of him, he exhaled sharply. "Anything particularly exciting happen since I have seen you last?"

Mary looked up at him in surprise, as if she truly had forgotten he was there. Then she frowned just a touch as she thought back. "Exciting? No, not particularly. Not anything you would consider exciting, at any rate."

He felt his brows snap together as if by a whip. "Something you found exciting, then?"

She waved a dismissive hand. "Oh, nothing so extraordinary. I had several callers this week, so many I had to dismiss them in order to eat a thing. I attended a gathering at the Duke of St. Martin's home for the unveiling of his gallery. He is quite a collector of art, you know, and has been cultivating a gallery for years. It was spectacular, you should attempt to gain admittance if you can. If you cannot, I shall be glad to obtain one for you. I have a long-standing invitation myself," she admitted with a flutter of her lashes that he found distracting and irritating.

He snorted. "I am perfectly well acquainted with St. Martin myself to garner my own invitations of him, thank you very much. We were at school together before he inherited."

She gave him a rather arch look. "Funny, he never mentions you."

Geoff glowered at her, which she pointedly ignored.

"I also received invitations to house parties hosted by Lord Oliver, Mr. Ashwood, Lady Frampton, I shall have to refuse hers, nobody of sense gets within ten feet of the Framptons if they can help it, and a card party hosted by Mr. Kent. I suspect he is still upset with me for trouncing him so soundly and wishes to have his revenge."

Geoff didn't doubt that. Kent prided himself on his skills.

"You know Society fairly well. Anyone you think I need to avoid?"

He was tempted, he was oh so tempted to lie. But he was an honest man to a fault. "Branson and Tremont are a seducers, Elliot a potential murderer, and Henley is too mysterious for anybody to trust. Other than that, I think you're safe." He managed to flick her a wan smile. "But you are quite right to refuse the Framptons, as delicately as you can. My stomach has not been the same since I attended one of their parties five years ago."

Mary shuddered in mock-revulsion, but smiled. "Very well. I'll take your advice into consideration, and probably heed it where those gentlemen are concerned. I have also received invitations from Lord Viskin, and Lady Wessex. Oh, and Mr. Burlington will be escorting me to the opera next Friday."

Geoff jerked in his seat with a cough. "The opera? He's taking you to the opera?"

"Didn't I just say that?" she said with impatience. "He has reserved a box for us and promised to show me off in grand style there. I have commissioned a new gown for the occasion."

Grand style she would receive, if Burlington were to be involved. They would be quite a spectacle for the eyes, and he was not entirely certain which of the two would attract more attention with their ensemble. Mary was the beauty, there was no doubt, but the extravagance that Burlington regularly employed for his own attire made the Prince of Wales resemble a cheap peddler in the gutters of London's darkest corners. And his conversation tended to be limited to himself, his clothing, and flattering women. People of sense could not abide the man.

Yet Mary was brimming with excitement.

"You cannot be serious."

One perfect brow rose with alacrity. "I'm entirely serious. Mr. Burlington is a fine man and one of my favorite admirers. He knows of my age and situation and isn't put off by it. He doesn't fawn as much as the others, and listens when I speak. He is complimentary and I enjoy his company. I would go to a great many more things if I knew he would be in attendance."

A wash of bile threatened to rise within him and it took all of his power to swallow it down. He wanted to ask if he had offered marriage yet, if he had made his intentions obvious, or if it was still a matter of flirtation. But he didn't want to know that any more than he wanted to know the future date of his death. "You hate the opera," he tried weakly, his head faintly swimming.

Again came her haughty look. "As it so happens, Geoffrey, I adore the opera." She turned to face the window, effectively shutting off any further conversation.

Geoff stared at her in his stunned silence, hardly breathing. She… she what? How could she possibly adore the opera when their entire lives she had groaned every time he took her? And the only reason he took her was because he knew she'd hate it, so he would be sure of a good laugh. She loved it? Why had she never told him that?

The dark feeling in his chest rose once more, becoming an old friend instead of an unwanted burden. He felt his face take on a careful, composed expression that showed absolutely no emotion whatsoever. If she could parade about falsely, so could he.

"There is a ball at the Duke of Ashcombe's townhouse that Friday to which we have been invited," he told her, keeping his voice formal. "Will you be attending?"

"Of course," she replied in a clipped voice. "I wouldn't slight the Duke and Duchess, nor Derek and Kate. Mr. Burlington will escort me there after the show, as he was invited as well."

"As you wish." It was now his turn to look out of the window, as still and unmoving as he could possibly be. He wished he were not going to the theater tonight. He wished he were any place else.

"I have arranged the date for Miss Arden's party," Mary said softly. "She was agreeable and generous, and very pleased with the opportunity. I think she does not receive such attentions at home."

"I would agree with that," he replied, keeping his tone as even and tempered as she had. He knew of the Ardens, but didn't know them well. All he knew was that the parents found it to be a great inconvenience that they only had daughters and took no pains with any of them. It was amazing that the elder two, who were the only ones out, actually seemed creatures of sense and grace.

"It will be two weeks from Tuesday. If you are still of a mind to attend..."

"I am."

"Excellent." She paused a long moment, then said, "I'll make sure that Winston unlocks the side door of the music room in case Fanny Harville feels the need to attempt to sing, so you have an efficient means of escape."

He couldn't help but to chuckle and looked over at her. "That would be most gracious of you. Why are you inviting Fanny Harville?"

She grinned and rolled her eyes. "Cassie is forcing me. Fanny is one of the only girls in Society who still speaks to her as if nothing had happened."

"I didn't know they were friends."

"They weren't. Friendly, yes, but never friends. Until now, apparently."

Geoff sighed and shook his head. "Very well, for Cassie's sake, I shall endure Fanny Harville."

"You don't have to. Hence the side door." She tilted her head in amusement, a small smile forming.

He inclined his head in gratitude. "Well planned, Goose."

Her smile faded and she looked down at her gloves. "You shouldn't call me that anymore."

He reared back. "What, Goose?"

She nodded.

"Why not? It's been my name for you for years."

"I know," she said, sounding apologetic. Or at least, pretending to be. "But it's too intimate and familiar. It's not proper for you to call me anything but Miss Hamilton anymore, or my given name if we are alone."

A cold chill ran up his spine and settled somewhere in his throat. He tried to swallow it down, but only manage to choke himself more in the process. When he could, he managed a weak, "If that is what you prefer."

"I would." Again she looked out of the carriage window as they approached the theater. "Now," she said, straightening up and giving him a brilliant smile that didn't reach her eyes, "let's enjoy ourselves tonight. It is a comedy, after all."

His entire life was a comedy these days. At his expense, of course. Now he had to address her as formally as he would any other woman in England? He had called her Goose since they were at least seven years old, and now, after mere weeks of playing the debutante, that, too, was gone.

They pulled up to the theater and Geoff alighted before they stopped completely, not even waiting for the footman. There were other carriages arriving and other guests that had yet to enter the theater, and so there was an audience for Mary's grand arrival. It took all of his considerable self-control to keep a glower from his face. He held out his hand for Mary, and she took it with delicate, graceful fingers, smiling as if all the people assembled had come for her.

And given their reactions, it rather seemed they had.

Whispers and smiles and little waves began the moment she began walking, and every eye was upon her, just as he suspected it would be. Every gentleman was transfixed, every woman envious, and it became quite obvious which men were married and which were not.

Geoff only prayed they could actually enter the theater before they would swarm in on her.

As it happened, that was the case. They entered the theater, her wrap and his hat were taken by servants, and as if on cue, admirers thronged. Unexpectedly, Geoff was bustled and bumped out of the way and before he could believe it, there were men at least four deep between Mary and himself.

He opted to sneak a little ways off and watch the spectacle. Just to see for himself if the stories were true. He hadn't heard anything about her lessons with Marianne, but he wasn't sure that was a good thing. Had she really changed all that much?

It didn't take long before he had his answer.

Mary was the perfect debutante. She was coy and flirtatious, encouraging yet giving no promises. She said volumes with her eyes, and not all of it was favorable to the beholder. She was hard on some, sweet with others, and somehow left all still wanting more. It was captivating to watch. Not that he was enjoying himself, for he could barely think of a time he had enjoyed less than this. And that was before the whispers began to reach him.

"Is that Harris over there watching Miss Hamilton?"

"Yes, the poor man. She will not give him the time of day."

"Poor man, indeed. There was a time when the two of them were thick as thieves. Can you imagine? Being put off now after all that history."

"Why should she keep him on? He obviously did not suit or she would have. She has better options now."

"Would you choose Harris when you could have Burlington?"

"She won't even let him near her, do you see?"

"He escorted her here, does that not mean something?"

"Nothing. A matter of convenience only."

A man snorted next to him. "Convenience, eh? Doesn't anybody remember where you live? If anything, your escorting her is a hardship on your horses and carriages, given how completely out of the way it is. And as for better options, well..."

He turned slightly to see Colin hiding a grin. "Not funny, Colin," he growled.

Colin quirked a brow. "Oh, did I say it was funny?"

"You're smiling."

"And you look like you are contemplating a murder," he replied without concern, still smiling. "My reputation has me being jovial at all times and not take anything seriously. So I smile. But tell me who your victim is, dear boy, and I shall offer you my sword."

Geoffrey sighed and looked back towards Mary and her admirers. "I am not going to murder anyone."

Colin snorted from his side. "Not today, at least."

"No, not today."

Colin waited only a beat before he said, "Have you spoken to Mary about those pesky rumors?"

"I have only heard them for myself just now," he muttered out of the corner of his mouth. "I haven't had time to inform Miss

Hamilton of anything."

"Miss Hamilton?" Colin said with great interest. "Since when are you so formal with her?"

"Since about half an hour ago in the carriage. It seems I am too familiar with her." His glower deepened as he turned back to watch.

"Are you indeed?" Colin murmured in a very soft, very unamused tone. "Fascinating news..."

Sounds from the orchestra met their ears and all turned at it. At once, realization hit the gathering that the show was destined to start shortly. At least four gentlemen offered their arm to Mary, but she politely declined them all.

Geoff could barely make out her voice above the noise. "Oh, thank you, Mr. Parker, you are too kind, but I already have an escort for the evening. Some other time, perhaps."

He grunted in satisfaction. So she did remember that he was here and that he had brought her. How nice to be considered after all.

She made her way over to him with a grand smile, the exact one she had been giving all night. "Well, Mr. Harris, shall we?"

He inclined his head politely. "At your command, Miss Hamilton."

She missed his irony and simply nodded, as if it was to be expected.

He glanced in Colin's direction to find his friend smirking, but his eyes showed far more understanding than Geoff had ever seen from him.

Geoff looked down at Mary, who was smiling and nodding to others as if she were a queen being adored by her subjects. He couldn't talk with her when she was like this, all false and condescending, with her waves and her smiles being restrained to that ridiculous polite one she always had fixed on her face these days. He wanted to speak to his friend Mary Hamilton, not Miss Hamilton the Adored.

But how to get her? She never let her guard down anymore, not even for him.

He caught sight of Fanny Harville and her mother and seized the moment. "Ah, Fanny Harville is here," he murmured, forcing himself to smile. "Do you think she will rush the stage to perform?"

Mary clamped her lips together so tightly they were white and her shoulders shook.

Geoff tried not to feel the delighted surge of warmth that raced from his chest to his fingers.

"I daresay her mother will bodily restrain her," Mary replied in careful, soft tones. "Mrs. Harville has always had a terrible fear of embarrassment."

Geoff snorted. "Bodily restraint, you say? Poor Fanny."

Now a laugh did escape from Mary and she clamped her hand over her mouth and looked up at him. Her eyes danced and for just a moment, his felt that his old Mary was returned to him.

"Don't say such things," she hissed, still smiling. "It isn't seemly for me to laugh so hard in public."

His warm feeling faded into a numbness. Since when did she care about what was seemly? Still, she was smiling. He might not have another opportunity. They approached the box and he stopped her, checked to make sure no one could see, then turned to face her.

"Mary, you have to stop being so flirtatious with your admirers when I am your escort," he said quickly.

Her brows rose in confusion. "What? Why?"

He sputtered and fumbled for a reason. "Because… because!"

She snorted and started to go past him. "Not good enough, Geoffrey."

He grabbed her shoulders and gently turned her back to face him. "Because it looks like I'm not enough for you," he hissed, looking around again.

She only gave him an arch look that quite plainly told him she was wondering if he was.

He took a steadying breath as his ire began to rise yet again. Really, he was going to have to do something about his control. "It reflects badly on me, Mary. People are beginning to talk."

"Oh, and since this is all about you, we must fix that right away," she said sarcastically, waving her hands for emphasis.

He put his hands on his hips. "That's not what I meant!"

She shook her head. "Bother with what you meant, Geoffrey.

None of the rumors will stick to you, whatever they are."

"But there are rumors, Mary, and I don't think you understand…"

She heaved a sigh, interrupting him and turned to go into the box. "Please, Geoffrey, the whole point of this was to have a laugh for my last season, not for you to suddenly become sensitive."

The glare he leveled at her retreating back would have made Colin run for cover, but it had no effect this time. "Who's laughing?" he muttered to no one in particular as he followed her into the box and sat for what was destined to be the longest evening he had ever been forced to spend in this blasted theater, and he had had several long evenings here.

So she didn't care what they said about him.

Well, he could play her game, too. If she would be proud and insulting and take no notice of him or their past friendship, then so would he. It wasn't all about her during this time, not anymore. If his name was being dragged into the mire, then he wouldn't stand by and watch.

The dark and bitter feeling in his stomach returned with a vengeance. He glared down at the stage where the actors were beginning their presentation. He paid them no mind. He found Colin in the box opposite, watching him steadily. Geoff stared back at him for a long moment, his expression very plainly telling his friend exactly what he was feeling at this moment.

Colin caught it, his smile disappeared, and he nodded, then looked towards the stage.

Geoff had absolutely no interest in the performance. If he were any less of a gentleman, he would have left at this moment and gone straight home, leaving Mary to fend for herself with her admirers and find her own escort home. But Geoffrey Harris was, after all and above all else, a gentleman. And so he would remain. He focused at the railing before him, and let his eyes unfocus for the rest of the time.

Chapter Thirteen

"Good morning, Mary!" Cassandra chirped as she fairly bounded into the breakfast room.

Mary winced and held up a hand. "Please, Cassie. Temper your tone. I am not quite myself this morning."

Cassie's eyes widened and she grinned mischievously. "Ah ha... You attended that dinner party at Lord Viskin's last night, didn't you?"

"Yes," Mary moaned, slouching in her chair, setting her head in her hands, and putting her elbows on the table, uncharacteristically poor posture for her. "And my head has been ill ever since."

"That's because," her sister continued in her brightest, most amused tone as she took a seat at the table, "Lord Viskin regularly tampers with the punch he serves. It is undoubtedly more alcohol than punch."

"You knew?" she cried, spreading her hands far enough that she could see Cassandra plainly.

Cassie snorted and reached for some toast. "Everybody knows that."

"I didn't."

She shrugged and took a bite. "Then it seems that, in spite of your best efforts, you are still not everybody." She smirked a little and filled her plate with food.

Mary glowered and rubbed at her temples. "Strike Viskin from the list. I cannot bear this."

"Honestly, I am surprised he made the list at all," Cassie said around a mouthful of food. "He is not only too old for you, but a complete bore."

A sigh escaped Mary and she craned her neck to try and work the kinks out. "He is not that old."

"Fifty if he is a day."

"And I'm twenty-seven."

"You are not in the ground yet, Mary. Don't pretend to be so desperate that even the old men looking for company actually interest you."

Mary gave that some consideration, and shrugged. "I haven't encouraged anybody of a certain age, but perhaps you are right. I'll stay within a decade of my own age, fair enough?"

Cassie snorted and shook her head. "I thought lessons with Marianne were going to help you to be more discerning, Mary. If age is all you require, then by all means, have at. But if you want suitors worth having..."

She cocked a brow at her sister. "I have been more discerning. I have lost multiple scholars because they bored me, rogues because their reputations preceded them, a few timid pups because they could not take a verbal lashing, and a few card players because I bested them. What else would you have me do?"

A strange light entered Cassie's eyes, and she almost seemed to sadden. "Spoken like a true debutante. I think my work here is done."

Mary laughed, a little uneasily. She didn't like the expression on her sister's face. It wasn't sadness or jealousy, it was... finality.

"I still haven't managed the grace to descend a flight of stairs with books on my head," she pointed out. "Shouldn't that be accomplished before your resign your position?"

Cassie rolled her eyes with impatience. "Yes, of course, you should. Really, I am surprised nobody has commented on your lack of grace as yet. Shall we work on that today?" she asked as she cut into her breakfast. "Or does your head need more time to recover?"

Mary groaned and gripped the back of her neck tightly. "I need the rest. But we have the Ashcombe ball on Friday, so I need to be graceful for that."

Cassie nearly dropped her fork. "We?" she asked, her eyes going wide. "As in…"

"Well, honestly, Cassandra," Mary said with a roll of her eyes and a mock grimace, "you can hardly expect me to go by myself. Who will remind me to be graceful if you do not?"

The smile that spread over her sister's face would have made Mary consider more seasons of such behavior from her if she had not already decided.

"Really?" Cassie squealed, her hands going to her mouth.

Mary nodded, smiling herself. "Really."

Cassie squealed again, which made Mary wince as the ringing in her ears recommenced. Then Cassie was silent and gave Mary an odd look. "I didn't think the duchess would want me anywhere near an event of her hosting."

A very mischievous grin crossed Mary's face just then. "Well, as I happen to be good friends with the duchess's son and daughter-in-law, not to mention I am a bit of a toast this season, she simply had to invite me, and Kate made it quite plain that it would be very rude to neglect you when they invite me."

"I see," Cassie said with a smug look on her face. "It certainly does pay to have important friends, doesn't it?"

Mary nodded. "It does indeed."

"I'll have to thank the marchioness when I see her next," Cassie mused. "She hasn't been by in some time, is she well?"

A hint of a flush crept into Mary's cheeks and she glanced down at her mostly empty plate. "She is. Her condition is not so bad as others I have heard of, and she doesn't require much rest yet."

"Then why haven't we seen her?"

Mary's gaze moved to her hands, knotting together in her lap. "I haven't had much time for visitors other than the callers."

Cassie had no immediate reply, so Mary ventured a look, only to find that her sister was surprised and disappointed at the same time. "Are you really too busy for your friends?"

She didn't need to hear this from her sister, of all people, who was the one reason Mary agreed to this ridiculous scheme at all. And now she would disapprove? She would not stand for it. She frowned, her brows snapping together, and rose from her chair.

"I will be at the opera with Mr. Burlington before the ball," she informed her, "so you will have to go to the ball alone."

"Alone?" Cassie cried in protest. "I cannot possibly go alone. That would be..."

"Then find your own escort," Mary barked, putting a hand to her head as it rang still. "I have neither the time nor the patience to deal with this."

Cassie scowled and sank in her chair moodily. "I will ask Geoffrey. He, at least, doesn't snap at me."

"Then you would be well suited, the pair of you," Mary sneered. "You can disparage me the entire ride there and back home again and I will not be able to have any say in the matter."

A confused frown appeared and Cassie tilted her head with concern. "Why would Geoff want to say anything bad about you? He would never..."

"Oh," Mary laughed without humor, "he would. He had all sorts of things to say. He has suddenly decided not to approve of my behavior. We had a miserable time at the comedy last week. We fought the whole way there, didn't speak at all during, and he ignored me almost the entire ride back, except for a few snide comments. I haven't seen or heard from him since, and the peace has been almost blissful."

That was an all-out lie, but there was no need for Cassie to know that Mary was more upset by Geoffrey's manner than she should be. It was as if he had suddenly lost his sense of humor. Oh, she knew very well that she was partially to blame, and that her behavior was less than admirable, but that was supposed to be part of the fun. And she was having so much success with callers and admirers and suitors that she might not have to give up her dreams of marriage and family after all. Why couldn't he see that? Nobody had wanted her as she was before, and they did now! He ought to have been pleased.

"Blissful, is it?" Cassandra asked as she stared at Mary with eyes that were too clever. "Seems rather boring to me." She shrugged and went back to her breakfast.

Mary stood there a little awkwardly for a moment, and then

turned for the hall. She rubbed at her brow with some concern, and sighed. Perhaps she ought to go back to bed and sleep this awful headache away. Blasted Lord Viskin and his terrible evening! She really would need some better advice for which events to attend and which ones to avoid like the plague. Surely there was some method to be employed somewhere.

Perhaps she should write to Kate after all. And Diana, too, if she was feeling well enough. Her son was only two months or so, and she had come to Mary's dress fittings... She needed friends to help her, now that Geoff had... Now that he...

Well, neither of them had behaved well, she was honest enough to say that.

But how could her oldest friend become her chief critic? She wouldn't stand for it. He thought her behavior disagreeable before? He had no idea what she was capable of. She could have more airs, more pride, more calm and cool detachment than the most hardened of females. Marianne Bray would be terrified by the creature Mary Hamilton could become. Let him watch her thrive against his wishes and expectations, let him see the sheer volume of worthy admirers she could attain, let him call her flirtatious and ridiculous and false all he wanted. She would pay him absolutely no mind unless she was forced to.

Let him see how his hated London would feel for him then.

Winston suddenly appeared and bowed before her. "Miss Hamilton, you have a visitor."

She groaned and rubbed at her temple again. "I thought I specifically said no callers today..."

"You did, Miss," he acknowledged with another bow. "But this gentleman says he has a note from you requesting a meeting."

That brought her head out of her hand and she stared at her butler in confusion. "A meeting? I set up no meetings."

"I know that, Miss, as does he. He said to forgive his impertinence, but he thought urgency might be best, once he received the note you sent."

Still confused, Mary followed the butler down the hall towards the foyer. "Who is it, Winston?"

"Mr. Bray, Miss."

Mary stopped in her tracks. "Oh," she said softly. She took in a deep breath, then released it slowly. This would be very unpleasant, she feared. "Right, I must see him. Where is he?"

"The drawing room, Miss. Shall I send for some tea?"

She almost laughed, but nodded. "Yes, I think so. And extra biscuits. If half of what I have heard about him is true, we will need quite a few of them."

"Very good, Miss Hamilton," Winston said with a low bow as he left her in front of the drawing room doors.

The footman moved to open them, but she held up a hand.

Duncan Bray was Geoff's best friend. Would he know about their disagreements? Would it factor into his treatment of her or his opinion? Would he believe her as readily as he might have a few days ago? She shook her head. Duncan was a sensible, kind man, despite his terrifying stature, and he had always treated her with respect and generosity. He would not be so crass as to be ungentlemanly simply because Geoff was out of humor with her.

She pulled her shoulders back, adjusted a stray wisp of hair, and nodded at the footman, who opened the door for her.

Duncan turned from the window at which he had been standing and bowed with a smile. "Miss Hamilton, I apologize for not setting a time for a meeting. I assumed you would be receiving today. I've heard you have a bit of a crowd control problem of late." His smile was warm, and his piercing eyes danced with restrained mirth.

She managed a comfortable smile of her own. There was no need for pretenses with him. "That I have, Mr. Bray. It seems better since speaking with your sister, however."

His smile dimmed a bit. "I was afraid of that."

"No, no, it's quite lovely," she protested, taking a seat on the divan and gesturing for him to take a seat as well. "I wasn't used to the degree of attention I was receiving, let alone the number of willing participants, and your sister has such experience…"

"Too much, in my opinion," he growled.

Mary could not help but smile at his response. "Perhaps, but nevertheless, she was a great help to me, and I hope I shall be able to help her in some way in the future."

That seemed to satisfy him. "Thank you, Miss Hamilton," he replied softly. "I should like for Marianne to be exposed to some sensible feminine influence. I fear only having an overprotective brother does not sit well with her much of the time."

Mary let out a small sigh, and swallowed. "I fear it is for that overprotective brother part of you that I have requested to speak with you."

He frowned sharply. "What do you mean?"

She started to bite her lip in anxiety, then remembered she shouldn't and opted to clench her fingers together instead. "Has Marianne told you anything about our day together last week?"

He slowly shook his head. "Not a word, beyond that she enjoyed herself."

"Yes, well, there was one part that neither she, nor I, enjoyed at all," Mary confessed. She hesitated, just for a moment, and then said, "I think now, as I did then, that you should hear about this from me, and then you may decide how best to proceed."

Chapter Fourteen

$\mathscr{T}$he ballroom at the home of the Duke and Duchess of Ashcombe was undoubtedly the finest ballroom in London, aside from perhaps the palace itself. But even then, it was unfathomable that any place could look as magical and elegant as the sight currently before those fortunate enough to be in attendance. Candles blazed in every chandelier and holder, the grand windows gave sight to the immaculate gardens, all glowing in the firelight of the torches along the path, and the stars winked in on the dancers and those persons who had ventured out to the terrace and gardens for a more romantic evening. The musicians were the highest quality that could be found anywhere and their instruments gleamed proudly in the light of the room. The ladies present were as beautiful and elegant and immaculately dressed as any to be found, made more enchanting by the excitement and hope in each pair of eyes. The gentlemen, more prone to groan at such events, were as eager as young lads, and such was the attendance that partners were plenty and time had ceased to exist.

Geoffrey Harris had no such illusions. He barely noticed the splendor of the location or the ladies or the night at all. His attention was entirely focused on one particular point, and had been for the whole evening.

Mary was sitting, for a change, surrounded by as many men as he had ever seen attend her. She had been dancing the entire night, each dance and each partner as equally delightful as the previous, if her expression was anything to go by. He heard her tinkling laughter above the sounds of the musicians and he cringed at the sound. It was so grating, so false, so… not Mary.

She arrived after he and Cassandra did, which effectively ruined his evening, pleasant as it had begun, as she had swept in on Mr. Burlington's arm. They were quite the pair together; there was not an eye in the place that had not been fixed on them for their grand entrance. The smile on her face was proud and radiant, and more than one gentleman had been scolded by his lady wife for lingering too long upon her.

Cassie had not said a word about Mary during the ride over, for which he was grateful. He was pleased to escort the girl, as everything was exciting for her these days. She had chatted cheerfully about who would be in attendance, made him tell her any gossip he knew of, and then shyly asked him if she looked presentable enough for a ball hosted by a duke and duchess.

He tore his gaze away from Mary and her menagerie momentarily to look for her, and found her sitting in the corner of the room with Christian, smiling at something he was saying. But not dancing. He frowned. He had already danced with her once, as had Christian. They each may be able to dance once more with her, but beyond that would be cause for comment. Time to call upon his friends, he expected.

He seized Colin's arm as he passed in front of him.

"Steady on, Harris," Colin barked, looking down at the hand holding him still. "Do you mind? I've just seen Elizabeth Nearing reenter and if I don't dance with her now, her mother won't let me at all."

"You are dancing with Cassandra Hamilton next," he informed him.

Colin's brows rose. "Am I?"

Geoff nodded in Cassie's direction and Colin looked, then his eyes narrowed. "Right you are, so I am. See you in a minute."

Adjusting his gloves and fixing his most charming smile, Colin Gerrard strode across the ballroom, crowds parting before him as the very Red Sea for London's very own Moses. Several gentlemen watched with interest, for where Colin went, others were sure to follow, and even as he led Cassie to the dance floor, a few gentlemen approached the chair she had been occupying, content to wait for the dance to be done before their turn. Such was Colin's gift. No one could really tell just when or how Colin had obtained his mysterious power, but there was no denying that he possessed something rare.

Satisfied that his duty was done, Geoff turned back to his previous activity.

Burlington was nowhere to be seen, which made him grunt in satisfaction, but there were plenty of other men to make him glower. She looked like an illustration he had seen once of a beautiful ancient queen with a bevy of slaves surrounding her, faces turned towards her in adoration, worshipping her with their eyes. The idea had made him chuckle before, but now it simply made him nauseated.

She knew he was here. He had met her eye at least twice already. Each time she had given him a cold consideration for only a moment, and then looked to others around her with a greater intensity. She avoided looking in his direction at all cost, which suited him just fine. He much preferred to cause a stir by glaring from across the room. Let the gossips and biddies make something of that, and see if word would not reach Mary's preciously ignorant ears. Whether or not she would act on them remained to be seen and even he, with all of his past knowledge of her, could not have predicted her reaction.

"Geoff looks terrible, doesn't he?" Derek whispered in a not-whispering voice.

"Awful," Duncan agreed, equally not keeping his voice down. "Don't think he's had a proper night's sleep in some time. I think he is still having the corridor dream."

"Ah, I heard about that," came Nathan's voice from somewhere near them. "And do you know if you have actually appeared yet, Duncan?"

"I haven't heard. Geoff, can you see me in that dream yet?"

"Or where you are going?"

"Or why you are late?"

"Geoff?"

"Geoff."

"Harris?"

Geoffrey blinked, but didn't answer any of them. He couldn't think about that blasted dream right now, not when Mary couldn't even be prevailed upon to acknowledge him in such company as this. She laughed again at something Jack Kent was saying and he felt his stomach churn. She turned to some insignificant puppy and smiled as if at an adorable child, which made the fellow beam as though she were heaven's most glorious angel.

She could have been a Grecian goddess in that gown, a rich cream color with gold trim swirling about it, hugging every curve. Pearls and gold dotted her hair, which was braided and twisted to contain them all, but looked as though at any moment or with the slightest tug, the whole coiffure would come tumbling down. Which, naturally, made her that much more enticing.

To other people.

It only irritated him.

She was the perfect debutante embodied. Even the way her head was turned seemed to be graceful and elegant. The turn of her throat was regal, the precise depth of her chin modest, and the neckline of her gown suggestive without being shocking. There was no fault to be found in her appearance even by the most stodgy of pious men. They would have flocked to her as well simply to hear her voice.

Geoff harrumphed and leaned against the pillar next to him, shifting his weight and folding his arms.

This was ridiculous. Did these men not realize that only a few weeks ago she was a wallflower? That they themselves ignored her? That she had been around for almost ten years without any hint of an admirer? And now, because she changed her hair and her wardrobe, because she was smiling and coy and flirtatious, because she was playing the game…

He hated this game, and he always had. But now he had more reason than ever.

"Are you going to look like that all night?" Duncan's voice growled low somewhere near him. "Or are you going to do something about it?"

Geoff shoved off of the pillar and very nearly marched directly over to where she sat, ignoring the whispers of people who saw where he was going, ignoring the people who darted out of his way after observing the expression on his face, and most of all ignoring how she was not even aware of it. She was apparently so absorbed in her conversation with John Godfrey that no one else existed, not even the others surrounding her. Funny, he never thought Godfrey had anything worth saying, but then, she had shown her tastes to be much different than he would have expected.

He stopped directly in front of her, despite the distinct lack of notice, and gave the most perfect bow he had ever bestowed on anyone. His mother would have shed a tear of pride. "Will you dance the next with me, Miss Hamilton?"

The buzz of conversation around her stopped and she reluctantly looked at him, her face as calm and composed as he had ever seen it. Only her eyes told him the truth; she was furious.

She looked him up and down once, as if in assessment. Then she offered the polite smile he had seen her use so often of late. "I pray you would excuse me, Mr. Harris. I fear the experience would not reflect well on either of us."

As if that settled the matter, she turned to continue her conversation with Godfrey, who was more than happy to oblige.

Geoffrey forced himself to smile, but it was the sort of smile he had seen on a cat when they saw a mouse to trap. "I pray *you* will excuse *me*, Miss Hamilton, but you owe me. Or have you forgotten our debt?"

Slowly, so slowly he quirked a curious brow, she turned to face him once more, her face still composed, but only just. Her eyes flashed dangerously, but she made no response.

"Do you need me to remind you, Miss Hamilton? I perfectly recall the situation, and I would be more than happy to..."

"That is not necessary, Mr. Harris," she said at once, her tone only a trifle louder than it had been, but he noticed. She narrowed her eyes and smiled tightly, which should have been a warning to him.

He didn't care.

"Of course, I had forgotten. You are correct, and I shall pay my debt."

He inclined his head and held a hand out to her, which she took and gracefully rose from her seat, giving a slight nod to her passel of prats. He led her out to the dance floor, his eyes finding his friends where he had left them, all of whom watched with interest.

"What are you doing, Geoffrey?" she hissed through her polite smile, now more of a polite grimace.

"Dancing with an old friend, isn't that obvious?" he informed her, his tone mockingly innocent.

She snorted and barely avoided rolling her eyes. "Friend. Is that what we are?"

He gave her a hard look. "You have a better definition?"

She glared at him as she took up her position. "My friends do not insult me."

He bowed with the other gentlemen. "No, they only have to flatter you. Look at your friends over there, Miss Hamilton, just waiting to flatter and fluff."

Her delicate brows snapped together. "Not all of the men who call on me are flatterers."

"Oh no?" he asked as he moved first in the dance.

"No. Just the other day, your friend Mr. Bray paid me a visit."

"Did he now?" Geoff looked over in Duncan's direction coldly. Duncan met his look with confusion.

Mary laughed her annoying, tinny laugh, and said, "Didn't know that? Pity, I thought everybody always told you everything."

Now he glowered at her as she passed in front of him with two other ladies, who were both terribly confused as to the disagreeable expressions they were privy to. He forced himself to take a quick breath and smoothed his expression back to complacency.

"I see Burlington has abandoned you," Geoff mentioned as lightly as if it were a comment on the weather. "Poor sot."

"He's done no such thing," Mary said with a scolding tilt of her head. "We are not bound to each other. We are good friends who enjoy each other's company."

Geoff snorted and gave her a hard look. "I can think of someone else who once filled that position."

Mary said nothing, but she looked away and focused on her

shoes for a moment.

His hand closed around the back of her waist, as the dance required, and he hissed, "Has he made his intentions clear, Mary?"

She jerked her head away and her eyes flashed up at him. "That is none of your concern."

"As your very old friend, who only wishes the very best for you..."

She barked out a hard, disbelieving laugh, which he ignored.

"...It is my duty, I believe, to ask if you are seriously considering his suit."

She separated from him, twirled, then returned to his side with an impertinent lift of her chin. "And what if I am? He's eligible."

"Is that all it takes?" he asked in surprise as he took her hand and led her down the column of other couples. "Well, then we should expand your menagerie considerably once that is made known."

"Stop it, Geoff," she whispered as he spun her around the last couple. "He is kind and principled..." She broke off for the next dance movement, but kept her eyes trained on him in warning. Then she was brought back to him. "...and refined, and he is..."

"The worst possible choice for you," Geoff interrupted as he took her hand once more.

"How can you say that?" she asked, looking up at him.

He laughed and gave her a disbelieving look. "Well, for one, he has no sense of humor. And you love to laugh, or you used to. Could you really be happy with a life devoid of any humor?"

"I could adjust." Her voice was firm, but her response came a little slowly as they waited for other couples to pass them.

He shook his head. "You would be miserable."

Up came that impetuous chin once more. "I would want for nothing."

They were forced together again and he took her hands. "You would want for everything," he assured her, his voice dipping lower.

She swallowed and spun away with the other women. "I don't think you are being objective."

He fought a grin, knowing he was getting to her. "Objectivity is not required here, merely sense. Do you even know his Christian name, Mary?"

Surprised lit her features and she blinked. "Of course, I do," she said quickly. "It's Henry."

His grin spread further. "No, it's not," he taunted as it was his turn to leave her with the other men. She looked completely exasperated as he faced her once more. When they were close enough, he adopted the most matter-of-fact expression he could. "It's Ferdinand."

Her nose wrinkled up in surprise, confusion, and the first instinct of distaste.

He nodded. "He chooses to go by Henry because even he cannot bear his Christian name."

She shook her head, tossing those tremulous locks temptingly. "That makes no difference to me."

He laughed once with incredulity. "So you would choose an idiot, a fop…" He lowered his voice as he saw a few heads begin to turn in their direction. "A boring, refined, completely uninteresting fashion plate of a man with a terrible name and no sense of humor merely because he is rich and kind to you?"

Her grip on his hand seized into a vice-like clench. "Don't assume you know my taste in men," she breathed, her teeth clenching so hard he would swear he could hear them.

"Choosing him," he replied in a similar tone, "would show absolutely no taste in men."

Mary sighed heavily and rolled her eyes towards him. "Well, then, Mr. Harris, who would you suggest? You?"

He reared back and stared at her. "What?"

She tilted her head ever so slightly, her smile become feline. "You are so concerned about my suitors. Do I detect jealousy?"

He laughed a little too loudly, a little too hard, and forced a smile. "My dear Miss Hamilton, you would only be so fortunate."

She snorted. "Should you suggest my suitors then? Must all pass your inspection before I myself may consider them?"

"Not at all, I have no such claim on you." The dance was nearing its end, and he turned to face her, taking her waist in his hand once more, as was warranted. "I merely demonstrate the facts. And now that we have a moment, Miss Hamilton," he said, lowering his voice, "might I tell you how becoming your new gown is?"

She glanced up at him in surprise. "What?"

He continued to look at her, staring into her eyes. "I found your tiny waist very impressive myself not so long ago. In this gown you put every man's deepest desires in the most innocent and elegant form of display. Who would know that such a figure lay hidden in you?"

Her lips parted in surprise, and he could hear the breath racing past her lips. "You shouldn't say such things," she whispered, her lips barely moving.

"Why not?" he asked in a low, rumbling tone as he spun her once more. "Surely a brother can."

Mary's eyes dropped to his cravat, and she swallowed with difficulty. "You are no brother," she murmured, her voice almost lost against the musicians' finale.

"No," he replied darkly, his breath seizing when her gaze rose to his again. "No, thank God, I am not." He brought her hand to his lips and kissed it gently, lingering longer than he should have, losing himself in her eyes.

Then, collecting what remained of his wits, he released her and turned away, striding across the room to the safety of anywhere else.

Mary felt cold standing there abandoned in the middle of the ballroom. That kiss… Through the fabric of her glove she had felt an almost painful heat racing up her arm, and it tingled still.

Applause filled the room and she was shaken from her stupor. She forced a bright smile and applauded the musicians with the others, then made for the terrace as fast as she could. She needed air. She needed space. She needed… to think.

What in the name of Medusa's great gorgons was that?

Her cheeks were on fire. She lifted the back of a gloved hand to one, then dropped it quickly when she remembered he had kissed that one.

"Mary!"

She moved faster, not knowing who was calling her, and not caring.

"Mary!"

Her sister's voice broke through her frantic haze. She cautiously looked over one shoulder and saw Cassie moving towards her with as much speed as one gracefully could in a crowded ballroom.

She almost left anyway.

"Mary," Cassie said with a smile as she reached her. "I'm so glad I have a moment with you at last. How was the opera?"

Mary exhaled harshly through her nose. "Cassie, I can't talk about it right now. Later?"

Concern darkened her sister's features. "What is wrong? Are you unwell?"

Unwell? Mary nearly laughed out loud. But her sister's confusion meant that she had somehow missed the last dance and therefore would have no idea of the turmoil she was facing. She forced a kind smile. "Just a bit overheated, I'm afraid. Too much dancing."

Cassie grinned and gave her the very briefest of eye rolls. "You still have a weak endurance for dancing. How sad."

Mary shrugged helplessly and turned to go out to the terrace.

"When you have recovered, dance with Christian, will you?"

She turned back with a question in her eyes.

Cassie smiled. "He told me he would like to, but he wasn't sure he could get to you. I think he is quite shy about that sort of thing."

A bit of breath escaped Mary's lungs without her intent and she glanced over to see Christian standing where she had seen Cassie earlier, watching the dancing with enjoyment. "Of course," she murmured as she considered him, a fond smile forming. "Of course, tell him I would be glad to. I only need a minute."

Cassie nodded and whirled about, practically skipping back to Christian to tell him.

Mary took her escape and fled to the relatively cool night, thanking the heavens that the terrace was, for the moment, empty. She rested her hands on the balustrade and took in several deep, cleansing breaths.

The smoldering anger between her and Geoffrey as they danced was so palpable she could still taste it on her tongue. Their emotions had been running high, even surrounded by other couples and in plain sight of the highest members of the London society. They couldn't say what they had wanted to say, and yet they had said quite enough. The rest of the argument had taken place in their eyes alone, and had been even worse.

His eyes...

She shook her head and took another, unsteady breath. She had never seen his eyes look the way they had when he spoke to her in that low voice. Impossibly, after all these years, he still had power to make her feel things she shouldn't. They had been friends for so long, she should have been accustomed to them, no matter how they looked.

No one could have expected those eyes to look like that.

She frowned and slapped the balustrade. No matter what she had been feeling in a moment of weakness, his words to her had been unpardonable. So taunting and superior and disapproving. As if he would know better than she who to consider seriously, or who would be a good fit. There hadn't been any offers or understandings at all as yet, and even if there had been, he wouldn't be consulted!

"Miss Hamilton?"

She closed her eyes and exhaled silently, then turned with her debutante smile. "Lord Oliver."

He bowed and offered his hand. "May I have the next?"

She blinked once, then shook her head. "I am so sorry, my lord. I'm afraid the next dance has already been spoken for."

He straightened and smiled kindly. "Then may I take you back in to your partner?"

She considered him with a curious smile, and nodded, smiling more broadly. "That would be delightful, my lord, thank you."

He held out his arm, which she took, forcing herself to maintain her composure as she reentered the ballroom. Let Geoffrey Harris think whatever he wanted. She would allow the men she wanted to court her, she would flirt and flatter and let herself be adored, and she would dance with whomever she wanted.

And at the moment, she was going to most heartily enjoy a dance with his brother.

"Single most uncomfortable moment of my life."

"Seriously, Colin?"

"You need to get out more."

"*I* need to get out more?"

"It was a touch nerve-wracking, I admit."

"Thank you."

"Did you see the way they looked at each other? I wondered who was going to start breathing fire and set the place ablaze."

A snort. "The gossips will love this. They're talking already."

"Are you sure he went down this way?"

"Positive. Duncan told me before he ran for safety. Geoff!"

Geoffrey made no move to approach his friends, but also made no effort to hide himself as he stared out of the window nearest him.

After his dance with Mary, he had felt the need to flee the scene of his crime as soon as was respectably possible. He wasn't sure what had happened out there, but that had not been him. He was neither that impertinent nor that petty. And yet, he felt justified in everything he said. He had been honest and straightforward, just as he always had been with her.

But he didn't like the bitter taste in his mouth he'd had ever since.

And he didn't like the way her waist had felt beneath his hand.

And he most certainly did not enjoy the way his voice had lowered of its own accord and rendered him a complete idiot who couldn't look away from her.

"Geoff, I think we need to work on your hearing," Colin announced as he approached, clamping a hand down on his shoulder.

Geoff snorted a light laugh. "I hear you, Colin, but it doesn't always require a response."

"Well said," praised Derek, coming around his other side and leaning against the wall. "So, Geoffrey, would you like to tell us what that was all about?"

He looked over at Derek in apparent confusion. "What are you talking about?"

Nathan made a noise of disbelief. "Do you take us for idiots? That little duel you had with Mary Hamilton in the middle of the ballroom for all of London to see. I thought you were going to lose your head."

"I thought she was going to slap him," Colin offered with a hint of disappointment.

"I was just having a conversation with an old friend," Geoffrey told them, keeping his face free from any residual emotion. "It was my only opportunity. She's too busy at other times to see anybody besides her fawning fools. Except rarely," he muttered as he recalled her words. "Where is Duncan?"

"He vanished some time before your grand finale," Colin said with a wave of his hand. "Something about his sister that needed his attention, I really haven't the foggiest."

Geoff glowered darkly, which was fast becoming an expression of frequency for his face.

"If it was just a conversation," Derek asked slowly, his voice even, "then I am curious as to why you have had that exact expression on your face the entire evening, particularly when you were staring quite fixedly at Mary?"

Geoff turned his gaze back to Derek, who didn't even flinch.

"And I myself am wondering," Nathan mused aloud, "what could possibly drive you, the most controlled man I know, to march across the entire ballroom and practically drag her on to the dance floor, away from her collection of men, and then engage in the most tension-filled dance I have ever had to witness in my life?"

"And I want to know…" Colin started, but Geoff just looked at him, and he clamped his lips together with a shrug and an impish grin.

"Things are… difficult at the moment," Geoff said, choosing his words with care.

"For whom?" Derek murmured, a strange smile forming.

"She is being unreasonable and ridiculous."

Nathan snorted. "And you are being mulish and gloomy."

"And you cannot sleep," Colin pointed out.

Geoff frowned at him. "That has nothing to do with Mary."

Colin shrugged. "Both have you wandering random corridors, I made a logical leap."

"Well, don't," he grumbled. He shoved off of the wall and looked at them. "And if you nannies are through with your interrogation, I'd like to return to the ball."

They all stepped back and gestured for him to lead on. Their timing was impeccable and they nearly burst out laughing as Geoff walked past them and back into the splendor of the ballroom.

"I think he's in trouble," Nathan muttered softly to Derek as they followed.

"Oh, he most certainly is," Derek agreed, grinning. "Beyond trouble."

"What sort of trouble?" Colin asked eagerly, earning himself a look from the others. "What? What trouble?"

Chapter Fifteen

$\mathcal{M}$ary sat among friends as she listened to Lily Arden perform her third piece of the evening, bringing sounds from the pianoforte that Mary had only fabricated in her wildest imaginations. The girl was supremely talented, and she was delighted that she had been able to have a hand in displaying that to the ignorant.

She glanced about her music room with a small smile, searching for the most likely candidates to approach Lily when she was finished. Mr. Parker, perhaps, as he was a great admirer of music and looked quite arrested at the moment. That would be a fine match, but Lily could do better.

Her eyes fell upon Thomas Granger, her roguish card player, and saw that, much to her surprise, he looked positively bewildered. His dark features were taut and his eyes wide as he stared at Lily in wonder. It was much to his credit, she suspected, that his mouth was not hanging open. Was he an admirer of music or just of Lily? She had no idea, but wouldn't that be something? He would make a good match. An excellent one, to be honest. He might have been a rogue and a skilled card player, but he was perfectly respectable, charming, surprisingly shy in temperament, and his fortune... Well, it would be safe to say that he had the means that even if he had lost Mary's entire fortune in a poorly played round, he would still have fortune enough to be wildly eligible.

The charming rogue and the modest beauty? She fought a mischievous grin as she looked between the two. That would be the most delightfully unexpected match.

Her glance about the room showed her who else was still in attendance, but none were paying so close attention. They were all politeness, and no doubt would applaud Lily most handsomely, but they were not awestruck. They didn't appreciate her talent as Mary did, nor some of the other ladies in the room.

She took a moment to consider Kate, a wonderfully accomplished pianist herself, sitting near her husband, and watching Lily with a fond smile. Well, that was well done. If Lily could receive the attention and good graces of the Marchioness of Whitlock, her popularity would positively blossom. And Kate was fiendish enough that she would undoubtedly have her own ideas for helping Lily make a good match.

Mary had to laugh at herself. Since when had she become such a devoted matchmaker? She had never cared about such things before, and rarely even paid enough attention to know about the matches being made. That was her sister's territory. And yet here she was, eagerly making matches for a girl who had made no such desires known, and with a man she herself was being courted by.

Not that she would consider Mr. Granger for herself. It had become obvious early on that they wouldn't suit, but they remained friends and he kept up appearances for no other reason than to give her a bit of a reprieve as needed, and to make her laugh. Not that his sense of humor was particularly ebullient, but he did say the most delightfully droll things when nobody was listening.

He would make Lily a fine husband, if they chose.

Lily finished her song, and smiled shyly at the gathering. Applause rang through the room, though some were only doing so because of appearances. Mary frowned as she noticed Lord Wofford only clapped twice, and then stifled a yawn behind his hand.

And he was not the only one to do so.

Attention turned to her as hostess and she adopted her public face and smiled. "Miss Arden's talented fingers surely deserve a rest after so difficult a piece, particularly when she performed it so masterfully. Don't you all agree that it was so?"

Now the applause was louder and more enthusiastic. Lily

blushed from her seat at the pianoforte, but made no attempt to temper her sweet smile.

"I believe we may take a break from the music for now," Mary continued, noticing out of the corner of her eye that Geoffrey was making his way to Lily with a cordial smile. Her tone slipped ever so slightly, but she managed to cover it with a laugh. "Unless anyone else should like a chance?"

"Will you not favor us, Miss Hamilton?" came the slightly higher-than-masculine voice of Mr. Beech, who was equal parts young and naïve, and too eager by half.

Other voices cried out for her, but she shook her head firmly. "No, I am not performing tonight." She looked over at Lily, who was smiling kindly at Geoffrey, now at her side. Mary would ignore him. "Particularly after so exquisite a piece as Miss Arden has just played. I cannot exhibit anything half so great. No, no," she insisted, holding up a hand at the protestations. "Not tonight, thank you."

"Miss Harville?" Geoffrey suggested suddenly, looking at the round-faced girl sitting behind Mary. "Would you not favor us?"

Fanny Harville looked stunned, but delighted enough and she nodded.

Mary looked back at him with widened eyes, but he appeared not to notice as he helped Lily from the bench. Other faces in the room looked equally as horrified as Mary felt. She glanced longingly at the side door, which Winston had been instructed to leave open. She could not in good conscience leave the room when she was hostess, and Geoffrey knew that.

Her guests had no such restrictions. Several of the ladies claimed to be warm, and not a few gentlemen rose to assist them as they left the room. Derek and Kate stayed, though Derek watched the others leave with longing. Cassie glared at the retreating figures, then smiled encouragingly at Fanny as she took her seat.

Mary sighed to herself and settled into her seat. If Cassie could be encouraging, so could she.

Surprisingly, Lord Wofford didn't leave the room. Nor did Lord Oliver, Mr. Timmons, Mr. Parker, or Mr. Burlington, all of whom appeared as though any other accomplished female were about to perform. Yet all of them, she was quite sure, had been a victim of Fanny Harville's voice previously. They showed no sign of wishing to be anywhere else.

Well. She would have to seriously reconsider a few of those gentlemen for herself. True gentlemen, it would appear.

Decidedly against her express wishes, her eyes scanned for Geoffrey. She frowned ever so slightly as he escorted Lily from the room, already engaging her in more than polite conversation. Not that she expected Lily to remain. The poor girl had already played three times and with very little refreshment between. But Geoffrey...

She couldn't help but flinch slightly as Fanny began with a truly horrific note that made her feel as though her stomach had been plunged into an icy trough. She glanced up to see if Fanny would look around at them all, but true to form, the girl was playing and singing with her eyes closed. Probably for the best. Mary closed her eyes as well, and tried to imagine something else.

"Pardon me, Miss Hamilton."

She opened her eyes in surprise as Mr. Granger was sitting beside her now. "Mr. Granger?"

"I'm afraid I must take my leave," he said softly so as not to disturb what was supposed to be music.

Disappointment hit her in the chest and she frowned slightly. "Oh." Then she leaned in and quirked a half smile. "Is the entertainment not to your liking?"

He flashed a very quick show of teeth with a roguish grin. "No, indeed, it's very fine..." He coughed softly with suggestion, and Mary fought the urge to snicker.

"No, I've had a pleasant evening," he assured her, his smile retreating back into hiding. "I simply... I feel it is time."

Concern knitted Mary's brow. "Are you certain? We will have some other entertainment momentarily, and perhaps some riddles. I could use your cleverness there."

He slowly shook his head, his eyes wandering to the door out of which Geoff and Lily had vanished. "I fear I will not be good company for you, Miss Hamilton. I really must take my leave."

That, at least, Mary could understand. She smiled softly and nodded. "Of course, Mr. Granger. Thank you for your attendance this evening."

He stood and gave her a slight bow. "Miss Hamilton," he murmured. Then he swept from the room, his eyes avoiding that side door entirely.

Mary frowned in earnest now. Could Geoffrey not have seen what was plain for all? She snapped open her fan and began to fan herself in irritation, though the room was cool enough. She would have to speak with Geoffrey after all, though she had fully intended to avoid him all evening. She had been surprised to see him arrive at all, but then, he had promised to come for Miss Arden.

His words to her the other night echoed in her mind: "you have that party and invite Miss Arden and I will be her chief admirer for the entire evening. I will be so full of compliments that you will think you invited one of your fops instead of me."

She snorted in memory. A fop he was certainly being, and certainly her chief admirer. But knowing Geoffrey, knowing his current feelings, he would do it merely to spite Mary, to throw it in her face that he was keeping his word.

A discordant chord on the piano caused her to jerk and she flexed her fingers painfully. She released a slow exhale and looked at her sister, whose face was frozen into polite support, but there was real pain in her eyes. Perhaps now they could prevent this from happening again.

At long last, it was over, and polite applause filled the room. Mary rose before anybody could be so cruel as to suggest another and smiled at the gathering. "Thank you, Miss Harville. It is so delightful to witness your improvements."

Fanny smiled and nodded in acceptance.

"If you all would care for some refreshment, a light spread has been provided in the dining room. Then perhaps, we can reconvene in here for some games, and a bit more music."

All rose and did as she suggested, finding the ones who had departed already in the dining room. Mary looked around for Geoff, who was still chatting with Lily. She walked over calmly as if she were merely taking a stroll about the room. Lily saw her approach and smiled.

"Miss Hamilton, thank you so much for this evening," the sweet girl gushed, absently pushing a stray lock of her brown curls behind her ear. "It has been wonderful."

Mary couldn't help but smile. "I'm glad you are enjoying yourself, Miss Arden. I trust you have received some compliments?"

Lily blushed. "Quite a few. It's a trifle overwhelming."

"But absolutely deserved," Mary insisted, putting a hand on her arm. "Now, if you don't mind, might I borrow Mr. Harris for a moment?"

Lily looked up at him and nodded with a smile. "Of course!"

As if Mary had summoned her, Kate was suddenly there with her dark eyes trained on Lily. "You, my dear Miss Arden, put me quite to shame."

"Miss Arden, you know the Marchioness of Whitlock?" Mary said quickly, making the proper introductions.

Lily curtseyed very prettily. "Only by sight, my lady. It's a pleasure. Thank you for your compliment."

Kate took the girl's arm. "No, the pleasure is mine. Now we must talk at great length, Miss Arden. Your largo was so moving, I could hardly speak." And with that Kate steered her away, taking her around the room.

Mary exhaled silently, then cast a look up at Geoffrey, who watched the ladies move fondly.

"You have to adore Kate, don't you?" he said on a sigh.

Mary glowered. "I believe most do. Geoffrey, what are you doing?"

He looked down at her in surprise. "Standing here talking to you. And before that, complimenting Miss Arden and having a most pleasant conversation."

"Well, stop it!"

He reared back in surprise. "Why? I told you I would come and compliment Miss Arden, and so I have. And not insincerely either, she's remarkable."

"Yes, yes, I know she is," Mary snapped, clenching her fan in one hand. "And I'm becoming terribly fond of her, which is why you must stop."

"Stop complimenting her?"

She huffed and turned towards him more fully so that others would not see her. "Stop monopolizing her. Don't you realize that others may want to speak with her?"

He looked at her with complete incredulity. "Are you serious, Mary? Monopolizing? So says you, who monopolizes all attention everywhere she goes these days."

She clenched her teeth together a little painfully. She must remain calm, she must remain collected. "Don't make her fall in love with you, Geoffrey."

"I have no such intentions," he began, his voice beginning to rise.

"Shh!" she hissed, looking around quickly. She opened her fan and held it before her face. "You have paid her your compliments, now leave her alone."

"I will do no such thing," he said, keeping his voice low as he smiled pleasantly at Kate from across the room. "I like Miss Arden, too, and I will converse with her as I see fit. No need to get all huffy because it means one less person is complimenting you."

Her mouth popped open in surprise and she sputtered. "That is not my... That is absolutely ridiculous."

He looked at her. "Is it? You have asked me to stop being pleasant with a young woman who you yourself decided to host an event for, because...?" He waited expectantly.

"Because others may want to have some of her time!" she hissed.

He shook his head with a laugh. "Absurd. They can come up and compliment her all they like no matter who she is conversing with. If they truly wished to, they would have. We were not being exclusive. And if I were to form any designs on Miss Arden, I do believe I could do so without having to confer with you."

She narrowed her eyes and snapped her fan closed. "Leave it alone, Geoffrey. And don't ask Fanny Harville to sing anymore unless you are prepared to endure it with the rest of us." She left in a swirl of skirts and huffed an impatient grunt of dissatisfaction. Impossible man.

"I thought, perhaps, we could now have a game of riddles."

Geoff turned with the other gentlemen in the room, and managed to stifle his groan. With the silly idiots she had collected here tonight, she wanted a game of riddles? The only creatures of sense here besides himself were Derek and Kate, and perhaps Miss Arden, though he didn't know enough of her to be able to determine that as yet. But none of Mary's scholars had attended, and certainly no clever man had. With the exception of Thomas Granger, who had wisely fled the evening some time ago.

He entered the music room with a heavy sigh knowing this was going to prove to be an exercise in restraint for him. All the rest seemed to be excited about the prospect of riddles, but he feared very much that Mary would use her now quite sharpened tongue upon those unsuspecting fools who thought her the epitome of all goodness. They had no idea how clever she was.

Grudgingly he took up a position along one wall, near enough to Derek and Kate that he would be able to hear their mutterings, which were destined to be hilarious, and far enough away from Mary that he wouldn't have to look at her if he chose not to. He glanced over to find that she was yet again surrounded by far too many gentlemen. And she was scolding him for monopolizing someone? He snorted silently.

"Shall I begin?" inquired Lord Wofford.

Geoff tried not to laugh, and saw Derek struggling as well. Wofford was notoriously stupid and the idea that he even knew a riddle was astounding.

"Of course, my lord," Mary said politely. "Is this for someone in particular, or for all?"

"Oh, for all, certainly," he puffed pompously. He cleared his throat. "What walks on four legs in the morning, two at mid-day, and three in the evening?"

Most of the room groaned and Geoff hid a smile behind a fist. The most well-known riddle of all? It was too perfect.

"Oh, it's a human," Cassandra announced with a roll of her eyes and a light laugh. "We all know that one." The room, including Mary, laughed politely.

The glare that the earl tossed in Cassandra's direction wiped Geoff's smile from his face. It was evident he knew exactly who had answered and exactly what rumors were swirling about her, and he held the same disreputable opinion of her as the rest of Society did. Mary didn't react at all, as she was engaged in conversation with Mr. Beech beside her. Geoff's fist clenched as he looked back at Wofford, still glowering at Cassie as if she were a viper, and he heard Derek murmur, "Steady, Geoff. Allow me."

He glanced down at his friend, only to find him glaring at Wofford. The earl saw it and managed to color slightly, and looked away. After all, Derek was a powerful man with a powerful glare, and anybody who wished to keep any standing at all in society would do well to avoid them.

"Thank you," Geoff muttered as a touch of satisfaction hit him. Derek nodded, barely.

"I shall go next," Mr. Parker said politely. "What can run, but never walks, has a mouth, but never talks, has a head, but never weeps, has a bed, but never sleeps?"

There were mutterings and murmurings around the room, and Geoff found himself watching Mary. Her forehead was furrowed, ever so slightly, and then it cleared. She looked up and Geoff knew she had the answer.

"A river," she said in clear tones. Then she smiled brightly at Mr. Parker. "Isn't it?"

He inclined his head proudly. "It is indeed, Miss Hamilton. Bravo."

Applause and laughter spattered about and Geoff shifted in annoyance, his eyes threatening to roll of their own accord.

Mary giggled, (she giggled? Since when did she giggle?) and turned to the gentleman beside her. "I have one for you, Mr. Timmons."

Timmons looked as though he'd just been granted a favor from the Queen. "I should be so honored, Miss Hamilton."

Geoff saw Cassandra bite her lip to contain her laughter and he wished he felt the urge to do the same. He only felt a crawling sensation in his stomach.

Mary smiled fondly at Timmons. "Here it is; give me food, and I will live; give me water, and I will die. What am I?"

Geoff stilled as he recognized that particular riddle as one from a book of riddles he and Mary had gone through one rainy day only a few years ago. It had been one of the most entertaining memories he had of them, and he'd assumed she'd forgotten. Obviously, she hadn't, considering the way her eyes almost unconsciously flicked in his direction, but never actually at him. He frowned and looked at Timmons, who was utterly bewildered and growing redder by the minute as he fumbled for an answer.

"Food, and I will live," he murmured anxiously, "water and I will die…"

"Do you need a hint?" Mary asked impatiently, her words now holding some bite to them.

"Oh, if you please, Miss Hamilton," he responded with immense relief.

Idiot, Geoff thought with a snort. It was a simple riddle, it didn't need…

"When I touch a finger," Mary said slowly, her eyes fixed on Timmons's, "it grows red."

Really, Timmons looked as though he were going to swoon under such attention, let alone the inviting tones of Mary's voice that made Geoff want to hit something.

Fire, he thought hard. Fire, you fool, the answer is fire!

"Fire!" Timmons cried, grinning wildly. "The answer is fire!"

He earned a faint applause from some, and Mary nodded regally, her hand touching Mr. Timmons' arm encouragingly. More than encouraging, as she rubbed it softly. She was flirting with the idiot! The man could not figure a simple riddle, and she had spoken harshly to him, and now she was flirting?

He forced his glower to abate, and looked directly at Miss Arden, who was watching the game with amusement. "I have one for Miss Arden," he said suddenly.

The room quieted, though excitement was still palpable. The corner of his eye caught Mary looking directly at him, and he could only imagine the glare that he was receiving.

Miss Arden looked at him in surprise, but nodded. "Very well, Mr. Harris. I am not particularly skilled with riddles, but I shall try."

He smiled at her. "I am sure you are too modest. Here it is; if you break me, I do not stop working. If you touch me, I may be snared. If you lose me, nothing will matter. What am I?"

She frowned ever so slightly, and Geoff took the moment to glance around a bit with his eyes only. Cassie looked astonished, but she had a smile for him. Mary's glare was indeed potent. The gentlemen in the room were thinking equally as hard. Derek and Kate on his other side were watching him carefully, a small, bemused smile on both of their faces.

Miss Arden's expression cleared a bit as she looked up at him. "Is it... might it be... one's heart?"

He smiled genuinely at her and nodded. "Indeed, Miss Arden, it is."

There was considerable applause for Miss Arden, and not a few of the young ladies now regarded Geoffrey with a bit more interest, which didn't matter to him. Miss Arden looked very pleased and smiled at him, then at the two girls beside her, who congratulated her.

Mary got to her feet, a little quickly, but her face was composed. "Mr. Harris, I wonder if you might oblige me with a word?" The room became utterly silent, as if they could sense the tension radiating from her.

"Confused about the riddle, Miss Hamilton?" he asked innocently.

Her eyes narrowed ever so slightly and her smile tightened. "Not at all, sir. I merely wish to discuss an alternative answer. Privately, if you don't mind."

He shrugged and pushed off of the wall, gesturing for her to lead the way out.

"Perhaps I should go next," Derek said a bit loudly, bringing the attention in the room away from them. "The man who invented it does not want it..."

Derek's voice faded as Geoff followed Mary down the hall, far enough from the room that they could hear voices, but not quite make out what was being said.

"What was that?" she hissed furiously, her composure gone in a blink.

"A riddle for Miss Arden," he said, as if that should be obvious.

"Geoff, I told you to leave her alone!" She looked back at the room, then up at him. "A riddle about the heart? Honestly!"

"Oh, and you are the only one allowed a little harmless flirtation?" he asked, his voice rough as his own irritation swept in.

She opened her mouth in affront. "I beg your pardon?"

"You were practically throwing yourself on Timmons in there," he said as he flung a hand towards the room. "The idiot who couldn't figure out what fire is, and you insult him, and then encourage him!"

"Insult him?" she cried. "When have I…?"

"A coffin!" someone shouted from the room, to the delighted cries and applause of the rest.

"When did I ever insult him?" she asked in a quieter, more deadly voice.

He snorted. "Your tone when you offered a hint. A man with any intelligence would know exactly what you thought of him from that."

"Don't be ridiculous, Geoffrey."

"I'm not the one giving false impressions to anybody who blinks in my direction." Her eyes were blazing now, but he wouldn't stop this time. "And yet, you would not even acknowledge when Lord Wofford was blatantly disrespectful towards your sister."

Mary huffed and put her hands on her hips. "I did not…"

"You did nothing," he ground out harshly. "If it wasn't for Derek, Cassie might have actually been insulted by the man in her own home. And you, too busy with your own attention, wouldn't have noticed. Are you so heartless now that you care so little for those who care for you? Or is everything about you?"

"Needle and thread!" a female shouted from the room to much applause and laughter.

Mary's eyes were ice cold and she lifted her chin. "You needn't

164

worry about being my escort this season any longer, Geoffrey. I have quite enough options to ensure that I have excellent company at my disposal."

He laughed and stepped closer. "Really? You mean those fops in there? They don't even know you, Mary."

"Oh, and you do?" she asked, tilting her head up to look at him more fully. "Those fops are the first gentlemen to ever show interest in me. Why shouldn't I receive their attentions and offers, if I find them agreeable?"

He ground his teeth and moved closer. "Because they are interested in who they think you are, not who you really are. They want this..." He gestured to her form, perhaps a bit recklessly, but it served his point. "The imaginary creature you have turned yourself into, the one who barely resembles the real you at all."

She backed away, her back now at the wall. "Did you ever think that perhaps this is who I am? Who I was meant to be?"

"Not possible," he said with a shake of his head, moving in on her again. He could hear her breath coming rapidly as her ire rose. Even like this, when he was so angry with her he could hardly see, some small corner of his mind registered the fact that she was beautiful. Breathtaking. Captivating.

He wanted to kiss her. He wanted to throttle her. He wanted...

She held up a hand to stop him coming any further, pressing against his chest. "Did you ever think that I might enjoy being this? Why should you hate that I have changed and now have suitors?"

"Because I want you to be who you were before!" he cried, his voice becoming pleading. "I don't want you to be this!"

The color faded from her cheeks and her eyes widened. Her mouth worked silently, and eventually, her voice breathy and weak, she managed, "You encouraged me to do this. You told me it would be fun."

"And I hate myself for it," he rasped, his eyes raking over her face. He could kiss her now. She would let him, he could see it in her eyes.

She said nothing as they stared at each other, breath uneven, emotions high, too close and yet not close enough.

"A turtle!" Applause.

"Miss Hamilton!" a male voice called urgently. "Miss Hamilton, are you returning to the game? We have need of your excellent wits!"

She cleared her throat and laughed a shadow of her merry debutante laugh. "Of course, Mr. Burlington! I shall only be a moment more! Save your cleverest for me!"

Geoff snorted, shook his head, and stepped away from her, ignoring the sudden cold that washed between them. "Perhaps you're right," he said, his voice hollow. "Perhaps I don't know you after all." He looked her up and down with distaste, his look becoming a sneer. "Perhaps this really is all you have to offer."

Mary's eyes widened, and her breathing faltered. She took in a shaky breath, then whispered, "Get out."

He jerked as if struck. "What?"

"Get out," she said again, her voice stronger, her eyes flashing as he had never seen them before. "Don't ever set foot in this house again."

"What?" he cried, stepping back as she advanced. "Mary!"

"I have nothing more to say to you, Mr. Harris. Not now, not ever." Her hands were balled into fists at her sides, and her voice might have been filled with icicles as cold and dangerous as it was.

"You don't mean that," he protested, his mind whirling, his head swimming through sand. "You... you need me!"

She laughed, then; a cold, heartless laugh that made him numb from head to toe. "Need you?" she laughed once more. "I never needed you." She gave him a hard look, and turned to go back into the room. "Not even once."

And with that, she reentered the gathering, apparently as bright and enthusiastic as she had been moments before, as if nothing had happened.

As if she had not just left her oldest friend in an empty hallway of her home, feeling just as empty himself.

He slowly turned away from the party and made his way down the hall, grasping onto random objects along the way to aid his progress. His chest ached as though there was a knife piercing his flesh, and he had to feel his chest just to be sure. He could barely see straight and wavered a number of times before he reached the door. A mindless footman saw him coming and opened it for him.

The night air was cool, pleasant, one might have said, but it hit him like a bitter winter wind and he shivered. He glanced back towards the room, utterly lost. How could he be furious with her and yet ache for her at the same time?

Laughter met his ears, and he could make out hers loudest of all. He swallowed with difficulty, and turned back to the night.

What had he done?

Chapter Sixteen

The wood on the table before him was positively ancient. He had never paid much attention to tables before, but after staring at one for a few hours, he began to notice all sorts of things. No portion of the wood looked the same. No swirl looked like any other swirl, no line was perfectly straight, and each plank of wood was a slightly different shade from the one next to it. The age of the wood was evident by the slight fraying on the top, not immediately noticeable to the untrained eye, or even to the hand as it rested upon it. But when noticed, it was difficult to not notice it. He could keep his hand just a breath above the table and run it carefully along the direction of the grain and there would be the very faintest tickling of miniscule slivers of wood against his palm. Fuzzy, that's what it was. There was a hint of fuzz to the table top.

And it creaked deeply every time he shifted the weight of his body against it, whether his elbow or his arm or his head, they all had experienced the sound and the vibration. He used to think creaking was a very high sounding thing. This table had proven him wrong.

He spun the tankard before him absently, staring at this old, creaking table. Would he become so scarred and noisy as he aged? Would he develop some almost invisible fuzz? Would ignorant eyes look at him and fail to see all that had transpired in his lifetime?

At least a sturdy, strong table like this one would never have to reflect back on its life with horror. Or regret. Or disgust. It would only have the fond memories; its previous life as a tree giving shade and possibly being a home for animals, then becoming this table which had undoubtedly supported thousands of grieving and despondent people in its time. It had probably even seen much celebration and joy. It might not have been a bad life, being a table.

"Oh, there he is, I see him."

"Holy mother of... He looks terrible."

"Is that a beard?"

"Not yet. But it will be."

"He looks like a ruddy sailor."

"Good heavens. Geoff?"

He grunted, still staring at the tankard as he spun it.

One by one his friends began taking seats around him, leaning their arms on his new friend, the table, as he was doing. Nice of them to join him. Then he remembered it was he who had summoned them here. Right.

"Geoff," Derek said in a careful tone, as if speaking with infinite patience to an out of control child, "how many of these have you had today?"

He looked up as Derek tapped the tankard with a finger.

He shook his head. "Just one."

Derek rose up and looked in, then sat back down heavily. "It's still full."

"Wait... you're not drunk?" Colin asked in surprise.

Geoff shook his head slowly, back and forth, then back and forth again.

"Someone go check on that," Nathan muttered, leaning down a bit to try and catch Geoff's eye.

A chair scraped against the stone floor sharply and heavy footfalls left. No one said a word; there was no sound except for the ones coming from Geoff's tankard against the table as it slowly spun in his hand.

The footsteps came back. "No, he's right," Duncan announced as he sat. "He's only been served the drink before him, and that was two hours ago."

Colin gave a low whistle. "Well, that's uncomfortable. He looks like that and he's still got all of his faculties."

Four pairs of eyes looked at him, waiting for him to say or do something. But he had nothing to say or do. He was simply numb, frozen inside, so exhausted that blinking was painful.

No one spoke, no one even moved.

Then Colin twitched a finger.

Geoff stopped spinning his tankard.

There was silence.

"Are you positive he's not drunk?" Colin asked at last, sounding more than a little terrified.

A longsuffering sigh came from someone and then a hand fell hard on Geoff's shoulder.

"Geoff, are you all right?" Nathan asked with surprising gentleness.

"It's been over a week since any of us have seen you," Derek said, sounding like the future duke that he was. "Not a word to indicate if you were alive or dead, no responses to any messages, and you refused to see anybody when we called."

"Even your brother is worried," Duncan added, "and says he's never seen anybody look like this."

"Start talking, or I swear, I will write your mother, and we all know what that means," Colin threatened, his voice sounding more serious than it had ever been.

It would have been comical to an outsider to hear a table of grown men gasp at such a threat, but an outsider did not know Martha Harris. The very thought was enough to make wars cease and plagues depart. Geoff looked up at Colin slowly, his eyes wide, his brain sliding back into place.

"You wouldn't dare," he rasped, his throat dry and raw.

Relief splashed across Colin's blue eyes, and he nodded. "I would and I do dare."

Knowing Colin, he really would, too.

Slowly, painfully, Geoff sat back against his chair, one hand still on the tankard. "I…" He sighed and shook his head. "I have been… an idiot."

Silence met his ears, and he blearily looked around at his friends, who still stared at him.

"Go on…" Colin prodded at last, trying not to smile.

Geoff swallowed and told them everything that had transpired that awful night just over a week ago. All the horrible things he said, how Mary had responded to his actions and his words, and the complete and utter shame that had been tearing him apart ever since. He told them how every day he seemed to be reliving his past, remembering how much Mary had meant to him over the years, and cursing himself for treating her so abominably after all they had been through together. He told them that he didn't see any point in remaining in London if he was going to sink himself so low that he was losing friends over it.

He spoke until his voice hurt, and then it faded altogether as he ran out of words.

No one said anything for a while, and he couldn't even bring himself to look them in the eye. These were great men before him, even Colin. They were respected and their opinions held in high regard. They had known him for years, for most of his life, in some cases, and they knew him well. He couldn't bear to see their opinion of him tarnished because of what he had done.

"Well," Derek said, after a long moment, "that was…"

"It certainly was," Nathan agreed softly.

Geoff nodded. He knew he was beyond words.

"What are you going to do?" Duncan asked in his low rumble.

Geoff barked a humorless laugh and looked up at his friend, whose face was full of concern. "Do? There's nothing to do! No apology is going to wipe away what I said."

"Have you tried to apologize?" Derek queried, folding his arms. "It really does go a long way, I know from experience."

Geoff swung his head in that direction. "And how would that go, hmm? How do you phrase that? Anyway, she wouldn't read anything I sent over, I know her. She'd burn it."

Colin sighed and gave him a hard look. "All right, why don't you just go over there and tell her you are sorry you made a complete arse of yourself?"

Geoff stared at him in confusion. He spread out his hands. "She's forbidden me from setting foot in the house."

Colin shrugged as if that made no difference. "Shout it from the street. She'll love it."

Geoff shook his head at him, and saw that he was not the only one doing so.

"Hopeless," Nathan muttered with a disbelieving laugh. "Absolutely hopeless. No more ideas from Colin."

"Amen," Duncan said, leaning back in his chair. He trained his ice-blue eyes on Geoff. "She'll come around, Geoffrey. She's a sensible girl, in spite of her current behavior, and she has a good heart and intentions."

That drew a snort from him and he raised a brow. "Has she?"

He received a brow raise in return. "You don't know that?"

Geoff groaned and put his face in his hands. "I don't know. I don't know anything anymore." He rubbed his face in agitation, then looked back at Duncan. "Why did you call on her the other day?"

Now both of Duncan's brows shot up to his hairline. "How did you know about that?"

An unbidden glare appeared on Geoff's features and his voice came out as a growl. "Mary threw it in my face when I said she had no time for anyone but flatterers and fools. She laughed when I had no idea you'd been to see her."

Duncan grunted and frowned at him in return. "Don't look at me like that, Geoffrey Harris, not when you are the one who has made a complete mess of his life by his own jealous hand."

"I'm not..." Geoff started in outrage, only to be silenced by a vicious glare from his most intimidating friend.

Duncan expelled a hefty breath and rubbed his jaw. "I wasn't going to mention anything to any of you simply because my reason for going turned out not to involve me at all. But as it is all taken care of now, and since you seem to require more things to feel guilty for, I'll tell you exactly what happened."

In low quick tones, Duncan told them everything that had been related to him regarding what had transpired between Mr. Townsend, Marianne, and Mary. He had the story first from Mary, and then had checked with his sister for any additional details. That part of the story alone had made each of his friends look murderous in turn, and Geoff put his head back into his hands with a groan.

Mary had been watching out for her friends. She had defended Marianne aggressively and swiftly, without even knowing the details of the situation. And she wasn't even that close with the girl. And then to tell Duncan about it? Mr. Townsend couldn't have had a more vicious punishment.

"What has happened to Townsend, then?" Nathan asked with a wicked grin.

Duncan quirked a half-smile. "He will have some trouble garnering invitations anywhere until his swelling goes down, but I think he received the impression that he is to keep his mouth shut concerning any behaviors of my sister. Or that of Kit," he added with a nod in Colin's direction.

Colin nodded once, his eyes blazing with fury.

Geoff looked between them briefly, wondering what had passed between them. Before he could ask about it, Duncan turned back to him.

"So, yes, I can say that Mary has a good heart," he told him firmly, "because I have seen it for myself, and I will be forever grateful that she didn't hesitate to defend my sister."

"And so fiercely at that," Derek murmured thoughtfully. "That was well done."

Geoff winced and looked at him. "I didn't know," he said, his words feeling like ash in his mouth.

"She defended her own sister no less fiercely."

"She what?" Geoff cried, his voice cracking. "When?"

"Some time after you left that night," Derek told him. "She completely shunned Wofford for the rest of the evening, and then as everyone was beginning to depart he approached her. Kate and I could only make out bits and pieces, but what we heard gave us a good idea of what went on. That and the fact that when Wofford left he was pale and shaking." Derek grinned at the lot of them in delight.

Geoff groaned and rubbed at his eyes with the heels of his hands. "I am such a fool."

Duncan laid a hand on his shoulder. "Just give her some time, Geoff. She will come around, you'll see."

"No," he said, grinding his hands in further, "no, she won't. I don't deserve anything from her. I just... I have to tell her that I... just how wrong I was." He removed his hands and slumped back in his chair. "How wrong I have been. I just... I have no idea how to make up for what I have done."

"You could start with an apology," Nathan prodded gently, "when she's ready."

"Then, I am afraid, you will just have to prove that you are," Derek added, looking grim. "We all know how badly I treated Kate all those years, and look at us now."

Geoff nodded slowly, having momentarily forgotten that. If Derek and Kate could become friends after the seething hatred that had always existed between them, maybe there was a chance for him to make amends as well.

Colin sighed and leaned forward. "But you really should bathe first, Geoff. And shave." His nose wrinkled up and he grimaced. "No woman will listen to anything you say looking and smelling like that."

For the first time in what seemed ages, Geoff's mouth stretched into a smile, and the rest of his friends chuckled, which he took to be an agreement.

Mary had always loved the smell of a fire. There was something very soothing about the aroma, something warm and comforting, something intangible that tickled her senses in a way that transported her from wherever she was and whatever she was feeling.

She inhaled slowly, letting the scent wash through her, evaporating the darkness that had been invading her mind of late. She could feel the warmth of the flames on her skin, sitting as she was in the chair nearest to it. She knew that sitting this close, particularly with her hair loose and unbound as it was, meant that the scent would linger upon her nightgown and her hair for quite some time.

She did not mind one bit.

It was worth it for a few moments of peace. To not feel the anguish in her heart, or hear the echoes of arguments past, or reek of self-loathing. For a little while, at least, she would be free of every memory of late, none of which she was particularly pleased with.

A knock came at her door, bringing her out of her reverie. She cleared her throat and called, "Come in."

Cassandra entered, ready for the day, her expression severe. "Ah, so you are awake. That is reassuring."

Mary frowned and tucked her shawl more securely around her. "What do you want, Cassandra?"

"You are not receiving this morning," her sister said, folding her arms.

"No." There was no need to elaborate, in her estimation.

"This is the third morning you have not received in a week, not counting Sunday."

"This is true," Mary said simply, giving her a searching look. "Do you have an opinion on the subject?"

"I have."

She was not surprised.

"And…?" she drew out slowly.

"You will lose all of the success you have gained if you continue to shut yourself up like this," Cassandra scolded.

Gained? What had she gained at all with this venture? The attention of men she would never have sought out? The envy of women she had never cared about? The knowledge that she could act with greater success and credulity than anybody had ever expected? What value was there in any of that? She had lost much more than she had ever gained.

"You cannot expect to maintain your popularity if you are not seen," Cassie continued. "I have not heard anything, as I never do anymore, but more than a week without being seen will make them quite forget you."

Mary frowned and opened her mouth to retort.

"Going to church service on Sunday does not count," Cassandra said quickly.

Mary closed her mouth, then muttered, "I was seen by a great many people then."

Cassie rolled her eyes. "Yes, yes, and you looked very pretty, everybody agreed. Though to tell you the truth, you looked so forlorn it might as well have been a funeral service."

"I was merely being solemn and reverent," Mary replied with a sniff.

Her sister snorted at this and shook her head.

"I went to see Marianne on Wednesday," she reminded her.

Cassie sighed and uncrossed her arms. "Mary, you know what I mean."

"I have not turned down any invitations."

"That is not the point. You have not been seen. Not really. Was your fight with Geoffrey really so terrible?"

Mary stilled and her eyes widened. "Who said I fought with Geoffrey?" she asked in a shaky, would-be obstinate voice that would convince no one.

Cassandra gave her a hard look. "Aside from the fact that we have not seen him since your party and the pair of you have been bickering like spoiled children for weeks?" She snorted and shrugged. "I drew my own conclusions, but I am fairly confident in them, particularly with you looking so ill."

Confident indeed, Mary thought. And very astute.

"It was very bad," Mary confessed, not wanting to relive a single moment, but knowing she had to give some answer. "I... behaved very badly. As did he." It did not seem right to blame him, not when she had fanned the flames herself. She ducked her head a touch with her residual shame. "Then I ordered him from the house."

She heard her sister gasp in horror. "Mary..."

"I know," she moaned with a wince, pinching the bridge of her nose. "I was a complete shrew, and I deserve his neglect." She sighed and looked up at her sister, whose expression had softened greatly. "It is done now, and I cannot take it back. I wouldn't even know how to begin an apology. I suppose I shall have to wait until I see him again. A note would not be good enough."

For a moment, she thought her sister would argue, but then, Cassie smiled with determination. "Well, you need not receive this morning if you wish it, but we are going out."

Mary laughed. "Are we, indeed?"

There was a fervent nod. "We are. I'll send Josephine up. Get dressed in something fetching. We are going to walk about so that people can see you are indeed alive and well, and all you will have to do is smile, make polite conversation, and bat those lovely long eyelashes of yours at the attractive men."

A hoard of giggles escaped Mary's mouth, and she covered it. Then she tilted her head. "You never told me I had long eyelashes."

Her sister grinned mischievously. "Well, I could not very well compliment you myself. Not when you've already been so puffed up by everyone else." She quirked her brows impishly and turned from the room.

"Wretch," Mary muttered with a fond smile. She looked towards the fire once more, allowing a small sigh to escape her. Cassandra was right; she would not do herself any good staying cooped up in her house in misery. Not that it had been her intention to do so, she simply had no desire to do anything. Colors ceased to be vibrant, sleep had ceased to be restful, and going out seemed wrong.

But a walk with her sister, with no expectations or plans, with fresh air and abundant sunshine, might do her good, and sufficiently distract her mind from other topics.

For while, at least.

The corridor was the same with its crumbling walls and echoing floor stones, with the same people in their finery blocking his path needlessly. The same sconces with flames alight guided his frantic steps around corners and straightaways. His friends, their faces shining with the same worry, all said the same words of warning.

"You're going to be late."

"Geoff, are you coming?"

"It's almost time."

He ignored them all, as he always had, and kept running. His clothes had the same rumples, his necktie flew in exactly the same directions, and his shoes skidded around the same corner. His chest ached in the same places from the run, and his heart raced with the same horrific anxiety. He couldn't breathe for the panic he felt.

At long last, the door was in sight. A brief flare of hope flashed within him and he ran harder.

His fingers grasped the wrought iron handle and shoved with all of his might, hardly hearing the horrible screeching such a heavy door was bound to make. It moved with him, and then he was in.

His breath caught in his chest at the sight before him.

She was loveliness itself. Her back was to him, but it made no difference. Her figure was divine from every aspect. Her gown was the color of clouds on a summer day, and her veil shimmered like the stars.

"You look beautiful..." he breathed, his chest heaving with his emotion.

He could not see her face, but he sensed a smile as she said, "Thank you." She adjusted her lace gloves and her bonnet. "What are you doing here?"

He swallowed with difficulty, his lungs remembering their exhaustion and panting with his previous exercise. "I had to see you. I couldn't... I cannot let you go through with this without telling you..."

"Tell me what?" she asked with a light laugh.

She never so much as turned in his direction. "Will you look at me?" he softly pleaded.

"Tell me," she said as she shook her head slightly, still adjusting. He took a deep breath. "I love you."

She froze, her hand still in the process of adjusting her glove. But he noticed, ever so faintly, that her breathing became heavier.

He wasn't sure if that was favorable or not, but he continued. "I have always loved you, and I am fairly sure I always will. I've been an idiot, and I must ask... is there a chance for me?"

"It's my wedding day..." she said, her voice wavering.

"There's time," he insisted. "If you love me, if you could ever love me, then we have all the time in the world."

At long last, she turned to face him.

Mary's lovely eyes were filled with sadness, the sheen of tears beginning to form.

He held out a hand to her, feeling his heart lurch to his throat. "Mary, please," he pleaded, his voice hoarse. "I love you. Come away with me. Run away with me now. Leave all of this. Leave him... Come home with me."

Her eyes were unreadable amidst the tears. She stared at him for the longest moment, so long he lost count of the number of heartbeats that thudded against his ribs. A solitary tear silently rolled down her pale cheek.

She drew in a quivering breath. "It's too late, Geoff."

His heart stopped in his chest and his knees faltered.

Mary wiped her cheek and glided past him. As he turned to watch, she halted, turned, and laid a perfect hand along his face. "It's too late," she said again, her voice soft and delicate.

She turned then and exited the room, the triumphant sounds of the church organ suddenly blaring into the joyous notes of processional.

The door closed behind her, before he realized it had even moved. He turned, only to hear it lock. "No!" he cried as his heart surged again. He ran to the door, banged on it with all of his might. It was not too late. He could not be too late. Not for her, not for this.

"Mary!" he bellowed, beating the door with his fists. "Mary, no! I love you! Mary!"

Geoff surged up from his bed with a strangled cry, completely disoriented in the dark of the room. Where was she? Where was she? His chest heaved with his breaths, still exhausted from running those corridors. And his heart...

It took him several moments of frantically turning his head to realize that it had only been a dream. He hadn't run the corridor any more than he had any other night he had dreamed it. There was no reason to panic, not single solitary one. Mary wasn't here, she wasn't getting married, and he was most certainly not too late.

"Too late?" he muttered to himself. "Too late for what?" He shook his head and swung his feet off of the bed, put a hand to his now-throbbing head, and heaved up to his feet.

The fire in the grate was nothing but coals now, which meant it was still the middle of the night. He grunted and sat in the chair before the fire, stoking the coals until a few flames flickered.

He stared at them for a long while, then sat back and put his hands over his now clean-shaven face. He had no idea his frantic corridor run would lead him to Mary, let alone in such a situation. How could he have? Weeks of the same dream over and over with no resolution, all to culminate in this?

"Ridiculous," he grunted with a snort and shake of his head. He dropped his hands and sighed. "Get a hold of yourself, man. You cannot be dreaming this, cannot keep panicking like this. There is no reason. Just because she's furious with you and you are in love her doesn't mean…"

He stopped suddenly, his eyes widening, his throat constricting. What had he just said?

He was in love with her? How was that even possible?

Yet instantly he knew it was true. Had always known it.

He loved her. Of course he loved her, how could he not?

He laughed once, breathless with the momentous realization, feeling his chest expand with delight. Then he covered his face again and groaned. He was, without a doubt, the biggest idiot that had ever walked God's earth.

He couldn't condone her consorting with other men because he had always considered her his. It wasn't vanity, it was nothing more or less than the fact that he loved her, and there could not be any other man for her but him.

Except he had just ruined that.

It really was too late.

He groaned and bent forward, his hands gripping his hair. Why had he been so stupid? She had every reason to hate him now and forevermore.

But he would do what his friends had suggested. He would do everything in his power to somehow apologize, on bended knee if she asked him, and then spend every day proving that he valued their friendship above all else, that she meant more to him than his pride.

That he loved her, if he could.

He leaned his head back against the chair and shut his eyes.

He was the world's most pathetic fool.

Chapter Seventeen

*H*e was running again, but this time it was no dream. He was properly dressed, his shoes did not skid, and there was no corridor about him. He could have waited for the carriage, but it would have taken too long. His heart thudded in his chest and his fingers clenched more tightly around the note in his hand.

It was a short missive, nothing out of the ordinary. He could recall the exact words as he had read it hundreds of times in half of the seconds;

> *If you could be so good as to come to call upon us at your earliest convenience, it would be most appreciated.*

> *Mary*

It was perfectly polite, and gave no indication of emotion of any kind.

To anyone else, perhaps.

But Geoffrey Harris had received thousands of notes from Mary Hamilton over their lengthy friendship and he knew the exact form of her writing and penmanship. These words had the slightest tremble to them and the alignment was poor. Mary had the steadiest hand of anyone he had ever known. Something was terribly wrong.

That had sent him flying about his house like a madman, calling for his brother to inform him what he was about, his valet to finish dressing him, and his butler to inquire after the carriage, only to be told it was not prepared and would take time. So, with no more ado than that which he had already created, he had fled the house on foot and run for it.

Finally her home was in sight and he ran faster, willing his mind to not conjure up disaster without cause.

He rang the bell and attempted to collect himself. The door was swung open and Winston let him in, looking as though he had been expecting Geoff to arrive exactly as he was.

"Winston," Geoff said, ignoring the way he was panting. "Where is she?"

"Geoff?"

He heard the gasp of his name and whirled. She stood in the hall, her eyes wide and red rimmed, her complexion drawn, her face haggard. He had never seen anything so lovely in all his life.

"Mary," he managed to force out.

Her throat constricted visibly. "You... you came."

He swallowed with no small amount of difficulty. "Of course, I came," he said softly as Winston made himself scarce. "How could I not?"

Her chin quivered and she ducked her head as her shoulders heaved with a single sob. Instantly he moved towards her and gathered her into his arms.

"Oh, Mary, what is it?" he asked, holding her as she trembled. "What's wrong?"

She shook her head and pushed back to look up at him. "It's not me, I'm well enough. I didn't send for you for me..." She looked away and shut her eyes.

His chest tightened. "Heavens above, Mary, what is it?"

He noticed then how her hair was simply plaited, her dress was rumpled, and her eyes puffy besides their redness. She looked absolutely exhausted. She faltered slightly against him, and he took greater hold of her.

"Have you slept at all?" he asked quietly.

She shook her head.

He led her over to pair of chairs against a wall and helped her sit, while he took the other. Then he took her cold hand in his.

"Mary, what is it?" he asked again, his voice gentle and calm.

She looked towards the darkened drawing room, whose door was ajar. Geoff followed her gaze but could see nothing within, and he wasn't about to leave her side until he knew everything.

"Cassie received a letter last night," Mary said at last. "From Felicity Wyndham."

Geoff felt a curl of dread begin in the pit of his stomach.

"It appears that Lieutenant Wyndham's ship has been lost at sea." Mary's voice wavered slightly. "Sunk somewhere around the Spanish coast, it is presumed. They've not recovered any survivors as yet."

"Oh no…" Geoff looked towards the room again, and this time he could see a lone figure sitting before the fire.

Mary swallowed hard. "She has been up all night, and so have I. I cannot get her to eat or to drink, and she won't even think of sleep. She is barely speaking a word, except when she cries. I've been unable to console or comfort her with any success. Geoff…" She shook her head and looked at him. "I didn't know who else to send for."

He searched her tired, tear-stained face for a moment, aching for her aches. He nodded and squeezed her hand. Then he rose and softly entered the drawing room.

The curtains were all drawn, letting in only the faintest degree of light from the morning outside. No candles were lit, and only the sound of the low fire crackling could be heard. Cassie stared into the fire, her hair in disarray, a shawl draped around her shoulders, but she didn't seem to notice.

She gave no indication that she saw Geoffrey as he came around and sank down before her. He reached for one of her hands, colder than ice and as limp as a rag doll, and held it tightly.

"Cassie," he said softly, trying in vain to get her to look at him. "Cassie, I am so very sorry."

She said nothing for a long moment, her eyes vacant. "He's gone," she finally said, her lips barely moving, her voice weak.

He squeezed her hand. "I know, pet."

"I loved him."

"I know."

She inhaled, her breath catching as she did so, and her face tightened. "I'll never... never see him again. No one will. I will never be able to tell him that I loved him... that I m-missed him. That I will always love him." Her whole body trembled with her suddenly erratic breathing. "He's g-gone..."

Stray tears fell from her eyes, but she didn't seem to feel them.

Geoffrey could not take this and seized both of her hands. "Tell me how to help you, Cassie," he pleaded earnestly. "Tell me what to do, anything, and I will."

She shook her head frantically, her breath catching, tears still absently falling. "There's nothing to be done. There's nothing anyone can do. Nothing." Her chin quivered and she erupted into pathetic, heart-wrenching sobs, and buried her face into her hands. Geoff immediately gathered her up into his arms and she clung to him like a child.

He soothed her softly, murmuring words of comfort and solace. He rose from the floor, holding her tightly, and moved to the sofa, cradling her in his lap, content to let her cry as long as she needed to.

Mary jerked awake for no apparent reason and blinked hard, her head still fuzzy. Her chair in the hallway was not comfortable in the least, so it spoke to her exhaustion that she had somehow managed to drift off at all. She craned her neck to one side, then the other, wincing at the stiffness that had set in. She couldn't hear anything but the ticking of the clock near her and stilled as she realized what that meant. There was nothing resembling sobs or sniffles coming from the drawing room.

She rose silently from the chair and went to the doorway, peering into the darkened room.

Geoffrey was sitting on the sofa, staring into the fire, Cassie still in his arms, her eyes closed.

Mary released a sigh of relief, and Geoff heard it, slowly turning his head to look at her.

"She's sleeping at last," he told her softly, readjusting the arm around Cassie's back. "Though it took quite a while to get there."

Mary nodded, a lump forming in her throat that she struggled to swallow. "Thank you, Geoff," she finally said. She swallowed again and took a deep breath, "After the things I said to you, I did not..." She couldn't even finish the thought. She didn't know if he would come. She wouldn't have blamed him if he didn't.

And yet he had come. With no explanation at all, he had come running, despite everything. She didn't deserve a friend like him. If they still were friends.

"Mary."

She looked up at his gentle use of her name, and found him smiling softly at her, holding out his free hand.

"Come here," he said, flexing his fingers ever so slightly.

Blinking back tears, she came and took his hand, sitting beside him on the sofa.

"I don't want to hear another word about that," he said firmly, giving her hand a tight squeeze. "I have treated you horribly, and you had every right in the world to toss me out of the house and worse. I need to apologize."

"No," she instantly argued, shaking her head.

"Yes," he insisted, his eyes silencing her. "Yes, Mary, I do. I am sorry, so deeply sorry, for all that I have said and all that I did to make you unhappy. It's unforgivable, one does not treat friends this way."

Mary's heart twitched with the faint stirrings of hope and she looked into his face eagerly. "Are we still friends, then?"

He gazed at her with a soft smile, then took the hand he held and brought it to his lips for a long moment. "You are my best friend, Mary Hamilton," he said as he squeezed her hand once more. "And you always will be."

The warmth that suddenly radiated from her heart coursed through her limbs and she could not help but to smile broadly at him. Her exhaustion evaporated and she felt as though she could run the streets of London without once feeling the least bit winded. He returned her smile with one of his own, and she felt, ever so briefly, the all-too-familiar twinge of butterflies in her stomach. She pushed that away immediately. She had just got her best friend back, she was not going to ruin the moment with long-forgotten romantic whims.

Cassandra shifted slightly, moaning sleepily and tucking herself more securely against Geoff.

They looked down at her, then back at each other with a bit of a smile.

"Do you think she will sleep in her bed?" Mary asked, pushing a bit of Cassie's hair out of her face.

"Probably," Geoff replied, grinning. "She's quite soundly asleep."

Mary looked up at him. "Can you carry her up?"

He gave her a look. "She's smaller than you are and I've carried you."

"Not in years," Mary reminded him with a bit of a snort as she rose and backed away to give him space.

He shrugged, tightened his hold around her sister, and rose fluidly. "Close enough. You haven't changed that much."

Mary shook her head, astonished at how quickly they had managed to pick back up where they had left off. It was as if the last few weeks had never happened, and she found she was perfectly content with that.

They slowly made their way up to Cassandra's bedchamber, accompanied by Mrs. Evansdale, who seemed to be on the verge of tears every time she looked at Cassie. They entered the room and Geoff gently set Cassie on the bed.

"I'll leave you to it," he told Mary softly, backing away.

She seized his arm. "Don't leave," she ordered, knowing she sounded severe, but not particularly caring.

He smiled and patted her hand, then removed it from his arm. "I'll wait in the drawing room." He nodded at Mrs. Evansdale, then left without another word.

Mary blew a puff of breath at a strand of hair in her face, and shook her head. She didn't want him to leave just yet, not when things had been so bad between them.

She looked down at her sister, finally at peace after hours of so much turmoil, and sighed. Everything would have to change now.

She could hardly stay and play debutante with Cassie hurting so, and the gossip would only get worse. Whatever games she had played, they were at an end now.

She worked silently with Mrs. Evansdale to change Cassie out of her dress from the day before and slip her beneath the bedcovers, then she turned her attention to the situation at hand.

Geoffrey.

She made her way back down the stairs, steeling herself and forcing her breathing to be natural. Geoff was her friend. He would help her decide what to do, and the misunderstandings of the past would be forgotten. If she could forget the look in his eyes when they danced or the heat of the moment that night of the riddles, nothing about Geoffrey would make her uncomfortable at all.

She hoped, at any rate.

He was in the drawing room, as promised, but the room could not have looked more different. The fire had been built up and the curtains pulled back, illuminating the room in a morning glow that made her wince a little. Geoffrey had pulled Cassandra's chair away from the grate and moved it to its typical position near the divan, and he was now sitting on the sofa he had so recently vacated.

He smiled fondly at her as she entered and rose.

"Oh, sit down," she said with a laugh, waving at him. "This is not a social occasion, no need for formalities."

His smile grew into his reckless grin she so adored, and he sat back down. "If you insist."

She sat on the other sofa opposite him, but matched his position, leaning one elbow on the armrest. She let her smile fade, and she glanced at the fire. "Thank you for what you did for Cassie. She was so distraught, and you've always been able to put her to rights."

"There's no need to thank me for that," he murmured. "I only wish I could do more."

Mary nodded, understanding only too well. "I don't know what else there is to do. The Wyndhams were so angry with her before, which crushed her, and now that he is gone…" She shook her head, willing fresh tears away. "I don't know if she will ever recover."

Geoff made a noncommittal sound, frowning as he stared off at nothing.

"What?" Mary asked, seeing his expression. "What are you thinking?"

"Do we…" He paused, as if trying to phrase it properly. He looked out of the room, then back at her. "Do we know that he was aboard?" he asked in a very soft voice. "I mean do we definitely know that he was lost with the rest?"

Mary's brows rose in surprise. "Well, no, I suppose we don't. I only have the note from Felicity and it seemed fairly certain, but as there has been no sign of the ship or any crew…" She shook her head once more. "It is highly unlikely, Geoff."

He sighed and sat back a bit. "Yes, it is." But he didn't look convinced. "It was considerate of Felicity Wyndham to write Cassandra about it."

Mary nodded, feeling grateful for one friend of Cassie's who was not casting her off. "She has always been a sweet girl, without the presumption of her family. She must obey their restrictions, naturally, but she makes every effort she can where Cassie is concerned. I cannot imagine what they must be feeling at this time."

"What will happen now?" he asked quietly, looking back at Mary. "Will the feelings against Cassie become worse?"

Mary sighed and rubbed at her head. "More than likely. I had hoped that my little scheme might help to smooth over some of those feelings, but now this…" She shook her head. "I'm not even sure I can bear to know."

Geoff smiled sadly at her. "I know. I'll do what I can, you know that."

She returned his smile. "You always do."

He shrugged one shoulder nonchalantly. "What will you do?" he asked her, turning serious. "Have you made any plans?"

She shook her head and looked towards the doorway. "I've been thinking about it all night, and I can't decide. Part of me wants to rush her off to the country right this minute, and part of me wants to wait and see. But waiting… I'm afraid waiting might make things worse."

"But you are determined to leave?" he prodded.

She looked back at him. "That was always the plan. Enjoy the season, and then leave for the country. George's house in Hampshire is available while they tour the continent."

"That's not so far away," he murmured, nodding slowly.

"The more I think about it," she said on a sigh, "the more I think we should just leave now, as soon as we can. Things are only going to get worse for Cassie, and I have no ties to bind me here."

"Not even your splendid conquests?" he teased with a grin.

She laughed softly and shook her head. "No, there was never anything serious. I thought perhaps there might have been, but…" She shrugged. "Nothing ever went beyond a surface flirtation."

He made no comment, which was probably wise, given their history of disagreements on the subject, but she distinctly saw a strange light steal into his blue eyes for a moment.

She cleared her throat. "Not to say I didn't enjoy myself, because at times I did."

"I know you did," he murmured, smiling. "I could see it."

"But not all the time," she admitted, feeling the color in her cheeks rise again, remembering all the times she had intentionally spurned him, how he had glowered at her, how they had fought.

"No, no, no," he scolded, shaking his head at her. "We've already discussed this. None of that."

"I was horrid," Mary protested, wringing her hands in her lap. "I was the worst sort of creature imaginable. I was vain, and cruel, and frivolous…"

"And I was rude, inconsiderate, and heartless," he interrupted firmly, looking faintly exasperated with her. "Not to mention immature, inappropriate, disrespectful, disloyal…"

"Stop!" she said with a laugh, covering her ears. "No more, no more."

He grinned, and sat back.

She removed her hands, and gave him a warning look.

"And I made a complete arse of myself, as Colin would say."

Mary couldn't hold back a laugh and clamped a hand over her mouth. Geoff didn't laugh, but she could see the mirth in his eyes.

"Would he really say that?" she asked when her laughter had subsided.

Geoff snorted. "He did say that."

Her eyes widened. "Really?"

"It was very distressing to find that all of my friends were on your side of the matter," he said with mock-annoyance, smiling a little.

She couldn't help it; she smiled back. "I'm sorry, Geoff."

He shook his head and held up a finger. "As I've told you, I'm the one who needs to be sorry."

"Well," she said, "it's all behind us now, and all is forgiven."

"Is it?" he asked, looking at her with concern.

"Of course," she replied simply.

"It shouldn't be this easy," he scolded with a stern look. "I have a lot to make up for."

She heaved a sigh. "Very well, I begin with reversing your ban on being in the house. We'll start there."

He nodded, fighting a smile. "Excellent, I'd hate to think I'm breaking rules by being here."

"And... you must help me pack up the house."

He sobered considerably. "Completely?"

She nodded and shrugged. "I see no reason to leave it open at this point. We're the only ones who use it, and none of my nieces or nephews are old enough to desire to come to London yet. It won't be good to anybody until then."

"Yes," he said slowly, "yes, I suppose you are right. Very well, I will help you, on one condition."

She narrowed her eyes at him. "What condition?"

"Don't look so suspicious!" he laughed. "I only ask that you give yourself a little bit of time. Cassie will need to be strong before you remove to Hampshire. See how she does, and allow yourself a little bit of amusement. Not quite the extent as before," he warned, a teasing half-smile on his lips, "but a little."

Mary pretended to think it over carefully.

"And if you do," Geoff added, leaning forward, "then I will personally help with your removal to Hampshire and will have my friends assist as well."

"Even Colin?" she asked dubiously.

He quirked his brows. "Especially Colin."

"Hmm…" she mused, tapping her chin. "I agree to your condition, upon one of my own."

He tilted his head in query, but said nothing.

She smiled shyly. "Would you agree to be my escort once more? I need to laugh more, and nobody makes me laugh the way you do."

The smile that spread across his face would have made the sun seem gloomy, and it made her toes tingle.

"That I can most certainly agree on," Geoffrey said, holding out his hand.

Mary took it, and shook firmly. "Done."

"Done. Now, you need to sleep yourself," he said as he stood and pulled her up.

"Oh, but I…" she tried.

He silenced her with a look. "You are dead on your feet. You need rest." He pushed her towards the stairs and shooed her up. "Go on, be off with you."

She started up, then looked back at him. "What are you going to do?"

He grinned and shrugged. "I'm going to rest myself. If I am going to be your escort, and I have to help you pack up the house, I'm going to need all the rest I can get." He bowed very smartly then turned for the door. "I'll call on the both of you tomorrow. Let me know if I am needed sooner."

"And if you are?" she asked, not entirely sure why.

He turned slightly and looked at her in surprise. "Then I'll come, of course. I am yours to command." He bowed once more and departed with a smile.

Mary remained on the stair for a moment longer, staring at the door. Then, almost without her noticing, she smiled too.

Chapter Eighteen

"*I* don't want to go."

"Mary, nobody turns down the Rivertons once they have already accepted."

"I don't want to go!"

Geoff growled rather uncharacteristically. "Mary, so help me, if you are not in the carriage in five minutes, I will throw you over my shoulder and carry you out myself."

She looked up at him, her blue eyes narrowing. "You wouldn't."

"Try me."

She frowned, then looked towards the door and sighed. "I don't want to leave her."

Geoff resisted the urge to sigh himself. They had been arguing over this event for the past two days, mostly because Mary couldn't make up her mind. One minute she wanted to go, the next she didn't. They had been over this time and time again, and up until half an hour ago, he thought it was settled. He had arrived to fetch her only to be told that in the middle of getting ready, she had yet again changed her mind. Now he was standing in her private sitting room while she fidgeted and paced around fully dressed, but hair only half done. It actually looked rather becoming, now that he studied it. The top half of her hair had been twisted up and pinned, while the bottom half hung long and loose down her back.

It was actually *very* becoming…

He forced himself to look away and clasped his hands behind his back, just in case he were more tempted than he already was to reach out and touch.

"She'll be fine," he reassured her kindly. "She is sleeping better, she ate a full meal today within my view, and I presume she ate others?"

Mary scowled, but nodded. "Yes, she did," she mumbled as she paced.

He gave her a look. "Then I think we can safely leave her for a few hours. Mrs. Evansdale is here, Winston is here, and I have asked Christian to stop by this evening and read to her."

That stopped Mary in her tracks. "You did?"

He nodded, unable to stop a smug smile from appearing. "I did. He has plenty of experience reading, you know. Our nieces and nephews beg for it often."

"Do they?" she asked, her voice ringing with suspicion.

"Would I lie to you?"

"Yes."

He chuckled and spread his hands out. "I promise you, he really does read well. We thought it would entertain her for a bit. If nothing else, they can play cards."

Mary chewed her full bottom lip in indecision.

He looked away then as well. Just to be safe.

"Mary?"

Both Geoff and Mary turned to see Cassie in the doorway, looking pale and small, but her eyes were clear and her long hair braided over one shoulder. Her shawl was wrapped around her tightly, though it was a warm evening. Still, she looked a good deal better than she had this morning, which was a good deal better than she had looked the day before.

Cassie stepped further into the room. "Mary, you should go."

Mary watched her with sad, concerned eyes. "Cassie…"

She shook her head. "I don't need a nanny. I'll be fine. Go to the Rivertons. Geoff is right, no one refuses them. It would be in very poor taste."

Mary stared at her sister for a long moment, her eyes searching her face and expression. Then, at last, she sighed and her shoulders relaxed. "Very well. I'll go."

Geoff nearly sighed himself with relief. Not that he was particularly desiring to go dine with the Rivertons, but he did have something to accomplish that would be much easier to do if he were there. And he much preferred to spend an evening with Mary without being reminded of the pall that was on Cassie during this time.

"Shall I prepare a report for you?" Mary asked, a small smile on her lips.

Cassie tried for a weak smile. "That would be lovely."

"Right," Geoff said, clapping his hands once. "Fix yourself up, Mary. You have five minutes or it is the shoulder for you."

Mary glared at him, then spun back into her room, her hair flying behind her.

He grinned and looked over at Cassie, who met his eyes.

"Make her have fun, Geoff," Cassandra told him softly. "I know she's thinking of moving us to Hampshire for a while, and being cooped up with me in George's house will hardly be enjoyable for her."

Geoff sobered at the thought, and he looked at Cassandra with a newfound appreciation. She was more astute than he had expected her to be. Perhaps a bit of Mary was rubbing off on her sister after all.

"So please," Cassie continued, "make sure she enjoys herself while she can."

He smiled and nodded. "That I can do, Cassie." He went to her and pressed his lips into her forehead, which earned him a smile. "Christian will be here in an hour," he informed her, patting her hair. "So pick your most disgraceful novel for him to read aloud and scold him soundly if he does not do it justice."

Another weak smile flickered across Cassie's face and she nodded, making her way out of the room.

Geoff smiled fondly after her, then turned to leave the room himself. "Four minutes, Mary!"

"Ten!" she hollered.

"Six and a half!"

"Go away!" she laughed from her bedchamber.

He grinned and went down to the foyer to wait.

Almost precisely six minutes later, she appeared at the top of the stairs and made her way down to him. She was watching her feet as she descended, which meant he could look at her the way he wanted to. Her gown was simple but elegant in its cut, and the pale green color made her skin positively luminescent. Her hair was twisted and pinned elegantly, which he found miraculous, given the state it was in only six minutes prior. He felt a twinge of sadness that it was completely up, but then she turned her head slightly, and the line of her throat was so graceful, so elegant, that he found himself swallowing.

What was the matter with him? He needed to have control or he was very likely to blurt out his feelings right here and now, and he could hardly do that. She would never believe him.

When she looked up at him, he was perfectly composed, and gave her an approving smile. She blushed with pleasure, and perhaps a touch of embarrassment, but smiled back at him.

"Impressive," he said in a low, teasing voice.

"What's impressive?" she asked with a tilt of her head as she neared him.

You, he nearly said. But he only smiled more broadly up at her. "You have gone from panicked and unkempt to poised and incomparable in six minutes." He shook his head and held out his hand. "No shoulder for you tonight, Miss Hamilton."

"More's the pity," she murmured, placing her gloved hand in his.

Her words and the teasing light in her eye sent a shocking jolt of pleasure into his chest, and it was only due to his long practice of polite and gentlemanly behavior that he managed to avoid dwelling overlong on the image of him carrying her over his shoulder into more entertaining spheres.

He would probably revisit the idea later, however.

For now, he merely smiled at his best friend and escorted her to their waiting carriage.

"How well do you know the Rivertons?" Mary asked as they began to move.

"Not particularly well," he replied with a shrug. "Not personally at all. Lord Riverton is well respected, and has a great deal of influence in the political scene, I understand. Lady Riverton is known for her vivacity and generosity, as well as being a fashion leader."

"My, my," Mary murmured, "however did I manage an invitation?"

Geoffrey grinned a bit devilishly. "They have a son."

That earned a dramatic roll of the eyes. "Oh, for heaven's sake."

"Now, now, Miss Hamilton," Geoff scolded with a warning finger, "you must not blame the poor viscount for his parents being overeager to see him well matched. I understand he is a very handsome man, and he's not yet thirty so he is right within your grasp."

"A viscount, did you say?" Mary mused, looking mildly interested.

Geoff nodded soberly. "A handsome one."

"Well," she replied, adjusting her gloves, "I shall be on my best behavior, then."

"Good girl."

She grinned at him, and he grinned right back.

"Well, attractive viscount or not, I'm glad you're the one taking me tonight, Geoff," she murmured, averting her eyes. "I... I missed you."

His heart stopped in his chest and he couldn't breathe. "I missed you, too," he finally managed, though there were three other words that he'd rather have said.

Their eyes met and held, and suddenly breathing was all but impossible. She was so beautiful he could hardly stand to look at her, but he would dare walking through hellfire before he would look anywhere else. Did she feel the heat that he did as it coursed between them? Was he the only one that had begun to feel a bit light-headed? Or was it possible that she could feel it too, that the bumps and rattling of the carriage had ceased to exist and all that remained was the two of them in this heady moment?

The carriage halted then, breaking their connection. They had arrived before a grand building, windows alight with candles, servants standing at attention all along the grand stairs of the entrance. Other carriages were emptying, their inhabitants excitedly making their way up, everybody in their finest ensembles. Geoff recognized a great many, all powerful in their own realms, whether they be lords or rogues, gossips or debutantes. It was a collection of the great influences of the London season.

He was fortunate that Derek had managed to get him an invitation. Powerful friends were convenient indeed.

"Heavens above," Mary breathed as he helped her down, her eyes taking in the spectacle before her. "They spare no expense, do they?"

He smiled and offered her his arm. "The Rivertons have always had a taste for finery. Which is undoubtedly why they have invited you this evening."

She glanced up at him with a half-smile. "You are full of compliments this evening. What are you planning?"

He gave her a look of pure innocence. "I'm not planning anything at all! Can't a man compliment a beautiful woman when she is on his arm and not have any ulterior motives?"

"Not when that man is you."

He chuckled and patted her hand. "I have much to make up for, my dear Miss Hamilton, so forgive my abundance of accolades where you are concerned, true though they all may be."

She giggled and held his arm a little more tightly. "I didn't say it was a bad thing. I merely point out that you're doing it."

He lifted a brow at her. "So I may praise you freely without punishment?"

"Oh, why not?" she replied with a laugh. "You will be the prelude for what is to come once we set foot in there."

They were almost inside already, and he sighed heavily. "Alas, that is not enough time to pay proper tribute to even your littlest finger."

Again she laughed, and it was music to his ears and soul. He could have ridden to Africa on horseback without food or water with only the promise of that laugh as his reward.

"Is that your favorite part of me, Geoffrey?" she asked as they entered the house.

He quirked his brows rather wickedly. "I'll never tell."

She rolled her eyes and handed her wrap to the servants, then led the way into the ballroom, as Geoff obediently trailed behind. They greeted the host and his lady, conversed only briefly, and then made their way around the room. It didn't take long for gentlemen to begin appearing to request a dance.

Mary looked at Geoff, who only grinned. "Behave yourself, Miss Hamilton. The viscount is watching."

She fluttered her eyelashes, and allowed Mr. Timmons to lead her to the dance floor, where the other couples were already lining up.

Assured that she would be occupied for quite some time, given the line of gentlemen that had assembled, Geoffrey began his search for Derek, his true reason for coming this evening. It didn't take long, as Derek was quite the popular gentleman, and if he had any more personality, he would have rivaled Colin in attracting listeners. The world did not need two versions of Colin Gerrard, which Derek knew full well.

Derek saw Geoff coming and excused himself from the group and came to him. "Are you ready?" Derek asked in a low voice, smiling for the benefit of others.

Geoff nodded, feeling the weight of what he was about to do. He glanced around. "No Kate?"

Derek shook his head. "She's unwell this evening, and has elected to remain at home, given her condition." He snorted and rolled his eyes.

"Is she not so very unwell?" Geoff asked, starting to smile a bit at Derek's reaction.

Derek grinned. "She is becoming self-conscious about how visible she is. I find it breathtaking, she finds it inconvenient." He shrugged. "Her gown didn't fit properly, so she is at home being unwell."

"She turned down the Rivertons?" Geoff laughed, keeping his voice low. Really, that was something to talk about. He hadn't thought Kate had grown that shocking in her opinions.

"The Rivertons are no match for my wife in a highly emotional state," Derek muttered, his eyes dancing with amusement. "I am to return to her side the moment our business is completed."

"I'm surprised she let you come at all."

Derek's amusement faded and he gave Geoff a serious look. "When I told her what we were doing, she turned me from the room and literally forced me out and into the carriage. She is in full support of this, and I have no doubt that she will be just as invested in it as the rest of us."

Geoff nodded without speaking, touched beyond words. When he had approached his friends only two days ago with his thoughts, they had latched onto it. They scoured their acquaintances for any that might be of use and were willing to throw their individual or combined influences behind whatever came of it. He was grateful for such friends and allies.

Tonight was the first opportunity they would have to begin.

Derek led him around and through the many guests in the ballroom, somehow managing to avoid becoming trapped in conversation with any of them.

Geoff was grateful. He had no wish to delay any further than they already had, and he had appearances to keep up, so he must dance and converse and dine as he usually would. There was little time, but they would make use of it.

"Now, we will be speaking, as I have told you, with Captain Riverton, late of His Majesty's Navy."

"Riverton?" Geoff interrupted, coming close to Derek's side. "As in…?"

"The second son of the earl," Derek replied with a nod. "The title and family name are the same. He is an old companion of David's and a very discreet gentleman. He has made his fortune and is preparing to resign his commission. I, however, have convinced him to wait for the time being."

They were nearing the man in question, Geoff could see from the uniform, and he turned to Derek quickly. "Does he know what we are going to request?"

Derek shook his head. "I didn't give him any particulars, merely that it involved his profession."

"And his reputation in the Navy?"

"Very well respected," Derek assured him. "He knows absolutely everybody."

Geoffrey nodded firmly and allowed Derek to lead the rest of the way.

Captain Riverton was a rather tall man, and had the same strong features as his father and brother, but with the fair coloring of his mother. He seemed a somber man, by appearances, which would have made him an odd companion for the wild and reckless Lord David Chambers. He was standing apart from all the rest, and seemed content to be ignored. Would a man such as he be willing to do so much for a man he didn't know purely on the word of one he did? He hoped so, as no other alternatives had presented themselves as yet and there was not time for reconsideration.

He saw them approach and turned at once, bowing smartly to Derek. "Whitlock," he greeted in a voice lower than Geoff had expected. "You haven't changed much."

Derek grinned and clamped a hand on the younger man's shoulder. "Only in wisdom and vigor, my dear chap. But look at you! So tall and tanned, you look like a foreigner rather than a specimen of His Majesty's Navy."

The captain smiled and inclined his head in acknowledgement. "There is no substitute for sea air, Whitlock. I'll outlive you and your brother by a full decade because of it."

Derek laughed out loud. "I have no doubt of it." He turned to Geoff. "Geoffrey Harris, may I present Captain William Riverton, of the Royal Navy. Will, this is one of my closest friends, Mr. Harris. It is he who has need of you."

Captain Riverton bowed again, then extended a hand. "A pleasure, Mr. Harris."

"For me as well, Captain."

"Whitlock said you have need of my connections," the captain said, taking no time for pleasantries. "How can I be of assistance?"

Geoff looked around, then back up at the young captain. "Might there be somewhere private we could converse? The situation is delicate."

He nodded. "Of course. Follow me, please." He turned and exited the ballroom, and they followed.

Not a word was said between the men as they passed servants bustling with food for the dinner and footmen standing silently in their livery, and it wasn't until they had entered what was undoubtedly Lord Riverton's study that the captain even faced them once more. He gestured that they sit, as did he.

"How can I be of assistance, Mr. Harris?" Captain Riverton asked once more.

Geoffrey looked at Derek, who nodded in encouragement, then returned his gaze to the captain. "What do you know of Lieutenant Simon Wyndham?"

Chapter Nineteen

What in the world had he been thinking?

It had seemed like a good idea, paying penance for his many sins where Mary was concerned. He had been abominable to her, and he ought to have to work to get back into her good graces. She would never have insisted on it herself, which was why he had suggested it. He thought she would be pleased to see that he was taking the mending of their friendship so seriously.

How bad could it be, he had thought. Groveling, heavy lifting, spending more money than he was comfortable with, he was prepared for all of that. She suggested he be her escort for the rest of the season. He could definitely do that. He had begged her to stay in London a bit longer, and he had been relieved beyond measure when she agreed. She had suggested he help her pack up the house in preparation for their removal. He was pleased to be able to help her. He had even envisioned moments of them laughing over old drawings and letters from him to her that had been long forgotten, perhaps even the box of costumes they had used during their many plays as children.

Documenting books for her to consider taking in the library by himself was not something he had expected.

He had already been at it for two hours and he was rather wishing the cord for the curtains had been a bit longer so he might more easily hang himself. He had made a proper list for her, he thought, and had even gone so far as to pile the books he was certain she would take in one corner. But not seeing her for two hours, knowing they were in the same place, not knowing what she was doing, made for a wandering mind and an overactive imagination.

She could be working with the kitchen staff on remaining menus or which members of the staff would be coming with them. She would be sitting at the table, poring over options and discussing merits of each. That unruly strand of hair would fall into her eyes, and she would push it behind her ear without even thinking about it.

He smiled. He loved when she did that. He wanted to do it himself.

She could be going through her wardrobe, wondering which gowns she should take and which she could do without. She would never take them all, she was far too sensible and practical. But she would have to try each on to see how they flattered her, which was most comfortable, which she could walk about the countryside in. He had his favorites of her dresses, but she was so self-conscious that he would never tell her. He would just smile and nod and tell her to choose the ones she liked best.

And enjoy the view.

She could always have come in here and helped him with his task. He wouldn't have gotten half of the things done he needed to if she had. He would have watched her move, watched her think, possibly caught her biting her lip in indecision. She may have met his eyes once or twice, and he would have let her see him looking. She might have blushed and continued her work, or she might have looked straight back at him. Daring him to do exactly what he wanted to do. He could have snuck up behind her and nuzzled the nape of her long, graceful neck. He could have bracketed her between his arms and the shelf. Would she have laughed as if it were a joke? Or would she have felt the simmering heat that he had come to accept as his eternal reaction to her? As if it had actually happened, he felt that same jolt of intense heat somewhere behind his navel.

He took a deep breath and released it quickly, shaking his head. He would get nowhere imagining things that weren't happening and may never. It would take time for him to convince her that he was in love with her, not for the changes that she had undergone, but for who she was and who she had always been. He was aware of it now, and that, at least, would never change.

He reached for another book he thought she would enjoy and tucked it into his arm. He reached up to straighten a fallen book when his hand felt something different. A strange, almost leather like texture; soft and worn, but bound like a book. He felt for the edge and pulled it down.

It was small, no larger than an average sized book, though a good deal thinner. He thumbed it open, and grinned at the handwriting. It was one of Mary's diaries, and from the date in the corner, from when she was sixteen. She had been an irregular author, going through spurts of time when she was dedicated, and then there would be months of famine. He had seen her scribbling away in one of these every now and then, but it had been years since he'd even thought about it.

Mary would laugh madly when she saw these.

He reached up to see if there were more of them on the shelf with this one. A wild grin crossed his face when he felt not one, but several more. He shifted the books in front of them out of the way, and then pulled all of the journals down. There were seven in all, now in his grasp, and who knew how many more there might have been lurking around the house.

A page fluttered to the ground, having fallen out of the oldest and most worn journal of the lot, whose pages all seemed loose. He adjusted his grip and turned that one so that no more pages were in danger of becoming lost. That done, he reached down to pick up the page and put it back where it had come from.

The date in the corner put it right around Mary's thirteenth birthday.

Her penmanship had improved a good deal since then, but he could see how carefully each word was written. The only perfection she had cared about back in those days was her penmanship, and he had teased her endlessly for it.

His name caught his eye as he perused the page and he grinned. He remembered specifically asking her once upon a time if he had ever made it into one of her journals. Young Mary had turned up her nose at him and insisted that only important people made it into the diary of a young lady.

He looked more closely, wondering what he had possibly done to warrant an entry.

Geoffrey came today with his family. I thought I might expire on the spot! His smile makes me feel warm and tingly, like I have been wrapped in a warm blanket and set before the hottest fire. I love him so much, but...

He stopped, his eyes transfixed by that one word.

Love.

She loved him.

Well, thirteen-year-old Mary loved him. The description of her feelings was a little juvenile, but at thirteen, he would not have done much better.

He read on.

I love him so much, but he will never see me as anything more than a friend. My love for him will forever be in vain. I shall become one of those pathetic women one reads about in novels that pines for her lost love, only mine shall never come to me. I shall let him tease me and tug at my hair and call me Goose for as long as he likes. So long as he is near me at all, my heart will want nothing else.

He stared at the page, his heart thudding against his chest with such force that he was light headed. He couldn't believe it. At one time, Mary had been in love with him. She had pined for him. His smile had made her feel something. He smiled now as he thought of it.

Mary at thirteen had been much the same as Mary now, only less graceful, less coordinated, and less witty. She had been a slender reed of a thing, but she was always amusing and had always made him feel as though he was someone special, which was a rare thing for a fourth son.

Now he understood why.

Had she ever tried to tell him? Had there been signs that he had missed? It wasn't possible, he would have known if she were really in love with him, wouldn't he? She must have kept that secret from him. With good reason, he was sure, for at thirteen he only thought of riding horses and joining the Army. He would never have taken her seriously, and it would have been difficult to be friends with a girl who let it be known that she was in love with him. Or would it have been different? He had always liked Mary, but had he ever thought of her beyond that?

She loved him.

She once had loved him.

When had that ceased?

Or had it ceased?

He looked down at the diaries in his hand, chewing his lip. No gentleman would intentionally venture into the secret diaries of a young woman. It was an invasion of privacy and could be perceived as disrespectful and disloyal. He could ruin everything he was trying to build by such a betrayal. Mary would be mortified by the knowledge that he had read what her younger self had written about him, particularly when such devout feelings were expressed.

Perhaps it was just the one page. Perhaps she had been in love with him for the span of a week. He remembered when his sister had been a young girl, and she had been in love with a new young man every other day, it seemed. If Mary were the same way, it would only be natural for her to think herself in love with him. He was the only young man she had any semi-regular interaction with outside of her brothers. He was the obvious choice. He supposed he should be grateful she had not mentioned his brothers.

He frowned and looked down at the diary from which the particular page had fallen. Perhaps she had gone through all of the Harris brothers at some point. That would take some of the weight away, and if that had been the case, she would be much more apt to laugh about the discovery than if it had been just him alone.

It would be best to check. He would need to know how to approach her about this and the proper context would be required if he didn't want to make an absolute fool of himself, not to mention what it could do to her.

He set the other diaries down on the nearest table and opened the oldest one. He found the place where the fallen page belonged, and then flipped to a few pages after that. Two months later. That should be plenty of time. He checked the door to make sure it was clear, and then read.

I went on a walk today and thought about Geoffrey. Of course I did, that is what one does when they are in love.

Geoff swallowed, and flipped a few more pages. Six months after her first entry.

The sky was a brilliant blue today. It looked like precisely the same shade that is in Geoffrey's eyes. I love his eyes. They are beautiful. I hope that our children will have his eyes.

His mouth gaped open as he finished. She imagined herself having children with him?

His stomach fluttered at the thought.

Geoff set the diary down and sank into the chair nearest him, rubbing his face repeatedly. This was a lot to take in. His best friend, the woman he loved, had spent at least six months at thirteen being so in love with him that she thought about him on walks and imagined herself having his children and comparing his smile to blankets and his eyes to the sky.

Six months at that age felt like an eternity.

He looked at the table, where the other diaries were neatly stacked.

He shouldn't even consider it. Why, this diary was written fourteen years ago, more time had passed since she had written the entry than the age she had been when she wrote it. It was incomprehensible that she would have felt this way forever, let alone if she would feel that way now. Her emotions were sure to have changed from year to year. Nothing should be taken seriously at thirteen.

The other diaries would prove that.

He ran his hands through his hair, staring at the floor. He was a gentleman. He would not peruse the private writings of a young woman for his own amusement or to fulfill his apparent need to have his own feelings reciprocated. He was delighted beyond words that one version of Mary had been in love with him. It meant there may be some thread of hope for him after all. That knowledge alone should have satisfied him.

He glanced at the diaries once more.

He would not read any more.

He would not.

He gnawed at his lip, for a moment, then groaned and pulled the entire stack into his lap.

He would need a diary at least one year after the one he had just read. He looked through a few, and finally found one from the summer she was fifteen. Fifteen was significantly more mature than thirteen. With a nod of satisfaction, he opened it up.

I found my diary from when I was thirteen as I was going through my trunk. What a laugh! I cannot believe that I was in love with Geoffrey Harris! Oh, he would positively expire with laughter if he knew! I will not tell him, of course, it would be mortifying to admit to such silly feelings. To be in love with my best friend? Ha!

Oddly, Geoff felt a significant twinge of disappointment at her words. He snorted as he closed the diary and set it aside. He was disappointed that her fifteen-year-old self had only thought of him as her best friend? Wasn't that what he wanted to be? Knowing that she had been in love with him once meant it might be possible for her to love him again, but there was no reason why being her best friend would not also give him an advantage.

It would be enough.

He nodded and sighed, sitting back.

She had loved him, she had not loved him.

She could love him again.

His brow furrowed. If she could love him again... perhaps she had...

He glanced down at the diaries and before he could stop himself with thoughts of what he should or shouldn't do, he was opening the rest of them to find the most recent one.

Ah ha! Eighteen years old. She had had her first season and had been exposed to some other men besides him and his brothers. This would tell him the truth.

The Thorntons had their ball last evening. Phoebe Thornton made an absolute fool of herself trying so desperately to get the attention of Robert Forsham. Geoffrey and I were beside ourselves with laughter. I thought we would make quite the spectacle of ourselves with our behavior, but Geoff assures me that nobody pays attention to anything but bad behavior and Colin Gerrard.

He had to pause for laughter at the memory. As it turned out, Phoebe Thornton had married Thomas Forsham, older brother of Robert, and nobody had spoken of either of them since. But he remembered that ball and laughing hysterically with Mary about it.

So they were merely friends at eighteen as well. He could live with that.

Then he saw the next lines.

I love laughing with Geoffrey. He makes me feel as if I am someone special. It does not matter if my first season had no success, I still have him. If only he could see how I really feel about him. There is nobody to compare to him in looks, in manner, in temperament… He is the perfect man, and he is perfect for me. Can he not see how I adore him? Is my love for him not plain for all to see in my eyes? I cannot bear to tell him. If he does not feel the same, it would ruin our friendship. I dare not risk it. My heart will have to be patient, to see if he ever figures it out. If he does not, all will be well. I need not be loved by him if we may always be friends.

Geoff closed the diary firmly and put it in the stack with the others, then stared at them for a long while. His chest ached, so much so that he had to rub it. She had loved him. She had loved him again. She had gone from loving him to not loving him to loving him again. Eighteen was no flighty age. Many young women were married at eighteen these days.

Had she really loved him? How long had it gone on? How deep had it been? Were there times he wondered? Had he ever given her a reason to stop?

His breath caught in his throat. Did she love him still?

He sat back heavily against the chair as his mind spun that idea. Eighteen was still a good distance from twenty-seven. Why, when he was twenty he had courted Lydia Fawcett, and he had no feelings for her that remained.

He winced as he considered that Mary might still have loved him at twenty. Had she been pained by the attentions he had given Lydia? He had spoken with Mary about Lydia! Not in depth, for he was not that foolish, but still. If she had loved him during that time, knowing he was courting someone else...

But here was proof. By her own hand, Mary had admitted her love for him. Repeatedly and over time.

His heart began to pound, and he glanced back up at the shelves. Were there more diaries? More recent diaries? Ones that might give him more reason to hope?

He shoved off of the chair and rushed back to the shelf, immediately checking the place the other diaries had been. No such luck. He frowned and began checking behind the books on the shelf below. He would tear apart this entire library if he must in order to find further proof that the woman he loved might love him in return.

"What have you found?"

He stopped, a book in each hand, and turned towards the door of the library. Mary stood there, simply dressed, but no less lovely in his opinion. He frantically searched for a response when he noticed that she was not looking at him.

She was looking at the diaries.

His mouth twisted slightly with interest. "You tell me," he said slowly, setting down the books he held. He picked up the stack of diaries and brought them closer. He hadn't moved three steps when her eyes widened and she froze like a statue. If he didn't know better, he would have thought she'd be near to fainting.

She swallowed hard and forced a smile that was more a grimace than a smile. Then she laughed that false, high-pitched laugh that had so grated on his nerves. "Oh, those are nothing," she said, closing the distance and taking them from him quickly. "Nonsensical scribblings of a silly girl. I could burn the lot and not miss a page."

She spun from the room so fast her hair bounced with the force. "Lunch will be ready soon, Geoff, if you are hungry," she called behind her, her voice still too high.

"All right," he said after her, knowing she wouldn't hear it, nor would she care.

He stared at the door, unmoving. Mary knew exactly what those diaries had contained. She'd been terrified that he would know. She had not asked if he had read them. She had no reason to suspect he would, as he was always the perfect gentleman and never did anything even remotely ungentlemanly.

His reputation had saved him from having to answer for his actions. Her diaries had saved him from doubt.

She had loved him. He could make her love him again. He could be everything she wanted, everything he had ever been to her and more. He was a man now, not a foolish boy who had unwittingly made a girl fall in love with him and hadn't even seen. He could treat her the way he always should have treated her, the way a man in love should treat the woman of his dreams.

She had loved him once.

And by God, she would love him again.

Chapter Twenty

"You have received another bouquet of flowers, Miss Hamilton."

Mary rolled her eyes, then held her head as the motion pained her. "From whom this time?" she moaned, rubbing her brow.

"Mr. Timmons, I believe," Mrs. Evansdale said with a bob of her head as she fidgeted with the tray in her grasp. She brought it to Mary and frowned, her round face bunching up with the expression.

Mary sighed patiently and held her arms out. "Here, I will take it in my lap."

Mrs. Evansdale nodded and handed it to her.

"And what did Mr. Timmons have to say?" Mary asked as she began the awkward attempt to eat properly whilst still abed.

Sweet Mrs. Evansdale had to think for a moment, though it could not have been more than ten minutes since the gentleman had come.

"Was it perhaps well wishes for my recovery?" Mary prodded, doing her level best to avoid smiling.

"I believe it was, yes it was," Mrs. Evansdale said with a fervent nod, as if she'd just had the recollection herself. "He said he was dreadfully sorry you were unable to attend the theater last night, and said they all missed you, and he was your devoted servant if you should need him."

It spoke as to how ill Mary felt that she did not roll her eyes at this. Mr. Timmons did not seem to understand when a lady was politely trying to refuse his suit. She would have to be more blatant upon her return to society. Subtlety was useless.

And he was not the only slow-witted one.

She had been unwell for two days now, and the attention she received for a simple cold that kept her in bed made her more keen to recover than any ill-tasting tonic she'd ever endured. It was absolutely ridiculous. Why, she was receiving more attention from being ill than she had in the last two weeks combined. Geoffrey had been true to his word and had been her permanent escort once again, but it had not changed anything. Her behavior had gone back to more of her natural self, and that had somehow only increased their sincerity.

She had lost track of who had brought her flowers and who had not. It made her head ache trying to remember, which was not much different from the headache she suffered from on a continual basis of late. The doctor had been by, thanks to Mrs. Evansdale's tendency to overreaction and fear of illness, and had given her strict orders to stay in bed until she was feeling her old self. It was maddening.

There was so much work to be done around the house as yet for their move to the country, and she could not very well accomplish any of it while she was confined to bed. Geoffrey promised he would do as much as he could, but he had not been able to come since she had taken ill. Some matter of business that he would not discuss with her, which was not unusual, and so she did not ask any questions.

But the admirers had come, and she had never been more grateful for the excuse to avoid them. She was done with this whole charade, and good riddance to the madness. She would not have minded a few admirers who were fervent, had some sense, and who happened to share interests and tastes she herself had. If she could have enjoyed a bit of that, she might have continued to be the debutante.

But alas, all she had were silly men with sillier attentions.

The sensible men that had come around had been kind enough, and she had the opportunity to see quite honestly that they would not suit, and no feelings were injured and no good feelings lost.

A knock at her door broke through her thoughts and startled her so she nearly upended her tray, which she had completely forgotten about.

"Come," she called, her voice still hoarse and her nose stuffed to such an extent her words were affected.

"Pardon me, Miss Hamilton," Mrs. Evansdale said softly, entering timidly.

Mary smiled at her with kindness and patience. "Yes, Mrs. Evansdale?"

"Mr. Harris is here, Miss," she replied with a quick bob. "I know you are not receiving in your condition, but as it is Mr. Harris..."

Mary could not help the grin that nearly exploded across her face. "No, you're right. I cannot come down, but you may send him up."

Mrs. Evansdale nearly fell over. "What, to your bedchamber?"

A snort escaped Mary, even with her illness, and she rolled her eyes. "Well, yes, Mrs. Evansdale. It's not as though I am naked, is it?"

The poor lady looked near to swooning, but somehow she managed a nod and left.

Entertainment at last! She sat up a little and made sure her dressing gown was properly tied. She was not entirely without decorum, after all.

There came another knock and she hid her smile. "Come."

Her door creaked open and she saw Geoff before he saw her. He was dressed as finely as he ever was, which never failed to make Mary wonder why any man ever dressed less finely, considering how splendid he always looked. His color was robust and healthy, and it was possible he looked even more handsome than when she had seen him last. Which was a silly thing, considering how handsome he always was, and had always been.

He took in her appearance and state and there was a flash of something hot, like fire in both heat and intensity, that made her breath catch in her chest. But then it was gone, without the barest hint that anything had ever occurred. He grinned her very favorite grin at her, and he kept one arm behind his back.

"My dear Mary, what have you been telling poor Mrs. Evansdale?" he scolded as he neared. "She looks as though a ghost has been roaming your halls."

She giggled and held out a hand to him. "I merely told her to have you come up, since I cannot go down, and you would have thought that I had asked her to catch a snail and eat it raw."

He tsked as he took her hand in his. "Bringing a man up to your bedchamber. Mary, you are quite shocking." He offered a half smile as he placed a very light kiss upon her hand.

It burned as if he had branded her with a hot iron. Somehow, she managed to smile. "You already knew that."

"I did," he agreed, sitting and giving her a singularly wicked look. "And it is quite possibly my favorite part of you."

She looked at him for a long moment, waiting for his composure to break. When it didn't, she burst out laughing, in spite of the ache in her head.

He laughed himself as he sat in the chair, and smiled as he looked at her. "It is good to hear you laugh, Mary."

She tilted her head at him with a smile of her own. "It feels good to laugh. Well, not at the moment, it feels quite horrid to do anything, but in my heart, it feels good to laugh."

"Yes, I wondered how the rest of you would be feeling at the moment," he said, looking at her a bit sadly. "And I'm not entirely sure you will feel up this now, but perhaps later…"

He reached behind his back, and Mary sat up a little, feeling as curious as a kitten.

To her surprise, he brought forth a book. He smiled and held it out for her to see. "I thought you might prefer this to more dying flowers."

She grinned and took it. "And you would be quite right!" She looked at the spine for the title, then looked back at him, still grinning. "Fairy tales."

He nodded, his own smile becoming quite smug. "Yes, in my cataloguing of your rather immense library, I discovered that you didn't have a collection of fairy tales, which seemed quite a shame, considering how fond you always were of fairy tales and how many hours I spent playing all the roles from the wicked witch to the dragons."

She giggled, which made her cough a bit. "Only because you

were so good at it," she insisted. She set the book down beside her. "Thank you, Geoff, it was very sweet and considerate of you. I'll read them when I can."

"Yes, don't strain your eyes," he said, his voice growing concerned. "I would hate to think that I brought something else ill upon you."

She gave him a disbelieving look. "Please, you could never bring anything ill upon me."

That seemed to surprise him, and he gave her a look that might have heated her from the inside out.

Then, unexpectedly, it was gone. "I never did hear, you know," he mused, folding his arms, "how was your meeting with the dashing Viscount Riverton? Two whole weeks with no report? I hope it is good."

Mary smirked a little. "Quite good. We danced twice, I think. I was very impressed with him, and shall retain a high opinion of his character. He has my good wishes and I hope we shall meet again on other occasions."

"But…?" Geoff prodded, keen eyes fixed on Mary.

She shrugged. "But we wouldn't suit. He is very pleasant, and dances very well, but he is not looking to settle yet, and he made that very plain."

"Did he, indeed?" he replied with a laugh. "And just how did that come about?"

"Oh, when we were dancing I mentioned that he danced well, and he replied, 'What, only well? Not like an angel or with the grace of a swan?', to which I replied, 'I know nothing of swans or angels, my lord, but I know enough about dancing, I am sure.'"

Geoff laughed loudly, grinning at her. "Nicely put. Then what?"

"Well," Mary continued, thinking back, "then he informed me that he had it on good authority from no less than three young ladies that he did, in fact, dance like an angel, and I said he could not argue with so many witnesses, but I would stand by what I had said. He seemed surprised by it, and asked me if I had any intention of flattering him at all."

Geoff's eyes narrowed slightly. "What did you say to that?" he asked her.

Now Mary smiled in earnest, still rather impressed with her daring from that night. "That I only flattered when there was something to flatter, and never falsely at that."

Now it seemed Geoff was fighting laughter, but it was there in his eyes.

"And after that," Mary said with a sigh, "the viscount laughed and stated that I had no intention of trying to marry him, did I, which, naturally, I had not."

"You told him that?" he asked, his smile turning crooked.

Mary nodded. "In no uncertain terms."

"And how did the dear viscount take the news?"

"Rather well. He laughed again and said he appreciated that, as he was not looking for a wife despite his mother's best attempts, and he would be glad to dance with me again later for a reprieve."

"And he did," he stated, looking oddly pleased.

Mary nodded. "And he did."

He paused for a long moment, staring at her. "Seems a good match to me," he said carefully.

Mary smiled and shrugged a shoulder. "Perhaps, but he would only be pursuing me to please his mother, as so many others have tried this season. I require more than that, I fear."

Geoff shifted a little in his seat, his eyes intense. "Do you?"

A knock on the door came and she rolled her eyes. "Oh, for heaven's sake. Come!"

"Busy day?" he asked in a low voice.

She sniffled into her handkerchief. "I find I am more popular when I am sick than when I am well. It is most distressing."

"Such a horrid life you must lead," he muttered, shaking his head.

Mrs. Evansdale entered once more, bobbing yet again. "Mr. Burlington is here."

"I am not receiving," Mary reminded her, ignoring the way Geoff had begun to snicker.

"I know, Miss," Mrs. Evansdale said with a motherly smile. "I just thought you ought to know. He left a lovely bouquet of flowers and expresses his most fervent wishes on a fast recovery with no lasting ill effects." She bobbed once more, and turned from the room.

"Oh, come now," Geoff said the moment she was gone. "You are going to see me, but not the standard by which all fops are measured?"

Mary expelled a burst of giggles and covered her mouth. "Oh, don't! He is quite a nice gentleman."

He shrugged. "I have no doubt of it. The epitome of a twit would have to be favorable in some form, or he would never get invited anywhere."

Mary clamped her lips together as more laughs shook her shoulders.

"But really," he continued as if nothing had happened, "you ought to at least take a look at the flowers he brought you. If the biggest waste of refinement and breath that was ever called a gentleman has gone to all the trouble of getting you flowers, without even checking to be sure if you like flowers, it would not hurt you to glance at the poor dead things."

Mary was now beside herself with laughter, which unfortunately made her cough even more. She hunched forward as she coughed, and suddenly felt a hand at her back, rubbing soothing circles.

"There, there," Geoff murmured, his voice soft and low, "there, now, I'm sorry."

She shook her head as she recovered and patted his chest before he moved. "Don't apologize," she wheezed, coughing slightly. She smiled up at him and lay back against the pillows as he resumed his position in the chair. "Never apologize for making me laugh."

He smiled uncertainly and rubbed his hands together. "But I should apologize for making you cough."

Again, she shook her head. "Breathing makes me cough at the moment. Not you."

Her errant strand of hair suddenly fell forward into her face. She went to move it, but Geoff's hand was suddenly there. He slowly moved the hair out of her face, tucking it softly behind her ear. His fingers brushed her cheek with the lightest touch as they came forward, and Mary felt her face heat beneath them. She chanced a look at his face, only to find his eyes fixed on hers.

Her heart began racing within her and her breath was suddenly hard to find. And it had nothing to do with her illness.

His eyes flickered down to her lips, where puffs of air were escaping in the most shameful pants. Then they were back on hers, and somehow, there was more heat, more emotion, more power in them. Something she felt all the way to her toes, which curled involuntarily beneath her bed sheets.

She could not be this vulnerable to him. Not anymore.

She drew in a shaking breath. "I think… I had better… rest now," she said in a soft, trembling voice.

His lips curved into the softest, sweetest smile. "Yes, you probably should, Mary." He sat back and prepared to leave.

She swallowed quickly. "That is not your name for me."

He turned in surprise and gave her a very serious look. "You told me not to use it any longer."

Impulsively, she bit her lip. His eyes followed. "I…" she began, hesitating. What would he think of her?

His eyes met hers again and she found confidence. "I miss it," she finally told him, smiling helplessly.

He stared at her for a long moment, hardly a reaction on his face. Then he sighed in apparent relief, and smiled once more. His smile was warm, tender, and something else she could not find a word for.

"Sleep well, Goose," he murmured, leaning forward and pressing his lips to her forehead. He touched her cheek, and she met his eyes. "Send for me if you need anything."

Somehow, amid her swirling senses, she nodded.

He moved to the door, grinning once more as if he had not just sent her mind and emotions and wits reeling.

Then he was gone.

She inhaled sharply and exhaled in one fell sweep, bringing her hand to her brow.

What in heaven's name had just happened?

She had not felt that fluttery with him in years.

He had never looked at her like that before.

He had ever touched her so gently before.

He had never...

She shook her head and put it into her hands. She was imagining things. She was in very great danger of falling head over heels over heart for him yet again, and as usual, her mind was playing tricks on her for it.

She rubbed her chest absently, still feeling the burn within.

He was not in love with her.

And she was not in love with him.

Not anymore.

Geoff inhaled deeply as he stepped out of doors, determined to cleanse his lungs with the fresh air. He sorely needed it. He had meant to visit Mary as a way of cheering her up, and instead he had been the one affected.

Not that he had failed to notice the effect he had on her. He knew very well that she was no longer immune to him, he could see it in her eyes, in the slight trembling of her body, the shakiness of her breath. But all of that did not amount to love. He could not deny he was pleased by it, but it was not enough.

It would never be enough.

He shook his head to clear away the fog within it, and got into his carriage with a firm nod at Dawes.

It had been several weeks since their reconciliation, and he was delighted with the progress he had made towards rebuilding what he had almost destroyed. And he felt even more confident that Mary could come to love him, assuming he did not make a mess of things again. With their history, and given her responses to his treatment of her, he thought it just might be possible.

But he could never be entirely sure. After all, she had loved him on and off for all those years and he had never noticed a thing.

He was watching now, though. He was keeping a close eye on her throughout this time, so that he could be sure to catch the first hint.

He could not shake the nagging fear, however, that throughout her time as a debutante, she had learned to be a better actress than he would have thought. What if she could hide her emotions from him, as she had so long ago? What if he never saw the slightest trace of softening on her part? Would he have to swallow his fear and pride and confess all?

Would she ever believe him?

He sighed and glanced out of the window at the passing London buildings and people. There was not time to dwell on all of this now. He'd been meeting with Captain Riverton frequently, and they had set many things in motion. Now results were coming into light, and he was pleased with the progress that had been made.

No one outside of his circle of friends and Captain Riverton had any idea what they were about, save for the few contacts that the captain had utilized. Determining the fate of a ship and specific members of the crew was a messy business and had to be done with a great deal of tact. They could not possibly find out the fate of all that should have been aboard, and if anyone knew of their plan, that question would be raised.

He could not make such a request of Captain Riverton, nor of his contacts. He was fortunate enough to have gotten as far as he had.

They knew a great deal at this point. They knew the ship and crew had been in a Spanish port some eight weeks ago, and that at that time, Lieutenant Wyndham had been with them. But considering what they had known before, which was nothing, it was a start. They had also received word of a potential epidemic of a rather potent stomach virus in the vicinity of the port, but they were waiting for more details on that subject.

The other information that was vital was the knowledge that the ship had indeed left the harbor in Spain, and had done so nearly six weeks previously. All they waited upon now was the information as to whether or not Lieutenant Wyndham had been with his shipmates at the time of their departure. Those details were difficult to come by, and it was this crucial detail that had taken so long.

The waiting had been tortuous.

Keeping the secret from Mary, and from Cassie by extension, was painful beyond expression.

But he dared not discuss it with them. Not until he had something concrete to tell. For all he knew, the lieutenant had perished with the rest, and there was no hope. He could not bear to raise that hope in vain.

And so he met with his friends and the captain every few days to gather what information they could. Between their combined contacts, influence and determination, they had been able to manage much, and their progress had been impressive. But if they did not receive answers, real answers, soon, it would be too late.

"Do not wait for me, Dawes," he told the man as they pulled up to the club. "I may be quite a long while. It is not far to home, I shall walk."

Dawes inclined his head with a quick, "Yes, sir," and was off again just as quickly.

Geoffrey entered the establishment, nodded to a few gentlemen he knew, and then spotted his friends and the captain at their usual table in the corner, drinks already in hand.

"Ah, Harris!" the captain called, standing and coming to shake his hand. "Good to see you."

"Riverton."

He nodded to his friends, who were not quite so polite nor so eager to see him as to stand for his arrival.

"How is Mary?" Nathan asked when he sat. "Moira is quite worried, but doesn't wish to trouble her."

Colin snorted loudly.

Nathan glared at him, even as the others fought to hide smiles. Captain Riverton looked as though he was not sure whether he was to be smiling with the others or frowning with Nathan.

"Something to say about my wife, Colin?" Nathan growled.

Colin shook his head, but said, "The very idea that Moira should be a trouble to anyone is absurd, Nate."

Nathan frowned more, then turned to Geoff. "So how is Mary?"

"Bored," Geoff said on a sigh. "Being confined to bed does not suit her. But she is in good spirits, though frustrated with the amount of flowers gathering in her foyer."

Now the lot snickered, save for poor Captain Riverton, who was still confused.

"You may tell Moira she would be more than welcome," Geoff told Nathan when they had settled themselves. "Mary was delighted beyond words to see me, I can only imagine how desperate that is."

Nathan and Derek hid smiles, while Duncan and Colin nodded soberly.

Geoff ignored the lot of them and turned to the captain. "Now, then, Riverton. What news do we have from your friends in Spain?"

Captain Riverton slowly set down his glass, and stared at it for a long moment.

The table became subdued instantly as all gazed upon the young man. Geoff felt his stomach sink in despair.

"Will?" Derek asked quietly.

Riverton glanced up, then smiled broadly. "I think we may have something after all."

Chapter Twenty One

"*C*assie, can you come and help me with this?"

There was no response.

Mary waited a count of thirty, and then tried again. "Cassie! I need your help!"

Again, her sister did not reply.

"If you don't come and help, I won't keep any of your gowns at all and you will have to go about the country in your mourning dress or stark naked!"

She grinned at her own threat. If that wouldn't send her sister scampering into the spare bedchamber used exclusively for Cassandra's wardrobe, nothing on earth would.

As it happened, it didn't. Not only that, but Mary heard no reply whatsoever. She set down the pile of gowns she had started to look through and put her hands on her hips. Despite her threats, she was not about to make any sort of lasting decision about which of her sister's gowns would be suited for the country, and which should be packed away for the rare London excursion. As well as Mary knew her sister, she was not at all versed in her taste for fashion.

If she were to make a mistake, the world might collapse in on itself and they would all be lost forever.

She turned from the room and set about to find her sister, drag her by the arm up to this room if she must, and force her to make these decisions for herself.

Cassandra had not lessened her behavior in the last few weeks.

She rarely left her bedchamber, and when she did, never ventured to the main floor. It was a very good day if her hair progressed beyond a loose braid, and an even more fortunate day if she was not wearing black. She was determined to mourn her "dear, sweet Simon" as if they had actually wed, which meant her current fashion was dictated by how mournful she felt that day, whether she wore black or merely something very drab and plain.

Either way, the change was not something Mary was prepared to deal with, though she knew she wouldn't have much of a choice. Cassie had been moaning about losing him for months now.

Recovering from his death would be much worse.

Her first stop was Cassandra's bedchamber, which had become her private sanctuary of late. If Cassie was ignoring her, she would be in this room.

She knocked softly, knowing it was unlikely she would respond now when she had not before. When she had no response, she entered of her own accord.

"Cassie! Stop ignoring me!" she scolded as she pushed open the door.

The room was entirely empty. The curtains were drawn, as they had been for weeks, and the room itself was as morose and solemn as Cassie herself had been. A mere five minutes in such a place and even the happiest of persons would find nothing to smile about.

She shuddered delicately and backed out of the room as quickly as she could.

Out in the hall, she frowned and placed her hands on her hips. If Cassie was not in her room, there was no telling where she might have gone, except she would stay indoors. Were they in the country, she might have walked about aimlessly for hours bemoaning her situation, but in the busy and Society-flooded London, she wouldn't risk being seen in such a state.

Her sister might have been an emotional and flighty creature, but she wasn't one to put on a show merely to gain attention.

For the public, at least.

Mary had seen a great many performances in her time.

She checked her own bedchamber, not that Cassie venturing in there was likely, but since Mary had acquired a few gowns that Cassie had envied greatly, it was possible, but that too was empty.

The other bedrooms, all typically empty but kept in readiness, were as vacant as they ever were.

She huffed in irritation and made her way down the stairs, frowning as she considered where to go next. She ought to just move on to a different project. One that would not require her sister's assistance.

She shook her head. This needed to be done at some point, and it might as well be done today. If Cassandra was so involved in her perpetual mourning that she couldn't assist in the preparations that Mary was undertaking to remove her to the country for a more private recovery, then all of the decisions would be made by Mary herself and very quickly, and they would be gone as soon as possible.

Mary took in a breath, and then released it slowly. She shouldn't be so quick to judge her sister, not when such a tragedy truly had occurred. It would have been difficult for any woman, and Cassandra had long proved that she was more emotional than the average woman.

She turned towards the back of the house, only to find Mrs. Evansdale sitting in a chair outside of the drawing room, her face in her hands.

"Mrs. Evansdale?" Mary cried softly, coming to her knees before her. "Whatever is the matter?"

The woman sniffled and raised her head, her plump cheeks red and stained with tears. "Miss Cassie h-has a visitor."

That was not the reply that Mary had expected.

"That is lovely," Mary said, choosing her words with care and keeping her voice calm. "Who is it?"

Mrs. Evansdale's lower lip quivered and she shook her head. She waved her handkerchief at the drawing room, where the door was very slightly ajar.

Mary restrained a sigh, and rose, moving to the room softly.

She shouldn't intrude upon her sister's privacy, but if she must...

She had to cover her mouth to keep from gasping at the sight.

Very rapidly she backed away, until the stairs met her back. She met Mrs. Evansdale's eyes, and found herself wanting to cry as well.

"Send for Geoffrey Harris," Mary whispered, her voice choking in her throat.

Mrs. Evansdale hiccupped, but nodded.

"Now!" Mary hissed, smiling.

The woman nodded instantly and darted away, her footsteps echoing down the hallway.

Mary clamped her lips together, and then felt giggles bubble up within her. She couldn't wait to see Geoff's face when he found out.

Geoff grinned as he approached Mary's house mere minutes after receiving the message that she needed to see him at once.

He had been waiting for this message for two days now.

He didn't wait for the carriage to completely stop before he stepped out and strode up to the door of her house, keeping his expression devoid of emotion. He knocked swiftly, and only had to wait a moment before Winston, with his inexorably good timing, opened the door for him and bade him enter.

Mary waited for him by the stair, her hands mangling each other in front of her, her teeth clamping down on her lip so fiercely she was likely to draw blood.

"What's the to-do, Goose?" he asked lightly. "Your note was rather cryptic, even for you."

She put a finger to her lips and waved him after her as she turned towards the back of the house.

He hid his smile and obediently followed.

They came to the drawing room door, which was open just enough for one to look in without being noticed.

"Who are you spying on this morning, Mary?" Geoff whispered, grinning.

She waved him into silence, her eyes widening, but he could see her fighting a grin. She pointed into the room and tilted her head in invitation.

He came over to her side and looked in.

Cassie sat in a chair by the fire, as she had done so many other days, but this morning, a man knelt before her. He was clasping her hands in his, then reached out to stroke one cheek, bringing a smile and a few tears to her face. He couldn't see the man's face, but the uniform upon his back and the tenderness in Cassandra's gaze told him everything he needed to know.

Lieutenant Simon Wyndham, not so very dead after all, had come again.

And if he had any understanding of men at all, there would be an engagement very shortly.

As if his thought had been said aloud, Cassandra suddenly burst into tears, frantically nodding, unable to speak. Simon kissed her hands, then rose and gathered his beloved into his arms.

It was a sight that stirred something within him, and he glanced down at the woman he loved, pressed almost entirely against his side as she watched the scene with him. He swallowed with more difficulty than he would have liked to admit.

"True love conquers all once more," he murmured so only she could hear, his eyes raking over any part of her they could see, hungry for such a scene himself.

She was not immune to the warmth in his tone, nor their position. Slowly her eyes came up to meet his, and in them he found the breathlessness that he was feeling. Her eyes had always and would ever be his favorite feature of hers. Not that he would ever tell her, but they held every expression in them, every emotion, every thought. And at this moment, he could not possibly comprehend all of the emotions he saw swirling in their beauty.

Without thinking, he leaned towards her, unable to stop himself from glancing down at her lips.

She noticed. And he didn't imagine the way her frame began to sway towards him, nor the way her lips parted under his watchful gaze.

His breath caught in his throat at the possibilities of the moment, and he wished, for one instant, that he would stop thinking, that she would stop thinking, and…

Mary's eyes met his once more, and thought vanished.

The moment hung there between them, tense and hungry and thrumming with every unspoken emotion. No breath, no words, nothing but the two of them, closer than they had ever been, a kiss away from changing their lives forever.

And then it passed.

Mary skittered away, struggling for composure, eventually managing a warm smile that didn't meet her still dazed eyes. "I think we should hide," she whispered, her voice shaking.

He raised a brow as he swallowed his flood of emotions and disappointment. He already was hiding, and far too much. "Hide?" he repeated.

She nodded. "They cannot know we have been spying!"

It took him longer than he would have ever admitted to realize what she was talking about. Then it dawned on him that was speaking of Wyndham and Cassandra. He had completely forgotten the amorous couple in the room just beyond.

But the idea of hiding anywhere with Mary... At this moment, that would not be wise.

He smiled and shook his head. "Alas, dear Goose, I cannot hide with you. I dashed off rather suddenly to come and see what you had to show, and now I must be off once more. I am expected at Derek and Kate's, though for what purpose I have no idea."

She looked a trifle disappointed, but smiled in spite of it. "That's a rather terrifying prospect. Kate might have you beat carpets."

He shuddered. "Heaven forbid. But I promise I'll come to collect you tomorrow for the masquerade ball."

Now it was Mary who shook her head.

"No?" he asked, his heart skipping with dread. Had she decided she had no use for him after all?

She smiled mischievously. "I will see you at the ball, Geoff, but you must not see me before. I intend to surprise you as well as the rest of London."

The relief he felt hit him squarely in the back of the knees and he almost buckled. He grinned at her, hiding his shameful rush of emotion. "A mystery, Goose?"

"See if you really know me, Geoff," she offered with a quirk of her perfect brows. "For if you don't, no one will."

He couldn't help the warmth that washed over him, nor that most of it would end up in the smile he gave her. He loved her. He loved when she was mischievous and impish, because it was the more entertaining side of her that very few saw, but also because it was absurdly attractive. And it made him want to kiss her quite madly. She thought he wouldn't know her? She could have come dressed as King Henry VIII and still he would have known her.

"Challenge accepted, my lady," he murmured as he stepped towards her and took her hand. "I look forward to it." He drew her hand to his lips and lingered longer than was appropriate. Why not? He could be just as mischievous and far more daring.

He released her hand and bowed, very politely, then smirked at her shocked expression. "I cannot wait to see you."

She swallowed hastily and nodded, apparently unable to speak.

Good.

He inclined his head and swept from the house, rather grandly, feeling supremely proud that he had managed, this time, to render Mary entirely speechless.

She would need to get used to that.

He had never been an anxious man. He had never been the sort to become distracted by his mind being somewhere else, or prone to sweaty palms, or flickering eyes. He had only ever been the epitome of a calm, collected gentleman.

Until tonight.

He was so distracted at this moment he didn't realize his drink was empty until he had tried to drink from it and found only air.

"Steady on, Geoff," Duncan's deep voice growled from nearby. "Save some of the beverage for the other guests."

"What?" he asked, looking at him quickly as he tore his eyes from the entrance to the ballroom.

Duncan, wearing an ornate mask and a turban that made him seem somehow even taller, leaned over a bit closer. "You have had four glasses already this evening, and I'm fairly certain you haven't actually tasted a drop. Are you drinking to forget something or...?"

Geoff shook his head rapidly, almost dislodging his own mask. "I have not had four. We've not been here nearly long enough for that many."

Duncan snorted and patted Geoffrey's shoulder. "We have been here for an hour and it hasn't stopped you from drinking faster than my aunt's housekeeper. What's the fuss?"

An hour? He would have sworn in church that they had been here for twice that long. He had mingled with the host and hostess, though at this moment he had absolutely no idea who they even were, and had paid his due diligence to all of the important members of society, as they would expect him to do, and since then he had only waited. And waited. And waited some more.

It was obvious to everybody who he was. He had made no attempt to disguise himself beyond a simple black mask and a cape, feeling the need to be as open as a masquerade would allow him to be. Why bother hiding at all when his presence was expected?

"Geoffrey Harris, are you ignoring me?" Duncan's voice reverberated in his ears.

"No," he said simply, keeping his eyes fixed on the entrance yet again. Now there was a low, rather amused chuckle.

"Right. Well, when Mary gets here and you have recovered yourself, should you have need of me, I will be elsewhere."

"What?" Geoff asked, only half listening.

Duncan's chuckle turned into full blown laughter. "Really, Geoff, if you weren't going to pay attention to anybody else, why did you come alone?"

"She made me."

"Made you? Did you anger her again?"

Geoff glowered at his turbaned friend. "No, thank you very much. She said she wanted it to be a surprise. That I had to see for myself if I would know her."

"Clever girl. And your reply was...?"

He snorted. "I accepted the challenge, of course. She cannot fool me."

"Oh, really?"

Geoff raised a brow rather imperiously. "You doubt me?"

Duncan offered a rather knowing look himself. "She has fooled all of London, you included, the entirety of the season. Why should tonight be any different merely because she will be wearing an actual mask? How can you be sure you will know her?"

Geoff turned and tilted his chin up to look his oldest friend as squarely in the eye as he could from his present height. "Never once has she walked into a room and I have not noticed. While she has blended into the background so easily for Society and the rest of you, I have always seen her there. I know the curve of her cheek, the exact shade of her eyes, and the very things that will make her smile in that perfect way to make knees tremble with delight. So yes, Duncan, I daresay I can be perfectly sure that I will know her."

It was much to Duncan's well-rehearsed credit that he kept his expression so impassive when his shock was so apparent. His eyes were wide, and his mouth would have hung completely ajar had his lips parted in the slightest. His thick brows almost entirely hid themselves beneath his turban, and it was difficult to tell if the man were even breathing.

Geoffrey felt the slightest flush of embarrassment start at the back of his neck and ears, but he continued to keep his gaze steady. He was not ashamed of anything he said, and he would repeat them to anybody that asked. Truer words had never been spoken, especially not by him.

"Well, damn, Geoffrey," Duncan said softly, his words almost lost amidst the murmuring around them. "If you love her that much, why haven't you done something about it?"

Geoff did not, after all, have Duncan's control, and his mouth did gape open.

Duncan clamped him on the shoulder. "What is holding you back, man?" He gave him a wry look and left without another word.

What did hold Geoff back?

He could not help but grin as his realization sank in.

Not a thing.

There was nothing in his way. He could tell Mary exactly what he felt, what he wanted. She would listen, and if their encounters of late would be any indication, she would not be entirely opposed.

He could tell her. He would tell her. Tonight.

The low buzz of the room suddenly dropped to nothing. It registered only dimly to him.

He could have Mary. He could have it all. He would no longer be afraid or cautious or reserved. He knew what he wanted and he was going to take it.

The noise in the room rose once more, louder and more insistent than it was before.

Slowly, Geoff turned to face the entrance, the focal point of every set of eyes and the topic of every gossiping mouth.

A vision in silver stood there, proud and aloof, her pale eyes shimmering beneath her mask like the very stars in the night sky. Her figure was perfection itself, draped as it was in the color of the delicate mist that hung in the early mornings over the Thames. She was a siren, calling all to her, even at their own peril. And all would follow, delighted to even take part in the journey. No one knew her, could not have even told what shade her hair was, as her mask encased it amidst tendrils of silken fabric that cascaded down her back. She was a mystery and the entire room trembled with curiosity.

All were clueless.

Except Geoff.

He knew what they did not.

Mary Hamilton had arrived.

Chapter Twenty Two

*M*ary couldn't breathe. Her dress was so tight it required a smaller set of her corset, which had not been possible since she was seventeen years old, and had only been made possible by not eating anything after breakfast and employing three maids and her sister to pull the strings. But the dress had been made for Cassie before her seasons had been given up, and just this once her sister had agreed that Mary had more need of it than she did. As it was, Cassie was around here somewhere with Simon, dressed rather simply considering her tastes. But no one would know that either, especially as they had arrived twenty minutes earlier than Mary and in Simon's carriage.

It took Mary three seconds to realize that all of her work, even the tighter corset, was worth it. Not a soul in the room knew who she was, and it titillated them. She practiced her best debutante poise and airs, pretending that she was a more mature, more experienced version of Marianne Bray. She would never even feel the panicked fluttering in her heart or the pulse throbbing in her throat or the slightest wobble in her kneecaps. She didn't feel anything at all for the public.

She saw her sister out of the corner of her eye, dressed in her rather plain costume, a perfect choice for Cassandra, as no one would suspect her in something so drab, and received the smallest of winks. She acknowledged it with her eyes only, then surveyed the gathering with practiced indifference. She couldn't care less about the rest of the people here or if they could figure out her true identity.

She only had eyes for Geoff.

Or at least she would have when she found him.

Of all the eyes staring at her, none were his.

She frowned, but only slightly. It wouldn't do to appear dissatisfied with such a splendid gathering of Society's finest.

After all that flirting and teasing yesterday, he wasn't even looking for her? She scolded herself and started her way into the room, ignoring how the crowd parted like the Red Sea before her. Geoffrey wouldn't do that. He had been more than curious about seeing her in her costume. He had even appeared intrigued. Very intrigued. So much so that it had made Mary seriously consider surprising him more often.

Or, at least, warning him of a surprise. As she had yet to see him, the actual surprise had not occurred yet.

Perhaps he was looking for her now.

She nodded and smiled at several people, all of whom seemed to think they knew her, though their confusion was plain to see. It was far more entertaining than the entire season combined. This would be her crowning achievement.

Geoffrey would be pleased to hear that.

Assuming she ever found him.

She had several admirers approach, each looking more mystified than the one before, but somehow she was able to embrace her best version of Marianne and send them away without crushing them. She couldn't escape a dance or two, but she couldn't mind that when it allowed her a greater opportunity to survey the crowd.

Where was Geoff?

At long last, she spotted him in a corner, engaged in conversation, though with whom she could not see. She completed her dance with Mr. Tremont, who had made his identity known from the first moment, which quite defeated the purpose, as she pointed out. He hadn't cared. Nor had he cared overly much when she bid him farewell. He had always been one who admired attention more than personal interaction.

She was almost to Geoff when Henry Burlington stepped into

her path. His ensemble was resplendent to the point of distraction, and his mask held more detail than the most intricate of gowns. He took no pains to hide his identity either.

"You, my dear, are the breath of fresh air that awakens spring after winter's chill," he said with a low bow before her. "The Lord has blessed you with an overabundance of beauty, it puts all other creatures to shame. The sun itself would hide its comparative wretchedness when it sees you in your glory."

Mary raised a brow, which he would not be able to see behind her mask. His words dripped with flattery and fluff, hardly the sort of thing she expected from him, given their history. He had always said kind things, sincere things, with maybe a touch of excess, but never outright fawning, and never something so ridiculous.

"Ah, I see you have been stunned into silence by my words," he said, taking her hand tightly in his. "I am afraid I can have that effect on women. Allow me to prove it to you?"

Mary rolled her eyes and tugged her hand away. "No, thank you, Ferdinand," she said in a voice lower than her natural one.

His eyes widened at her use of his name.

"I prefer to keep my ears unsullied by too much hot air. Good evening." She inclined her head and swept around him.

Her eyes caught sight of a simply masked Colin Gerrard standing nearby, currently stifling laughter into his fist. Ah, so he had heard her. That made her absurdly delighted.

"Couldn't have said it better myself," he murmured with limited composure as she walked by.

"Coming from you, Mr. Gerrard, that says a great deal," she replied with a dip of her chin.

He saluted her with his glass, but made no further attempt to pursue.

She was grateful. She had to speak with Geoff now before anything else prevented it.

His back was to her, which suited her even better as it meant she would be able to sneak up on him without suspicion. A slow, catlike smile crossed her lips and she headed straight for him.

He shifted his weight and his companion was revealed.

Mary stopped dead in her tracks.

Lily Arden.

She was grateful that her mask covered half of her face, for it saved her the trouble of being completely in control of her expressions. Lily wore a small mask, but hardly enough to hide her identity. Not that it mattered, she was a breathtaking sight as it was. The violet ensemble made her skin seem perfectly translucent and her dark eyes looked even darker. Anybody would have been captivated.

But Geoff...

Just then Lily smiled, nodded, and walked away without looking back at him. But she still smiled.

Geoff watched Lily go, his expression furtive. Then it cleared and he started to scan the room.

The cold feeling in her stomach melted a little, and a satisfied smirk threatened to make an appearance. He was looking for her.

But first, a little fun.

She forced her face to be perfectly composed, with only the smallest of smiles tilting one side of her lips. She exhaled briefly, then started forward until she was just behind his left shoulder.

"Looking for someone in particular?" she asked, keeping her voice in that same low voice she had used with the others.

"As a matter of fact, yes," he replied, only glancing behind him for a second, as if he could not have cared who was addressing him.

She hummed a small laugh. "Perhaps I can help you look. I can be very useful when I put my mind to it."

He seemed to chuckle, then turned to face her. "Are you indeed?" His eyes met hers and she could see interest flare in them. "And have you put your mind to it?"

Mary allowed herself to smirk ever so slightly. "Would you like me to?"

His lips parted on a breath, which caught in his throat. He swallowed and Mary tilted her head ever so slightly up at him. "Something wrong?"

"No," he said softly, slowly shaking his head. "No, not a thing. Forgive me, but do I know you?"

Mary had to fight to keep from laughing. So he didn't know her.

He was so sure he would, and here he was, just as clueless as everyone else.

She smiled indulgently. "Perhaps."

"You will not tell me?" His eyes flashed again, this time with amusement. His mouth curved up in her favorite smile. "How can I know, then?"

"Why, you must discover for yourself, Mr. Harris." She batted her lashes flirtatiously. "It wouldn't do for a lady to reveal her secrets."

He laughed softly and gave her a small bow. "Of course not, my lady. I apologize. Perhaps I may tempt the lady with a dance? I wish to discover all that I can." He held out a hand to her expectantly, though his eyes never strayed from hers.

She seemed to consider the idea for a moment. A rather long moment. Enough that it started to draw comment from the people around them, who hadn't been paying attention until this moment. A lesser man might have faltered or begun to worry.

Not Geoffrey. His hand was as steady as his gaze, which only grew in heat and intensity the longer she waited. When she thought her toes would melt into the floor, she gave a little sigh and slid her hand into his.

"I suppose I must," she said airily. "I would dearly love to see you attempt to identify me."

He kissed her hand suddenly, making her gasp in shock.

"Who said I wanted to identify you?" he murmured as he came closer and began to lead her to the floor. "Perhaps I take great pleasure in mystery."

A hot shiver raced up Mary's spine. Now would be the time for her to say something witty, to keep the mystery alive, yet the only thoughts coursing through her mind were those that screamed that if he really knew her, he wouldn't say such things. He wouldn't look at her with such heat, nor tease her so suggestively.

She ought to tell him now, before things got out of hand. Before he said something he would regret when he knew who she was. Before she was overcome.

Something was happening to her that she couldn't pretend to

identify. Something only Geoff could do, whether it was the thought of him or the look of him. Something that had been coming on for some time now, but she hadn't noticed until this moment. She felt… alive. Excited.

Hopeful.

She couldn't tell him. She wanted to know what he would say now, what he would do next. She wanted to see him look at her this way for as long as possible. She wanted to keep the mystery alive herself. This was her last chance to be someone other than who she was, and heaven help her, she wanted this moment.

"Then a mystery you shall have," she murmured back, glancing at him from the corner of her eye.

He was smiling at her again, the sort of smile that made one's toes curl up and fingers tingle and breath quicken

He was no longer looking around the room.

He only looked at her.

It was heavenly. Except…

"What of the woman you were looking for?" she asked with a tilt of her head as they took their places.

He bowed with the men. "I never said who I was looking for."

She smirked. "True. But I have kept you from your looking. Should you not like to find them?"

He took her hand and led her through the dance. "Who says I haven't?"

Mary swallowed hastily and forced herself to take a quick, quiet breath to still her beating heart. Geoff was just as full of riddles as she herself was. It was maddening.

It was also a tantalizing sort of fun.

She tossed her hair, sending the tendrils of fabric dancing down her back. "Oh, I shouldn't like to make a certain other female angry by taking you from her."

"Must we talk of other females?" he scolded as he passed by her. "I wish to talk of you."

"There is very little to tell."

He turned with the movement and stared at her intently. "Oh, I doubt that very much. Come, tell me something. Anything."

What could she say? She wouldn't lie outright, but he already knew so much about her... Was there anything she had not told him?

"You must not tell a soul," she breathed as they proceeded down the line of couples, "but my late arrival tonight was a complete accident."

"You had no intention of making a spectacle of yourself?" he replied, his voice also low.

She hummed a low laugh. "Of course, I did. But I intended to be earlier."

"What kept you, pray tell?"

"My dress. Some rather important stitches had come undone, and one whole section of the skirt threatened to fall out of place. I would have tripped on it the moment I began to dance, and then quite a scandal would have erupted." She shuddered in horror—it really had been terrifying. "But as you can see, all is mended."

He made a soft noise of assent. "Quite mended," he murmured. "Looking at you, one would never have suspected. You are the epitome of perfection, and there is not an eye in this room that is not more fortunate for having seen you."

There was no breath left in her lungs. She almost swooned, but he held her still as they moved through the motions.

"You must not say such things, Mr. Harris," she attempted to scold. "A lady does not know how to take such praise."

"If you wish it, my lady, I will be silent on the subject. But you had to notice how the others stare."

"I had not," she said with the shrug of one shoulder. Oh, all right, so she could outright lie, but only when it didn't matter. "I pay little attention to what others think." That, at least, was truth.

He looked rather impressed. "You are more and more a mystery, my lady."

"A good mystery, or a bad one?" she could not help but ask.

His blue eyes blazed in their intensity as he looked at her. "Oh, a good one. Very, very good."

Mary swallowed hard and prayed she would live through the evening.

Geoffrey needed to be more careful. More than once already he had nearly revealed that he knew exactly to whom he was speaking. But how could he help it when Mary was being so maddeningly alluring? He had thought this whole charade of the masquerade would be hilarious, but he was so far from laughing it unnerved him. All he wanted to do was take Mary from this overcrowded, overheated ballroom and run away with her into the night. And she was willing, oh was she willing. Or at least, her character was. He had to believe that it was not entirely an act. She could not hide what was in her eyes, and in them, he saw interest, enjoyment, and at times, the same desire that swirled in his stomach. But she was playing a role, and he would let it play out.

But he would not make it easy for her.

Their dance had been delightful and full of shameless flirts and teases, and the two following it had been so full of unspoken emotion he'd nearly choked with it. How he was managing to at least appear so calm was beyond his comprehension. She was giving him her undivided attention, and that in excess. It had been almost two hours since she had arrived, and yet it seemed only minutes. He could have stayed with her like this for years…

His breath caught at the sudden pain in his chest. He wanted her for the rest of his life. He wanted her as she was tonight, as she had been yesterday, as she would be any given day or time. He wanted her. And more than that, she was his. There would never be anyone else for him, not in a million lifetimes. No one knew him so well, no one made him feel as she did, no one had such power over him, and no one could ever mean more to him than she did. She was his.

He looked down at her, only half listening to whatever it was she was saying. Had he never noticed how her lips moved so perfectly with every word she spoke? He was so captivated that he missed a question, which he discovered as she tilted her head up at him and said, "Well?"

He shook his head and smiled at her. "I apologize, my lady, what did you ask?"

"I am boring you," she pouted, turning on her heel to leave.

He seized her arm in a vice-like grip. She was not going anywhere. "You are not boring me."

She turned her head only and looked back at him. "Then why were you not listening?"

"I was thinking about you."

Her eyes widened in surprise. "You were?"

He only nodded.

"And that took all of your mental capacity so that there was no room for listening?"

He grinned at her wit. "When in the company of a captivating mystery such as yourself, merely thinking about you can absorb quite a good deal of mental capacity. I have been attentive this whole night, does that not signify?"

She shook her head firmly, pursing her lips together. "Attentiveness does not signify true attention. I've had many suitors that were the most attentive of men who never heard a single word I ever spoke. It was the most tiresome thing on the planet."

Geoff could not help it; he burst out laughing, turning a few heads in their direction. He knew she spoke truth from her experiences, and he loved that she would share that with him. It made his heart swell with pride and hope.

Mary turned to him fully, smiling herself. "You find me amusing, sir?"

He kept his hold on her arm, but gentled it considerably. He gave her a warm look. "Terribly so. And breathtaking."

She gave a little laugh that he heard the smallest sounds of surprise in. "Breathtaking? Surely not."

"Surely yes," he murmured, pulling the arm he held so that her hand rested on his chest, where his heart had begun to pound wildly. "Can you feel that?"

Her eyes dropped to her hand where it lay on his chest, and he saw her fight for a swallow. "I think... you flatter me, Mr. Harris."

"Oh, I hope I flatter you," he said earnestly, his eyes raking over her. "I hope I inspire you. I hope I steal into your dreams at night and never leave them."

Mary's chest heaved with her breaths that panted between her lips. Still she didn't meet his eyes. "I think you've said quite enough," she whispered.

"I don't think I have said nearly enough," he breathed, his own breath hard to come by. He had not said enough for a lifetime. "But if you cannot bear to hear any more, then I will be silent."

There could not have been anyone else in the room but the pair of them, not when he felt this intensity surrounding them, not when his pulse pounded in his ears, not when she stood before him in this way, so shy and modest, yet her hand rested over his heart. The heat pulsating from her touch coursed through his limbs, and he almost could not bear it. But he would bear it, and much more, if only...

She swallowed with great difficulty. "What else would you say?"

He had almost missed the words, so softly were they spoken. She wasn't attempting to mask her voice any longer, and he heard raw terror in it. Yet she had forced them out in spite of her feelings. She wanted to know.

He reached out his fingers and tilted her face up so she would meet his eyes. The lights of the ballroom danced within her incomparable eyes, glittering like diamonds in the heavens. He stroked the soft underside of her chin once.

"That you are exquisite," he told her, his voice low and warm. "That I have forgotten any other woman exists. That my heart has never known sensations like this. That one evening with you would never be enough. That I have realized that no one else will ever do for me. That I want nothing else but to adore you all the days of my life."

He leaned in as if he would kiss her. He had to kiss her. He wanted nothing more in the world than to kiss her.

She gasped, but he heard something in it and pulled back to look at her. Her eyes had filled with tears and she fought for composure.

"I have to go," she managed, her voice choked with emotion.

"What? Why?" he asked suddenly, bewildered as to what had happened.

Her face nearly crumpled and she shook her head. "You don't

know," she whispered harshly, yanking her hand from his chest and his hold. "You don't even know." She whirled away and ran, darting in and out of people so fast he had not the smallest hope of pursuing her.

People turned and stared at him, then whispered amongst themselves.

He didn't care.

Mary was gone.

What had he done?

"What in heaven's name did you say to that goddess?" Colin asked as he suddenly appeared at Geoff's side. "I thought the pair of you were getting on rather well."

"I told her the truth."

Colin winced and hissed loudly. "Never a good idea, old chap. Lies are much better."

Geoff didn't reply. He ached in places he didn't know he could ache, yearned for the moments to roll back, that he could live in those precious seconds where time had ceased to exist and Mary had been his.

"So what great truth did you reveal to the siren, hmm?"

"That I love her," Geoff murmured, still staring at the now vacated entrance where Mary had disappeared from view. "Well, not that, but that I adore her, and that I wanted to do so for the rest of my life."

Colin whistled low. "Bravo, Geoff," he chuckled. "Pity it didn't go over so well. Do you know who she was?"

"Mary." Even her name ached as it passed his lips.

"Pardon?" Colin asked as he took another glass from a passing footman, apparently having not heard.

"It was Mary."

Whatever beverage had been in the process of being drunk suddenly came blasting out of Colin's mouth, and unfortunately misted the nearest guests. But Colin, being Colin, didn't notice any of it as he stared at Geoff with large eyes. "That was... that was Mary?"

"Of course, it was Mary," Geoff snorted. "Who else?"

"Stop," Colin said, shaking his head quickly. "Stop, that couldn't have… Mary, really?"

Geoff rolled his eyes and moved to the nearest wall of the room and leaned on it, tilting his head back with a groan. "Who else, Colin? You think I would have said that to just anybody?"

"Wait, you knew it was her all the time?" Colin asked as he followed and stood facing him.

He nodded. "She didn't know that I knew, but I did. How could I not? I love her."

Colin paled. "I beg your pardon?"

Geoff glared at him. "I love Mary," he said in a slow, deliberate tone that left absolutely no room for misinterpretation. "I always have."

"Oh," Colin said softly, blinking in confusion. He swallowed and took another long drink of his beverage. "Correct me if I am wrong, I know so little of these things…"

Geoff waited, tempted to roll his eyes already.

"But… should you not have… run after her, then?" He gestured faintly in the direction of the exit once, and then again for effect.

Geoffrey winced and looked up at the ceiling.

"Would that not be the romantic thing to do?" Colin prodded thoughtfully, starting to smile ever so smugly, gesturing one last time towards the exit.

Geoff exhaled forcefully and took the liberty of banging his head against the wall repeatedly. Those nearest looked at him with concern, but quickly skirted away.

Colin watched with interest, then cleared his throat. "Oh dear. Geoffrey Harris, by all the authority given me by the Society of London, I hereby proclaim that you utterly fail at being a romantic hero."

Geoff glared at him again, which only served to make Colin chuckle.

"Come on," Colin said cheerily, throwing an arm about his shoulder. "Let's go somewhere much more suited to my taste and your stupidity. All these masks are making me very uneasy."

Geoff resisted. "Colin, I am not in humor for…"

"For an expeditious gathering of our friends to plot how to put you back on the romantic road and see you collect the fair hand of your lady love?" Colin finished with a wry rising of one brow. "Are you sure?"

Geoff opened his mouth in shock.

Colin grinned broadly. "Nice to know I can still take you by surprise, Harris. Come on, we've work to do."

Chapter Twenty Three

Three days. Three long and lonely days with nothing to do but sit in anguish and ponder over her abject stupidity. How could she have been such a fool?

She had fallen in love with Geoffrey Harris.

Again.

She slapped her bedcovers as she lounged against her headboard. She was a complete idiot. She had fallen for his charms, his goodness, and the way he made her feel. She had let herself become soft where he was concerned, and in spite of every attempt, she had let him take her heart.

And he didn't care at all.

How dare he make her fall in love with him again, after all this time, after all the fighting, after all her tricks of the season and his ill-humor and rudeness, after everything they'd come through, and then to make violent love to a perfect stranger in a mask? The gall of the man! Had he no decency or sense or honor at all?

And what of Lily Arden? He had fawned over her before, and again at the ball, when he was supposed to be waiting and looking for Mary, he had been at it once more!

She thought she knew him. She thought she could trust him. She barked a laugh at herself and closed her eyes. She had thought she could love him. Worse than that, she thought it might be possible for him to love her.

It was a ridiculous notion. He would never love her. Oh, he was a good friend when he chose to be, and she had no doubt he loved her dearly. But it would never be how a man should love a woman.

How she wanted him to love her. It didn't matter that lately he had been sweet and charming and made her feel things she'd thought her heart too sensible to feel again. It didn't matter that his eyes had somehow developed the power to melt her bones and set her heart aflame.

He had nearly professed his love for the stranger she had been that night. He was supposed to be looking for her, the real her, not the version of herself she had come as.

She screeched and slapped at the bed once more. It was maddening, this torment of reliving every aching moment. But she had to endure it. She had to live through it. It would be the only way she could shut him out of her heart for good.

Her heart was putting up an incredible resistance.

This had become a frequent occurrence since that night. She had refused all callers and notes, forcing Cassie to be her guard and postmaster for good measure. She couldn't see anybody and wouldn't hear from anybody until she had regained the good sense that had once been hers.

And she absolutely would not under any circumstances hear from, see, or have anything to do with Geoffrey Harris.

That she had been absolutely resolved upon.

Cassandra knew most of the story, and had been understandably confused, but as Mary had been prone to uncharacteristic outbursts of raw emotion of late, she was quite amenable to all of Mary's demands. She never once scolded her for the behavior, nor did she give her own opinions on the subject. She became, as it were, the Mary to Mary's current Cassandra.

It was quite revealing.

She didn't see much of her sister, as Mary chose to spend much of her time above stairs just to be safe. But Cassie would come and remind her that there were things to do, and Mary could only wallow in her self-inflicted torment for so long. She had completed much of the packing she needed for the countryside, but since Cassie had entered into an understanding with Lieutenant Wyndham, the plans for leaving were on hold.

Cassie would undoubtedly stay now that she would be restored to her position of former glory.

Mary would leave. As soon as she could.

Eventually she would return to her normal, sensible self. She would forget everything about this season, everything she had been and become, everything that had thrilled her and hurt her. She would go back to that girl who was ignored but respected, who could do as she pleased without care, and who had a heart strong enough to withstand love and disappointment.

She would forget it all.

Except she would not, could not, forget him.

And that infuriated her.

She couldn't sit here anymore, not today. She needed something to do. She thought about everything she could possibly do that didn't involve going down to the kitchens and scrubbing the floors until her fingers bled, although that held a certain poetic justice in her mind.

With another groan of frustration, she realized that everything she could do had been done.

Except one.

She gasped in relief, bounded off the bed, and dashed out of the door. She was halfway down the stairs when she caught sight of her sister's intended.

"Lieutenant Wyndham!" she called, gripping the railing as she almost tripped.

He stopped and looked up at her with a smile, completely ignoring her horrid state. "I do believe I have asked you to call me Simon, Miss Hamilton, as we are to be family."

She smiled as she reached the bottom of the stairs and looked up at him. "My apologies, of course. Simon."

"Yes, Mary?" he responded politely.

"Are your parents planning on hosting an engagement party or ball for you and Cassie?" she asked in a careful tone, hoping her eyes didn't look as wild as she currently felt. "Because I would dearly love to be able to do something, and I know that there is so much to be done..."

"You are too generous, as always, Mary," Simon gently interrupted with a smile. "My parents are not hosting a party for us, because someone else already insisted."

Mary frowned. That was odd. Not shocking or scandalous by any stretch. But simply... odd. "Oh, really? Who?"

"Colin Gerrard."

Mary's jaw would have hit the floor if it could go that far. She sputtered for a few moments, then managed, "C-Colin Gerrard?"

Simon seemed to realize he had said something he shouldn't, and his eyes immediately shifted for an escape. "Erm, yes."

"I was not aware you were acquainted with the Gerrards so well," she said slowly, her eyes narrowing.

"We're not," he fumbled. "That is to say, we were not. But recently we have..."

"How recently?" Mary interrupted, far less gentle than he had been with her. "You've been thought dead for weeks and you only just returned to life days ago. How have you become friends with Colin Gerrard?"

Simon's eyes widened and he stepped back hastily. "I didn't know this would be such a problem, Mary, I just..."

She forced herself to take a deep breath and release it slowly. "It's not a problem," she replied in a remarkably controlled voice. "Not at all. I'm very fond of Colin Gerrard. However, I am curious as to how the two of you have become so closely connected that he wishes to host a party for your engagement to my sister. Now, can you elaborate on that?"

The poor man struggled for words, and Mary felt the smallest bit of pity for him. Eventually, he sighed. "Colin was one of the men who was instrumental in seeing me returned to England and having the rumors of my demise quieted. He is the one who brought me to my family and then directly here to your sister."

Mary frowned and bit her lip. "That is even odder. Colin would have no knowledge of your particular situation of late, the only person I told was..." Her stomach dropped to her knees and her eyes widened.

Simon backed up another few feet.

"Simon," Mary said slowly, wetting her suddenly parched lips, "who told Colin Gerrard about your situation?"

"I don't know all that transpired, Mary, believe me, and..."

"Simon."

He winced, and released a heavy sigh. "All right, I was sworn to secrecy, but I'll tell you, Mary, because I love your sister, and I hope to one day love you as my sister, and at this moment I am very afraid of you." He hesitated, then shook his head on another exhale. "Colin was acting on orders of Geoffrey Harris. He organized the whole thing. He and his friends discovered what had happened, where I was, and worked with the Navy to bring me home to England swiftly. Colin wishes to host the event because it will highlight my safe return as well as thrust your sister back into the popularity she enjoyed before I left with the benefit of his approval. This, I believe, was also Harris's doing."

Mary couldn't breathe. The room spun. She grabbed at his wrist to keep herself from falling.

"Mary? Are you all right?" Simon's voice reached her ears as if from a great distance.

"Fine," she whispered, fighting to keep a clear head and her wits about her. "Why couldn't you say anything?"

"I don't think that signifies."

"Tell me," she insisted, gipping his wrist more tightly.

He sighed and took her arm to steady her. "Because Harris didn't want anyone to think he had done this for any personal reasons. I could tell Cassandra, but no one else, not even you."

"Not me?" She looked up at him in confusion. "Why not me?"

"From what Colin told me, you and Harris had only just made peace with each other. He didn't want you to think he did this to improve his standing or to put you in his debt or anything of the sort. He just wanted..."

"To make Cassie happy," Mary murmured.

Simon nodded once, watching her carefully.

"He's a good man," she forced herself to admit, feeling as though her words were ripped form her.

"The best," Simon agreed. He had the decency to sound

reluctant as he said it, and he kept his hold on her firm.

She couldn't hate Geoff. It wasn't in her. She loved him, and that was his fault. He made her love him, and she hated him for it. Even when she was hurt and furious with him, he did something to make her love him even more.

It was the most infuriating thing about him.

She wouldn't let him do this to her.

She nodded at Simon and quickly made her way past him.

"Mary? Where are you going?" he called after her, sounding more than a little worried.

"The kitchens!" she replied in a tense voice. "I feel the need to scrub some floors."

The urge to scrub floors had only lasted a few minutes. The cook, a dear sweet woman who was Irish by nature and had the temper to match, had quickly and most emphatically sent Mary from the kitchens with screeches of dismay that could be heard up and down the streets of the neighborhood. Mary had tried to protest her case, but her words fell on deaf ears. Only on her exit from the kitchen did she notice the scandalized expression on the kitchen staff's faces. Surely it was not so shocking that she wanted to work her fingers to the bone out of frustration over a man who simply refused to get out of her head and heart.

Then again…

She set her jaw determinedly and moved on to the housekeeper's closet and began working at polishing the silver. She had seen Winston and Mrs. Evansdale do this for years, surely this was something she could manage without offending anyone.

It was an oddly soothing task. The harder she rubbed at the silver, the sooner its surface gleamed in the afternoon light. She imagined doing the same thing to her soul, rubbing at the stained and tarnished parts that kept her from shining the way she had once done. She imagined scrubbing Geoffrey out of her mind, forcing away all thoughts of his smile and the warmth of his smile, forever erasing the need to find him first when she entered a room or the jump her heart made when he called on her. She was a pathetic creature and he had done that to her.

She muttered angrily as she replaced the spoons moved on to candlesticks, rubbing at them with just as much determination. He would not get the best of her; he would be gone from her heart and her mind. He could be as good a man as ever lived, and probably was, her softer side interjected, but that did not mean she had to worship the ground upon which he walked.

If only that ground didn't call to her as a paradise in the desert to a wanderer.

A brief growl escaped her as she rubbed harder at the candlestick.

How dare he make such declarations to a strange woman when he made her feel this way. How dare he!

A distressed screech met her ears and she turned to find Mrs. Evansdale staring at her in horror, her plump hands clasping over her mouth, and Winston by her side, composed but for his eyes, which blinked slowly in disbelief.

That was it, then. Mary sighed and handed the candlestick over to Mrs. Evansdale and made for her room without protest. It was the one place she was of use to anybody anymore. Or at the very least it was the one place she could go without making any trouble.

After nearly half an hour of attempting to read, fix her hair, organize her wardrobe, and sort her personal library, she had to admit that she was absolutely useless to everybody, including herself. She could go call on Kate. She was growing large with her first child and could probably use some cheering up.

That would not be wise, she reconsidered. She had no cheer to spread, and Kate would become a victim of hearing all of her troubles, which would lead to her wanting to fix them, which would only depress Mary further as she knew there was no hope for her.

She flopped herself back onto her bed and tossed an arm over her eyes with a moan. She had never been so miserable in her life. How did a man turn a sensible woman into a weeping mess of feelings, and when the tears had run dry, into an angry collection of nonsensical thoughts and wild emotional bursts? Her heart felt stretched and overworked, and she feared it was headed for the all-consuming numbness her sister had spoken of only days ago.

Perhaps her life wouldn't seem such a mess at that point.

Rapid knocks suddenly sounded at the door.

"Who is it?" Mary called, not moving an inch.

"Mary, open up."

She moved her arm quickly and looked at the door in disbelief. That was Geoff's voice. At her door. Ordering her. She scowled and replaced her arm. "Go away."

"No."

"I am not receiving. Go home."

"No, Mary. Open the door."

"How many times do I have to say no for you to understand that I don't want to see you?"

"As many as you feel like saying. I'm not leaving until I see you."

"Fine. Stand there all day. Stand there all week, I don't care."

"Mary, don't be an idiot."

She barked a laugh. "You are the one ordering me to let you into my bedchamber after I have repeatedly refused. Who is the idiot here?"

She heard him shuffle and exhale sharply. "Mary, I won't ask again."

She snorted and shook her head. She would not say another word. He could demand all he liked, she would remain firm and resolute.

He knocked more loudly. "Mary, I'm serious. You have to talk to me."

She did not have to do any such thing. She settled herself more completely onto her bed, smirking in satisfaction.

His knocks became a pounding. "Mary! You have been avoiding me for three days, I will not be ignored any longer!"

She rolled onto her side, facing the wall. She would be strong. She would be indifferent. She shut her eyes tightly as a protection against his words.

"I will break down this door."

Her eyes snapped open. He what?

"I will count to three, Mary, and if you do not let me in, I will come in on my own. One."

She rolled over and looked at the door in horror.

"Two."

She jumped from the bed and scrambled back. He couldn't break in. Her door was too sturdy, and Geoff was not that strong.

"Three."

The next instant her door nearly exploded off of its hinges and it swung open, hitting her wall with a loud bang. Geoff stood in the doorway almost majestically, his eyes instantly finding hers, and they blazed with fury. It was a powerful sight, and much to her self-loathing, her heart skipped several beats.

He did not say a word as he stared at her, though he took in her rather unkempt state with interest.

Mary found her spine and swallowed, forcing her face into a glower. "Happy now, are you?"

"Do I look happy?" he asked in a careful voice that didn't bother to hide the anger emanating off of him.

"You look like a wild animal," she informed him with a snort. "What, was my no so offensive to your ears that it unleashed you?" She glanced at her door, then back at him. "You owe me a new door."

"Forget the damned door. Why have you refused to see me?"

"I had no idea you had been trying to see me," she sniffed, feeling rather proud that her words were true.

He took two steps towards her. "I have called every day, three times each. I was refused every time."

"Except this time," she muttered, "so obviously something went wrong."

"And I sent notes."

"I never saw them."

"I figured as much."

"I should think the point rather evident by now."

His eyes narrowed. "Quite. Which is why I am here now."

"In my bedchamber," she reminded him. She tilted her head up at his set face. "Do I need to scream for help?"

His shoulders drooped ever so slightly, and the tension in his jaw relaxed. "What happened, Mary? Why do you suddenly hate me?"

She scoffed and looked away, feeling her knees begin a traitorous quiver at the hurt she could hear in his words. "If you have to ask…"

"Of course, I have to ask!" he yelled as he threw his arms out wide. "I don't understand you!"

"Well, that we can agree on!" she yelled back, pushing off of the wall she had been standing against. "If you did, you wouldn't be such an ignorant, arrogant louse who barges into a woman's room when she expressly tells him no!"

He snarled and ran his hands through his hair. "You have this impossible ability to drive me to my wits end, Mary! It's maddening to the point of insanity, which, yes, led me to break down your door just so I could talk to you!"

"If I am so maddening," she sneered, "then why bother coming at all? I was well enough off ignoring your existence, you have not done me any favors today."

"I am well aware of that!" he bellowed. "And I'm wondering that myself." He whirled away, clenching his hands. "I have never been so furious in all my life, and it's your fault. I should never have said those things to you at the masquerade!"

Mary opened her mouth to argue back, and then realized what he had said. Words evaporated.

He looked back at her when she didn't respond.

"Wh-what things?" she finally said, her entire body still.

His look softened and he shook his head. "Mary. Did you really think that I didn't know it was you?"

Her mouth dropped open, and she couldn't feel anything.

He straightened and faced her fully. "Did you really think that I would say such intimate things to a stranger? Mary…"

"How could you possibly…?" she began as her heart unsteadily began to beat again.

"I knew it was you from the moment you entered the room." His words were soft, but they echoed as if he had shouted them. They replayed in her mind over and over, and each time it made her pulse pound ever harder.

"I knew it was you," he said again, coming towards her. "And every word I said was meant for you and you alone."

Her mouth worked in disbelief. "Why would you...? How could you...?" She sputtered hopelessly as she tried to get out a single coherent thought. "What you said... You weren't serious?"

"I was serious. In fact, I believe I have never been more serious."

How could that be? His words had belonged in the mouths of lovers and rogues, and were said to other sorts of women than she. She could only form the questions in her eyes. "But... but Lily Arden..." she stammered.

"...is a sweet girl who is madly in love with someone else and needed a friend. She has no more interest in me than I in her." He gave her a soft smile that made it impossible to disbelieve him. In fact, it made her fall even more in love with him.

Could it be possible? Could he really have meant everything he had said to her? All of those things she felt... could it have been real?

He took pity on her, closing the distance so that there were only a few feet separating them. "Mary, you know me. I am no flirt, I'm not a rogue, I couldn't care less about Society and reputations, and I loathe consorting with husband hunters. I could never say such things merely to say them. I meant them for you." He stepped closer, his expression earnest.

Her heart fluttered in spite of herself. "Geoff," she said softly.

"I have no expectations," he told her quietly. "I'm not asking for anything. I just..." He trailed off uncertainly, his eyes searching hers.

"Just what?"

He sighed softly. "I love you."

She blinked slowly, sure she had heard him wrong. "You... what?"

"I love you, Mary."

Her knees, so unsteady under pressure, gave way completely and she grabbed at her bedpost. "You... love me?"

"I do," he said simply.

She shook her head. No, it was not possible. She loved him. And he felt nothing. That was how this worked, how it had always worked. But he sounded so sure, so calm. Perhaps she could forgive him for being stupid at the masquerade, but that didn't mean that he could just say these things to her. Didn't he know what it cost her to even listen?

He said her name softly, but she couldn't look at him.

"Mary," he murmured again, "I love you."

She bit back a gasp and looked at him in disbelief. "Why now, Geoffrey?" she asked, not bothering to keep the quiver out of her voice. "After all of these years, why now?"

He shook his head and shrugged helplessly. "I don't know. That is the most maddening part of this whole affair. How long? I don't know. Why now? I don't know. When? I don't know. All I know is that I love you, Mary Hamilton, and all I want is for you to give me a chance."

A chance? She almost laughed, except she failed to find the humor. Her heart ached with his words, her mind raced with her doubts, and her hands clenched the bedpost more tightly to keep her upright. "I don't know if I can believe you," she whispered. "With all that we have been through this season, how can I believe what you are saying?"

He nodded in understanding. "Would you believe that I come to town just for you? That I have for years?"

Her eyes widened and her breath caught. "That's not possible," she managed.

"It's the truth," he assured her in soft, warm tones. "You know me, Mary. You know I hate Society and balls and parties and clubs and theater. I detest London and everything about it. You know that. But every season, I come. I ask myself why, and the answer is simple; I come because you are here." He shook his head and came closer until he was so close to her that she could feel the warmth of his body. "And I always have, and always will, want to come just to be with you." He cupped her cheek in one hand and stroked it softly with his thumb. "It's all the reason I will ever need."

She couldn't believe him. She couldn't...

"Mary," he whispered, looking into her eyes with such tenderness her heart nearly burst. "I love you. I have been in love with you for years, I was just too blind to see it. I want to be with you today and tomorrow and every day after. And unless you tell me otherwise, I am going to kiss you now, because I cannot bear not to anymore."

She would never breathe normally again. Her eyes dropped to his mouth, and her lips parted of their own accord.

He leaned in, stroking her cheek softly once more, and then pressed his lips to hers. Soft and sweet, his lips caressed hers, more perfect and magical than even her most vivid imaginations. It seared her soul as if he had branded her with his passion, simmering so near the surface. She was his. She would always be his.

He loved her. She could feel it, could taste it, and she wanted it.

Before she could arch up for more, encourage him, or make any sort of sound, he pulled back, as breathless as she was. He touched his forehead to hers, still cupping her cheek in his hand. "Think about it, Mary. I love you. I want… all I want is you." He sighed, pressed his lips to hers once more, and left the room quickly, as if he couldn't bear another minute.

Slowly, very slowly, thought and sense and feeling returned to her. She stared out of the open doorway, ignoring the splintered wood around the locking mechanism, ignoring the crooked manner in which the door hung against the wall, ignoring everything.

Geoffrey Harris had kissed her. Had professed his love for her. Wanted her.

She gasped a shuddering, body-shaking gasp and sank to the chest at the foot of her bed with a sharp thud.

Heavens above. What had just happened?

Chapter Twenty Four

"What did Geoffrey want?"

Mary blinked slowly and looked back at the doorway. "Pardon?"

Cassie's brows rose with interest. "What did Geoff want? For once, I didn't eavesdrop, so I really have no idea what went on up here." She looked at the door for a long moment, but didn't comment as she looked back at her.

Mary swallowed and shook her head, trying to diminish the fog that had formed. "Don't pretend that you had nothing to do with it," she scolded, trying to sound firm. "I know you sent for him."

"I didn't," Cassie insisted, shaking her head quickly.

Mary gave her a look. "You did so. You disapprove of my behavior and sent for him. I know you, Cassie."

"No, Mary," Cassandra said again, growing very serious. "I didn't. I have been vigilant in keeping him from coming inside the last three days. I've taken all of his notes and kept them from you, as you requested, and not said a thing about it."

Mary hummed in disbelief. "Yet he came."

"Winston answered the door, and I didn't get to him fast enough. But Simon and I tried to stop Geoff from coming up. I told him you weren't receiving, not even for him. We stood in the stairwell and barred him entry."

That surprised her. "You did?"

Her sister met her eyes and sighed. "He threatened me, Mary. Geoffrey Harris, undoubtedly the sweetest and most gentleman-like man in England, threatened me. And he threatened Simon, who is larger and stronger, I daresay. And I can see he broke your door," she said with a flick of her wrist.

Mary looked at the door again.

"I think he wanted to see you, Mary," Cassandra said unnecessarily. "At any cost."

Unbidden tears sprang into her eyes and she clamped her lips together. She glanced back at her sister, who smiled softly at her tears.

"Have you... have you refused Colin's party tonight?" Mary managed to squeak out.

Cassie's brows furrowed in confusion. "No, of course not. We must see what his ballroom can accommodate for our engagement party, so of course Simon and I are..."

"I mean for me," Mary interrupted gently, allowing a smile to cross her lips. "Have you refused for me?"

Now Cassie grinned broadly. "No. No, I have not."

"Good." Mary sniffed back the last of her tears. "I'll need you to help me get ready, Cassie. I have something very important to attend to."

Her sister's grin turned positively fiendish, and right away they went to work.

It was several hours before they were able to depart for Colin's party, but she was satisfied that it would be well worth it. She had chosen to wear the one gown he had insisted she get; the dark blue that shimmered like the night sky. She had already worn it this season, which would undoubtedly scandalize those who thought she had been permanently transformed into one of the more extravagant debutantes of Society. She didn't care. That had been the first instance where she had seen something other than friendship in his eyes. Now that she knew he loved her, she wanted to see that look again.

The carriage ride was unbearably long. She didn't live far from Colin Gerrard, but when one was as popular amongst society as he was, the sheer volume of guests in attendance was astounding. The line of carriages hardly seemed to move at all. It didn't help that her heart raced so fast that she thought she'd faint.

She fidgeted with her hair, which was more intricate and

elaborate than any style she had attempted yet, and felt as though it might all tumble down at any moment. She had been repeatedly assured that it wouldn't; that it was, in fact, very secure, and beyond that, quite becoming on her. She was not so sure, but she was willing to trust that her sister would not let her make a fool of herself on such an important occasion.

There was nothing Cassie appreciated more than a stunning entry and the reputation to sustain it.

Mary didn't care about either of those things. She just wanted to see Geoff.

The entire afternoon she had been an absolute mess, fluttering between ebullient joy and helpless tears of disbelief. And she hadn't even spoken with Geoff yet. He didn't know her feelings. He might have suspected, given her reaction to his words and his kiss, but he hadn't let her respond.

And she very much wanted to respond.

At long last, she was in the ballroom with the rest of London. It really was a stunning room, and would definitely suit a party given for her sister. Grand steps led the way down from the doorway onto the dance floor itself with fine balconies overlooking the dancing. All railings were congested, as no sensible person wanted to be among the first dancers. Yet dancing was occurring, and it was plain to see that the party was well under way.

She had to find Geoff, but in this crush, she couldn't even find Colin and he was the host.

She released an irritated sigh and looked longingly towards the wall where she would have situated herself only months before. But she had promised Geoff that she would enjoy the rest of the season, and she would live up to it. She made her way down the stairs to the dance floor, knowing that it wouldn't take long for one of her former admirers to ask her for a dance. She prayed it would be one she could tolerate.

"Miss Hamilton."

She smiled, not bothering to hide her relief as Thomas Granger approached. "Mr. Granger. I hope you are here to ask for a dance."

"I am indeed." He bowed smartly before her, returning her smile and holding out a hand for her.

She took it and curtseyed. "Then lead the way, good sir."

He took her to the head of the line of couples just as the music was beginning again, and soon they were dancing with the rest. Mary hoped Geoff would be here soon. She wasn't sure how long she could wait.

She smiled at Mr. Granger as she passed him, and plotted how she could discover his true feelings for Lily Arden. Or perhaps she could plant a seed...

Mary laughed merrily as she completed yet another turn of the jig. She was dancing with Lord Oliver now, and he had always been one of her favorite dance partners. He was a lively and entertaining dancer, and never presumed, which was a refreshing change from some of the others.

This was her fifth dance in a row, and still she hadn't seen Geoffrey. She'd tried to look for him as best as she could, but it was proving difficult with the sheer volume of guests in attendance and the movements of the dancing were not particularly conducive to looking. Still, she was enjoying herself now that the majority of her more ridiculous suitors had moved on to other ladies.

Lord Oliver himself had joined the pursuit for Miss Catherine Blythe, just returned from her tour of Switzerland. Mary didn't know her, but hoped the girl was ready for the onslaught of admirers.

As she waited for her turn in the next movement, she took the opportunity to look up at the balconies and guests at the rails on the landing. All were filled with various members of Society, some who watched the dancing, others merely conversing while fluttering their fans. It was amusing to watch even from this distance.

Her eyes suddenly clashed with a very familiar pair of blue ones, and her heart leapt into her throat. He was on the landing, standing alone, watching her. Only her.

He didn't flinch or look away when she stared back. He didn't move a single muscle.

She nearly missed the next movement of the dance so entranced was she by his expression and intensity. She continued to dance, looking back up at him as often as she could. He watched with all the steadiness of a hawk and looked just as predatory.

What was he thinking? How did he feel? Could he possibly be angry with her for not seeking him out? For dancing with other men? His expression was impossible to translate, even for one as fluent in all things him as she was.

She turned and twirled and hopped as the dance required, but always her eyes returned to him, wanting him to indicate something, anything to her. A wink, a smile, a frown, any show of emotion to indicate where she stood with him at this moment. He loved her, he'd said as much, but she knew full well what a torment of emotion that alone brought.

When the dance was over, she would tell him everything. Absolutely everything.

Again she met his eyes, and this time, she held his gaze even through the dance. Her heart pounded so hard against her chest she couldn't breathe. But she would keep watching him, beg him to wait for her.

He pushed off of the balcony and began to move, keeping his eyes on her as he did so.

Where was he going?

She watched him walk, panic rising. What was he doing?

His eyes, so powerful even from this distance, held her captive, stared at her as he walked along the railings.

And then he was gone. He was lost in the crowd and she couldn't see him. For what felt like ages she scanned the crowd, but she never saw him.

She couldn't restrain a horrified gasp. He couldn't have left!

Emotions welling within her, she fled the dancing, ignoring the other dancers and Lord Oliver. She weaved in and out of other couples, running as hard as she could for the stairs. She had to find him, had to tell him now, before anything else happened. She would embarrass herself in front of all of England and more to confess everything.

She pushed through people clogging the stairs and panted with her frantic exertions. People cried out in dismay at her behavior, but she ignored them all. She had to find him, she had to tell him, he had to know…

A sudden force stopped her on the stairs and nearly sent her tumbling. Strong hands gripped her arms to keep her steady, and she glanced up to find herself face to face with Geoffrey himself.

"Geoff!" she gasped in panicked relief, half of a sob, and more than a little breathless.

"Mary?" he asked in soft confusion, his eyes searching hers with concern.

She inhaled shakily, tears rising, wondering what to say. But looking into his eyes, seeing what he felt, words were meaningless. She swallowed and reached up to touch his jaw softly, her lower lip quivering.

He exhaled a soft sigh even as his eyes widened at her touch.

She couldn't take it any longer.

She slid her hand around to the back of his neck and pulled him in, although who kissed whom first would be up for debate. He seized her lips instantly, and she was just as fierce. There was no holding back, no restraining the heat and desire and emotions rising and thriving between them. She poured every ounce of herself into this kiss, her lips molding and caressing as his were possessive and hungry. One of his hands gripped her hair and pulled her in impossibly closer, while the other reached around her back and supported her. She fisted her free hand in his coat and tugged him as close as she could. It wasn't close enough.

Everything she had ever felt for him rose to the surface. There were no secrets any longer as love, passion, and need all burned like fire. This was no mere kiss; he was claiming her as she was claiming him, and it was long overdue for them both.

The room vanished, time ceased to exist, and it seemed as if the music from the orchestra swirled around them, a symphony to their moment. It was too perfect, but she would take it. She would take eternities of such moments, such feelings, with him.

Someone very close to them cleared their throat rather loudly.

"Begging your pardon," Colin's voice muttered, breaking the moment. He coughed politely, then said, "But the two of you need to disengage and come with me. Now."

For a moment, they only stood there, suspended in the aftermath, foreheads touching, their breath mingling together.

Again, Colin cleared his throat. "Now."

Slowly, very slowly, Mary pulled back. Then it occurred to her that there was no music playing. Not a single sound in the entire overcrowded ballroom. Every eye was fixed on them, and in just a quick glance, she saw shock, dismay, abject horror, and in some rare cases, unfettered delight.

She felt her cheeks flush immediately, but then Geoff slid his hand into hers and interlaced their fingers, giving her a gentle squeeze. She looked up into his face and saw that he was fighting laughter.

The same urge welled up in her, and she grinned at him. With a faint wink, he squeezed her hand again, the promise of things to come.

Obediently they followed Colin down the rest of the stairs and out of the ballroom, not meeting any eye but those of their friends, all of whom were either delighted or stunned or both. Mary faintly heard Colin's brother Kit instruct the musicians to start up again, the room once more turned to a buzzing of conversation, and presumably, the dancing continued. They kept walking, however, Colin leading them and not saying a single word.

When they could no longer hear the music or the chatter from the room, Colin turned down an empty corridor. Only then did he turn and face them. His expression was vacant of any emotion.

"All right," he said quietly, looking at them both, "if anybody asks, I was a perfect host and scolded you soundly for such a scandalous display in my home. And thereafter I was a perfect chaperone and never let the two of you out of my sight." He turned to Geoff with the barest hint of a smile. "Geoff, I hereby rescind my proclamation where you are concerned. Consider yourself a roaring success." He bowed smartly, then walked passed them back towards the ballroom.

They were alone.

Entirely.

Mary exhaled, and looked up at Geoff, who had already been looking at her.

Without a word, he pushed her against the wall and once more his lips were on hers, just as insistent and hungry as they had been moments before. His hands held her face, her hands latched into his hair, and she matched him kiss for bone-melting kiss. Then it occurred to her, ever so faintly, that she had yet to actually tell him what she needed to.

"Geoff," she murmured when he let her breathe.

His lips had no reprieve for her as they made their way up her jaw.

"Geoff!" she hissed as her eyes fluttered helplessly.

"What?" he said against her skin, perfectly content to continue tormenting her.

"I have something to say."

He chuckled breathlessly. "Oh, have you?" He took her lips in another long, lingering kiss.

With a whimper, she broke off and put a hand on his chest. "Yes," she said, her voice sounding like a mix of a whisper and a sigh, but it was firm.

He sighed and looked at her, still keeping her face between his hands. "What is it, Goose? Make it quick, I have work to attend to." His eyes told her exactly what he meant by that, and her stomach nearly burst into flame.

She swallowed hard, then cleared her throat. "I... I thought about what you said."

One side of his mouth curved up in a grin. "Yes, I gathered as much from your delightful ruse on the stair."

She blushed and ducked her head. He was quick to tilt it back up.

"Don't be embarrassed," he laughed softly. "I loved every second of it."

"I thought you were leaving." Strangely, she found herself close to tears again and she shook her head. "I thought you were angry and leaving, and I couldn't..."

He laughed again and stroked her cheeks. "I was coming to dance with you, Goose. I'd had enough of watching you dance with other men. I wanted to claim what I have always thought was mine."

A hot thrill shot through her and she smiled at him. "Then why, if you felt that way, didn't you let me answer you earlier today?"

He groaned and dropped his hands to her shoulders. "I was so headstrong, bursting into your room like that, and then telling you all of those things... I didn't want to presume to..."

"I would have said yes."

He stopped talking and stared at her, eyes wide.

Mary smiled and touched his chin softly. "I was going to say yes."

Geoffrey stared at her for a long moment without speaking. Then he shook his head on an exhale, then leaned forward and gently kissed her, nuzzling softly.

Mary felt the emotion in his kiss, the disbelief, the joy... She understood, and her heart thudded with the same emotions. "Geoff," she whispered, laying a hand on his cheek.

"Yes, love?" he murmured as his lips dusted her cheek.

It took her a moment to find words after the endearment, and she absently toyed with his waistcoat. "I was in love with you."

She felt him stiffen. "Was?" he asked slowly.

She nodded, still not looking at him. "For most of our friendship, even at the beginning, I was in love with you."

He chuckled in a low tone. "I know. I found your diaries."

She closed her eyes as more embarrassment rushed in.

"Mary..." he said softly, touching her cheek.

She nuzzled against his touch and met his eyes. "Then I grew up and I was so sure, so determined that I wasn't in love with you. I knew you'd never love me in return, so it was easy to believe."

He shook his head, his eyes full of anguish. "I am so sorry."

"I'm not blaming you," she assured him, laying her hand on his chest. "You were just too perfect, and I was... Well, I was me."

"I love you," he said fiercely, placing a hand over hers. "Just as you are, just as you always have been."

She smiled and pulled his hand to her lips. "I had hidden my feelings so deep I didn't even know I still had them. It didn't occur

268

to me until recently that they had always been there." She shook her head, tears threatening once more. "I had roomfuls of men. Great men, fine men, fops, rogues, scholars… Roomfuls of men, and all I really wanted was to see your face among them."

His breath caught and she stroked his cheek gently. "I just wanted you. I love you, Geoffrey Harris, and I only want you."

This time, she pulled him in for a kiss, and this one was long, leisurely, and so filled with passion and promise that it made her weep. They had all the time in the world to be together, to love each other as they should have done years ago and every day since.

A screeching filled the corridor and Geoff broke off with a groan. He touched his forehead to Mary's and looked towards the sound.

Cassie and Simon stood at the entrance, looking bewildered and delighted.

"It's your sister," he murmured, turning back and closing his eyes.

"I figured as much," she muttered back.

"Geoffrey Harris," Cassie called, her grin evident. "What are you doing with my sister?"

"Cassie, go away!" Mary yelled back with a roll of her eyes.

"Be nice," Geoff whispered, unable to keep from smiling himself.

Mary gave him a look. "What transpired before she appeared, that was nice. That scene in the ballroom, also quite nice. Being interrupted, not so nice. I'm entitled to being more than a little agitated."

He swallowed and let out a shaky chuckle.

"Ahem," Simon called out.

"Oh, lord," Mary moaned, dropping her head back against the wall. "I may kill them both."

"Harris, I believe as the future brother-in-law of the woman you are with at this moment, I must ask… what are your intentions?" Simon asked, sounding innocently concerned.

Cassie giggled. "Yes, Geoff. What are your intentions?"

Now Geoff growled. "You impertinent children. Very well, my

intentions are to continue my activities with Miss Hamilton here, marry her as soon as we can manage, and spend the rest of my life giving you ungrateful cretins as many nieces and nephews as I can. Fair enough?"

While Simon coughed in surprise and Cassie squealed with glee, Mary grinned rather salaciously at him. "My, my, that does sound appealing," she murmured.

"Don't you start," he hissed, giving her a warning look. "I'm on thin ice as it is."

"Well, perhaps we should announce your engagement presently? Quite a few people are talking about it," Cassie said, her voice sounding rather authoritative. "Reputations must be preserved, and all that. Simon and I will start spreading the word that the two of you have been engaged for some time, but due to his misfortune and then reappearance and our subsequent engagement, you chose to keep your own a private matter. I think your friends will corroborate it."

"Whatever you like, Cassie," Mary called out with a sigh. "You know best."

Geoff bit back a laugh and touched his forehead to hers again.

"And you had better be married as soon as banns can be read," Cassandra continued, as if she hadn't said anything. "Three weeks. I'll get to work on that right away."

"Very good, Cassie," Geoff said, staring at Mary with warmth. "It sounds grand."

"You need to make a re-appearance," she went on. "People may think you've run off to Gretna Green, and that wouldn't be…"

"Thank you, Cassie," they chimed in together.

"Darling, let's go back in and start quelling rumors," Simon said quietly, though his voice carried. "They'll be along shortly. Now, who do you think we should start with?"

"Oh, Geoffrey's friends, absolutely," Cassie said as they turned to go and continued down the hall. "We need their cooperation first of all."

When it was silent once more, Geoff and Mary burst out laughing together.

"Well, it appears your sister is now planning our wedding,"

Geoff said when he could speak.

"So it would seem," Mary replied with a sigh, her hands sliding around his neck.

"I suppose the polite thing to do would be to officially ask for your hand in marriage," he mused, his hands finding her waist.

Mary nodded soberly. "That would be very polite, yes."

He cleared his throat and became serious. "Mary Hamilton, would you do me the honor of consenting to marry me?"

"Geoffrey Harris, I would be delighted," she replied very properly. "Now stop talking and kiss me."

He grinned rather wickedly. "I love you."

She matched his grin. "I love you."

And then Geoffrey, being the epitome of a gentleman, after all, complied with the lady's request.

Epilogue

The hallway was littered with men. It couldn't be helped when they'd all arrived in such haste and without plan, and considering the bustle of the house, there were no servants available to prepare a room for any of them. No one complained, not even the stray servant that had to weave between the lot of them to get by.

Not that Geoff cared about his companions or their well-being. He had quite enough to be getting on with.

No one was telling him a blasted thing.

He had been sitting out here in the hall for hours without any idea of what was going on. Duncan paced anxiously back and forth, Colin sat against a wall and stared at the ceiling as if it held all the answers, Derek stood like a soldier by the stair in preparation to ride off as needed, and Nathan leaned against a wall nearby with his head bowed. All of them seemed as anxious as he, but that wasn't possible. They had all lived through this. They were all fathers multiple times over.

But Geoff, despite his almost six years of marriage, was not.

He knew how Mary had ached for children, cried in the night when she thought he was asleep, and wondered if her advancing age had prevented it being possible.

She was not that old, as he was constantly reminding her, and women of thirty-three had children all the time. But she was convinced that this was all her fault, that she had missed her opportunity, and she had prevented him from the joys of fatherhood.

He'd done everything in his power to persuade her otherwise, and assured her that being with her was enough.

The six years they had spent together had been the best years of his life. He had grown to love her more and more every day. Not that theirs was a perfect marriage, for they had their share of disagreements and disputes. But at the end of the day, there was friendship and love between them, and there was no obstacle that they didn't face together and no problem they couldn't solve.

Except this one.

His heart had come close to breaking for her, knowing what an extraordinary mother she would be, if given the chance. She couldn't know that those nights that he held her when she cried, he'd cried as well. He would have moved heaven and earth for the merest chance of granting this dream for her.

And then… the most miraculous thing had occurred. Seven months ago, Mary had told him over his breakfast that she was with child, and then after enduring his ebullient celebration that involved him swinging her around and around, and then waltzing with her around the breakfast table, she'd become sick all over his shoes. It was his first inkling that the pregnancy might not be as smooth as that of his friends and their wives.

She had been sick for her entire pregnancy and only recently had been feeling well enough to let her friends visit. Geoff had been tending to her the entire time, waiting on her hand and foot for months, and apparently, he'd made quite a nuisance of himself, as she had forbade him from doing anything anymore.

Last week she'd insisted that he accompany his friends to one of Derek's northern estates to oversee some repairs. He'd utterly refused, with her being only weeks from her time, but she had been adamant. More than that, she had already arranged for Moira and Kate to be with her while he was gone. As those two women were mothers multiple times over, he was relented. He still had his doubts, but when his wife had her mind set on something, there was no sense at all in arguing the point.

They'd only been gone one night when he received word from an express rider that the baby was coming and he needed to return.

It spoke of the quality of the men he called friends that they had not only come back with him, but had ridden just as hard.

They arrived with the word that the baby had not come yet, that Mary did not want him in the room, which perturbed him on a great many levels, and that the doctor was feeling encouraged by her progress.

So here he was out in the hall he was with his friends, trying his best not to turn completely insane with worry and anxiety. He'd started with pacing the halls, then turned to sitting and fidgeting, then finally took up a position just before the door, facing it, waiting. Faintly, he could hear the sounds of distress from their bedchamber and each sound gripped his heart in a vice and made his hand clench to reach for the doorknob.

He asked every fifteen minutes if he was needed, but she always refused. It troubled him. Moira had called for Nathan during her first delivery, and he had been just as present for the subsequent children. Kate, on the other hand, never allowed Derek on the same level of the house as she was when she delivered. He had attempted to barge his way in with their first son, but she'd made Duncan carry him from the house and contain him in the garden until the child was present. As far as he knew, they still fought over it, but Kate was always victorious.

Geoff loved his wife, and respected her a great deal, but he now understood Derek's frustrations. His place was in there with her, not out here wondering what was going on, wondering how much longer she would have to endure this, and wondering, God forbid, if she should live or die. He'd never let his mind dwell on the possibility, but now it loomed before him with terrifying power.

A series of short and very young cries emanated from the room beyond him and he felt his chest expand with surprising swiftness. He faltered a bit as he became slightly light-headed, but Duncan held him steady.

"Congratulations," Duncan said with a laugh as he pounded his back. "Your child has quite the set of lungs."

Geoff laughed himself and turned to embrace his friend tightly. The others eagerly extended their felicitations with hugs and handshakes and back thumping. He would later recall seeing the slight sheen of tears in Colin's eyes, but at this moment, he could only stare at the door in anticipation. His child… their child… continued to wail from inside, and he grinned at the sound.

When no one came to bring him in, he started to feel the slightest rise of panic.

"Oh, it can take a while," Derek assured him with a hand on his shoulder. "When Helena was born, Kate had me wait an entire hour before I could even go into the room. You all left before that happened, but I was a mess. Turned out Kate wanted to sleep before I came in to bother her. Didn't see the need to have me informed of that."

"Moira did the same with Lizzie," Nathan said with a laugh. "Kicked me out of the room once she was born and wouldn't let me back in until she had rested. Perhaps this means you have a daughter, Geoff."

He smiled at the thought, but it didn't make him worry any less.

He could hear the room bustling beyond, but no one made any sounds of distress or horror or mourning that he could hear. Even the child had stopped crying, for whatever reason.

The wait was agonizing. Colin resumed Duncan's pacing, Derek sat where Colin had, Duncan stood next to him, and Nathan took up his former place on the wall.

He started bouncing on his heels when Duncan muttered, "Easy, Geoff. If there was a problem, you would have been informed of it by now."

"Doctor Durham is the best," Colin said even as his pacing increased. "Just ask Thomas Granger, he wants the man petitioned for Sainthood, I swear."

The others nodded in affirmation of his claim.

As the Grangers lived only two estates over from this house, Geoff was inclined to believe him. But he would make a point to verify that with Granger once things were settled here. Colin didn't know all the particulars of the Granger's story, or perhaps he did, as it was Colin, after all, but the others knew even less.

Still, Mary was in capable hands with Moira, Kate, and the

inestimable Doctor Durham. He exhaled slowly and waited.

Just when he thought he was about to be driven mad, he could hear the baby cry again and laughter resounded from the room. He felt himself breathe easier. Laughter was a sound he had nearly forgotten in his wait.

"How long was it?" he murmured to Duncan.

"Twenty-five minutes," he promptly replied, checking his pocket-watch.

Geoff nodded, narrowing his eyes. "She'll pay for that."

All of the others laughed loudly. "I think she just did," Colin crowed as he came over.

"You'll never win another battle again," Nathan assured him with a slow nod. "After what she has just endured... You'll never match it."

Geoff sobered slightly, knowing it was true.

The door opened and Kate appeared, looking rather haggard, but beaming. Her hair, normally so perfect, was in a bit of disarray, but she didn't seem to care. She looked straight at Geoff with a smirk.

"Well?" he said with a touch of impatience when she didn't say anything.

"Mary did beautifully," Kate replied in a soft voice, smiling. "I've never seen a woman deliver so quietly, but she is very strong, your wife. She is tired, obviously, but altogether quite well."

He swallowed down a rather extensive lump of emotions that had lodged in his throat. "Can I see her?" he rasped without shame.

She smiled. "Of course. But don't you want to ask after anyone else?"

The others chuckled, and Geoff grinned. "How is the baby, Kate?"

Now she seemed to have difficulty swallowing, but she smiled through her sudden tears. "They are fine."

Which of his friends gasped, he couldn't tell. He only knew that he couldn't breathe and the sounds of jubilation coming from the others, the pounding on his back, all went unnoticed as he stared at Kate open-mouthed in shock.

"They?" he finally managed.

She nodded, grinning. "You have two children, Geoff. Two beautiful, healthy babies."

"Are… are you sure?" he stammered, shaking his head. "We've been trying for so long…"

She laughed and put her hand on his arm. "I'm quite sure, Geoff. I was there the entire time. You have two perfect children, your wife is delirious with joy and doing well, and if I stand here talking to you about it any longer, she will never forgive me." She stepped back and gestured for him to enter.

He didn't need any further encouragement. He raced into the room and saw the doctor washing his hands in the sitting room. He smiled cordially at him.

"All well, Mr. Harris," Doctor Durham said cheerily. "I shall be back tomorrow morning to see to all three, but I don't foresee the slightest hiccup of a problem."

Geoff nodded and shook his hand repeatedly. "Thank you."

"My pleasure, to be sure, to be sure," he replied with a chuckle. He picked up his bag and left the room with a bow.

Geoff would seriously consider taking up that petition with Granger for getting the good doctor sainted.

He turned with breathless anticipation to the bedroom. Slowly, almost hesitantly, he stepped in, his eyes instantly clapping on Mary, who was pale, drawn, completely disheveled, and so beautiful it made his chest ache. She was staring down at the bundle in her arms, smiling with a serenity words could not describe.

He hated to disturb the scene, but he couldn't contain himself. "Mary," he breathed.

She looked up at him, her eyes shining with tears, but her smile broad. "Come meet your son, my love."

He moved to her side and looked down at the child in her arms.

"A son," he murmured, reaching out to touch a small hand. The fingers spread out instinctively, and he was struck by the perfection of this infant. He shook his head. "He's beautiful."

"And he's the oldest," Mary informed him with a laugh, "and quite impatient."

"This little one, on the other hand," came Moira's voice from somewhere behind him, "is the sweetest little angel that was ever born."

Geoff turned to see Moira sitting in the chair with a second bundle. His eyes immediately fixed on it.

"That is our daughter," Mary murmured softly, a smile evident in her tone. "She took a little coaxing."

Moira stood and brought the baby over to him, laying her gently in his unpracticed arms.

Geoff stared down at the baby, a new and confusing twist of emotions playing within him. He felt a surge of pride that inexplicably caused his eyes to water and his throat to close. These were his children.

He was a father.

He tried to speak, but couldn't. He shook his head at the embarrassing show of emotion and the nondescript sounds that emanated from his throat.

Moira smiled and put a hand on his shoulder. "I'll leave you alone to have this family time. Come and fetch me when you need a reprieve."

He nodded, knowing he would probably want to hold his children for the rest of their lives, and also knowing that was not going to be true in coming weeks and months. But for this moment, it was.

Moira left the room and the only sound heard was the fire crackling in the hearth nearby.

Mary suddenly touched his arm gently, and he was drawn out of his reverie. He looked down at her with a bewildered smile.

"Two?" he asked.

She grinned and blushed a bit. "I've suspected for some time, but it seemed impertinent to vocalize them when we were already blessed to have been pregnant at all."

He could understand that. "You could have told me," he scolded softly, sitting on the bed next to her carefully so as not to jostle his daughter.

She shook her head. "You would have worried far more than you already did, and what if I was wrong?"

"Did Doctor Durham suspect?"

She nodded. "Towards the end, when he saw my size, and when I explained how I seemed to be feeling kicks and movements in different areas. But we were not sure until... well, until I had delivered him and the pains didn't subside."

Geoff looked at Mary more carefully, taking in every aspect of her appearance. "How are you?" he murmured with concern.

She smiled and put a hand on his cheek. "Perfect. Tired beyond belief, but I'm so happy at this moment, I can barely feel it."

He doubted that, but smiled all the same. "I wanted to be here with you," he whispered. "I could have been here."

She stroked his cheek softly. "I know. I'm sorry, but I just... I wanted to be strong, and I knew immediately that I couldn't be. I didn't want you to see me like that."

He leaned in quickly and kissed her hard. "Don't protect me, Mary Harris," he whispered. "I love you. For better or for worse, I am yours and I will support you. Let me."

She sighed softly and brought her lips back to his.

He hummed with pleasure as she pulled back and she quirked her brows at him, then looked back down at their son.

"I suppose we should name them," Geoff said with a light chuckle. "Though what names we could use that haven't already been taken up by our siblings and friends..."

"I have been thinking about that, actually," Mary replied. "For him, how do you feel about William?"

He nodded thoughtfully. "William is a good, strong name. I don't know a single William that I don't like."

Mary snorted and shook her head. "High praise, indeed."

He nudged her with his shoulder, but otherwise ignored the comment. "And this little angel?" he asked holding his daughter a little closer.

"I don't know how you will feel about this," Mary said slowly, "but I've always loved the name Julianna. I know it is a little grand for so small a person..."

"I love it," Geoff interrupted. "It is perfect for her."

Mary beamed at him and kissed his cheek, then rested her head on his shoulder with a sigh. "William and Julianna. Welcome to our family."

Her voice squeaked with emotion, which made Geoff smile, and he pressed his lips to her hair. They sat together for some time, watching their children sleep.

Only when Mary yawned herself did Geoff come to his senses.

"You need sleep as well," he told her, rising gently. "I'll fetch Moira or Kate to take him."

Mary sighed and looked at William. "I don't want to let him go."

Geoffrey chuckled. "Darling, he is ours forever. He won't go anywhere, unless the girls run off with him, which I don't believe their husbands will allow, as they have children at home. I can have them brought back to you the moment you are awake."

"I suppose so," Mary allowed with a frown.

"I insist that you rest," he told her with a look. "Would you like me to go?"

She bit her lip, chewing thoughtfully. "If you don't mind, I'd like you to stay. And hold me."

He smiled, loving the warmth that he still felt when she asked such things of him. "I don't mind at all." He went into the sitting room and opened the door to the hall, calling for Moira and Kate, who were quick to respond. Kate eagerly took Julianna from him, and Moira rushed to Mary and claimed William.

Moments later, the room was quiet and still once more. Geoff returned to the bed and lay beside his wife, opening his arms for her. She nestled against his side and rested her head on his chest. "You know what I was thinking this morning before the babies came?" she asked softly.

He chuckled. "I haven't a clue. What was going through that devious mind of yours?"

"You never told me what your favorite part of me was."

He looked down at her in surprise. "What?"

She met his eyes. "Before we were married, when we were just friends, and then into that melee of a season, you always complimented a part of me, and I asked if it was your favorite, and…"

"And I never told you," he finished, nodding thoughtfully.

"Well, my dear, I suppose now is as good a time as any. Nothing has changed after all these years of marriage and your miraculous bearing of two children in one afternoon. My favorite part of you is and always will be… you."

She frowned. "I don't understand."

He shrugged. "How could I ever have a favorite part of you? There are so many parts to love, but when it comes down to it, the combination of everything that you are and everything that makes you up is my favorite part. Your mind, your body, your heart, your wit, your lips, your laugh, your hands, your toes, that freckle on your back that looks like France…"

Mary burst out laughing, but clamped a hand over her mouth and beamed up at him.

He shook his head and pulled her in tight. "I just love you, Mary. You are my favorite part."

She kissed his chest directly over his heart. "And you are mine."

She tilted her head up and kissed him, long, slow, and tender.

"None of that, Mrs. Harris," he scolded as he broke off. "Your wiles must wait. You must rest now, and if I'm too distracting, I will leave."

She giggled and wrapped her arms around him. "You are too distracting, but you can't leave. I forbid it."

He sighed a very long-suffering sigh. "Very well, if the lady demands. Shall I tell you a story to help you sleep?"

"Yes, please," she said on a yawn.

He nodded with a smile. "Once upon a time, there was a girl who was vibrant, brilliant, beautiful, and clever, which is quite the combination to be proud of in a sensible girl. Her name was Mary, and she made even the most unruly flowers sing."

Mary snorted, and he felt her shake her head against him.

"At any rate, Mary had this quite slow, rather stupid, and almost completely blind friend named Geoffrey, who really wasn't good for very much, but he tried."

"Oh, be nice," she murmured.

"Shush," he scolded. "I'm telling this story. Anyway, they became friends as children when Mary was found in a tree one day…"

Coming Soon

The Dangers
of
Doing Good

"A generous heart is a risky venture."

by

Rebecca Connolly